## Also by Sharon Sala

# the Best of Me

# SHARON SALA

sourcebooks
casablanca

Published by Sourcebooks Casablanca, an imprint of Sourcebooks
P.O. Box 4410, Naperville, Illinois 60567–4410
(630) 961-3900
sourcebooks.com

Printed and bound in Canada.
MBP 10 9 8 7 6 5 4 3 2 1

# CHAPTER 1

THERE ARE PLACES ON EARTH SO PERFECTLY ALIGNED WITH the universe that they develop a rhythm…like the heartbeat of a living, breathing thing. And when something comes along that threatens the life flow and the sanctity of those places, the people within rise up as one to protect that which is theirs.

Those places hold and shelter the best of humanity, and the humanity within holds fast to the blessing and gives back the best of themselves.

And so it goes in Blessings, Georgia.

Those who are hurt are healed.

That which is broken is fixed.

That which threatens one threatens all.

And such a tragedy or intrusion is not to be taken quietly or lightly.

———————

The Greyhound brakes were squeaking in protest as the long, gray ride pulled up and parked at the bus stop next to the Blessings police station. Intermittent clouds of black smoke were coming from the muffler, as if in protest of the pause in its journey, when the bus door abruptly opened. The driver, a slightly rumpled middle-aged man in need of a shave, jumped off and headed for the luggage compartment.

Behind him, a gaunt young woman emerged, staggering slightly as she reached back to the little girl with her and took her hand to steady her as she came down the steps.

The driver had two suitcases out on the sidewalk.

"Shirley Duroy?"

"Yes. That's me," the woman said.

"You just had the two suitcases, right?" he asked.

Shirley nodded, then glanced at the blanket and stuffed toy her daughter, Carlie, was clutching and brushed a stray strand of blond curls away from her forehead.

The driver eyed the dark circles beneath the woman's eyes and the tremble in her hands and voice. He'd been concerned about her ever since their boarding in Little Rock, Arkansas. She looked like death warmed over, but now that she'd debarked, her journey was none of his business.

"Well then, thank you for traveling Greyhound," he said, then climbed back on the bus and drove away.

Carlie looked up. "Mama, is this it?"

Shirley choked back tears. "Yes, this is Blessings. It's going to be your new home. Can you help me pull our suitcases to that building?"

Carlie laid her blanket and stuffed rabbit on top of one suitcase, grabbed the strap on the wheeled suitcase, and began pulling it toward the door. As soon as she got it off the street, she ran back to get the other one and pulled it up as well, then ran back to her mother.

"Hold onto me, Mama."

Shirley took a quick breath. Everything was spinning. The sun was hot, and she needed to get in where it was cool. Her heart was pounding in her chest in an erratic rhythm that did not bode well for her, but she already knew her fate. It's why she was here.

Then she felt her daughter's hand in hers and looked down at her through a veil of tears. *This isn't fair. But Carlie Duroy's existence is not, nor has it ever been, based on fair.*

It felt like forever, but they finally reached the door to the police station. Shirley grabbed the knob, gripped it with all the strength she had left, and turned it. The door swung inward, and Carlie grabbed her blanket and toy from the suitcase and led her mama straight into the front lobby. She sat Shirley in the first chair they came to, dumped her things in the chair beside her, then went back to drag in their bags.

Shirley was in something of a panic. She was realizing that the time she'd counted on settling Carlie in wasn't going to be given to her. Her heart, which had been pounding, was suddenly skipping beats—a lot of beats, and she was losing her breath.

*Oh God. I needed more time. I needed more time.*

Avery Ames, the dispatcher, jumped up the moment they came inside and ran to them, then didn't know who to help first.

"Ma'am?" he asked.

Shirley pointed at the open door and Carlie, who was trying to drag a suitcase over the threshold.

"Help..." she whispered.

"Yes, ma'am," Avery said and ran to the door. "I'll get that for you, honey," he said.

"We have two," Carlie said.

"I'll get them," Avery said.

Carlie went back to her mother, pushed her blanket and toy aside, then sat down beside her and reached for her hand. Her shorts and T-shirt were rumpled from traveling, and the backs of her bare legs were sticking on the wooden chairs, but her only concern was Mama.

Avery pulled the bags over to where they were sitting and then paused in front of the woman.

"Ma'am, how can I help you?" he asked.

"Chief..." she mumbled, and then leaned back and closed her eyes.

"Yes, ma'am," Avery said and bolted down the hall and into Lon Pittman's office without bothering to knock. "Chief! Come quick. There's a woman with a little girl in the lobby. The woman looks bad sick, and she asked for you."

Lon was on his feet and running, with Avery right behind him.

One look at the pair sitting in the lobby, and Lon knew something dire was happening. The little girl looked terrified, and the woman wasn't breathing right.

"Avery, get an ambulance here, stat."

"Yes, sir," Avery said and ran back to his desk.

"Ma'am, I'm Lon Pittman, the chief of police. How can I help you? Are you sick?"

Shirley moaned. "Carlie…sorry, baby, sorry."

"Mama's dying," Carlie said.

Lon reeled as if he'd been sucker-punched, staring at the little girl and the tears shimmering in her eyes.

"How do…? What's your mother's name?" he asked.

"Shirley Duroy."

Lon was checking the woman's pulse as he spoke, and it was blatantly obvious the kid knew what she was talking about. The woman's heart was barely beating.

"What's wrong with her?" Lon asked.

"Her heart is sick. I take care of her."

*Oh Jesus.* "How old are you, Carlie ?"

"Seven…almost eight," she said and started shaking. "Mama can't live no more. I have to live for both of us. I have to be good and do right." Then she turned and hid her face against her mother's shoulder.

The last time Lon had felt this helpless was the day he thought his wife, Mercy, had drowned. Only she hadn't been his wife then, just the love of his life. He could only imagine what this little girl was feeling.

"Do you have family here? Is this why you came to Blessings?"

Carlie shook her head, then sat up and wiped her eyes. "Mama has a letter in her purse. It tells you what to do."

Lon was reaching for Shirley's purse when they began hearing sirens.

Carlie wrapped her arms around her mother's neck.

"I love you, Mama. I will be good."

Shirley opened her eyes, thrust her hand in her daughter's hair and held her close. "The best of me," she whispered, then looked at Lon and whispered, "Call Ruby Dye," and exhaled.

Her eyes closed. She never took another breath.

Avery was crying and made no attempt to hide it.

Carlie was still clutching her mother's arm.

"Come back, Mama. Come back. I need to talk to you," she sobbed.

Lon was choking back tears as he felt for a pulse, but there was none. And then the ambulance was outside. He stood, grabbed the blanket and stuffed toy and Shirley's purse, then lifted Carlie out of the chair next to her mother's body.

"She's gone," Lon said. "Avery, you fill them in on what happened. Give them her name. I'll get the rest of her info to them later. Right now I'm taking Carlie back to my office."

"Yes, sir," Avery said, then wiped his eyes and blew his nose as the chief left the lobby with Carlie Duroy in his arms.

Lon got back to his office, sat down on the old couch with her still in his arms, and just held her.

She was sobbing.

"I'm so sorry, Carlie. I'm so, so sorry. You said there was a letter in your mama's purse. Do you want to get it for me?"

He handed her the purse, then watched as she stroked the soft brown leather before opening it and pulling out a long white envelope.

"The 'structions are in there," she said.

Lon grabbed a handful of tissues and gently wiped her face and eyes.

"Do you know what they are?" he asked.

Carlie nodded, then hiccupped as she took a breath to answer.

"Mama said Miss Ruby is gonna guard me and take care of me. Miss Ruby is her friend."

Lon frowned. The last thing Shirley Duroy had said was Ruby's name. But the name she used was Ruby's name before she and Peanut Butterman got married. He wondered how long it had been since they'd been in contact. He snuggled the little girl up against his chest as he opened the letter.

There were several pages.

The first was a personal letter to Ruby. He laid it aside without reading it, but he did read the official, notarized court document naming Ruby Dye as the legal guardian of Carlie Jo Duroy. There was a birth certificate and medical info about her childhood immunizations, the name and address of the pediatrician who had Carlie's health records, and the last school she'd attended in Little Rock. Basically, the sum total of Carlie's seven-plus years on earth.

He put everything back in the envelope, then got more tissues, scooted Carlie off his lap onto the sofa, and began wiping her eyes and then her nose. She was so still, with her blanket and her stuffed rabbit clutched against her chest. He was heartsick for her, imagining how scared she must be.

Lon glanced at the calendar. Monday, July 21. Ruby didn't work on Mondays. Whatever she'd been planning to do today had just gone to hell in a hand basket.

"Are you hungry, Carlie? Do you need anything?" he asked.

"The bathroom?"

"I'll show you where it is," he said, then led her to his private bathroom. "Can you reach everything?"

She looked, then nodded.

"I'll be right outside the door if you need help," he said.

The moment he closed the door, he reached for his phone and made a quick call to Peanut Butterman. As he was waiting for Peanut to answer, Lon heard more sobs and gritted his teeth, waiting for Peanut to pick up, and then he did.

"Hello?"

"Peanut, this is Lon. We have a serious situation here at the station. I need you to get Ruby and get down here as soon as possible."

"Get Ruby? What the hell's going on?"

"It's complicated. Just get here."

"Yes, okay, but I'm already at the office. It'll take a few minutes to get home and pick her up."

"That's fine. See you soon," Lon said.

A few moments later, Lon heard the toilet flushing, then water running at the sink. When Carlie opened the door, her hands were dripping.

"I can't reach the towels," she said.

Lon quickly pulled down a couple of paper towels and handed them to her.

She dried with the precision of a little old woman, and he wondered how long she'd been "taking care of Mama," because it appeared all aspects of her childhood had been abandoned. He took her by the hand and led her back into his office. She crawled up onto the sofa, rolled herself up in the blanket, tucked the rabbit beneath her chin, and never took her gaze from his face.

"Are you hungry?" Lon asked.

She shook her head. "Where's my mama?"

"They took her to the hospital in the ambulance," he said and sat down in the chair opposite the sofa.

Carlie took a slow breath. Tears were rolling again.

"Do you have family somewhere?" he asked.

She shook her head.

"What about your father? Who is he? Where's he at?"

Carlie shrugged. "He's dead. Mama didn't talk about him. She took care of me. Then she got sick."

"Do you have grandparents, or an aunt, or an uncle?"

She shook her head again. "Not anymore," she said, but now her voice and body were shaking. "Did you call Miss Ruby? Mama said she'll know what to do. Mama said she is a nice lady. Mama said she was her friend."

"Yes, I called. Ruby is married now. She and her husband are on their way here."

Carlie glanced nervously at the door. "Does she know my mama died?"

"I didn't tell her yet, but it will be okay. Ruby has never let anyone down in this town. She won't let you down, either."

Carlie shuddered, rolled over onto her side on the sofa, and closed her eyes, then abruptly opened them again.

"Don't go away," she whispered.

"I won't. I promise," Lon said.

Her eyes closed again. Tears continued to roll from beneath the lids, but she was finally silent.

Lon couldn't breathe without wanting to cry with her. She was so little and broken.

He sent Avery a text and told him to send Peanut and Ruby back to his office as soon as they arrived, and then began making copies of Shirley's ID, all of her insurance cards, and everything else the hospital would need for their records. He put the originals back in her purse and sat in silence, listening for the sound of footsteps out in the hall.

———————

Peanut called Ruby on the way home. She answered on the second ring.

"Hey, honey," Ruby said.

"Are you dressed?" Peanut asked.

"Yes. I was just getting ready to run some errands. Why?"

"Stay there. I'm on my way home to get you. I got a call from the chief. He said for me to bring you to the police station ASAP, that they had a serious situation."

"What does it have to do with me?" Ruby asked.

"He didn't say. Just grab your purse. I'm coming down the street now."

"Okay," Ruby said. She hung up and ran to get her purse before heading out the front door to meet him. She jumped in the car and buckled up without saying a word, and then Peanut took off for the station.

Ruby gave him an anxious glance as she settled back in the seat.

"You swear you don't know what's going on?" she asked.

Peanut frowned. "I would never lie to you…or deceive you. I know nothing beyond getting the phone call. I asked, but he said it was complicated, and to get you and get to the station. That's all I know."

"Sorry. It just freaked me out a little," she said.

"Well, I'm somewhat freaked myself," he said.

She nodded, but her heart was pounding.

"I have a feeling that something terrible has happened," she said.

Peanut reminded her, "Whatever it is, we'll deal with it together."

"Yes, you're right. I'm sorry. I guess it's just the unexpected suddenness of the summons that has unnerved me."

"We're about to find out," Peanut said as he pulled up and parked in front of the station.

They got out, then entered the station together.

Ruby saw two large suitcases pushed up against the wall and then glanced at Avery. He just pointed down the hall.

"The chief is waiting for you in his office," he said.

Peanut frowned, then led the way, with Ruby right behind him. The door was open. They walked in and saw a little girl lying on the sofa and Lon in the chair beside her. She was clutching a blanket and stuffed toy—a brown and white lop-eared rabbit. The moment she saw them, the girl sat up, leaned back against the sofa, and looked at Lon.

"Is this Miss Ruby?" she whispered.

Lon nodded. "It's going to be okay. Don't be scared."

Ruby didn't know what was happening, but the look on that child's face broke her heart.

"What's going on?" she asked.

Lon stood, then handed Ruby the letter. "This is Carlie. Her mother died in the lobby about fifteen minutes ago, so she's having the worst day of her life right now. Have a seat, both of you. I'll sit by Carlie."

Ruby gasped, then stared at the little girl in disbelief. She felt Peanut's hand on her shoulder. They pulled their chairs close and sat down, then opened the letter and began reading it together.

*Dear Ruby,*

*If you are reading this letter, it means the heart disease I contracted years ago has won, and I am dead.*

*I have known for two years that this was imminent, but without any family left, I could not bear to think of my baby…my Carlie…winding up an orphan in the foster care system. She is the best of me. She's all I have left that is good in this world, and now she has no one.*

*Mom and Dad died during Hurricane Fanny. Her father was just a man who broke into my house and raped me. He wasn't caught then, but was killed a few weeks later while trying to rob a liquor store. This was before I even knew I was pregnant. Carlie does not know the circumstances of her birth, other than that her father is dead.*

*I have been working for Lloyd and Lloyd CPA in Little Rock for years, and after Carlie was born, I continued to work for them from home so I could also take care of her.*

*There is a man named Bart Carlson who works at the same firm. He knows about the money I inherited after Mom and Dad* died. He also knows I have a life insurance policy with Carlie as the beneficiary. There is no history between us. He's just someone I know from work. But the sicker I became, the more he pressured me to let him and his wife raise Carlie. I know enough about him to know he just wants his hands on the money. I don't want him anywhere around her, which is what prompted me to find a legal guardian for her that I trusted. I did that almost two years ago, and that's where you come in.

At my last doctor visit, it became painfully obvious that my days were numbered. Despite the legal papers I had set up for Carlie, I was afraid of what Bart might do if I died without letting you know what I'd done.

Yesterday, I packed our bags and we headed to Blessings on a Greyhound. Forgive me for the presumption in naming you her guardian without asking you. Since you're reading this instead of hearing it from me, you realize I had hopes of getting to you and explaining. But time and life got away from me. I just needed to make sure I got her to you before it was too late.

You are the only person I knew from my past who I trusted enough to see to her best interests and welfare, even though I want you to understand that I am not assuming you would want to raise someone else's child.

What I am asking is for you to be her spokesperson—her legal guardian—until her future can be decided in a careful and loving manner. If you pursue finding a wonderful family to adopt her, then so it is. If you find yourself falling in love with her and wish for her to stay with you, my gratitude will be eternal.

I have sent Carlie's information regarding school, her health records, and the legal guardianship papers. I had the money in my bank account transferred to the bank here in Blessings before we left Little Rock. You are named as the person to access it. You'll need some to bury me. Keep it simple and graveside. Likely no one here will remember me. The money is the inheritance *from my parents' deaths and my savings. The bank will have a signature card for you to sign. It is yours as needed to see Carlie to where she needs to go. There is also a $250,000 life insurance policy with Carlie as the beneficiary. Fortunately, I got that before I became ill. That will get her through college and set her on a good path in life. The policy and the papers to access it are in my purse.*

*She is seven years old, almost eight…and has been taking care of me for the last two years in the times when I could not take care of myself. She has lost her childhood. She has lost the safety a child should expect as a given. And now she has lost me.*

*She is such a good girl. I've told her all about you and what I can remember of Blessings and the people in it. She knows what I'm asking of you. She knows you as Miss Ruby. She knows you gave me my first job when I went to work for you cleaning up in the Curl Up and Dye after school. I was fifteen years old, and you were so beautiful I wanted to be you. I wish we had never moved away, but one cannot change the past.*

*I have never forgotten what a loving and wonderful woman you were to me.*

*I know right now that my baby is so scared.*

*Please help her feel safe again.*

*I need you to help her find her place in the world because I cannot.*

*With apologies,*
*Shirley Duroy*

Ruby read in total silence. The magnitude of the request was beyond anything she could ever have imagined, but she never once showed her shock. She looked at Peanut, saw his instant agreement and understanding, then laid the letter in his lap.

She got up and went to the sofa where Carlie was sitting, sat down beside her, and scooted her into her lap. As she did, Lon got up to give them space. She wrapped the blanket tighter around Carlie, tucked the rabbit in the little girl's arms, and then pulled her close.

"Hello, sweetheart. I'm Miss Ruby. I'm so sorry about your mama, but you are right where she wanted you to be, and we will do everything for you that she wanted us to do, okay?"

Carlie looked up at Ruby and took a slow, shuddering breath.

"Mama died."

Ruby's eyes welled. "I know, baby. I'm so sorry. She was my friend."

"They took Mama away," Carlie added.

"I know. Don't worry about anything more. You don't have to take care of your mama now. We're here to help."

Carlie looked over at Peanut. "Will Mr. Ruby help, too?"

Peanut walked over to the sofa and lifted her out of Ruby's arms. "Yes, Mr. Ruby will help. Are those your suitcases in the lobby?" he asked.

"Those are the ones they came in with," Lon said.

When Ruby stood up, Lon gave her Shirley's purse. "I'm so sorry," he said.

Ruby was teary-eyed as she nodded. "So am I."

Lon led the way back to the lobby. "I'll get the bags. You get the door," he said.

Ruby got into the back seat with Carlie and buckled them in. The back door was still open as they watched the men loading her bags into the trunk, and then as Peanut got in, Lon paused where Ruby was sitting and looked in.

"Carlie, I'm going to check on your mama now. And I'll make sure the doctors know what her last wishes were, okay?"

"I need to talk to my mama," Carlie whispered, then covered her face with her blanket.

Lon looked at Ruby and grimaced in dismay as he closed the door between them.

At that point, Ruby unbuckled Carlie's seatbelt and pulled her into her lap. "Drive slow and careful," Ruby said. "I'm not letting her go."

Peanut glanced up in the rearview mirror. Their gazes met. Then he backed up the car and drove away.

Ruby felt Carlie leaning into her and held her close. She didn't know how in hell she was going to make this work, but she'd figure it out one day at a time. The first thing was rescheduling her upcoming week at the salon. The clients who didn't want to wait would have to be worked into Vesta and Vera's schedules, because this week was about putting Shirley to rest and Carlie at ease.

"Honey, did you eat breakfast this morning?" Ruby asked.

"No," Carlie said.

"Well, we have all kinds of things to eat at home. We'll find you something," Ruby said and heard Carlie sigh.

Even though Carlie witnessed her mother's life coming to an end, Ruby knew she hadn't really grasped what it meant. Her grief was real. Her need to know what had happened to her mother was a necessity. They couldn't just whisk away Shirley's body and pretty up Carlie's life. The child needed to see the finality of death. She needed time to grieve and understand what *gone to heaven* meant.

Ruby already knew Peanut was on board with this. She'd heard his breath catch as he'd read Shirley's letter with her. She'd seen the tears in his eyes and the look he'd given her. He was with her all the way, of that she was certain. How the rest of this all played out was yet to be determined, but she intended to make sure that whatever it was, the final choices would be Carlie's.

———

Peanut tapped the brakes as he turned the corner leading to their house. This morning, their lives had changed forever. Not in a bad way, but in a shocking way.

After so many years of being single, and then falling in love with a woman who could not have children, he'd given up the idea of fatherhood without hesitation. Ruby was his life. Whatever came with her was exactly what he wanted.

And now this.

His heart was breaking for the child, but if there was one thing he knew, it was that without knowing it, Shirley Duroy hit the jackpot when she named Ruby as her daughter's guardian. Ruby had all the love in the world to give to a child. All the understanding and patience she was going to need, and Miss Ruby had her own lawyer on board. Then he tapped the brakes again as he turned up the drive and parked at the house.

"We're home," he said. "You two go on inside. I'll get the bags."

Ruby gave Carlie a quick hug and then unbuckled the seatbelt.

"We're here, sugar. Let's get inside where it's cool and find you something to eat."

They got out of the car in silence, and then Carlie reached back for her blanket and rabbit.

"Want me to carry them?" Ruby asked.

Carlie shook her head and clutched them against her.

Ruby took her by the hand and led her all the way to the front door, unlocked it, then led her inside.

Peanut was right behind them with the bags, but instead of carrying them back to one of the bedrooms, he left them in the hall, then followed them into the kitchen.

Carlie was sitting at the table, eyeing everything around her in wide-eyed wonder at how shiny the appliances were and how big the house was compared to where she and her mother had lived, when Peanut paused behind her chair and gently cupped the back of her head.

"Is there anything I can get for you two before I head back to the office? I so wish I could stay, but I have two appointments I need to keep," he said.

"We're just fine," Ruby said. "I'll call if I need you."

He nodded, then turned and spoke directly to Carlie.

"I have to go back to work now, but I work right here in Blessings, so I'm always close. I'm so very sorry about your mama, but she chose us for a reason. She knew we would take very good care of you, okay?"

Carlie nodded. She liked the sound of his voice. It was soft and deep. And he'd mentioned Mama. Just the thought of her was settling.

Peanut smiled. "Ruby, honey, I have to be in court right after lunch, so I won't be home until the hearing is over. Are you going to be okay?"

Ruby turned to look at him. "Of course. We'll talk tonight. Have a good day," she said.

Peanut blew her a kiss, winked at Carlie, and then left the house.

Ruby turned to the table where Carlie was sitting.

"Which would you rather have for breakfast? Scrambled eggs with jelly toast, or cereal? I know we have Rice Krispies."

"I like that kind," Carlie said.

"Then Rice Krispies it is," Ruby said, giving Carlie's shoulders a quick pat of reassurance. She got the cereal from the pantry, then a bowl and glass from the cabinet. After fixing the cereal, she poured up a small glass of milk and carried them both to the table. "Who knew you and Mr. Ruby would like the same cereal?" she said.

Carlie thought about that. "He likes this kind, too?"

"It's his favorite," Ruby said. "You two are going to be the best of friends. I can tell."

Carlie picked up the spoon and shoved it in the bowl, scooping up a bite of cereal and milk and poking it in her mouth.

She ate until the bowl was empty and most of her milk was gone.

"I'm full," she said.

"Good. Nobody goes hungry in this house," Ruby said. "Now you get to make another decision. We have two spare bedrooms.

How about we take a tour of the house, and you can pick out the bedroom you want for your own?"

Carlie grabbed her rabbit and blanket, slid down from the chair, then followed Ruby out of the room. She didn't know what to think or how to feel. All she knew was this was where Mama wanted her to be, and so she accepted that with all the innocence of the child she was.

Ruby took her all through the house and showed her where her and Peanut's bedroom was, and then the two spare bedrooms across the hall with the Jack and Jill bathroom between them.

"You choose which one you want to be yours," Ruby said. "Whichever one you choose, there is a bathroom between them. I call this one the yellow room because the bedspread and curtains have yellow and white flowers on them."

Carlie hung onto Ruby's hand with a death grip. The bed looked huge. Her bed at home had been a twin size. This one looked scary.

Ruby didn't know what Carlie was thinking, but she didn't like the look in her eyes.

"Let's look at the other room, okay? We can walk right through the bathroom, see?" she said and led the way.

The moment they walked into the other bedroom, she heard Carlie sigh and felt her grip easing.

Carlie looked up. The ceiling was blue like the sky, and there were two small beds in this room with blue and white comforters and white bed skirts. The little table and chair at the window between them was almost exactly like the little table and chair she'd had in their apartment.

She clutched the rabbit a little closer and looked up at Ruby. "I choose this one, Miss Ruby."

Ruby smiled and, without thinking, brushed the stray strands of hair away from Carlie's forehead.

Carlie closed her eyes when it happened, because it felt just like what Mama always did, then leaned against Ruby's leg, hanging onto the fantasy that it *was* Mama and that everything that had happened this morning was a bad dream.

"You like blue," Ruby said.

The fantasy ended with the sound of Ruby's voice.

Carlie blinked, then nodded. "It's Mama's favorite color, so it's mine, too. The beds are my size, and the ceiling is blue like the sky."

Ruby knelt and hugged her.

"You are a darling, and I am so sorry for all that's happened. But this is where you're going to be safe, and one day, maybe you'll be happy here, too."

"You and Mr. Ruby don't have any kids?"

Ruby took a slow, shaky breath. "I lost a baby once before it was born. I can't have any more."

Carlie slid her arm around Ruby's neck.

"We both know how to be sad, don't we?"

Ruby ran her finger down the side of Carlie's face.

"Yes…I guess we do. But I also know how to be happy here. And Mr. Ruby makes me very happy. His name is really Peanut… Peanut Butterman. He's a lawyer."

Carlie listened and then discarded the information.

"Does Mr. Ruby snore?"

Ruby smiled. "Sometimes. Why?"

"Back home, we had a neighbor in the next apartment who snored really loud at night. His bedroom was next to my bedroom. It scared me. Then Mama told me it was just Larry snoring, and when you know what something is, then it's not scary anymore."

Ruby sighed. "Your mama was really smart."

Carlie leaned over and whispered in Ruby's ear. "Will I get to tell her goodbye?"

"Absolutely," Ruby said. "But you will have to understand how—"

Carlie interrupted her. "I know what being dead means. Mama

told me lots of times. I will see her but I can't hear her anymore. And when I tell her goodbye, her spirit will be too far away for me to hear her answer. I'll have to feel it…in here," she said and patted her heart.

It was all Ruby could do not to break down in tears.

"Yes, baby. That's right," she said, then got up. "You try out the beds and see which one you want to sleep in, and I'll go get your bags and we'll unpack."

# CHAPTER 2

RUBY WAS UNPACKING THE SECOND BAG WHEN SHE FOUND a big manila envelope with Shirley Duroy's name on it. When she pulled out the contents, she quickly realized these were Shirley's health records and contact info for the doctors who'd been treating her in Little Rock, as well as contact information for her place of employment, with a note attached asking that they be notified of her passing.

Ruby was saddened by what she read. Shirley's diagnosis had been severe cardiomyopathy with complications, whatever that meant. She could only imagine how horrified Shirley must have been to learn this.

It occurred to her that the doctors at the hospital who would have had to pronounce Shirley's death might need this info for their records. She glanced over at Carlie, who was busy pulling out toys from one of the bags.

"Carlie, honey, you can put the toys wherever you want them. This bench beneath the window opens up, see?" She raised the seat, revealing the storage area beneath. "There are also shelves in your closet, and the stuffed toys can all go on your other bed."

"Okay," Carlie said, and began pulling out her other stuffed toys and lining them up on the pillow of the extra bed.

As soon as Ruby was satisfied the little girl was preoccupied, she stepped out into the hall and called Lon's cell phone.

"Chief Pittman."

"Lon, this is Ruby. I just found a manila envelope full of Shirley's health records in one of the suitcases. I thought maybe you, or the doctor, would need these. It might save an autopsy."

"I was getting ready to take copies of her ID and insurance info to the hospital. Is it okay if I swing by and get that stuff, too?"

"Of course, but if you don't mind, I'm going to leave it out front on the porch swing. Carlie is calming down a little, and I think seeing you again would set off a whole other set of concerns."

"Absolutely," Lon said. "Is she doing okay?"

"I don't know. She isn't talking much, but she's not crying right now."

Lon sighed. "God, I can't imagine the shock of this for you. If there's anything I can do, don't hesitate to ask."

"I learned a long time ago that life doesn't always go as expected. Right now, this sweet baby is the one I'm worried about. Peanut and I will be fine."

"Okay. I'll be there in a few minutes."

"I'm putting the packet on the swing right now. Oh… There's a note inside asking someone to notify her place of employment that she has passed," Ruby said.

"I'll see to that," Lon said.

"Thanks," Ruby said. She went up the hall and out the front door, left the envelope on the seat of the porch swing, and went back inside.

She was walking back down the hall when she heard Carlie's voice. Reluctant to interrupt, she paused just outside the door to listen.

"Mama is gone, Hoppy. It's me and you now, and we're not gonna cry, 'cause we don't want Mr. and Miss Ruby to get tired of us and give us away."

Ruby started to rush in there to reassure her, and then stopped. This child had been through enough today. Time would do what no amount of words could ever do. Carlie would learn to trust them, and then she wouldn't feel so insecure.

As she walked back to the front of the house, Ruby heard a car pulling up in the drive. Likely the chief. She heard him on the porch and then again as he was driving away, and then she sat down to make some calls.

The first call was to the funeral home. After she briefly explained to the director, he reassured her that he would check with the hospital, and when the body was released, they would pick it up.

"Thank you," Ruby said.

"Of course, and we're very sorry for your loss," he said.

Ruby disconnected, then paused, trying to remember where she'd left her appointment book, and groaned. She was pretty sure it was still at the shop. Well, she needed it, and she still needed to get groceries and pick up cleaning and get supplies for the shop. For one of the first times in her life, she was the one needing help, so she called Vesta and Vera Conklin, identical twins who were the other stylists at her shop.

Vesta answered, and Ruby could tell she was eating because she was chewing in Ruby's ear. "Hello, Ruby, this is Vesta."

"I need some help," Ruby said.

Vesta coughed. Ruby never asked anyone for help. She swallowed and was suddenly all business. "What do you need, honey? What's wrong?"

Ruby began to explain, and by the time she was through, Vesta was in tears.

"Oh dear lord," she said. "That poor baby. Tell me what we can do."

"I'm going to need help with my appointments this week. My book is at the shop. If you and Vera would get it and see how many you could work into your schedule and how many would be willing to reschedule with me for next week, I would hugely appreciate it. There's also a list on my workstation of supplies we need for the shop. I'll Venmo you the money to get them."

"You'll do no such thing. We'll keep the receipts for you, and we can settle up when we see you again."

Ruby sighed. "Thank you. This is so helpful. I need this week to get Shirley buried and Carlie settled in a bit. Right now, she doesn't know what to think."

"I'm just sick about this," Vesta said. "I remember Shirley. She was a real sweetheart. That's so sad. I wonder what happened to her parents. Why aren't they in the picture?"

"According to Shirley's letter, her parents died during Hurricane Fanny. There's no one left."

"Oh lord. We all sure remember that storm. Well, you don't worry a bit about the shop. We've got it covered, and let us know if there's anything else we can do. We love you dearly."

"I love you all, and please let Mabel Jean know what's happening," Ruby said. "I'll check in with you in a day or two."

Now that she'd settled the immediacy of restructuring her workweek, she hurried back down the hall to check on Carlie and found her curled up asleep on her bed, the rabbit tucked beneath her chin and her blanket over her shoulders.

Ruby sighed, then got the afghan off the other bed and covered Carlie the rest of the way up, turned off the lights, and left the door open on her way out.

All of the errands she had planned still needed to be done, but Carlie was in no condition to be dragged all over town. It was time to call in more help, and Lovey Cooper was the first person she thought of. Even though Lovey was always at her café, there were plenty of people who could stand in for her for a while.

Ruby went back to the kitchen, got her grocery list, poured herself a cup of coffee, and sat down at the table to make her call.

———

Lovey was at odds with the world today. Her son, Sully, was working in her place at Granny's Country Kitchen, and she was giving herself a leisurely day at home, doing whatever the hell she wanted, even if it was nothing.

But when her phone rang and she saw it was Ruby, she smiled. The Curl Up and Dye was always closed on Mondays. This might mean she was going to hang out with her best friend.

"Hi, Ruby! What's going on?" she asked.

Ruby sighed. "Lovey, I need you. Can you come to my house?"

Lovey's heart sank. She'd never heard those words come out of Ruby's mouth.

"What's wrong? Are you okay?" she asked.

Ruby sighed again. "We're fine. I'll explain everything when you get here."

"I'm on my way," Lovey said. She disconnected, grabbed her purse, and raced out the door, then tried not to panic on the way over. When she pulled up in the drive and got out, her stomach was in knots. But before she could ring the doorbell, Ruby was standing on the threshold.

"Thank you so much for coming," Ruby said.

Lovey hugged her. "Of course."

"I want to show you something, but you have to be really quiet. I don't want to wake her up."

Lovey frowned. "Wake who up?"

"You'll see," Ruby said and led her down the hall to the open door, put a finger to her lips, and then pointed at the little girl curled up on the bed sound asleep.

Lovey gasped, her eyes widening, and then followed Ruby back into the kitchen.

"Who is she? Where did she come from? And why is she in your house?"

"Do you remember the Duroy family who used to live here? Their only daughter, Shirley, worked for me at the Curl Up and Dye after school for an entire year. She was a pretty little thing with a turned-up nose, blond hair, and blue eyes."

"Yes, I do remember her, but what—?"

"Shirley and her daughter got off the Greyhound this morning. They got as far as the lobby of the police station, and then Shirley died."

"What? Oh my God! What happened to her? Is that her daughter?"

"Yes, that's her daughter, Carlie. Shirley had an incurable heart condition and she knew it. All of her family is dead. That baby in my bedroom isn't quite eight years old, and she has been taking care of her mother for the past two years, doing what Shirley could not. She knew her mama was dying. She knew she was coming here. She knew Shirley named me as her legal guardian and asked me to see that Carlie did not wind up in foster care. Carlie was in her mother's arms when she took her last breath in the lobby of the police station."

Lovey's eyes welled. She was thinking back to the day she'd left her own baby behind, and how heartbroken she'd been. The fact that she was still living when Sully finally came to find her was the best thing that ever happened to her, and she could not imagine how afraid and lost that little girl must feel.

"Oh my God. Bless her sweet heart," Lovey said. "What are you going to do?"

Ruby sighed. "Try as hard as I know how to help her feel safe again. Love her as much as she'll let me. The saddest day of my life was being told I could never have babies again. And now God has given us a little girl to take care of. Maybe we're going to get to be parents after all."

Lovey leaned over and hugged her. "What can I do?" she asked.

Ruby grimaced. "Today? Pick up my cleaning and shop for groceries. This week I have to bury Shirley and settle Carlie into something of a routine before I go back to the shop. The girls are taking my clients this week."

"What are you going to do when you have to go back to work?" Lovey asked.

"Take her with me. She's an adorable little girl who is scared half out of her mind, afraid to misbehave because we might not want her. I'm not leaving her anywhere with anyone. Where Peanut and I go, she goes. And when school starts next month, she'll be in third grade, and we'll figure that out as we go, too."

"Good enough," Lovey said. "Now, where's your grocery list, and what else do you need done today?"

Ruby handed her the list, then added, "There are a dozen of Peanut's dress shirts at the cleaner, too."

"I'll have Melissa drop them off here," Lovey said. "Since she owns the cleaners, she'll know what to pick up."

"Tell her I'll pay her when she brings them by," Ruby said. "And I'll pay you for the groceries when you bring them, okay?"

"Sure thing, honey, but I'm guessing you wrote this list before you knew about Carlie. Are there things you want to add to the list now?" Lovey asked.

"Oh. Good call," Ruby said. She grabbed a pen, thought for a few moments, and then wrote down a few more things.

She pushed the list toward Lovey, and then they both heard the pad of little feet coming up the hall and Ruby called out.

"I'm in here, honey!" Ruby said.

Carlie paused in the doorway, a little startled by the stranger sitting at the table with Miss Ruby.

"Come sit in my lap," Ruby said, then smiled and patted her knee.

Carlie walked in without hesitation, the blanket over her shoulder, the rabbit under her arm. She climbed up in Ruby's lap, then leaned against her without taking her gaze from Lovey.

"Carlie, this is my best friend. Her name is Lovey Cooper. She owns the café downtown and it's my favorite place to eat."

"Is it Granny's?" Carlie asked.

They both stared at her. "Yes. How did you know that?" Lovey asked.

"Mama told me lots of stuff about Blessings. Are you the granny?" Carlie asked.

"No, that's just the name of my business. I don't have any grandchildren," Lovey said. "But I wish I did."

Ruby patted Carlie's shoulder. "Honey, Lovey is going to get groceries for me today. Next time, you and I will go together and you can help me, but is there anything special you like to eat for treats? Any kinds of fruits? Or chocolate milk? Or cookies? Things like that."

"I can pick?" Carlie asked.

Ruby nodded.

"I like 'nanas, and animal cracker cookies with icing. And ice cream. I like 'nilla best."

"I'm adding them to the list," Lovey said.

"Now I know some things you do like to eat, but I don't know things you don't like to eat. What might that be?" Ruby asked.

"Things that hurt my mouth," Carlie said.

"You mean spicy food…like things with hot sauce and tacos? That kind of hurt?" Ruby asked.

Carlie nodded. "Yes. Like that."

"Duly noted," Ruby said. "Okay then. No spicy foods for Carlie."

Carlie looked up at her. "Mama always ate my hot stuff."

"Mr. Ruby eats mine," Ruby said.

Lovey grinned. "Mr. Ruby?"

"Carlie named him. He likes it," Ruby said.

Lovey stood. "Carlie, it has been a pleasure to meet you. I'll see you soon when I bring back the groceries."

"Thank you, Lovey. You're the best," Ruby said.

Carlie's eyes lit up. "Mama said I was her best."

Once again, Ruby was struggling not to cry. "I know. She told me in her letter, and I can see why."

"I'm out of here," Lovey said. "Back later." She left before she started bawling where she stood.

Ruby stood and then took Carlie by the hand.

"Let's go finish unpacking your bags, okay?"

"Okay," Carlie said.

Lon went back to the station long enough to run copies of all of Shirley's info. Since she died on the premises, he would have a file on her, and this was just more info to add.

He went in through the jail in the back and into his office, and started making copies. He found the note and made the call to the CPA firm where Shirley Duroy was employed.

"Lloyd and Lloyd CPA. This is Moira."

"Moira, this is Chief of Police Lon Pittman in Blessings, Georgia. I need to speak to Edward Lloyd."

"One moment, please," the woman said.

Seconds later, a man answered.

"Hello. This is Edward Lloyd. How can I help you?"

"Mr. Lloyd, I'm Lon Pittman, chief of police in Blessings, Georgia. I'm very sorry to inform you that one of your employees—Shirley Duroy—passed away here in Blessings this morning. She asked that you be notified."

"Oh no! I'm so sorry to hear this. Of course we all knew of Shirley's diagnosis, but this is still a terrible thing to hear. What about her daughter, Carlie?"

"She was with her mother when it happened. But she's now in the care of the woman Ms. Duroy named as her legal guardian."

"Oh. I don't guess I knew she'd done that," Edward said.

"It appears she'd been preparing for this for some time," Lon said. "All of the paperwork was in order, and her daughter, Carlie, already knew the people's names and that they were going to take care of her when this happened. Again, I'm sorry for your loss," Lon said. "If you have any correspondence you need to send regarding her, send it to Butterman Law Office, Blessings, Georgia."

"Yes, I'll make note of that," Edward muttered, writing quickly before he forgot. "Thank you for calling."

Lon hung up, then finished making copies before getting back in the cruiser and going straight to the ER with the originals to find Dr. Quick.

"Hey, Doc, are you the one who pronounced Shirley Duroy?" he asked.

Dr. Quick nodded. "Just to make it official. She was already deceased when they loaded her in the ambulance, and she never responded to the CPR."

"This will explain why," Lon said and put Shirley Duroy's health records in the doctor's hands. "Ruby found them in her daughter's luggage."

Dr. Quick pulled them out of the envelope, scanned the pages, and then sighed.

"Okay, this explains a lot. I'll be calling her doctor to confirm all this, but given the information here, I don't see a reason to perform an autopsy. She did not pass unattended, and it appears she'd been warned her days were swiftly coming to an end."

Lon nodded. "Ms. Duroy has a seven-year-old daughter. She made Ruby Butterman the child's legal guardian. They got off the Greyhound, got as far as the lobby of the police station, and that's where she died. Her little girl was expecting it. It appears she's been helping take care of her mother for the past two years. I'll admit, it just about broke my heart."

"So the deceased woman knew Ruby?"

"Yes. The Duroy family was originally from here. Shirley once worked for Ruby. That little girl doesn't know it yet, but as we all know, her mother hit a home run when she picked out Carlie's guardian. Ruby has the biggest heart in Blessings."

Dr. Quick shook his head. "What a tragedy for the child and her mother."

"For sure," Lon said. "I better get back to work. Let me know if you need anything else."

Quick nodded, then took the paperwork to his office to make some calls before another emergency came in.

Peanut called home twice between appointments until he went into court, making sure Ruby and Carlie were okay. But after Ruby assured him the second time that all was well and everything was under control, he quit worrying.

"I love you," he said.

Ruby sighed. "I love you, too, honey."

"Our life just changed. Are you okay with that?" he asked.

"Yes, I am. We have everything we'll ever need, and this child has nothing and needs everything, most especially love. Whatever we need to do, I'm in."

"So am I. Don't doubt that," Peanut said. "Oops, it's time to go into the courtroom. See you later."

"Okay, honey. Do your stuff."

He chuckled as he disconnected. Ruby shivered. His laugh made her toes curl. She dropped the phone in her pocket, then took a load of clothes from the dryer and carried them to her bedroom.

Carlie was across the hall, playing, but when she heard Ruby in her bedroom, she came to the door to see what she was doing.

"Hey, sweetheart. I have clothes to hang up. Want to come sit on my bed and talk to me while I work?"

Carlie nodded.

Ruby dumped the clothes on the bed and then turned around to help her up onto the high mattress. As soon as Carlie was on the bed, she scooted toward the pile of warm clothes.

Ruby pretended she didn't see her thrusting her bare feet and legs beneath the pile as she began sorting the pieces and getting hangers.

"I helped Mama do laundry," Carlie said.

"I know you did," Ruby said. "The next load of laundry that's dried will be towels and washcloths. Do you know how to fold washcloths?"

Carlie nodded. "I like to help."

"That's wonderful," Ruby said. "I have lots and lots of towels to fold at my shop. Maybe you can help there, too. Have you ever been to one?"

Carly shook her head. "No. Mama cuts my hair."

Ruby saw the expression that washed over Carlie's face when realization hit. No more Mama meant no one left to cut her hair. There were going to be many moments like this in the coming days. Sad moments. Moments of feeling lost.

"Don't worry. I know how to cut hair, too. It's my job," Ruby said.

"Mama's job was counting numbers for people," Carlie said.

"Your mama used to work for me. Did she tell you that?" Ruby asked.

Carlie nodded again.

Ruby smiled. "She used to fold the towels in my hair salon."

"I can do that," Carlie said.

Ruby sighed. Bingo! Just what she needed—a willingness to go to the shop with her.

"Then that's what we'll do. We still have a little bit of summer vacation left, but school will start next month. You can come to work with me every day until school starts. There is a break room in the shop that has a bathroom, a table and chairs, a refrigerator, and a little sofa where you can nap if you get tired. And there are always snacks and the nicest ladies ever who work there. Will that be okay with you?"

"Can I bring Hoppy and my blanket?"

"Absolutely," Ruby said.

Carlie sighed. There were so many new things to remember.

Ruby stopped what she was doing and sat down on the bed beside Carlie and hugged her.

"Don't worry about all that now. We'll figure it out as we go, sweetheart. But I want you to promise me something, okay?"

"Okay."

"When something happens that scares you, or you don't understand, you come tell me or Mr. Ruby. We're here for you. Your mama made me your legal guardian because she knew I would take the best care of you when she couldn't. I know this is a very hard, sad day for you. And nothing can change that. Right now, all you need to know is that you're safe."

Carlie looked up at Ruby and then came out from under the warm clothes and crawled up into her lap.

Ruby was struggling not to cry as she wrapped her arms around the little girl and held her close. They sat that way without moving until there was a knock at the door.

"I'll bet that's Lovey with the groceries. We better let her in and get that ice cream in the freezer before it melts."

The thought of ice cream lifted Carlie's spirits. She nodded, scooted out of Ruby's lap, and then hurried with her into the foyer to answer the door.

It was Lovey, but Melissa was right behind her with Peanut's dress shirts from the cleaners.

"We're back!" Lovey cried. "I'll take the bags to the kitchen," she said.

"Where do you want the shirts?" Melissa asked.

"Do you mind taking them down the hall and putting them on my bed? It's the first door on the right."

"No problem," Melissa said and took off down the hall, only to come hurrying back moments later.

"Thank you so much," Ruby said, then laid her hand on Carlie's shoulder. "Carlie, honey, this is another friend of mine. Her name is Melissa. She's married to Lovey's son."

Melissa knelt down so that she was on Carlie's level.

"I'm very sorry about your mother," she said softly.

Carlie nodded, then backed up against Ruby's leg.

Ruby could see it was time to change the subject. "Melissa, I so appreciate you bringing Peanut's shirts. Wait while I get my purse so I can pay you."

Melissa stood. "Why don't I just bill you? That way you can deal with it when you have more time."

"Thank you. That would be helpful," Ruby said.

"Then I'll be going," Melissa said, and left.

"We better go help Lovey put up that ice cream," Ruby said.

Carlie nodded. "Before it melts."

Ruby smiled. "Yes, ma'am. Before it melts."

Lovey had everything out of the bags and on the counter, making it convenient for Ruby to put things away.

"I just put the ice cream in the freezer," Lovey said. "Oh, and there's a little something on the table for Carlie, from me."

Carlie's eyes widened, and then she looked straight at Ruby.

"Better go see what it is," Ruby said.

Carlie hurried over to the table and reached into the sack. She pulled out a coloring book and a big box of crayons.

"Do you like to color?" Lovey said.

Carlie nodded. "Thank you for the surprise."

Lovey wanted to hug her, but not today. Not when Carlie's emotions were raw enough to bleed.

"You're welcome, honey. Now, I better let you two get back to business. Ruby, if you need anything else, call. I'm home all day."

"Thank you so much," Ruby said.

"Anytime," Lovey said, then like Melissa, just waved goodbye to Carlie, and left.

"I'm going to put the groceries away before we go back to hanging up clothes," Ruby said. "Why don't you look through your new coloring book and find a picture you might want to color?"

Carlie didn't have to be told twice. Coloring and drawing were two of her favorite things to do.

A few moments later, Ruby looked over her shoulder.

Carlie was on her knees in a chair, the box of crayons open beside her, head down and coloring intently.

*Thank you, Lovey.*

# CHAPTER 3

THE TRAUMA OF THE MORNING BLED OVER INTO NOON WITH a withdrawal that Ruby couldn't crack as she watched Carlie pick through lunch with tears in her eyes.

As for Carlie, the reality of everything that she knew being gone was starting to soak in.

She was used to their little first-floor apartment and the small kitchen with a tiny table and two chairs. They'd left behind their cans of food that Mama kept in the cabinet to the right of the sink. And coloring in her new coloring book had reminded her of the pictures at home that were still on the refrigerator, stuck there with the magnets Mama collected. She knew, because it was one of the last things she remembered seeing as they walked out the door.

Her heart began to pound. What was going to happen to their things? Did they die like Mama? Or would someone rescue them like Miss Ruby rescued her? Compared to losing Mama, it was a small thing. But it was the culmination of all of it that became too much to bear. When she finally put her head down on the table and started to cry, the tears wouldn't stop.

Ruby jumped up from her chair and picked her up, grabbing Hoppy and the blanket. She headed for the rocker-recliner in the living room and plopped down with Carlie still in her arms. She tucked the rabbit beneath Carlie's chin and wrapped the blanket around her.

"It's okay, baby girl. It's okay. Cry all you want. Cry until that hurt inside you lets go enough to breathe. I know...I know."

And so she rocked, and hugged, and patted, until Carlie cried herself to sleep. And even then, Ruby didn't put her down. She was a problem solver, but there was no way to fix what was broken. All she knew was that when this little girl woke up, she must not wake up alone.

———————

She was still sitting there two hours later, still holding the sleeping child in her lap when Peanut walked in the door.

He took one look at the stricken expression on her face and knew they were struggling.

"Oh, honey...you're both breaking my heart here," he said softly as he knelt at Ruby's side. "What can I do?"

Ruby looked up. "The funeral home called a while ago. They want to know about Shirley's burying clothes. They're in a bag on our bed. Would you run them by? Everything they need is in it."

"Of course," he said and then patted Ruby's knee. "Do you want me to pick up food from Granny's for supper tonight? I think cooking is going to be one thing too much today."

Ruby sighed. "She had a bowl of cereal this morning, but didn't eat hardly anything at noon. I don't know what she likes, or what would tempt her. But whatever you get, make it kid friendly and not spicy."

Peanut leaned over, brushed a kiss over Ruby's lips, and then kissed her again, lingering on the softness. "This is the worst day of this child's life. And it's the first day of the rest of ours. It will all work out."

"Promise?" Ruby whispered.

"I promise. You love stronger and better than anyone I've ever known. You'll find the way to her heart. We both will, but it's going to take time. Now don't worry. I'll get the clothes to the funeral home and then swing by Granny's."

"Thank you," Ruby said.

Peanut gave her a thumbs-up, then went to get the bag from their bed. He blew her a kiss on the way out the door and then quietly closed it behind him.

Carlie whimpered in her sleep.

Ruby pushed off in the rocking chair with her toe to start the chair rocking again, and then reached for the remote and turned on the TV. She hit Mute while she searched channels for cartoons. Only after she found some did she turn the sound back on, and then kept rocking, letting Carlie wake up on her own to the familiar sounds of childhood.

———

It hadn't taken long for the town to learn about the young woman who got off the Greyhound this morning and went straight into the police station to die, or that she'd brought her daughter to Ruby to care for.

It was the greatest tragedy to come along in Blessings in quite a while, and it left the residents somber from the shock of it.

They all wondered about the little girl. What did she look like? How was she reacting to the death?

They were also curious about Ruby and Peanut. Why would this woman, a stranger, choose Ruby as the guardian? What was the mystery that linked them? Was Ruby related?

The stories were random, wild misconceptions, but typical of Blessings. In time, the connection would be made, and the questions would cease once they learned the dead woman's name. Then someone would remember the Duroy family, and Lovey would remind them that Shirley Duroy once worked for Ruby, and that would be that.

So when Peanut walked into Granny's later to order food to go, the diners began peppering him with questions. By the time he headed home, curiosity and suppositions were coming to an end, and facts were beginning to circulate.

Ruby had turned off the ringer on her phone, letting everything go to voicemail, answering only the texts from Vera and Vesta, and reassuring Lovey they had all they needed for now.

And then Carlie woke up in Ruby's arms.

"Hey, little one," Ruby said softly. "You had such a good nap."

Carlie nodded as she rubbed the sleep from her eyes.

"I need the bathroom," she said.

Ruby leaned down and kissed the end of Carlie's nose.

"Then hop to it," she said and slid the girl off her lap.

Carlie looked back at her toy and her blanket, but Ruby was all business.

"Hoppy wants to watch cartoons right here until you get back. Is that okay with you?"

Carlie blinked, then looked at the television, suddenly realizing her favorite cartoons were on.

"Yes," she said and took off running down the hall.

By the time she came back, Ruby had gotten up and gone to the kitchen, leaving Carlie to have the sofa and the cartoons all to herself.

It was a good move. When Peanut returned with their supper, Carlie was all curled up in a corner of the sofa with the rabbit in her lap and the blanket over both of them, glued to the show on TV.

"Hey, darlin'," he said as he walked into the house. "I brought supper from Granny's, and Lovey says hi. Are you hungry?"

She nodded.

He winked. "Then follow me. We have good stuff, and Lovey told me that there's ice cream for dessert."

Carlie climbed off the sofa, tucked the blanket around Hoppy, and left the cartoons playing. She ran to the kitchen and climbed up in her chair, parking in the seat on her knees to watch what was coming out of the sack.

"Fried chicken! Good choice!" Ruby said.

"And mashed potatoes and gravy, corn, green beans, and Mercy's wonderful biscuits. They also included a few chicken strips, in case Carlie preferred boneless," Peanut said.

"Just open all of the cartons and I'll bring plates and forks," Ruby said.

Carlie watched them laughing and talking as they moved about the kitchen. Mama was right. Miss Ruby was a really nice lady. But Mama never mentioned Mr. Ruby. And having never lived with a man in their house, Carlie didn't exactly know what she thought about him. But she liked the way he touched Miss Ruby's shoulder, the twinkle in his eyes, and the sound of his voice.

She was thinking about their old apartment again, and remembering how uncertain she felt when people above and around them got too loud…or had fights. And after Mama got sick, Carlie had to be afraid on her own.

But here in this house, no one was sick. These people were happy, and Mr. Ruby's voice was deep and soft. There were no neighbors above them, and the neighbors on either side had houses of their own. Besides, Mr. Ruby was so big that he made her feel safe. If anyone came knocking on this door and shouting at them to be quiet, he would tell them to go away.

Ruby brought a small glass of milk to the table, then stepped up beside Carlie's chair and began pointing to the open cartons and containers.

"Okay, sugar. We have fried chicken and boneless chicken strips, mashed potatoes and gravy. Also corn, and green beans, and the best biscuits ever. So, your job is to point to what you want on your plate, and I'll put it there."

"Are you going to fix my plate, too?" Peanut asked.

Ruby grinned. "No, sir, I am not. You're a big boy. You can fix your own."

Peanut laughed and waggled his eyebrows at Carlie, which made her feel happy inside, and when he picked up a piece of chicken and put it on his plate, Carlie pointed at the chicken strips.

"I like those, and 'tatoes and gravy, and corn, please."

Ruby put some of all that on Carlie's plate, then halved a biscuit, buttered it, and added it to her plate.

"Do you eat your chicken strips plain, or do you like to dip them in something?"

Carlie glanced at Peanut, who had just cut a bite from the chicken breast on his plate and dunked it in the gravy on his potatoes.

"Gravy?" Carlie whispered.

Ruby smiled. "Again, just like Mr. Ruby. Who knew?"

Carlie looked at Peanut again, and when he winked at her, she smiled and then ducked her head.

"Finally, someone who likes stuff like I do," Peanut said.

Ruby thought it wasn't possible to love this man more than she already did, but she knew what Peanut was doing and wanted to hug him where he sat. The best part was that it appeared to be working on Carlie.

Ruby got a little dish from the cabinet, poured some gravy into it, and then put it on Carlie's plate beside the chicken strips.

"There you go. Enjoy," she said.

Peanut squirted a little bit of honey on his biscuit, then took a bite.

"Yum," he said and rolled his eyes, then held up the little squirt bottle. "Want to try a drop on your biscuit, too?" he asked.

She nodded.

He squirted a tiny bit on the edge and then kept eating, satisfied that she'd taken a healthy bite of it, as well as a big scoop of mashed potatoes and gravy. Then he watched as she dunked her chicken strip in the gravy and took a bite.

"Yum," she said and proceeded to watch Peanut as she ate. Whatever he took a bite of next, she followed suit.

Ruby smiled. This appeared to be a case of love at first sight, which meant Carlie was smarter at knowing a good thing when she saw it than Ruby had been. Ruby had been oblivious of Peanut's affections toward her for ages. She sighed and, for the first time today, felt a tiny bit of relief.

Peanut and Ruby talked to each other for a while, purposefully leaving Carlie to eat on her own so she could relax.

Carlie liked listening to the conversation. She and Mama used to talk like this. Sometimes they talked about her school, and sometimes about the work Mama did online for her job. Mama's job was about numbers, and Carlie could count to almost a hundred, but she still got mixed up at the eighties and nineties.

Finally, she had eaten all she wanted and was sitting back waiting for someone to say *dessert*.

"Are you finished with your plate?" Ruby asked as she stood up to begin clearing off the table.

Carlie nodded.

"Did you save room for a little ice cream?" Peanut asked.

"Yes. I saved room," she said.

"Awesome. Me too," he said. "But it will cost you one smile. Do you have one smile to spend?" he asked.

She blinked.

Ruby rolled her eyes as she got the ice cream out of the freezer. "He's just teasing, honey. Mr. Ruby is full of funnies and jokes."

Peanut grinned.

Carlie was intrigued by the idea of paying for ice cream with a smile, and when Ruby brought her ice cream to the table, she looked up at Ruby and smiled.

Ruby smiled back and patted the back of Carlie's head.

"Your mama sure raised a sweetheart."

The thought of Mama made her heart tug, but the sweet bite of ice cream on her tongue eased the pain. She ate a little more, then paused and looked up.

"Who feeds Mama now?" she asked.

Ruby frowned, pretending to think about it. "Why, I suppose the angels are serving supper right about this time, too. Wouldn't you say so, Peanut?"

He glanced at his watch.

"I'd guess they are already through. It doesn't take as long for angels to eat as it does for us."

Carlie slid another bite of ice cream into her mouth, interested in this concept, and as soon as she swallowed it, she asked, "Why not?"

Peanut shrugged, then leaned forward and lowered his voice. "Well, I always heard that the food in heaven just melts in your mouth…like that ice cream you're eating. You don't even have to chew, and nobody is sick in heaven or ever gets hurts. Everyone is all well there."

"Then can you come back?" Carlie asked.

Peanut shook his head. "No. But everyone who goes there waits for their loved ones to grow old, and then when it's time, they come to get us so we don't have to travel to heaven by ourselves. I like knowing that."

Carlie blinked. "Did someone come to get Mama like that?"

"Sure, and I'll bet I know who it was," Peanut said.

Carlie leaned forward. "Who?"

"Your grandparents. Your mama was their little girl, just like you were hers. They're taking care of her now, just like we're going to take care of you…which is what your mama wanted, right?"

Carlie nodded. "Yes. Mama said Miss Ruby will take care of me."

"And me… Don't forget me!" Peanut cried.

She giggled. "And Mr. Ruby."

"Thank you," he said and scooped the last bite of ice cream into his mouth and let it melt on his tongue. "Ice cream is the best thing ever," he said.

Carlie ate her last bite. "Ever," she echoed.

Ruby listened to the story Peanut was spinning and thought to herself that she'd never heard a more touching way to soothe a child's concerns. It also dawned on her then, as she watched them chatting away like two old friends, what an amazing father Peanut would have been—was going to be.

She turned her back to them so they wouldn't see her tears, and kept cleaning up and loading the dishwasher, then putting away the leftovers. When Peanut carried their empty ice cream bowls to the sink, she turned around and hugged him.

"Well, thanks, but what's that for?" he said, chuckling.

"Lovey always said, if you wanted to, you could talk a pig into laying an egg, and now I see how that happens. You are an amazing orator and lawyer, but you are an even more amazing man. I love you so much."

Peanut hugged her close. "Love you more," he whispered, then turned around and looked at Carlie. "Hey, Carlie, after I change into my old clothes, want to come outside with me and help water Miss Ruby's flowers?"

"Yes!"

Peanut gave her a thumbs-up, then left the kitchen at a lope.

Ruby saw Carlie pushing hair out of her eyes and dug in her pocket for a hair band and headed for the table.

"How about we put your hair up so it won't be bothering you while you and Mr. Ruby water my flowers?" she asked.

"Okay," Carlie said and sat still while Ruby began combing her fingers through Carlie's hair to smooth it out, then pulled it all up and put it in a ponytail.

"Now then. That will be cooler and won't get in your eyes. Does it feel better?"

Carlie nodded, and when she did, the ponytail bobbed up and down. She felt it and smiled. She was still smiling when Peanut came back, and he was barefoot.

He pointed to the sandals on her feet.

"Girl, you can't water flowers in those shoes. We're doing this barefoot."

Carlie looked up at Ruby.

"That's a good idea," Ruby said.

Carlie came out of her sandals in seconds and jumped out of the chair.

Peanut gave her little ponytail a quick tug and then opened the back door that led out onto their patio.

"Miss Ruby, we will be giving your flower babies a drink now," he said.

"Thank you both. They will appreciate it, for sure," Ruby said.

She was smiling as the door closed behind them.

Carlie gasped the moment she exited the house. She'd never seen a backyard look like this. There were a bajillion colors of flowers, and stones laid down in curvy lines to walk on, and a little round white shed out in the middle of the yard that had a floor and a roof, but no walls, just posts to hold up the roof, and seats beneath the roof so you could sit in the shade.

"What's that?" she asked, pointing to the little white house without walls.

"That's called a gazebo. Miss Ruby and I like to sit there sometimes and watch the hummingbirds feeding, the birds splashing in the birdbaths, and the butterflies and bees in her flowers."

Carlie was in awe. It looked like the magic garden in one of her storybooks.

"Are there fairies here?" she whispered.

Peanut paused, looked down at the little blond standing beside him, and thought, *Besides the one standing beside me?*

"It's hard to tell. You know how fairies are. They don't like to be seen," he said. "Now we better get busy here. If you're going to be my watering buddy, you need to learn the ropes. The first thing is watering everything in the pots and flower beds, and then when we've finished, we'll turn on the sprinkler system and it will water everything else. We don't have to do the sprinkler but about once a week, but we water the flowers in the pots and beds every day when it's hot. Miss Ruby does love her flowers."

"I love flowers, too," Carlie said. "And fairies. I love fairies a lot."

Peanut found a little watering can in the shed, filled it partway with water so it wouldn't be too heavy for her to hold, and then pointed to the pots on the patio.

"You can start with those. Let me show you once, and then you can do the rest." He tilted the can, letting a good amount of water shower down onto the soil around the pink petunias in the pot, and then handed the can back to her. "Now you do the others just like that, and if you run out of water, tell me and I'll fill it up for you again, okay?"

"Okay," she said.

Her expression was serious, but her eyes were alight with glee. Peanut watched for a couple of seconds and then stepped off the patio with the hose and began watering the larger flowering bushes below the patio deck.

And so it went, with Peanut refilling her can and Carlie following him farther and farther out into the yard until they were all but walking in step, watering and talking and looking for fairies.

Ruby watched from the window, relieved that for the moment grief had been replaced by such a simple thing as tending to something in need. And that's when it hit her. Carlie had been taking care of her mother for a long time. She just needed something else to take care of until she remembered she was still a little girl and no longer the one in charge.

———————

Almost an hour passed before Peanut came into the house with Carlie riding piggyback and ducked when they came through the doorway to keep her from bumping her head.

"Hey, Ruby, we're wet," Peanut yelled.

"Then wipe your feet. I already put down a mat," she yelled back.

Peanut looked down, saw a door mat just in front of him, and laughed. "Oh. Right!" He set Carlie on her feet. "Wipe good so you don't slip and fall on the tile," he said.

Carlie wiped her feet and then danced across the floor to the chair where she'd been sitting and reclaimed Hoppy and her blanket just as Ruby came into the kitchen.

"Such hard workers," she said.

"We looked for fairies," Carlie said.

Ruby gasped. "Oh my! Did you see any?"

Carlie shook her head. "No, but Mr. Ruby thinks fairies are shy. We'll just have to pay 'tention."

"Thank you both for watering the flowers for me today," Ruby said. She gave Carlie a quick hug and then gave Peanut a hug.

But instead of just letting her hug him, Peanut swung Ruby off her feet and danced her around the room in his bare feet until she was laughing and begging him to put her down.

Carlie was delighted. She'd never seen grown-ups playing.

And the minute Peanut put Ruby down, he swung Carlie up in his arms and danced her across the floor and back, with Carlie giggling and squealing every time he swooped.

When he put her back down, she picked Hoppy up and danced him around the kitchen so he wouldn't feel left out.

Ruby and Peanut watched, their arms around each other, hoping this one pure moment of joy on Carlie's face was but a hint of the years to come.

———————————

Ladd Daltry was the third generation of his family to grow up on their farm, but he had been struggling to keep it running ever since the death of his father earlier in the year.

Deborah Ryman, his first love, had grown up across the creek from the Daltry farm, enamored with Ladd, and he with her. When he graduated from high school two years ahead of her, he went away to college and for some reason just let go of Blessings and everyone in it. Suddenly, the two-year difference in their ages sent their lives in two different directions. By the time she graduated from high school, he was into his junior year in college, and she was just a teenage crush that had come to an end.

When Ladd came home after graduating from college, he thought of Deborah and was thinking of looking her up when they told him Deborah was long gone, in college in Oklahoma studying to become a veterinarian. He was struck by a sudden emptiness, knowing he'd let go of someone who still mattered. And then his visit was over, and he left to begin his new job as an architect for a firm in Atlanta.

After that, the times between visits to Blessings became longer as he got busier, and time passed. His mother, Anne, got cancer and died so fast he didn't have time to process it. He came home for the funeral, hugged his father goodbye four days later, and went back to his life in Atlanta, and more years passed.

Then he got the phone call that his father, Walter, was ill, and a wave of guilt swept over him that he still carried. He came home to help, thinking his father would get better. Instead, he died, and for some reason—maybe more guilt—Ladd stayed.

He picked up some work part time for an architecture firm in Savannah and had an office set up in the house, attending meetings via Zoom—when the Wi-Fi wasn't down. He worked the farm the rest of the time, barely making ends meet. He needed to devote all of his time to one or the other, but it was the architect job that was keeping the farm afloat.

He was at the point of thinking he needed to sell off the livestock and put the farm up for sale, but he had to get things mended first. It wasn't what he wanted to do, but he knew his limitations, and there just wasn't enough of him to go around.

This morning he'd gotten up, gathered up the stuff to fix fence, and was in the back pasture getting ready to mend a downed wire when he heard a snort and then a bellow. By the time he got turned around, a strange bull was in his pasture, between him and his pickup truck, and coming at him at a run.

"Oh shit," Ladd muttered and started running for the clump of trees about twenty yards away. He was tall and his legs were long, but it would still be a miracle if he made it.

Deborah Ryman was back on the family farm. She'd driven in from outside of Louisville, Kentucky, where she worked as a big-animal vet, and had been home only three days. But the news that awaited her was already a heartbreaking reality she'd tried hard to ignore.

Deborah's father, Josh, was in a nursing home in Blessings, and had been for almost four years now, since suffering a stroke. He was never going to get better, and both she and her mom, Maggie, had accepted that fact.

But living out on the farm alone and driving into Blessings several days a week to spend time with Josh was wearing Maggie down. So she called Deborah and asked her to come home and help her get the farm ready to sell so she could move into Blessings to be closer to him.

It was, for Deborah, something of a shock. She'd known this day would come, but it was still hard to accept, and today her mother had gone to town to visit Josh, leaving Deborah to do as she wished. So she chose to walk the land one last time while it still belonged to the family.

It was July, and even up in the hills it was hot as Hades. But she wasn't at some lake sunning on the shore and knew better than to take off through the trees and underbrush in a pair of shorts and a tank top.

Instead, she'd put on the oldest jeans she owned, chosen an old white T-shirt and boots, and was halfway out the door when she thought about snakes, stopped, and went back to the closet where they kept her daddy's hunting rifle. She checked to make sure it was loaded, then slung the strap over her shoulder and left the house.

She walked without aim for about half an hour until she realized she was just across the creek from the Daltry place. Her mom had already mentioned Ladd had come home after his dad got cancer and then stayed on after Walt Daltry died. When she said he was single, Deborah changed the subject. She didn't want to know anything personal about him. It was safer that way.

He was her first love, and he broke her heart when he left for college. After all they'd meant to each other, it was as if she'd never existed. He would be in his mid-thirties by now. Hopefully, he'd gotten fat and bald.

When she came to the creek separating the properties, she stood there a few moments, looking through the trees in disbelief. Damned if Ladd Daltry wasn't in the pasture right in front of her, working in plain sight. And, from where she was standing, she could see he wasn't fat. Then when he took his cap off to wipe the sweat off his forehead, she saw a full head of dark hair and a face that looked more like actor Jesse Metcalfe than the boy she remembered.

*Okay. Fine. So he's still the same good-looking Daltry he'd always been. Just older. Means nothing to me.*

But when she saw him suddenly stop and turn, she could tell by the set of his shoulders something was wrong. Within seconds, she saw the charging bull and realized it was between him and his truck.

As Ladd took off for the trees, Deborah tore through the brush, slid down the creek bank on her bootheels, ran up the other side, and leaped the fence. Before she had time to fire off a shot, the bull caught up with Ladd, butted him hard in the back, and tossed him up into the air.

Now Deborah was running and screaming, but the bull didn't stop, and as she was pulling the rifle strap from her shoulder, Ladd landed facedown and got stomped in the back.

Deborah wasn't fifty feet away when she fired one round up into the air, hoping the bull would run. Instead, it turned, saw her, and began pawing the ground.

She raised her arms and the gun up in the air and began waving and shouting, and then fired the gun again, shouting as she began to approach the bull.

The bull bellowed and tossed its head, and when she fired off the rifle the third time, still shouting and waving her hands, the bull turned toward the break in the fence and ran back into his own pasture.

Within seconds, Deborah was running toward Ladd's truck. She jumped into the driver's seat, started the engine, and took off toward where he was lying as fast as she could go, sliding to a stop a few feet from him. She jumped out on the run, then dropped to her knees beside him to feel for a pulse.

It was there!

"Thank God," Deborah muttered and then started looking for wounds.

There were hoofprints and blood on the back of his shirt, and a long gash on the back of his head was bleeding profusely.

She grabbed her phone, only to realize there was no reception down in this low valley. Her only option was to get Ladd in his truck and head for Blessings. She would drive into an area with cell reception and be able to call for help as they went.

But she needed something to stanch the blood, and without hesitating yanked off her T-shirt, wrapped it around his head, and tied it off over the wound.

"Now to get you in the truck," Deborah muttered.

She jumped back in it, turned it around so that the passenger side was nearest him, got out and opened the passenger door, and reclined the seat.

Deborah was almost six feet tall and strong from all the years of working with big animals, so she had faith that she could do this. But when she bent down to grab him beneath his shoulders, he stirred and then groaned.

She'd hurt him, and God only knew what the bull had done to him internally.

"I'm so sorry, but you got yourself into a mess. Bear with me," she muttered, and then looked in the back of his truck, saw a big tarp folded up in the corner, and grabbed it.

She unfurled it, then carefully rolled him onto the tarp before using bungee cords to keep the tarp wrapped around his waist and legs. It was the only way she could stabilize him and hope she wasn't hurting him worse. Then she grabbed hold of the tarp and started pulling his body toward the truck.

It took every ounce of strength she had to drag him into the reclining seat. Then she slid her arms beneath him and lifted him the rest of the way up and buckled him in. She was already inside and buckling herself up when she realized the bull was back in the pasture again.

"Eat my dust," she muttered, slammed the truck into drive, and took off through the pasture, heading toward the cattle guard. Once she crossed it, she drove into the back pasture behind the barn, then past the outbuildings and the main house, and headed down the drive. She kept glancing at him as she drove, making sure Ladd was still breathing. There was blood all over the inside of the tarp, and he was moaning.

"Don't you die on me," she shouted. "Do you hear me, Ladd Daltry? Don't you dare die!"

She slid and skidded through gravel until she reached blacktop leading to the highway and floored it. She knew the road like the back of her hand, and the ride could have been worse. His truck was a late model with good shocks, and Deborah was fearless behind the wheel.

When she reached the highway, she finally had time to check to see if she had enough bars on her phone to make a call. She pulled out onto the highway, the wheels humming as she drove, and made the call to 911 and put it on speaker. The speedometer read 98 miles per hour when she heard a dispatcher's voice and was so relieved she wanted to cry.

"911. What is your emergency?"

"This is Deborah Ryman. I'm bringing in an injured man to the ER. He got stomped by a bull and has not regained consciousness.

I'm about eight minutes outside of Blessings, and I'm coming in hot. Can you clear Main Street all the way to the ER?"

"We'll do our best, but be ready to slow down anyway, just in case."

"Yes. Okay," Deborah said and gripped the steering wheel a little tighter to take the upcoming curve in the road.

# CHAPTER 4

AFTER AVERY, THE DAY DISPATCHER, TOOK DEBORAH'S 911 call, he dispatched the info to all officers on duty.

Chief Lon Pittman had just made a U-turn at the far end of the street when he heard it. It wasn't the best of choices to bring an injured man in like this, but he knew how far the Daltry place was from Blessings, and without firsthand knowledge of the injuries, he wouldn't second-guess Deborah's decision. So he keyed up the radio, issuing orders to all the officers on duty as he went.

"Get on the loudspeakers. Turn on your sirens to get people pulled over. We need to clear Main Street from the north end of town all the way to the hospital. Just keep issuing the order to park or get off Main. We don't have much time."

Within seconds, sirens were blaring all up and down Main and vehicles were pulling to the curb to park. Deputy Ralph Herman was on the loudspeaker, repeating the order to clear Main Street.

People in cars either pulled to the curb and parked or took off onto a side street to park. Shopkeepers and customers came out of the stores, lining up along the street to see what was happening, and it didn't take long.

They heard the whine of the engine before they saw the truck. Many recognized it as Ladd's, but he wasn't the one driving it. From what they could see, a nearly naked woman was at the wheel, and she was flying.

Lon clocked her at 81 miles per hour as she came toward him, and as soon as she took the turn off Main heading toward the hospital, he got on the radio.

"Resume normal traffic," he said, and followed her to the ER.

Deborah came to an abrupt stop in front of the doors to the ER and got out on the run. But she didn't have to go inside for help. They came to her, transferring Ladd, tarp and all, from the front seat of the truck onto the gurney, then heading inside with Deborah running beside them.

They got him to an exam room, and within seconds Dr. Quick and his team began questioning her as they removed the tarp and cut off Ladd's clothes.

"What happened?" Quick asked.

"A bull was chasing Ladd and hit him from behind. It tossed him in the air, and then he came down on his belly," Deborah said. "I know the bull stomped him at least once in the back, but I didn't take his shirt off to see. All I know is by the time I got to him, the back of his shirt was bloody and his head was bleeding. The bull had horns. I guess they caused the head wound. I used my shirt for a bandage."

"Has he regained consciousness?" Quick asked.

"No, sir."

"Then how did you know what happened?" Quick asked.

"Oh. Our properties are separated by a creek. I was walking our fence line when I saw him and the bull, almost at the same time. I saw him take off running for some trees, but I couldn't get to him in time to stop the bull. I did finally run it off by firing my rifle several times. Ladd was in a back pasture down in a low spot, and there was no cell service, so I loaded him up and headed to Blessings."

Quick kept examining the patient as Deborah talked, and when they rolled him over on his side and found the cut on the back of his head, along with already darkening bruises where the bull stomped him, there was a communal groan around the exam table.

"His blood pressure is up but stable, and his heartbeat is fairly steady. I need full body pictures," Quick said. "Get him to X-Ray stat."

They were taking him out of the room, bed and all, when Chief Pittman came running down the hall. He recognized Ladd, bloody, pale, and unconscious, and Deborah standing in the doorway wearing boots, blue jeans, and a bra, and covered in blood.

"Is any of that yours?" Lon asked as he approached.

Deborah blinked, then looked down at herself and sighed.

"No."

"I know his dad recently passed, but would you happen to know who his next of kin might be?" Lon asked.

"He's an only child. All of his immediate family have passed."

Lon nodded. "Okay, thanks. Did you say he got stomped by a bull?"

Deborah nodded, then explained once more how she came to be involved.

"I don't know anything else to tell you, but Mom and I are his closest neighbors and oldest friends, if that counts for anything," she added.

"I'm sure it will count for a lot to Ladd when he wakes up and finds out you saved his life," Lon said. "Hang on a sec. I'll be right back," he said and headed out of the back of the ER through the ambulance bay.

Deborah looked down at herself and shuddered, then headed into a nearby bathroom to wash up. When she came back out, the chief was standing in the hall with a T-shirt.

"Here you go," he said, and handed it to her. "Blessings PD always comes prepared."

"Oh wow… Thanks, Chief. I was beginning to feel the chill of the air-conditioning," she said and pulled the dark-blue t-shirt over her head.

"No problem," Lon said and then also handed her a set of keys. "I moved the truck out of the ER entrance for you. It's parked on the front row out in the parking lot, next to the row of handicap parking places."

"Thanks again," Deborah said, and dropped the keys in her pocket.

The police chief left, and Deborah went back into Ladd's exam room and sat down and called her mother.

———————

Maggie Ryman was feeding Josh. He'd never regained his motor skills after the massive stroke he'd suffered years earlier, and his mental and physical decline were obvious and pronounced. She was waiting for Josh to swallow when her cell phone rang. She glanced down, saw it was Deborah, and then patted Josh's leg.

"Just a second, honey. It's Deborah. I'd better answer."

Josh didn't indicate by so much as a blink that he even remembered who Deborah was, as Maggie laid down the spoon and picked up the call.

"Hello."

"Hey, Mom, can you talk a minute?" Deborah asked.

"Yes, sure. I was just feeding your daddy his lunch. What's up?"

"I'm in town. I brought Ladd Daltry to the ER."

"Oh my lord! What happened?"

Again, Deborah repeated her story, and by the time she was through, Maggie was in disbelief.

"I cannot believe that happened. Thank God you were there. Ladd is alone now. No one would have known he was missing. Do you know how bad he was hurt?"

"Not yet. They took him to X-Ray. I'm in his exam room, waiting for them to bring him back."

"Did he say—"

"I haven't talked to him at all, Mom. He was unconscious by the time I got to him, and he has yet to wake up."

"Oh no. I don't like that," Maggie said. "I'll finish feeding your daddy and then be right there."

"Okay, but don't freak when you see me. The blood on my clothes isn't mine. It's his."

"Lord. Well, a few prayers wouldn't hurt while you're waiting," Maggie said. "I'll be there as soon as I can."

———————————

Ladd woke up in X-Ray, in more pain than he'd ever felt in his life. He groaned, trying to figure out what was wrong, but the moment he opened his eyes and saw hospital personnel, he remembered.

*That damn bull. I didn't make the trees, but how...?*

"Hang on, Ladd. Hold your breath for just a few seconds more."

Ladd closed his eyes. Hold his breath? He couldn't inhale enough to stay conscious.

"That's good. We've got what we need," the X-ray tech said. "You can take him back now. Tell Quick I'll send him the X-rays on his laptop."

Ladd felt like he'd been split open from the back of his head to his waist.

"Am I still in one piece?" he mumbled as they turned his bed around and started moving him down a hall.

"More or less," one of the orderlies said, then grinned and patted him on the shoulder. "Just lie still, buddy. Dr. Quick will get you fixed up."

Ladd moaned. *Lie still. Like I have any other options.*

They wheeled him back to the ER and then into an exam room.

"He woke up," the orderly said as a nurse and the doctor came back into the room.

Deborah stood, anxiously watching.

Now that Ladd was conscious to answer questions, Dr. Quick began questioning him, but he didn't have much to say.

"I don't remember anything but seeing the bull and running for the trees. I don't know how I got here, and I don't know how I'm still alive."

And then a woman moved to the foot of the bed and into his line of vision.

———————

It had been years since they'd seen or spoken to each other, but Deborah could tell by the way Ladd was staring at her that he didn't recognize her. That was fair, since she was a good six inches taller and a woman, instead of the leggy teen he would have remembered.

Ladd frowned. The woman at the foot of his bed was obviously not hospital staff. She was tall, tan, and lean, and there was blood all over her jeans.

"Who?" he asked.

Deborah sighed. He was awake. It didn't appear he was going to die.

"I'll be in the waiting room," she said and walked out.

"That's the woman who saved your life," Dr. Quick told Ladd. "She said she was your neighbor."

Ladd frowned. Neighbor? And then it hit him.

*Oh shit. That was Deborah? If she saved his life, then how did she get the bull away from him? And how the hell did she get him into the truck? He thought of the blood on her and wondered, did she get hurt, too?*

Then he saw the X-rays on the light panel and pointed.

Dr. Quick glanced over at the X-rays. "Yes, that's you. Broken ribs, a partially collapsed lung, and we'll be stapling up the back of your head."

Ladd groaned. The news sucked. The room was beginning to spin, and when he closed his eyes, he passed out.

———————

Deborah was in the lobby in the ER, waiting for Dr. Quick, when her mother came hurrying inside. She spotted Deborah immediately, hurried over, and plopped down in the chair beside her.

"What's the verdict?" she asked.

Deborah shrugged. "He woke up. Didn't recognize me. I'm waiting for the doctor to come tell me what's up."

"Well, thank goodness he woke up," Maggie said. "And I'm not surprised he didn't recognize you. It's been years since you two have seen each other."

Deborah wasn't going into their history together, but she thought it was weird as hell that a guy wouldn't remember the girl he'd grown up with and had sex with multiple times in the loft of his daddy's barn.

However, her mom was right. It had been years. And he'd just had his head split open.

"How's Dad?" Deborah asked.

Maggie shrugged. "The same, maybe weaker. What can I do for you?"

"I don't know, Mom. I need to know Ladd's condition before I figure out what to do next. I'm sure they'll keep him, but I want to know if he's going to need surgery. If he's here for a few days, I'll drive his truck home and see what livestock needs to be tended."

"The cattle are on good grass. He's not feeding them. He let the chickens go. The place was too much for one man to take care of, and it was losing money. I know because he and I talked about the fact that we were in the same boat. We needed hired help or to restructure. I didn't have the heart for it, and I know he's lonely there."

"Oh wow," Deborah muttered, trying to imagine the Daltry place going under.

Maggie shrugged. "Times are hard. You need money and warm bodies to work in this business, and we couldn't pay anyone enough to make it worth their while to work for us."

Deborah reached for her mother's hand and held it.

They were sitting in silence when Dr. Quick came out into the lobby looking for Deborah, then headed for her and sat down in the chair beside her.

"How is he?" Deborah asked. "Is he going to need surgery?"

"Not at this point," Quick said. "He has a partially collapsed lung, but he's on 100 percent oxygen right now, and I think the lung will correct itself in the coming hours. He has some broken ribs, which we have since reset, but I'm not wrapping them. That would restrict his breathing, and that lung needs to have breathing room to inflate. I put eleven staples in his head. The bull stomped his back, but not his head. I don't know how that got cut, but the X-rays don't show any internal injuries and no cracks in the skull. Maybe he got grazed by a hoof?"

"The bull had horns. The tips were missing, but there was about eight inches of thick horns sticking out like clubs. You're keeping him, right?" Deborah asked.

"Yes, ma'am, for several days."

"Then, when he wakes up again, tell him I took his truck home, and that I'll make sure to lock everything up before I leave. I'll take the keys with me, so when it's time for him to go home, someone call me. I'll come get him."

"I can do that," Dr. Quick said. "And just for the record, you are an amazing woman."

"It was a fluke that I was even there to witness it," Deborah said. "Is it okay if I come back tomorrow and visit him?"

"Sure. Barring any complications, he'll be in a regular room until he leaves."

"Thanks," Deborah said, and then she and her mother got up and left the building. "Are you going home now?" Deborah asked.

"No. I need to stop by the Crown to pick up some groceries first."

"Then I'm going to take Ladd's truck home. Will you come pick me up there and save me a half-hour walk home?"

"Absolutely," Maggie said. "I won't be far behind you. Oh… there is still one animal on the place who needs daily feeding. His name is Sam, the big yellow tomcat that lives in the hay barn. If there's any cat food in the granary, you might want to put some

food out. Even though the cat is there to keep the rodent popula-
tion down, I think Ladd's been feeding him."

"I'll check," Deborah said. "Take your time and drive safe."

"I will," Maggie said and got in her car, while Deborah headed
for Ladd's truck.

This was not what she'd expected when she got out of bed this
morning, but life seemed to have a way of changing people's plans.

---

Deborah made it back to the Daltry house, parked the truck in
the garage, and recovered her rifle. The inside of Ladd's truck was
bloody, so she went into the house from the garage, found cleaning
supplies and a bunch of paper towels, and went back to the truck.

As soon as she was satisfied all of the blood had been cleaned
up, she left the window down a bit in the truck to air it out, dumped
the bloody paper towels in the garbage can outside, and went back
in the house, turning off all but one light in the hall and making
sure everything was good to go before she locked up.

She was still carrying her rifle when she headed for the barn to
check for a cat. She was looking for a feeding pan when she opened
the first granary and saw a pan beside a little bed of straw, and a
bowl of water. She put some dry cat food in the tin bowl beside the
water, then looked around for the cat.

It didn't take long for her to hear a slight meow from above her
head and look up. A big yellow tom was walking a rafter toward the
open top of the granary.

"Well, hello, Sam. You are a fine-looking fellow. Your pal had a
run-in with a bull, but he's going to be okay. He'll be home in no
time, but don't worry. I'll make sure you don't go hungry, okay?"

The cat paused on the rafter above her head, then climbed
down the old wooden step ladder leaning against the wall.

"So that's why there's a ladder in an empty granary," Deborah
said.

When the cat head-butted her foot, she reached down and scratched it between the ears.

"Such a good boy," she said, and when the cat quit her for the bowl of food, she jumped out of the granary, fastened the door behind her, and headed back toward the house.

She was sitting on the porch, rocking in the porch swing and remembering sitting here with Ladd and sneaking kisses, when she saw her mom's car coming up the drive.

"And there's my ride," she muttered, grabbing her rifle from the front porch step and going to meet her mother. She put the rifle in the back seat, got in, and leaned back with a sigh.

"That Coke is from Broyles Dairy Freeze. It's for you. Relax. We'll be home soon enough."

"Oh, thanks, Mom. You are the best," Deborah said.

The cold drink burned her nose and the back of her throat as she took a quick sip, and then she did as she was told and relaxed all the way home.

---

Bart Carlson's office was at the end of the hall at Lloyd and Lloyd CPA. He always worked with the door shut because voices distracted him, but even with the door closed, he could hear more than the normal murmur of voices coming and going out in the hall. He was on the verge of complaining when there was a knock at his door, and then his boss was standing in the doorway.

"Bart, sorry to interrupt your work, but we got a call regarding Shirley Duroy. You know how ill she's been... Well, she passed away this morning."

Bart gasped. "Oh no! I'm so sorry to hear this. What of sweet baby Carlie? Who's taking care of her? My wife and I are free to step in if—"

"Oh...Shirley passed away in Georgia. She was in some place called Blessings when it happened, but Carlie is with her legal guardian now. There's nothing more for us to do, other than we'll be sending flowers from the firm. Carry on," Edward said and pulled the door closed as he backed out.

Bart was in shock. Georgia? Legal guardian? How did all of this happen without him knowing it? He'd been certain Shirley would eventually come around about him and Mila taking Carlie. He didn't know what he thought about this, but he was going to do his own investigating before he let this go. He needed to let Mila know what had happened. Granted, they might have assumed too much, but they'd had plans.

He grabbed his cell phone and sent her a text.

> Shirley Duroy passed away. Her daughter is in the custody of some guardian in Georgia. This is not what we expected. I will be investigating the legalities of this. TTYL, Bart.

It was raining when Bart left the office, and he'd already fielded two texts from Mila wanting him to stop off on the way home to pick up wine and the meal she'd ordered for curbside pickup.

He readily agreed, but it ticked him off.

Mila didn't work.

He paid people to clean their house, and the majority of their laundry went to the cleaners.

She shopped.

And she got massages and pedicures and manicures.

And called herself a homemaker, when in fact she was more often a pain in the ass.

But she was pretty, socially adept, and came from money, all of which were reasons why he'd dated and married her.

The only big thing they butted heads over was that she refused to have children and lose her figure and freedom. That's why the idea of taking in an orphan had occurred to him.

Bart had already married money, and now taking in a kid who'd inherited money seemed like a good idea—like adding to the plan to be rich. And Mila was amenable, as long as she didn't have to grow one inside her to get it. There were always nannies and babysitters. She wouldn't be disadvantaged in any way, and they'd be doing a good deed. It never occurred to either of them that the child would be anything but grateful—or they would be expected to expend emotion, to bond and show love.

But now that plan appeared to be moot. It had blown up in Bart's face, and he'd never seen that coming. He wasn't sure what he was going to do about this, but he felt like he owed it to himself to at least follow through—just to make sure the child was in good hands.

Lord only knew what kind of people Shirley had chosen as guardians. He'd never been to her home, but he knew the area in which they'd lived in Little Rock and it was nothing to write home about.

So he was in a mood when he parked at the supermarket to run in to get a bottle of wine and was soaked by the time he got back to the car. He headed off to the restaurant to pick up the food Mila had ordered. As soon as he arrived, he called in, and they brought the order out for curbside pickup. He tipped the server extra for having to bring it out in the rain and then headed home.

The windshield wipers were on high, and the thunder and lightning within the storm made driving dicey. By the time he pulled up their drive and into the garage, he was in an even worse mood. He hit the remote and lowered the garage door, which finally muted most of the storm.

His steps were measured, his feet dragging as he carried their dinner into the house and set everything on the counter before heading back to their bedroom to change.

Mila was lounging on their bed, video chatting on her phone when Bart walked in. She saw the state he was in and frowned.

"Bart! You're tracking on the carpet!"

He began stripping as he went, leaving the sopping clothes in piles. He was naked by the time he got to the bathroom and slammed the door shut.

Mila gasped, then pretended to be amused. "Carol, I have to go. Bart came home in a snit." She disconnected, then leaped off the bed and began gathering up his clothes and running with them through the house to the utility room.

She saw the wine and their dinner on the cabinet, glanced out the window at the downpour, and sighed.

"Okay, fine. You got wet…and now you're in the shower getting even wetter. Explain the difference to me," she muttered and began taking containers out of the sack, checking to see if everything she ordered was there, and then eyed the wine he'd brought home before getting down two wineglasses.

She had the table set, the wine chilling in an ice bucket, and music playing softly in the background when he came into the kitchen, his hair still wet from the shower.

Mila glanced at him, waiting for him to start the conversation. When he did not, she realized there was more to his ill humor than running errands in the rain. That's when she remembered the text about that woman dying.

"I'm sorry about your friend passing away," she said.

"She wasn't a friend. She was an acquaintance…a coworker. Her daughter has been placed with some guardian. This is not what we talked about."

Mila frowned. "I didn't know she'd ever agreed to us taking the child."

Bart shrugged. "She didn't agree, but she also never said no. I just assumed since she didn't have family, she would be grateful for the offer."

"Oh well," Mila said. "The kid is not our responsibility. She's wherever her mother wanted her to be. The end."

Bart glared. "Yeah, the end of a quarter-of-a-million-dollar life insurance policy and the money Shirley inherited when her parents died in Hurricane Fanny."

Mila blinked. "Really? That much?"

"Yes, that much. I'm going to follow up anyway, just to make sure Carlie is okay."

Mila shrugged. "Whatever. Just remember, if there are any kids in this family, someone besides me will be raising them. I am not the motherly type."

Bart sighed. "What did you order for dinner?"

"Beef bourguignon, with a fresh baguette to soak up all those good juices, and Italian cream cake for dessert," Mila said.

"Sounds good. Where's the wine?" Bart asked.

"Chilling."

"I'll get it," he said, and a few minutes later they sat down to their meal and ate in mutual silence.

———

Back in Blessings, Carlie was letting Miss Ruby help her out of the bathtub and into her pajamas. Miss Ruby was doing everything right, just like Mama did, but after a day of fear and grief, the adrenaline crash was inevitable, and so was another round of tears. It was becoming obvious that Mama wasn't going to be there to tuck Carlie into bed or read her a story. She wasn't going to be the one to come running in the middle of the night if Carlie had a bad dream or to snuggle in beside her when it stormed.

Ruby saw the meltdown coming.

Carlie's eyes were shimmering with unshed tears as Ruby pulled the top of her pajamas down over Carlie's head. Carlie thrust her little arms through the sleeves, then put them around Ruby's neck and laid her head on Ruby's shoulder.

"I know, I know. It's all different and so sad. I saw you have books on your bed table. Do you want me to read to you until you fall asleep?"

Carlie nodded.

"Are you afraid to be in the room alone?" Ruby asked.

Carlie shrugged.

Ruby sighed. "Okay, we'll just play this by ear. Come pick out a book. I'll bet you can read some of those books yourself now. Can you?"

"Yes, but I miss some of the words."

"I think you're very smart to already know so many," Ruby said. "Do you want to read one to me, and then I'll tuck you in and read one to you and Hoppy?"

"Okay," Carlie said and ran from the bathroom into her bedroom. Ruby already had the bed turned back, so Carlie crawled up in her bed. As she did, Peanut knocked on the open door and then stopped at the threshold.

"I just wanted to tell you good night and remind you that our bedroom is just across the hall. The door will be open and there are night-lights in the hall, so we'll hear you if you call out, okay?"

"Okay," Carlie said.

"Thank you for helping me water the flowers today," Peanut said.

"Welcome," Carlie said.

"See you in the morning at breakfast," Peanut said.

Carlie nodded.

As soon as he was gone, she picked up a Dr. Seuss book and opened it to the first page, put her little finger under the first word and began to read.

"'One fish. Two fish. Red fish. Blue fish.'"

And so it went.

Ruby sat quietly, watching Carlie sound out the words when she got stuck, and then when she glanced up at Ruby for help, the haunted look in her eyes was almost gone. And when she got to the end of the book, there was a sense of satisfaction on her face when she closed it.

"Good job!" Ruby said. "You are such a good reader!"

Carlie looked pleased, and then picked up her *Frog and Toad are Friends* book and handed it to Ruby.

"Scoot down and get all comfy," Ruby said. "Here's Hoppy. He looks so sleepy. I won't read too loud in case he falls asleep."

Carlie tucked the old lop-eared rabbit beneath her chin, pulled the little blanket over her shoulders, and sighed when Ruby pulled up the other covers and tucked her in.

The sheets smelled like flowers, and they were cool and soft against her skin. She thought of Mama and then looked at Ruby. They didn't look anything alike, but Miss Ruby's cheeks were pink, and she could talk and laugh without losing her breath. And Mama said Miss Ruby would take such good care of her. It had to be enough because it was all she had.

Ruby winked at Carlie, smoothed the hair away from her face, then opened the book to the first page and started to read, keeping her voice soft but full of expression as she began.

"'Frog ran up the road to Toad's house. He knocked on the door...'"

Carlie sighed. She knew the book by heart. It was one of her favorites. She pulled Hoppy closer and let Miss Ruby's voice carry her to sleep.

Ruby read the book all the way through, even though Carlie was already out. And when she had finished, she turned off the lamp by the bed, made sure the night-lights were on in the bathroom and in Carlie's bedroom, and then turned out the overhead light as she slipped out of the room.

She paused in the doorway and looked back. All she could see was the top of Carlie's head and one long, brown-and-white rabbit ear lying on top of the covers.

Ruby sighed, smiled, and tiptoed out of the room and then across the hall to their bedroom.

Peanut was in bed with his laptop, working, but the television was on. It was typical of their nightly routine, and after the day Ruby had had, it was reassuring.

Tomorrow would likely bring a visit to the funeral home and certainly a trip to the bank to sign the signature card to access Shirley's money. They would need to pick out flowers for the casket, too, and Ruby was hoping that taking Carlie to help do all that would help her see and accept the finality of what had happened.

Peanut looked up from his laptop.

"Come to bed, darlin'. I'll shut this work down."

Ruby sighed. "You don't have to stop on my account."

"But I want to stop on your account because I love you," he said. "You look as lost as that little girl across the hall. You don't have a blankie or a rabbit, but you have me to cuddle."

Ruby's eyes welled. She turned out the overhead light and then crawled into bed as Peanut put his laptop on the end table and turned out the lamp.

The night-light in their adjoining bathroom left their room in shadows as she turned toward him. As he put his arms around her and pulled her close, he heard her sigh.

"It's okay, honey. Whatever happens, I'm with you one hundred percent. I'll see to the guardianship papers tomorrow and make sure they're legally binding. You have a married name now, but that's just a legality to update. We'll protect her, come what may. Now close your eyes and rest while you can."

"I don't know what I'd do without you, but I love you forever," Ruby said.

Peanut rested his chin on the top of her head and closed his eyes.

"And I love you more."

# CHAPTER 5

*THE ROOMS WERE WRONG. THE FURNITURE WAS GONE. MAMA WAS gone. And Carlie didn't know where she was. She kept running from room to room, calling, "Mama! Mama! Where are you?" But Shirley never answered.*

*Carlie could hear footsteps in the room above her, and people knocking on the walls around her, and the sounds were coming closer and closer. Without any furniture to hide behind and no way out, Carlie threw back her head and screamed, "MAMA! MAMA!"*

———————

Ruby woke with a start and was out of bed and flying across the hall to Carlie's bedroom without turning on a single light. She found Carlie sitting up in bed, sobbing.

Immediately, Ruby turned on the lamp by Carlie's bed, pulled her into her arms, and started rocking her.

"It's okay, baby. It's okay. You're safe. You just had a bad dream!"

Carlie was sobbing. "I was trying to find Mama but she's gone. People were coming after me. I could hear their footsteps."

Peanut came into the room only moments behind Ruby.

"Bad dream?" he asked.

Ruby nodded.

"Would a little bit of ice cream take away that bad dream?" he asked.

"It couldn't hurt," Ruby said. "We need something new to focus on."

Peanut held out his arms. "Then give her to me, and you go dip ice cream. We're right behind you."

He took Carlie out of Ruby's lap, grabbed the blanket and

Hoppy, and they all trooped up the hall and into the kitchen, turning on lights as they went.

"It's been a while since I had ice cream at three in the morning," Ruby said as she got out the container and filled three small dishes with vanilla ice cream, then carried them to the table.

Carlie was still sitting in Peanut's lap when the ice cream arrived. She slid off into the chair beside him, grabbed her spoon, and took the first bite.

"Did it work yet?" Peanut asked.

Carlie paused. "Did what work?" she asked.

"Did the ice cream take away the bad dream yet?" he said.

"Almost," Carlie said, and took another bite, and then a third, and they all sat in mutual silence, eating until their dishes were empty.

"I feel better," Peanut said.

"So do I," Ruby said.

"I feel better, too," Carlie said.

Ruby smiled. "Good. Let's make a quick trip to the bathroom and then see if we can all get back to sleep, okay?"

Carlie nodded. "Yes. I can sleep now. I have sugar on my tongue."

Peanut grinned. "We all have sugar on our tongues. I'll bet we sleep all the way to morning."

Ruby put the bowls in the sink and turned out the lights as Peanut carried Carlie back to her room. He gave her a quick kiss on the top of her head as he put her down, then winked at Ruby and left.

"Bathroom, then bed," Ruby said, and Carlie ran into the adjoining room and came back a couple of minutes later.

"I washed," she said, holding up both hands.

"Awesome," Ruby said, then tucked her back into bed. "Are the night-lights enough, or do you want the light left on in the bathroom?"

"Night-lights are enough," Carlie said. "Hoppy doesn't like lights in his eyes."

"Ah...good to know," Ruby said, then leaned over and kissed Carlie's cheek. "You're okay. Remember that. And I've already scolded the bad dreamers for interrupting your sleep, so you'll be fine now."

Carlie sighed. "Thank you, Miss Ruby."

"You're so welcome, sugar," Ruby said, then reached over to turn off the lamp.

They were both in shadow now, and still Ruby stayed, her hand on Carlie's shoulder to remind her she was not alone. She sat until she heard Carlie's slow, steady breathing and knew she'd fallen back asleep.

At that point, she got up and walked to the doorway before looking back.

One small child. One tiny lump beneath the covers—with the top of her head and one rabbit ear showing above them.

"God be with her, and us," Ruby said, and then went back across the hall and crawled into bed beside Peanut.

"Where were we?" he mumbled as she snuggled up against him.

"Right about here," Ruby said, and closed her eyes.

———

The alarm went off at 7:00 a.m., just like it did every morning.

Peanut rolled over to shut it off as Ruby jumped out of bed and ran to check on Carlie. Satisfied that she was fine and still asleep, she went back to get dressed. Peanut was already in the shower, so she headed to the kitchen. Since she wasn't going to have to leave for work this morning, she had the time and luxury of being able to make breakfast for everyone.

She was at the stove frying bacon when Carlie came into the kitchen, dragging her blankie, and with Hoppy propped on her hip like a mother carrying her toddler. The flyaway blond curls were everywhere, but she was smiling.

"I smelled bacon," she said.

"So do I," Peanut said as he walked in behind her.

She giggled and ran to her chair and climbed up.

Not for the first time, Ruby thought how fragile Carlie was. Not very tall. Tiny bones, tiny feet, and a shade too thin. Love and time would take care of part of it, and DNA would take care of the rest.

Ruby took the last of the bacon from the pan and then turned around.

"Peanut, honey… How do you want your eggs cooked this morning…fried or scrambled?"

Peanut glanced at Carlie. "How do you like your eggs to be fixed?"

"I like scrambled," she said.

Peanut nodded. "We'll have scrambled this morning, please and thank you. And toast. I would like toast and jelly," he said, and got up and poured coffee for him and Ruby and carried the mugs to the table.

"I would like toast and jelly, too," Carlie said as Peanut brought her a small glass of milk.

Ruby hid a grin. "Coming right up," she said, and put four slices of bread in the toaster and pushed the lever down, then began cracking eggs in a bowl and whipping them with a fork before pouring them in the skillet to cook.

Within a couple of minutes, she was carrying plates of fluffy yellow eggs, crisp slices of bacon, and buttered toast cut in halves with grape jelly already spread on it.

"This looks delicious," Peanut said, and took a bite.

"Delicious," Carlie said, and took a bite of egg, followed by a bite of jelly toast.

Ruby picked up her fork and started eating, pleased that this morning was starting off better than yesterday.

"I have court in Savannah today," Peanut said. "And I'm taking those papers we talked about last night to get updated."

"Thank you," Ruby said. "They're in the library on your desk. I was going to have you put them in the safe."

"I will when I come home this evening. After Carlie and I water flowers."

Carlie's eyes lit up. "I know how now," she said.

"Yes, ma'am, you sure do. But while I'm gone today, I want you and Miss Ruby to do me a favor."

Carlie glanced at Ruby, then nodded.

"Okay."

"I know you two have business to take care of today, but when noon rolls around, I want you both to get some food and have a picnic in the park. The change of scenery will do you both good."

"Can we, Miss Ruby? Are there swings at the park? Can I play there?"

Ruby thought of the upcoming trip to the bank and the funeral home and nodded.

"Oh yes, there are swings, a slide, a little merry-go-round, and all kinds of things to play on, and yes, we can most certainly go there. I think it's a fine idea. But right now, finish up what you want of your breakfast and then you can help me make the beds."

And so their morning began.

The dishes were done. The beds were made, and Ruby dug through Carlie's clothes to find something for her to wear downtown. It was already in the high eighties outside, so jean shorts and a blue and white T-shirt seemed appropriate for the weather.

"Since we're going to the park later, let's do sneakers instead of sandals," Ruby said.

Carlie nodded and slipped her little feet in the shoes and fastened them with the Velcro strips, then looked back at her blanket and rabbit, and took a deep breath.

"Hoppy says he'd rather stay here," she said softly. "I'll put him over here with my other friends so he won't get lonesome." She scooted the stuffed toy in between a stuffed turtle and a yellow duck.

"What a good idea," Ruby said, watching as Carlie covered them over with her blanket and then looked up.

"I'm ready, Miss Ruby," she said and reached for Ruby's hand.

The hand Ruby held was small, but the trust Carlie had given her was huge.

"So am I, baby girl. Let's go see what we shall see."

---

It had taken hours before Deborah had unwound enough to fall asleep last night, and now here she was, awake before daylight and thinking of Ladd Daltry again. Before the literal bullshit of yesterday, he had been little more than a sweet memory of her past. But now he was all she could think about.

She'd come home to help her mom, and this had happened.

The thought of him alone and injured bothered her. And alone was what he'd be when he was released. She'd come home to help her mom, not babysit an old lover, but they both needed help. How in the world was all this going to play out?

She padded quietly through the house on bare feet to make coffee and then took a cup outside to the back porch, sat down in an old wicker chair, and curled her feet up beneath her before she took her first sip. It went down her throat in a wash of warmth, carrying that jolt of caffeine she was waiting on. A couple more sips, and she had enough in her to focus on the day at hand.

The sight of the old homeplace tugged at her heart. She couldn't imagine what it would be like not to have this place to come home to. She knew her mom wasn't looking forward to leaving, either, but living out here alone when her heart was with Josh no longer made sense.

Deborah knew the cattle were gone, and the pasture was going to seed. And depending on who bought the place, they may or may not want the chickens.

"Ah, Mom… I can't imagine what you're feeling, but I'm sad

this day has come. For all of us," she muttered, then sat watching the sun come up over the land.

As soon as they got the morning started, Deborah needed to make a quick run into Blessings and check on Ladd. She wanted to make sure he knew they'd watch over his place until he came home. Watching that happen to him yesterday had been traumatic, and she needed to reassure herself that he was truly going to heal.

---

Ladd had the night from hell. It hurt to breathe. It hurt to move. It hurt to even close his damn eyes because one of them was turning a gruesome shade of black with purple undertones. And there was no sleeping happening until the nurses eased up on the welfare checks because of the concussion he'd suffered.

So, since he had plenty of time to pass, he kept thinking about Darren Payne's herd bull. He'd seen it plenty of times from the road as he was driving back and forth from town and never once suspected it was that aggressive. He needed to let them know the fence between them was down, and what the bull had done before someone else happened to be in the wrong place at the wrong time. Like Deborah…or Maggie. He didn't want to think about what might happen if that damn bull decided to wander again.

He was still in shock at seeing Deborah. Compared to the teenager she'd been when they were dating, she'd turned into an Amazon. He'd seen the long, lithe muscles on her arms and shoulders, and her tight, flat abs. A body like that didn't happen by accident. She either worked hard or worked out, and he was curious to find out how his rescue had happened.

---

Melvin Lee Wilson was stressed.

Grandma had gone to the store.

Mama was in the shower.

Dad was at work.

And he'd been left in charge of his younger siblings…again.

Willy and Arnie were in the living room wrestling and punching at each other, even though he'd told them countless times to stop.

His sister, Lucy, who everyone called Sissy, was walking around the house dragging a rag doll by one arm and whining for "Mama."

And Davie, the baby, was lying in his crib bawling.

Melvin Lee dug the pacifier out of the blankets and had just poked it in Davie's mouth when he heard someone puking in the hall. He ran out of the nursery and saw Sissy wiping her mouth with the hem of her shirt.

"I frew up," she said.

Melvin Lee was horrified and trying to think what to do about it when he heard a crash in the living room and turned and ran.

Willy and Arnie were standing near a window. Willy's nose was bleeding, and Arnie had a button and most of a pocket torn off his shirt. And Mama's lamp was in the floor in pieces.

Melvin Lee groaned. "I told y'all to quit wrestlin' and now look what happened! Mama's gonna be mad at me for what you two did." He grabbed Arnie by the arm and dragged him to a chair at the end of the room. "Sit down and don't get up until Mama says you can," he muttered, and then went back, grabbed Willy and dragged him to the kitchen and set him down at the table, then got a wad of paper towels wet, wrung them out, and shoved them against Willy's nose. "Hold that there until Mama says it's quit bleeding."

Willy had the wet towels pressed against his nose. His eyes were huge and welling with tears. "I'm a'bleedin'," he said.

"Your own durn fault," Melvin Lee said. "Don't move. Don't get up. I gotta tend to Sissy."

He was on the way back up the hall when he heard more gagging and spitting and groaned. Sissy wasn't through puking after all. And the baby was crying again.

"Dad-burn it!" Melvin Lee took off for his parents' bedroom at a lope and didn't bother knocking. The bathroom door was still closed, and he could still hear the water running. It took Mama entirely too long to take a shower. Melvin Lee could take one in two minutes flat.

He ran across the room and flung the door open.

Junie Wilson was just turning off the water when she heard the door hit the wall and groaned. She'd forgotten to lock it. And then Melvin Lee was yelling, and she grabbed a towel and peeked out from behind the shower curtain.

"What in the world is the matter with you, coming in here like this?" she snapped.

"You better get on out of that shower right now because Sissy's pukin' in the hall, Willy and Arnie were wrestling in the living room and broke your lamp, Willy tore Arnie's shirt, and Willy's nose is bleedin', and Davie is cryin' again."

Junie groaned. "Dang it, Melvin Lee. All I asked you to do was watch the kids for just a minute and—"

"You took longer than a minute, Mama, and I can't be in three places at once. None of them mind me, and I can't stand the smell of puke. I'm gonna go sit out on the back porch until you get that cleaned up," he said, and walked out of the bathroom like the mini-version of his daddy that he was.

"Oh, crap on a stick," Junie groaned, and started drying off at warp speed, then dressed and ran.

Sissy was sitting in the hall next to her third puddle of puke. Davie was bellowing now, completely displeased at being in his room alone, and she could hear one of the boys crying in the kitchen, and the other one yelling from the living room, "Can I get up now?"

Junie felt like Melvin Lee. She wanted to go out and sit on the back porch, too, but that wasn't going to happen.

She knelt down, stripped her daughter out of her clothes, and carried her to the bathroom to clean her up, then took her to the room she shared with the baby.

The minute they walked in, Davie pulled himself up to a standing position and started bouncing and laughing, happy that he had visitors. He yelped and chattered while Junie got clean clothes for Sissy out of a dresser.

As she was helping her dress, Junie realized Sissy's skin felt hot. Oh, great. She had a fever, which likely meant that whatever Sissy was getting, the rest of them would, too.

"Sissy, honey, do you feel like you might throw up again?" Junie asked.

"No. My tummy's not hurting now."

"I want you to lie down here in your little bed. I'll turn on the television for you and Davie, and you just rest while Mama cleans up, okay? And…if you feel like you might throw up again, throw up in the wastebasket," she said. She shoved it beside Sissy's bed, then left the room at a run, sidestepping the mess in the hall as she went to check on the other two boys.

As Melvin Lee had warned, her lamp was broken, and the second she walked into the living room and saw Arnie sitting in the chair with a button missing and most of a pocket dangling from his shirt, she frowned.

"I'm sorry, Mama," Arnie said. "Can I get up now?" he asked.

"You should be sorry, and no, you may not get up," Junie said.

Arnie laid his head down on the arm of the chair and started bawling, but Junie still had one more kid to check on and followed the sounds of wailing coming from the kitchen.

Willy was sitting at the table with bloody-pink paper towels smashed up against his nose, and his face was streaked with tears.

"I'm a'bleedin', Mama," Willy said.

"Because you and Arnie were wrestling again. And you broke my lamp," she added as she took the wet paper towels from him and began dabbing his nose to see if it was still bleeding.

"Are you mad at me?" Willy asked.

Junie frowned. "Yes, I think I am. You and your brother did not mind Melvin Lee. And look what happened."

Willy's eyes welled. Tears rolled.

She refused to feel sorry for either one of them. She tossed the wet paper towels and got fresh ones, dampened them just a little, and then handed them back to him.

"Here. Hold this against your nose a while longer, and tilt your head back a little. It's about to stop bleeding. I've got to sweep up broken glass and then mop up puke, so stay where you are until I say you can get up. Understand me?"

"Yes, Mama. I'm sorry, Mama," Willy said.

"I'm sorry, too," Junie muttered, and went to the utility room to get a broom and a dustpan.

She glanced out the kitchen window to check on Melvin Lee, just to make sure he was where he said he'd be, because she sure didn't want him running away again like he did before.

He was there, drinking a bottle of pop and swinging in the porch swing. She frowned. She didn't allow her kids to snack between meals, but this seemed like a good time to pretend she didn't see that, so she headed for the living room. With five kids in the house, getting the broken glass off the floor was the first task. Mopping up puke would be next.

"Please, God, send my mother home now. I need some help here," Junie muttered.

---

Ruby had to buckle Carlie in the backseat of the car, but she was so small, Ruby didn't think she looked safe.

"Did you ride in the back seat like this with your mama?" Ruby asked.

Carlie nodded. "In a car seat, but not like the kind babies use."

"Ah, a booster seat! We need to see about getting one for you here, too. I'll text Peanut to go by Walmart and get one before he leaves Savannah."

So Carlie watched while Ruby sent her text and then started up the car and backed out of the driveway.

"We're going to the bank first," Ruby said, and winked at Carlie in the rearview mirror before accelerating up the street.

It didn't take long for Ruby to get to Main Street, but the stoplight was red. As they waited for it to turn green, Laurel Lorde and her daughter, Bonnie, drove past and honked and waved at Ruby.

She smiled and waved back as Dan Amos drove through the green light going the other direction and waved at Ruby. Again, she waved back.

And then a third driver and a fourth did the same, one honked, the other waved, and Ruby kept waving and smiling, unaware of how intently she was being watched. When the light turned green for them, she turned right and drove toward the bank. They parked and Carlie was unfastening her seat belt when Ruby opened the back door.

Carlie paused and looked up. "Miss Ruby, do you know everyone in Blessings?"

Ruby grinned. "Well, I guess I do, but that's how small towns work. There aren't many strangers in town, and if they're here long enough, then they aren't strangers anymore."

Carlie slid out of the back seat and took Ruby's hand as they started walking toward the entrance to the bank.

"Miss Ruby, someday will everyone know me like they know you?"

"You bet they will," Ruby said. "You just wait and see. Blessings is a very friendly place to live. I know it's all very new to you right now, but it won't take you long to figure stuff out."

"Okay," Carlie said, and took a little skip to catch up as they were walking.

That's when Ruby realized she was walking too fast for little feet and slowed down. They were just about to walk into the bank when her phone signaled a text. She paused and read the text, then sighed and sent back a quick reply before dropping it back into her pocket.

It was the funeral home. They wanted to speak with her about a casket and services at her convenience.

The moment they entered the bank, Ruby felt the curious glances and knew they were for the little girl beside her. God bless the Blessings grapevine. At least no explanations would be necessary. According to Shirley's instructions in her letter, all Ruby needed to do here was sign a signature card to access the money needed to bury her, so she headed for the front desk to speak to an associate.

A woman named Evelyn was staffing the desk today and smiled when she saw Ruby approaching.

"Good morning, Ruby. You have a very pretty helper with you."

"Yes, I do, Evelyn, and her name is Carlie Duroy. I believe there is a signature card here awaiting my signature. Do you know anything about this? It would be money that Shirley Duroy transferred here before she left Little Rock."

"Why don't you two have a seat while I pull up the info?" Evelyn said, and reached for the keyboard to her monitor.

Ruby sat down in one chair while Carlie sat in the other, but the child was quiet again, and Ruby knew it was because they'd mentioned her mother's name.

"It's okay, Carlie. We're just doing what your mother told me to do in her letter."

Carlie nodded. She remembered the letter, and Mama telling her it was important.

"Okay, here we are," Evelyn said. "Yes, I need you to sign a signature card, and then we'll get you set up to access the money." She glanced at Carlie, then looked back at Ruby. "Is it too early in the morning for a little treat?"

Ruby knew about the lollipops all of the cashiers kept at their windows.

"We're making all kinds of concessions today, and a treat would be appreciated," Ruby said.

Evelyn pulled a mug full of bright-colored lollipops out of the drawer of her desk and scooted it toward Carlie.

"Help yourself, honey," Evelyn said.

Carlie's eyes widened as she eyed the colors within the clear cellophane wraps, then slid out of the chair and moved to the desk.

"What's your favorite?" Ruby asked.

"I like the orange ones," Carlie said, and picked an orange sucker from the mug and then leaned against Ruby's knee.

Ruby put her arm around Carlie's shoulders and gave her a quick pat, then leaned forward and signed the card.

"Perfect," Evelyn said. "If you'll give me a few minutes, I'll get a debit card and some checks ordered. Do you want to pick out a design?"

"No, just standard ones are fine," Ruby said, and as soon as Evelyn left her desk, Ruby helped herself to a green lollipop.

"These are lime. I like them best," Ruby said, and then pulled off the wrapper and took a quick lick. "Yum."

Carlie pulled the wrapper off hers and licked, too.

"Yum," she echoed, and leaned against Ruby while they waited.

Everything about Carlie's life was new now—like a baby who had been born anew. She didn't know anyone here but Mr. and Miss Ruby…and the policeman. She knew him because he helped her find Miss Ruby.

But all of her friends from school were back in Little Rock. She wasn't ever going to see them again, or the lady who lived across the hall who used to babysit Carlie when Mama had meetings.

But that was before Mama got sick. Everything changed after that happened, and now she was gone, and Carlie was here, afraid to say or do the wrong thing. Afraid to make the people who were taking care of her mad. She knew about the foster people who took kids with no parents. They got paid money to take care of them, but they didn't have to like them, and sometimes they were mean to the kids who lived with them. That's what Mama told her, and Mama's word had always been Carlie's law. Now Carlie had new people with new and different rules taking care of her. But they weren't fosters. They were guarding her. She thought that was better and trusted Mama not to have given her to bad people.

However, it was scary to be Carlie Duroy right now, so she kept licking on the sweet sucker and not fidgeting and not making noise.

# CHAPTER 6

RUBY AND CARLIE LEFT THE BANK WITH THE SWEET TASTE of candy still on their lips and had plans to go straight to the shop. Ruby owed the twins for getting the shop supplies yesterday and wanted Carlie to see where she worked, because the Curl Up and Dye was going to become her home away from home.

"Where are we going now, Miss Ruby?" Carlie asked.

"To my hair salon," Ruby said.

"Is it the same one where my mama worked?"

"Yes, and the same ladies who work in the shop with me also knew your mama. They are very sad for what happened to her, and for you, but you're going to like them, I know."

Carlie wiggled in the seat. She was excited to see the salon and the people. Anyone with a connection to her mama made her feel less anxious.

As always, Ruby drove around to the back of the building to park; then she and Carlie went in the back door.

Vera was blowing out LilyAnn Dalton's hair so she could get back to the pharmacy where she worked, and Vesta was giving Myra Franklin a haircut, which meant Myra's husband was minding their flower shop until she returned, and Mabel Jean was finishing Rachel Goodhope's manicure.

When the scents of hair spray, shampoo, and nail polish met Ruby and Carlie at the door, Ruby inhaled, savoring the familiar, while Carlie wrinkled her nose.

Everyone stopped what they were doing and turned around. One look at the little blond with Ruby and they all wanted to talk at once but were uncertain what to say, so Ruby led the way.

"Hey, everybody! Carlie and I are out running errands this

morning. She wanted to see where her mama used to work, and I wanted her to get to meet you all. Carlie, honey, these—"

Then Ruby saw Carlie's face and stopped.

"What's wrong?" Ruby asked.

"They have the same face," Carlie whispered.

Vera and Vesta giggled. They liked confusing people as to which was which.

"We almost have the same name, too," Vera said. "I'm Vera Conklin, and this is my twin sister, Vesta. And yes, we knew Shirley when she worked here. She was a very hard worker and a sweetheart."

"We're so sorry about what happened," Vesta added, and then gently touched the top of Carlie's head. "You sure do look like her. Same pretty blond hair and blue eyes. You don't have to remember which name goes with which sister. Just say, 'Hey, twin,' and you'll be fine."

Carlie giggled.

Ruby pointed at the woman over at the manicure table by the window. "The pretty lady with all the nail polish is Miss Mabel Jean. She does manicures and pedicures."

Mabel Jean winked. "Hi, Carlie. If it's okay with Ruby, we'll have to pick out a nail polish and paint your fingernails some time."

Carlie immediately looked up at Ruby for verification that she could do that, because nail polish was something she liked.

"It's always okay with me," Ruby said, then pointed to the clients in the styling chairs. "And the ladies in the chairs are our clients, but they're also all our friends. That's Miss LilyAnn. She works at the pharmacy. That's Miss Myra. She and her husband own the flower shop. And that's Miss Rachel. She and her husband own a bed-and-breakfast. That's like a little hotel that serves food to their guests."

"Hi, Carlie," they all said and waved.

Ruby took Carlie by the hand. "I want to show you something

else," she said, and led her back to the break room. "This is where we come when we want to take a break. There's a refrigerator, a table and chairs, and a couple of comfy easy chairs and the sofa. I've taken many a nap on that sofa, so you can, too, if you get tired when you come to work with me."

"Can I bring things to play with?" Carlie asked.

"Oh yes. You can even bring Hoppy and your blanket if you want, and your crayons and coloring book, and we'll get Mr. Ruby to hook up a television in here so you can watch cartoons, too. Okay?"

Carlie nodded, trying to absorb how this new location would play into her life. It sounded like a good thing, but there would be lots of people coming and going.

"Do kids come here, too?" Carlie asked.

"Only if they have appointments. They don't come here to play."

"Why not?" Carlie asked.

Ruby sat down on the sofa and pulled Carlie into her lap.

"Mostly because their mothers want this time to themselves. And the other reason is some of them are not very well mannered, and would be running and screaming and messing with things that might hurt them. So, the only kids who come here are here for haircuts."

"I have good manners. I won't run or scream," Carlie whispered.

Ruby hugged her. "Oh, baby, you have nothing to worry about. I own this shop. I'm the boss. And where I go, you go. We're going to figure all this out together. And when we're home in our own house, you can run and play all over the house, or outside in the backyard. And when school starts, you'll make friends at school and have playtime there as well, okay? In the meantime, you're with me."

Carlie hugged Ruby and buried her face against Ruby's neck. She didn't say anything, but the tension in her shoulders was

gone and that was enough for Ruby. And Ruby was coming to realize that kids and bathrooms were going to take on a whole new
meaning for her.

"There's one other thing. The bathroom is through that door.
Sometimes our clients use it, but mostly it's just all of us. If you
need to go before we leave, there's your chance."

Carlie nodded and slid off Ruby's lap and went into the bathroom. A couple of minutes later, Ruby heard the toilet flush and
then water running. When Carlie came out, she was smiling.

"You have Frog and Toad, just like in my book," she said.

At first, Ruby didn't know what Carlie was talking about, and
then remembered the two little china frog figurines that Vera and
Vesta had added to the decor some years back.

"Why, yes, I guess we do," Ruby said.

When they came out of the break room, the stylists and clients
were finishing up on their appointments.

LilyAnn was blinking back tears when she saw them emerge.
Just thinking of dying like Shirley had and leaving her beloved
husband and her little boy without a mother was horrifying.
While Myra Franklin had never had children, she knew she'd be
doing flowers for Shirley Duroy's funeral. She remembered the
Duroy family, and she remembered Shirley working here. But
seeing Carlie, the only child left of those people, made her heart
hurt.

Rachel Goodhope was sitting quietly as Mabel Jean finished
up her manicure, just watching and listening. She'd heard all about
the tragedy, and while she had not known Shirley Duroy, this tiny
little girl with the big, sad eyes had stolen her heart. She could only
imagine how confused and strange everything must seem to her.
But if there was anyone who could put her world back together
again, that would be Peanut and Ruby Butterman. The misfortune that had befallen her had also brought her to the people who
would save her.

But Ruby had come here for two things—to introduce Carlie and pay back the Conklins for doing her chores yesterday.

"Okay, you two. Who do I owe money for picking up the supplies for the salon, and how much?" Ruby asked.

Vesta laid down her comb and scissors and opened the top drawer to her station.

"Here's the receipt, but there is no hurry."

"I know, but I really appreciated your help," Ruby said, and quickly wrote the check and gave it to her.

Vesta put it in her pocket and grabbed the curling iron to finish up LilyAnn's hairstyle.

"We'll be leaving now," Ruby said. "Ladies, if you have an emergency, you know how to find me." And then they were gone.

"Where are we going next?" Carlie asked as Ruby was buckling her up in the back seat.

Ruby paused. "We need to go to the funeral home and pick out a pretty casket for your mama. Do you know what a casket is?"

Carlie nodded. "It's a little travelin' house for people going to be angels."

Ruby was dumbstruck. That was the most perfect, beautiful thing she'd ever heard come out of a child's mouth.

"Who told you that?" she asked.

"Mama. She had to get them for Granny and PawPaw after they died in the water. Can I help pick out Mama's house?" Carlie asked.

"Yes. I think Shirley would love that," Ruby said. "What say we go to do that right now. And I can sign the papers and set a date for the burial service while we're there. Are you all buckled in?"

Carlie patted the buckle on the seat belt.

"I'm buckled," she said.

"Good girl," Ruby said, then closed the door and hurried around to the driver's side and got in.

They drove to the funeral home without talking and parked in the shade. It was already getting hot and Ruby wasn't so sure about playing at the park later, but one thing at a time.

This time when Ruby went to open the door to help Carlie out, she was already unbuckled and waiting. They walked in together hand in hand, and not for the first time it struck Ruby how easy it felt to slide into this relationship. But that was how it seemed. She had no idea how Carlie felt. She hoped with time Carlie would become as comfortable with them as they were with her.

It was cool and quiet inside the front lobby, but before Ruby had time to orient herself as to where the office was, Niles Palmer, the funeral director, came out of a hallway into the lobby.

"Hello, Ruby. Thank you for coming."

"Of course, Niles. This is Shirley Duroy's daughter, Carlie. She wants to help pick out her mama's casket."

Niles looked down at the little girl clutching Ruby's hand and was struck by the weary look in her wide blue eyes. She'd seen too much suffering at such a young age.

"My sympathy for your loss, Miss Carlie, and to you as well, Ruby. If you'll follow me to the showroom, we'll get started. Once you pick out what you want, we'll do the paperwork and set a date for the service."

He nodded at the both of them and then turned around, leading the way.

Ruby looked down at Carlie. "Are you ready to do this?"

Carlie nodded. "Mama likes blue."

"Then we'll look for something blue," Ruby said.

What most might have thought unseemly—a child picking out her mother's casket—turned out to be something that gave Carlie peace. She'd never been to a funeral. But she'd held her mother as she took her last breath. There was a tempering of loss in knowing there was still something she could do for her. One last thing for Mama. And that's what she did. Going from casket to casket, touching, rubbing the chrome and the polished wood, with Niles carrying a little step stool so she could see how it looked inside.

And then they came to a pale-blue casket with a pearl finish and wispy clouds painted on the interior of the lid.

Carlie climbed up to look inside, saw the white pleated satin and pale-blue pillow, and patted Ruby's arm.

"This one, Miss Ruby."

"Then this one it is," Ruby said. "You did good, sweetheart. Your mama would be so proud of you."

Niles made a note on his iPad. "Excellent choice. Now, if you'll follow me to the office, we'll get the papers signed and set a date."

And so they did.

About a half hour later, Ruby had Carlie in the car again. She started it up to cool off, and while she was waiting, she turned around to gauge Carlie's state of mind. Carlie looked pensive, and she was quiet again. But it was a quarter to twelve. Almost noon. She didn't want to disappoint Carlie about the park and the picnic, but at the same time, if she wasn't in the mood, Ruby didn't want to make her do it just because they'd planned it.

"So, how are you feeling?" Ruby asked. "Are you too tired to get a picnic and go to the park? We can always do that another day, if you are."

"Do I get to see my mama again?" Carlie asked.

"Yes. Mr. Niles said we could come back tomorrow morning. So that's when you'll get to see her, but remember she can't talk anymore."

"But I can talk to her. I need to tell her something," Carlie said softly.

"And so you shall," Ruby said. "Now, do you want to eat inside where it's cool, or get the picnic and eat at the park?"

"Eat at the park," Carlie said.

Ruby winked. "That's my girl. So, if we go to Broyles Dairy Freeze, do you want a hamburger or a hot dog?"

"A hot dog with ketchup," Carlie said.

"Do we want to share some fries, or would you rather have potato chips?"

"Fries…with ketchup," Carlie said.

Ruby laughed. "What do you like to drink with your hot dog? Dr Pepper? Root beer? Pepsi? Or maybe you'd rather have milk or water?"

"I like Dr Pepper," Carlie said.

"Without ketchup?" Ruby asked.

Carlie giggled. "You're not a'post to have ketchup in your drink."

Ruby grinned. "Just making sure," she said. "So, off we go to get our picnic, and then I know a really shady place with a nice picnic table where we can eat, okay?"

"Okay," Carlie said, and wiggled back against the seat and clasped her hands.

She watched the back of Miss Ruby's head as they drove and was thinking about the shop and the time she would spend there, and then her room at Miss Ruby's house and watering flowers with Mr. Ruby. For now, that was the breadth and scope of her new life.

Unaware of the chain of Carlie's thoughts, Ruby got in line at the drive-through at Broyles Dairy Freeze, ordered their food, and then headed to the park. Once there, Ruby let Carlie out and then grabbed the food.

"That little house is like the one in your backyard," Carlie said, pointing to the gazebo.

"It sure is," Ruby said. "Want to sit there to eat?"

"Can we?"

"Absolutely! The park is for anyone who wants to be here."

"Yay! Yes!" Carlie said, and was almost bouncing as she walked beside Ruby, chattering about the trees and the birds and the gazebo, and there might be fairies here as well.

She ran up the steps ahead of Ruby, then ran around inside the gazebo before coming back to the table in the center, where Ruby was taking out the food.

"I'm hungry," Ruby said.

Carlie nodded. "I'm hungry, too."

"Here, let's clean our hands with some of this," Ruby said, and pulled out a little bottle of hand sanitizer and squeezed a few drops in their hands, then rubbed them together. "Okay, we're good to go," she said.

They sat side by side on the bench facing the street so they could watch people walking and driving past as they sorted out their order.

Carlie immediately ate a bite of hot dog and then reached for a french fry and dunked it in the ketchup Ruby had squeezed out for her. She popped the fry in her mouth, chewed and swallowed, then took a drink of her pop.

"Does it taste good?" Ruby asked.

"Yes. When I'm finished eating, can I go swing?"

"When you've finished eating, you can run and play all you want, sugar."

Carlie smiled as she took another bite and began eyeing the slide, and the swings, and the little merry-go-round as she ate, wondering which to try first.

---

Back in the Wilson house, Junie finally got her sons patched up and made them sit in their rooms on their beds without TV or talking until she called them to the kitchen for lunch.

Lucy was still running a slight fever, and food was the last thing she needed on her stomach, so Junie gave her Pedialyte to drink and one saltine cracker, and took the baby into the kitchen so he could crawl around while she made lunch. He liked to crawl under the table, and because he was teething he would chew on the table legs. Junie would have freaked out that this was happening when her first two sons were toddlers, but at baby number five, if he was quiet and not bleeding she considered it a gift.

By the time she was stirring cheese into the cooked macaroni, her mother was pulling up the driveway. Junie opened the back door.

"Melvin Lee, your grandma just drove up. Please come help her carry in the groceries."

"Yes, ma'am," he said, and barreled into the house at full speed and ran straight to the front door and out onto the porch.

Junie rolled her eyes and then realized Davie was no longer under the table. She turned around just as he was crawling over the threshold and out onto the porch, and sighed. Lord! Melvin Lee forgot to close the door.

"No you don't, mister," she said. She scooped Davie up, then closed the storm door and the interior door. She was putting him in the playpen in the corner of the room just as Minna and Melvin Lee came in with the bags.

Minna set the bags on the counter and turned to look at her daughter.

"I hear you had quite a morning."

Junie rolled her eyes. "It's dealt with. Lucy has a fever. They'll all probably be getting sick now."

"Maybe not," Minna said. "I'm going to scrub down their bathroom. Make them wash up before they eat."

"Mom, I already scrubbed everything after I cleaned Lucy up. I'm not a complete idiot," Junie muttered. "If you would, please go tell the boys they can get off their beds now and come eat. Lucy is having Pedialyte and crackers."

Minna nodded and left the kitchen.

Melvin Lee was emptying sacks, putting everything on the counter and staying quiet. Grandma was here, which meant the pressure was off him now. She was his good-luck charm. She'd moved in with them before Davie was born to help out, and his life had never been better. And now that they were alone, except for Davie, who didn't count, Melvin Lee paused.

"Hey, Mom?"

"Hmmm?"

"Reckon after I eat I could go to the park for a while?"

"Yes, if you take your brothers," she said.

"They don't mind me. They fight. Everywhere they go. They embarrass me. I don't wanna go no more," he muttered, and walked out of the room.

Junie sighed. If she could just do one whole day of her life of motherhood and get it right, she'd be over the moon. She'd talk to him later. Right now, she just needed to get everyone fed, so she finished stirring the cheese that was melting in the pasta.

———————————

Deborah finally got the chores done and headed to Blessings to check on Ladd, leaving her mom going through her dad's old farm clothes.

Maggie watched Deborah drive away, then went back to sorting, remembering that when Josh first had the stroke, they had all expected him to get better and certainly be well enough one day to come home. But that had not been the case.

One week rolled into two, then a month, then months rolled into years while she kept doing her laundry and hanging her clothes back in the closet beside his, just like she'd done for the past thirty-seven years. Even after it became obvious that Josh Ryman's life would end in a nursing home, Maggie could never bring herself to get rid of his clothes. To do so was like throwing Josh away, and she'd never do that. But now, because she was leaving the farm to go to Josh, she had to give up the pieces of himself he'd left behind.

While Maggie was putting away part of her past, Deborah was thinking about her past with Ladd.

She'd loved him with all of the passion of a first love, and losing that bond had left her reluctant to ever give that much of herself away again.

She'd had relationships since, but nothing serious. And now life had drawn the two of them together again, and it remained to be seen what that meant.

She reached the city limits of Blessings, then drove up Main to the hospital much slower than she had the day before. What she knew for sure right now was that her stomach was in knots, and her heart was beating too fast, and she refused to ask herself why.

———————

An orderly walked Ladd to the bathroom, and he thought he'd die before he got back. He was muttering and cursing whoever thought this had been a good idea, and broke out into a cold sweat as they started back.

"Just in time," the nurse said, as she walked in with a syringe full of pain meds and saw the orderly helping get him back in bed.

Ladd groaned as he eased onto the pillow. "And keep 'em coming. The next time I need to pee, I'll just pee on the floor. I know I am not getting up again unless I'm numb or high."

The nurse burst out laughing and was shaking her head as she pushed the meds into his IV, then pulled the guardrails up on his bed.

"Just lie back and let the meds work. Here's your call button. Buzz if you need help."

Ladd felt the drugs beginning to kick in, and lay back and closed his eyes. God…all he wanted to do was sleep until he was well, and go home. He was drifting in a pain-free cloud when he heard a knock on his door and then footsteps. He opened his eyes, expecting another hospital employee, and then watched Deborah walking toward him with a slow, steady stride, her gaze locked onto his like he was being stalked. He had no idea how she'd come to find him, but he'd been told that she saved his life.

"So you are real," he said. "I thought when I first saw you yesterday that you were a hallucination."

Deborah shrugged. "You're forgiven. That bull was a monster. Was it one of yours?"

"No. I think it belongs to Darren Payne."

Deborah frowned, but said nothing.

Ladd felt the silence as something of a rebuke, but wasn't sure how to respond to it.

"I'm riding a drug high right now. Didn't know you were home, but I'd sure like to know how the hell you found me," he said.

"I came home to help Mom get the place ready to sell. I wanted to walk the old homeplace one last time, so I took Dad's hunting rifle and started out. I had walked all the way to the creek when I saw you through the trees. I was thinking how long it had been since I'd actually seen you, when I saw you turn and run, and then I saw the bull. I crossed the creek about as fast as I've ever moved and jumped the fence just in time to see it toss you in the air. You fell facedown and got stomped in the back. I shot the rifle up in the air and started toward it, waving my arms and shouting. It threatened to charge me, too, but I kept shooting off the rifle and shouting. It finally turned tail and ran back through the broken wire in the fence."

"Jesus, Deborah. He could have killed you."

"No. I would have shot him where he stood."

Ladd couldn't quit staring. She was one cool lady.

"Thank you," he said quietly.

She nodded. "Of course. I want you to know that Mom told me your cattle were in the grazing pasture and should be okay, but she wasn't sure about Sam. So when I took your truck back to your house, I fed your cat and locked up your house. I took your keys home with me. I'll continue to feed Sam daily until you're well enough to go home. And if I'm still home, I'll help you until you're back on your feet."

Tears welled. Ladd silently blamed it on the drugs, but part of it was just knowing he wasn't dealing with all of this on his own.

"What about your job...your family? Will they—"

"Mom and Dad are all the family I have. Have ever had."

"Where do you live?" Ladd asked.

"Just outside of Louisville, Kentucky. I'm a big-animal vet. Our clinic deals mostly with racehorses in the area."

"Well, that explains how you were strong enough to get me in the truck," he said.

"There was no cell-phone service down in that valley. I didn't have a choice. I wrapped my shirt around your head, rolled you onto the tarp that was in the back of your truck, wrapped the bottom half of you up in it and fastened you in with bungee cords, then pulled you up in the cab as if you were on a sled and drove like hell."

His hand was shaking as he felt the staples.

"I will never be able to thank you enough. I owe you," he said.

And for the first time, Deborah smiled. "Get well, and I'll send you a bill for the shirt."

Ladd was out of breath and fading.

"Deal. Sorry. Can't talk more."

"Do what they tell you, and don't be a hard-ass. I'll be back tomorrow," Deborah said. She hesitated, then patted his leg just below the knee. "You and me...we were good together. I didn't want to watch you die."

And then she was gone.

Ladd closed his eyes, but she was still there, drifting in and out of the haze in his head—the teenage girl lying beneath him in the hay and the tall, indomitable woman she was today.

———————

When Deborah left Blessings, she headed straight to Darren Payne's ranch, wondering if he was aware of what had happened.

She wasn't sure what she was going to say to him, but if he didn't know, then he'd better be penitent when she told him.

By the time she reached the ranch and pulled up at the house, it was nearly noon. Two dogs on the porch began barking when she started toward the house, and then the front door opened and Cheryl Payne, Darren's wife, came out of the house.

"Deborah! I didn't know you were home. I haven't seen you in ages."

"I've only been here a few days. Is Darren around?"

"Yes. He's washing up for dinner. Come on in."

"I'll just wait outside on the porch, if you don't mind," Deborah said.

Cheryl shrugged. "Suit yourself. I'll go in and tell him you're here," she said, and let the storm door swing shut behind her as she went.

Deborah turned her back to the front door, shoved her hands in her pockets, and took a deep breath. She needed to calm down. There was no need starting a war over this, unless Darren wanted to be an ass—in which case he was going to wish he'd made other choices.

A few moments later, the door opened behind her. She turned just as Darren Payne came out of the house, with Cheryl behind him. They'd all gone to school together, him and Cheryl, Deborah and Ladd. But she hadn't seen Darren in years, and it appeared he was the one who'd gotten fat and bald.

"Hey, Deborah. Long time, no see. Cheryl said you wanted to talk to me."

"Did you know your herd bull broke the fence between you and the Daltry place?"

He frowned. "No, I did not, but if Ladd is pissed off about it, then why isn't he here talking to me about it?"

"Ladd is in the hospital with broken ribs, a partially collapsed lung, and a bunch of staples in his head because your bull attacked him yesterday. Tossed him in the air and stomped him after he was on the ground. I just happened to witness it as it was happening, or he'd be dead right now."

"Oh my God!" Cheryl said as all the color faded from Darren's face.

"You're not serious?" he said.

"Yes. Yes, I am," Deborah said. "And if I hadn't had my rifle with me, that bull would have charged me, too."

"Rifle? Did you shoot it? Dammit, Deborah, that herd bull cost me almost ten thousand dollars."

She stared at him until he was the first to look away. Only then did she answer.

"No, I didn't shoot it. But if it's on Daltry or Ryman land again, I will. Why would you buy something like that? You want that kind of behavior bred into your livestock?"

"Actually, yes. I'm breeding rodeo bulls. They like them with a fighting spirit," Darren said.

Deborah took a slow, deep breath to keep from punching him in the face.

"Then you're about to become persona non gratis around here. You might as well be raising wolves to get in everyone's chickens. If people can't feel safe on their own land, they're gonna all start carrying their hunting rifles, and they're not going to give that son of a bitch a second chance to kill them. You better pen that baby up good and build fence like you're protecting Fort Knox, because your bull took that five-wire fence down like it was string."

"Oh God. Look. I'm sorry. I'll fix the fence. And tell Ladd I'm sorry I—"

"You tell Ladd face-to-face whatever it is you want to say. I'm just here telling you what I had to say, since I was nearly the second victim yesterday. Do you understand me?"

Darren nodded. "Yes, ma'am. I do."

"Then I'm done here," Deborah said. She walked off the porch, got back in her truck, and drove away.

Cheryl grabbed her husband by the arm and yanked him around to face her.

"You purposefully brought a mean animal onto our property?

Did you once give a thought to what might happen to our boys if they'd wandered off into the wrong pasture?"

All the blood drained from Darren's face. "I didn't think of that. The bull was in the far pasture. There are fences and gates between him and the house," he muttered.

"Obviously, fences don't mean much to that animal," Cheryl said. "You get in the truck and you go make sure that fence your bull broke between us and Ladd's place is fixed, and then you load that damn bull up into a trailer and sell it. I won't have an animal like that on our property!"

"It cost ten thousand dollars," Darren shouted.

"We didn't have ten thousand dollars…except in the boys' college fund. Please tell me you did not—"

Darren glared at her. "I was going to make that back a hundred times over by selling the bulls out of him as rodeo stock."

"Then you just learned a very expensive lesson. Get. Rid. Of. That. Bull."

The door slammed shut behind her as she went back in the house, leaving Darren on the porch upset and angry. He'd never seen this coming, but he knew she was right.

"Mother trucker," Darren muttered. He took the phone out of his pocket and made a call to the stockyard. He couldn't load that bull in his little stock trailer. He needed men to help him and a big livestock hauler to get the bull off the property.

———————

Deborah drove back home, so angry she was shaking. By the time she got there she'd made herself calm, but then she walked into the house and found her mother in tears.

"Mom! Are you okay?" Deborah cried as she ran to the kitchen table where Maggie was sitting.

Maggie nodded. "I didn't think it would be this hard. I don't know what to do with your daddy's things. I don't want to give them to the Charity Closet in Blessings and then see people all over town wearing his clothes."

Deborah hugged her. "Just pack them up. I'll take them to Savannah to one of the places there."

"Thank you, baby. I don't know if I could be doing this without you," Maggie said.

"It's why I'm here," Deborah said. "Now, have you eaten anything?"

Maggie shook her head. "I'm not hungry."

"That's no excuse. You have to eat something. Go wash your face. I'll figure out the food situation, and we'll eat together. And I'll tell you what I found out about Darren Payne and his bull."

It was enough to refocus Maggie from grief to curiosity as she hurried out of the kitchen, while Deborah began looking through the refrigerator for stuff to make sandwiches.

# CHAPTER 7

WHILE DEBORAH WAS STARTING LUNCH, JUNIE WILSON WAS in the kitchen cleaning up the remnants of theirs. She'd been at it about thirty minutes when she realized Melvin Lee was noticeably absent.

She hung up the dish towel and went looking for her mother, and found her in the living room, rocking Lucy to sleep.

"I think her fever is breaking," Minna said.

"That's good," Junie said. "Have you seen Melvin Lee?"

"He's in my room," Minna said.

Junie frowned. "What's he doing in there? Why isn't he outside playing? It's a pretty day."

"Because Willy and Arnie are outside, and he says he's had enough of them today. I swear, Junie. He's a kid. He is not their referee. He is not their father. He is their brother. But he doesn't get to be just a brother. You're still dumping your responsibilities on him. You could have waited for your shower until I got back from the store. If you had, you'd still have your lamp, Willy wouldn't have a bloody nose, and Arnie's shirt wouldn't have gotten torn. And…you might have noticed Lucy wasn't feeling well before it was too late."

Junie glared. She wanted to argue, but her mother's presence here was a huge help and saving her sanity. And her mother was right, so there was that.

"Okay, fine. I screwed up again. He wants to go to the park to play a while, but in this day and age, I'm not comfortable letting any of the kids out on their own."

"I'll go with him, and take Willie and Arnie, too," Minna said. "You tend to Lucy and Davie."

Junie sighed, and then threw her arms around her mother's neck and hugged her.

"You're the best. Thanks, Mom," Junie said.

Minna nodded. "I'm going to put Lucy in her bed to nap, then grab some bottles of water and take them in my shoulder bag. It's pretty hot out right now, and it's not going to get cooler until the sun goes down. We won't stay too long. Go tell Willy and Arnie if they want to go to the park with me and Melvin Lee that they have to come in the house and pee first. Last time I took them, they both took off to the creek to pee in the bushes. They can't do that in public."

"I know, I know," Junie said, and went out the back door, yelling at the boys to come in.

A short while later, Minna and the boys were on their way to the park, and she was issuing orders as they went.

"Willy…Arnie…we will play, but we will not fight. We will not wrestle, and you two will not run out of my sight. Do we understand each other?" Minna said.

"Yes, ma'am," they said.

"If you do, not only will we quit playing and go home, but I will report your behavior to your daddy when he gets home."

"No, Grandma, don't tell Daddy," they whined.

"Then don't misbehave," Minna warned.

"We won't. We promise," they said, and immediately ran on ahead.

Melvin Lee sighed.

"They ain't gonna mind, Grandma."

Minna patted the top of her oldest grandson's head. "Never you mind, honey. I've got this."

Melvin Lee grinned, then took off at a jog and ran to catch up with his brothers, with Minna a few yards behind.

They were all the way in the park and racing toward the monkey bars when Melvin Lee saw people in the gazebo. When he recognized Ruby, he stopped and waved.

"Hi, Miss Ruby!"

"Hello, Melvin Lee."

Carlie turned around, then got down out of her seat and went to the railing around the gazebo to see who Ruby was talking to. When she realized there were kids in the park, she stared.

And when Melvin Lee saw the little blond, he froze. She was a stranger. And pretty as a new puppy.

Moments of silence passed as they looked at each other, and then Minna caught up, waved at Ruby, and off they went.

Ruby saw the look on Carlie's face. It was a recognition of one's own kind…one kid to another…without the need for introductions or grown-ups.

"Carlie, honey, have you had all you want to eat?"

She was still watching the new arrivals, and nodded.

Ruby began gathering up their garbage and carried it to a trash can.

"Are you ready to go swing?" Ruby asked.

"Will you push me in the swing?" Carlie asked.

"You bet I will," Ruby said.

"I don't like to go high," Carlie whispered.

Ruby picked her up and hugged her because she couldn't resist, which made Carlie giggle.

"Then we won't go high," Ruby said, and put her down.

As they were walking toward the playground, Carlie glanced up.

"Miss Ruby?"

"Hmmm?"

"Do you know that boy?"

Ruby smiled. "Oh yes. Just about everybody in Blessings knows Melvin Lee. Those other two boys are his younger brothers, and there are two more kids at home. The lady with them is their grandmother, Minna. I guess Junie, their mother, is at home with the two youngest."

"Is he nice?"

"Who? Melvin Lee?"

Carlie nodded.

"Yes, he is a good boy who was given too much responsibility at a very young age. Kind of like you, taking care of your mother."

Carlie thought about that all the way to the swings.

Ruby set down her purse, helped Carlie up into the seat, and then gave her a little push. The smile that lit up Carlie's face was the best thing Ruby had seen all day.

"More?" Ruby asked.

"Yes! More," Carlie said.

"Hold on tight," Ruby added, and gave her another little push.

Carlie felt like she was flying. It was the best feeling. Like she had wings. Ruby pushed, and Carlie soared.

The sun was behind them, casting their own shadows onto the ground in front of them. Carlie could hear those boys laughing and talking as they climbed upon the monkey bars, and then all of a sudden that same boy with brown hair was walking toward them, and the swing was slowing down, and then he was standing in front of them, his hands in his pockets, and he was staring at her again.

Melvin Lee knew everybody in town—except this girl. So now he needed to know her, too.

"Hi, Miss Ruby. Is this your girl?"

"Hi, Melvin Lee. This is Carlie. She's living with us now."

Melvin Lee walked a little closer. "She sure is pretty," he said.

Carlie didn't know what to think about this. Grown-ups said stuff like that, but no kid had ever said that to her before.

"Can she talk?" Melvin Lee asked.

"She's just shy and a little sad," Ruby said.

Then out of the blue, Carlie blurted out, "My name is Carlie. I'm almost eight. My mama died yesterday."

Melvin Lee felt like someone had just punched him in the stomach. He didn't know how to say *I'm sorry that happened.* He didn't know how to express the empathy he was feeling. He'd never thought about mamas dying before. All he knew to do was be Melvin Lee. And so he walked straight up to the swing where she was sitting.

"If you want, I will be your friend," he said.

Carlie looked at Ruby, and then back at Melvin Lee.

"All my friends are where I used to live," she said.

"Then you're going to be needin' a new one, and I'm your man!"

Ruby didn't know whether to laugh or cry. The innocence of children never ceased to amaze her.

Melvin Lee had no name for the sadness he felt in her, but he wanted to make her smile.

"Wanna go meet my grandma? She helps take care of us. Don't worry. My brothers are goofy, but they're not mean."

Carlie didn't know how to answer and, once again, looked to Ruby for help.

"That sounds like a good idea," Ruby said. "I want to say hi to Minna anyway. We'll both go."

Carlie slid out of the swing as Ruby grabbed her purse. But Melvin Lee had already taken charge of Carlie and was talking about school and teachers and the giant playground there.

"Do you like hot dogs?" Melvin Lee asked. "Last year they had hot dogs in the lunchroom every Tuesday. Hot dogs are my favorite," he added.

And then the miracle happened right before Ruby's eyes.

Carlie smiled. "I like hot dogs, too."

Melvin Lee nodded. "Then you're gonna love that lunchroom. Except for recess, it's my favorite part of school."

Ruby laughed. She couldn't help it. Melvin Lee was a mover and a shaker. God help the girls when he hit his stride as a teen.

Minna saw them coming and waved. She'd already heard the story of the woman dying and Ruby and Peanut being the child's guardian. But seeing the little girl up close was a little bit heartbreaking. She couldn't begin to imagine what this child must be thinking and feeling when everyone around her was a stranger, and her own mother had died in her arms.

"Grandma, this here girl is Carlie. She's sad, so we're gonna go down the slide for a while. You'll like it, girl. Going down that slide is like jumping from a plane without a parachute...only safer."

Minna rolled her eyes and looked at Ruby. "It's hard to say what's gonna come out of this boy's mouth, but I sure do love him. He'll be careful with her. He's used to taking care of all his siblings."

"Do you want to go slide?" Ruby asked.

Carlie nodded.

"Then let's go," Ruby said, and quickly took up a position at the bottom of the slide, waiting to catch Carlie, but it was the shriek of delight as Carlie came flying down that made Ruby smile. Peanut was brilliant. This had been a really good idea.

As soon as Carlie's feet hit the dirt, she went straight into Ruby's arms.

"Did you see how fast I was going?" Carlie asked.

"I sure did," Ruby said, and they stepped off to the side out of the way for Melvin Lee, who was the next one in line.

He waved from the top of the slide and yelled, "Watch this!" and then came down the slide, waving his arms like he was trying to fly.

Minna sighed. "I swear to goodness. Where do boys get all that energy?"

Ruby laughed, and the minute Melvin Lee's feet hit the ground, he whooped and grabbed Carlie's hand.

"Wanna do that again, girl?"

She nodded, and off they went to the back of the slide again. Ruby was a little anxious about her role as a caretaker and was watching as Carlie started climbing up the steep steps, when all of a sudden Melvin Lee started climbing up behind her.

"Don't worry, girl!" Melvin Lee said. "I'm right behind you, so I'll catch you if you fall."

Carlie heard and, with all of the innocence of youth, believed he was capable of doing just that and kept climbing. So up and down they went until Carlie's face was pink and sweaty, and the day was getting hotter.

"Goodness, that sun is sure getting hot, don't you think?" Ruby said.

Carlie nodded. "Yes, I'm hot and thirsty."

"Oh…I've got water!" Minna said. She pulled an unopened bottle of water from her tote bag and broke the seal before she handed it over. "Here you go, sugar."

"Thank you," Carlie said, taking the bottle with both hands. She tilted it to her mouth and drank thirstily. When her thirst was quenched, without thinking she handed it to Ruby, just like she would have handed it to her mama. "Your turn," she said.

"Thank you, honey," Ruby said, and took a big drink, then screwed the lid back on the bottle. "And thank you, Minna. I did not come prepared for this, but I'm learning."

"And God bless the journey," Minna said, then frowned when she saw Willy and Arnie arguing at the monkey bars. "Looks like they've had enough of playing and of each other. We better be heading home."

"We can give you a ride if you want," Ruby said. "It's sure hot."

"Thanks, but it's less than two blocks. Maybe they'll be so tired when we get back they'll take a nap." Then she winked at Carlie. "Thank you for playing with us."

"Welcome," Carlie whispered, and then reached for Ruby's hand as Melvin Lee came running.

"Grandma, the boys are—"

"I saw them," Minna said. "I'll go get them. I think it's time to go home. Tell Carlie goodbye."

Melvin Lee didn't want to tell Carlie goodbye. He liked looking at her. And except for when she was laughing, she was quiet. He liked quiet. There wasn't much of that at his house. Sweat was running out of his hairline and down the back of his neck, but he was oblivious. All he saw were her big blue eyes.

"We had fun, didn't we, girl? You did good on that slide."

She nodded, pleased that he approved.

"Thank you for being such a good friend, Melvin Lee," Ruby said.

He grinned. "Welcome, Miss Ruby. See you around, girl," he said, and took off running toward his grandma and brothers.

"Come on, sugar. Let's go home," Ruby said and gave Carlie's hand a quick squeeze.

Carlie followed her, thinking about home. For a second when Miss Ruby said that, Carlie pictured the apartment in Little Rock, and then remembered that place wasn't theirs anymore, and she and Miss Ruby had picked out a little house for Mama to go to heaven. That would be Mama's new home, and Carlie's new home was here.

She squeezed her eyes to keep from crying, and as soon as they got in the car, she asked for the water again.

Ruby handed her the bottle and then buckled her in before starting up the car to cool it off.

Carlie sipped water as Ruby drove, and by the time they got home, the need to cry had receded. Carlie was thoroughly hydrated and mostly cool, but she clammed up again as soon as they walked back in the house.

Ruby saw the look on her face and knew she was shutting down again. "Let's go wash up," Ruby said, and led the way to the little bath in the hall to help Carlie wash up. She'd gone quiet again, and Ruby knew the only way she'd know what was wrong was to ask.

"Are you okay, honey? Did you get too hot?"

Carlie shrugged.

Ruby turned off the water, grabbed a towel, and handed it to her, then sat down on the side of the bathtub. The minute she got down on Carlie's level, she knew something was bothering her and pulled her into her arms.

"What is it, honey? You can ask me anything."

"What's going to happen to Mama and her little house?"

Ruby sighed.

"When people die, their spirits go to heaven, and we bury their bodies because they don't need them anymore. You know, you don't have to go do all that if you don't want to. They can bury your mama without you there."

Carlie's eyes widened, and she began to panic. "Oh, but I have to. I do things for Mama now that she can't do for herself."

"After the service, you won't have to do things for her anymore. After that, she won't need either one of us ever again, and your job will be to be a little girl again and let the grown-ups worry about the hard stuff, like getting you enrolled in school here."

Carlie thought about school and Melvin Lee. He liked recess and lunch. Maybe she would, too.

"Will that boy be in my class?"

Ruby frowned, remembering that Melvin Lee had been held back a year because his mother kept him home so much to babysit that he got behind. "Maybe. There will be lots of girls and boys for you to get to know."

"Sometimes kids are mean," Carlie whispered.

Ruby laughed. "And sometimes so are grown-ups. But I know how to deal with that, and so does Mr. Ruby. All you have to do is tell us, and we'll help you, okay? Now, let's go see what you have to wear to your mama's service."

"I have my Easter dress. I still fit it," Carlie said.

Ruby nodded. "Then let's go check it out, in case it needs to be washed or ironed before you wear it."

"Okay," Carlie said, and led the way back to her room.

Minna and the boys walked into the Wilson residence, hot, sweaty, and unusually quiet. They were tired and hungry.

"If you'll all go wash, then come back to the kitchen, I'll have snacks for you," Minna said. "But be quiet. Lucy isn't feeling well, and Davie might be napping."

They nodded and tiptoed down the hall to their bathroom and began washing up, while Minna washed her hands in the kitchen then began making bologna and cheese sandwiches. She cut each of them in four pieces, piled them on a plate, and poured three small glasses of milk. She had it all on the table, and when they came back, they were so hungry that they ate without talking.

Minna smiled. She loved them all dearly, but there was something special about Melvin Lee. She didn't know what he was going to be when he grew up, but whatever it was, she knew he would rock it.

They were just finishing up when Junie came into the kitchen with Davie on her hip. She sat down at the table and looked at her boys.

"Did you have fun?" she asked.

Minna nodded. "We had a great time. Ruby Butterman was there with Shirley Duroy's little girl. Her name is Carlie. She played on the slide with the boys."

Melvin Lee looked up then, eyeing his mother and little brother as if he'd never seen them before.

Junie caught him staring and frowned.

"What's wrong?" she asked.

"I didn't know mamas could die," Melvin Lee said, and then got up and went straight to his mother and wrapped his arms around her neck.

Davie immediately began pulling his hair, but he didn't care. He just needed to reconnect.

"Well, honey, bless your heart," Junie said, then put Davie in the floor and wrapped her arms around Melvin Lee. "I'm fine.

That little girl's mama was sick. There was something wrong with her heart."

But Melvin Lee didn't say anything. He just held on.

———

Bart Carlson didn't know the name of the people who had Carlie Duroy, but he was going to Blessings and he'd find out when he got there.

He'd already contacted his lawyer to see what he would need to take with him that the guardian might want to see regarding he and Mila adopting Carlie. He had impeccable references and, thanks to Mila, an even better financial status. Nobody in their right mind would think he wasn't well established. He also had prior knowledge of Carlie and had discussed this with Shirley more than once, so he felt like he at least had his foot in the door.

He never once thought about what Carlie might want. She was just a kid whose mother had died, and wherever she went, it would still be all new and strange. He had the drive, he had the paperwork in hand. But what he didn't have was Mila on board with going after the kid.

"Look, Bart. You need to get over yourself," Mila said. "It wasn't meant to be. Shirley gave legal guardianship to someone else, which means you lost out."

Bart didn't like to lose at anything. And he didn't like being told what to do.

"If I can adopt her, you will be her mother, whether you like it or not," he said.

"If you adopt her, you better have a nanny on board, because I am not going to be the soccer mommy or the one putting her to bed. And don't forget she might live under the roof of this house, but not under my wing, and you can't bully me into anything I don't want to do."

"Does this mean you're not going with me to Blessings?" Bart asked.

"That's exactly what that means. I'm not humiliating myself by chasing all over the South trying to find some dead woman's kid, and if you had a brain in your head, neither would you. That money you keep talking about is a pittance," she muttered.

"Look, just because you have a trust fund and get a butt-load of your daddy's money anytime you ask doesn't mean I have the same luxury," Bart said. "I work hard for the money it takes to give you nice things and a nice home."

"So you're saying you'd actually agree to adopt a kid just for the money that comes with her?" Mila asked.

Bart flushed. "That's not it at all."

Mila shrugged. "Yes, that is it. In a nutshell. I'm just telling you now. If you are successful at doing this, and that kid interferes with our lifestyle and vacations, you may find yourself living the life of a single parent."

Bart was stunned. He did not want to lose Mila and started backtracking on being assertive.

"Honey, I feel like I need to follow up only because Shirley and I had discussed this more than once. If I'm satisfied that she's okay, then that's the end of that and I'll forget they ever existed."

Mila sighed. "Okay, I see your point. And honestly, I think it's kind of sexy that you feel any kind of responsibility for an orphan."

Bart hugged her.

"Thank you for understanding, darling. I'll be leaving in about an hour. It's about a ten-hour drive, so I'll stop somewhere tonight and get there around noon tomorrow. Blessings is a small town. It shouldn't take me long to find out what I need to know. I'll call you and let you know when I'm starting home."

"Safe travels," Mila said. "I'm going to get my nails done."

She blew him a kiss and left the house without looking back.

Bart sighed. Mila could be a little coldhearted, but he was honest enough to admit that he had a tendency to be greedy. Their worst traits seemed to complement their lack of compassion for anyone but themselves. They were an odd match but, for the time being, oddly suited to each other.

Mila was backing out of the driveway as he went to get his overnight bag. He tossed it in the trunk of his Lexus and jumped in behind the wheel. After double-checking to make sure he had his briefcase, he backed out of the drive and headed for the nearest on-ramp to the interstate.

———————————

Peanut drove back from Savannah with Ruby and Carlie on his mind. He couldn't explain the feeling of anticipation of going home, because he always looked forward to seeing Ruby. He'd been in love with her for so long before he ever got the guts to tell her, and he now considered himself the luckiest man on earth to have her.

And then Carlie happened, and the parameters of their world exploded. They were scrambling to find the new borders to include this child who was dropped as rudely into their lives as she was ripped from her own.

He'd thought about Ruby and Carlie all day. Was everything going okay, or was Carlie coming undone? He couldn't imagine what was going through her mind, but she was already in his heart.

When he went to Walmart to get the booster seat Ruby wanted, it took him right past the toy aisle, and before he knew it, he had a dollhouse in the basket, too. Now all he wanted to do was get home and see the girls. He needed to know for himself that they were coping.

Even though it took most of an hour to get home, Peanut felt a great sense of relief as he turned the block on his street and headed to their house. The anticipation of seeing them both again was making him antsy. He drove up the drive and parked, and the first thing he did when he got out was install the booster seat in the back seat of Ruby's car.

He'd just shut the doors and was going back to his car to get the box with the dollhouse when the front door opened. He turned around, and Carlie was standing in the doorway, waving.

"Hi, Mr. Ruby," she said.

Ruby walked up behind her and waved. "Hi, Mr. Ruby," she echoed, and smiled.

He sighed. Thank God. They appeared to be okay.

"Hey, you two. Give me a second. I have to get something out of the trunk." He popped the trunk, got the box, and locked the car with the remote as he headed up the steps.

Ruby grinned. "What did you do?"

"I might have bought a dollhouse for a little doll," he said. "Who wants to help me get it all out of the box?"

Carlie was beside herself. She could tell from the pictures on the outside of the box what was in it and immediately raised her hand.

"I'll help," she said.

"I'll help," Ruby added.

He grinned. "Awesome. Then where do you think we should put it?"

"Not in our bedroom," Ruby said.

"Yeah, not a good idea to put it there," Peanut said.

"What about the living room?" Ruby said.

Peanut frowned. "Maybe, but I like to put my drink and snacks on the coffee table," he said.

"How about Carlie's room? We can bring that little maple table down out of the attic. It would fit against the wall at the end of the other twin bed," Ruby said, then turned and looked at Carlie. "Would you mind having the dollhouse in your room? For always?"

"No, no, I wouldn't mind," Carlie said. "I would like to play dollhouse."

"Then it's settled. And if we ever want to play, too, then we could come to your room to play with you, right?" Peanut said.

Carlie's head was bobbing like a cork on a fishing line. "Yes! Right!"

"Then lead the way," Peanut said, and followed his girls, knowing he was carrying far more than a dollhouse. He had hope, and joy, and something new—something Carlie hadn't brought with her from before.

He set the box down in Carlie's room and then headed up the attic stairs to get the little table Ruby wanted. By the time he came back, they had everything out of the box and spread out on the extra bed.

"Oh, it's dusty," Ruby said, when Peanut set the table down against the wall. "I'll go get a rag and some lemon oil while you two start getting the house set up."

By the time she came back, Peanut and Carlie were head to head, talking about dollhouses and fairy houses and little people in general. Carlie was holding Hoppy as Peanut worked.

"Hoppy is watching Mr. Ruby work," Carlie said.

"Hoppy will be happy to have a new friend in the dollhouse, just like you have a new friend from the park," Ruby said.

Peanut paused and looked at Carlie. "You made a new friend?"

Carlie nodded. "Melvin Lee. We went down the slide about a bajillion times."

Peanut grinned. "You sure know how to pick 'em, sugar. Melvin Lee is quality in my book."

"Melvin Lee was quite taken with Carlie, too. It was something to see," Ruby said.

Peanut arched an eyebrow. "Oh wow… Is this how it begins?"

"Well, you're the guy. You tell me," Ruby said.

Peanut shook his head, popped the last piece of the roof into place, and set the house on the table.

"Now it's ready for furniture and people, and that's for you and Carlie. I'm going to go change so I can water Miss Ruby's flowers," he said.

Carlie turned and threw her arms around Peanut's neck.

"Thank you for the dollhouse. I will help you water."

The feel of those little arms and hands around his neck were his undoing.

"You don't have to, honey. You can stay here and play this time, since your dollhouse is new."

"No. A promise is a promise," Carlie said.

Peanut nodded. "All right, then. Let me get changed, and we'll go look for fairies while we're at it."

# CHAPTER 8

THE FLOWERS GOT WATERED. SUPPER WAS EATEN, AND CARLIE played in her room until after 8:00 p.m. Finally, Ruby got her bathed and into pajamas, and then Carlie put her new doll to bed, too.

"Did you name your doll?" Ruby asked as she settled in with an Amelia Bedelia book.

Carlie nodded.

"What did you name her?"

Carlie pulled the covers up to her chin. "It's a secret," she said.

Ruby smiled. "Okay. 'Nuff said, right? Now, are you ready for *Amelia Bedelia's First Day of School*?"

Carlie nodded again and then lay back watching the way Miss Ruby's mouth said the words. She closed her eyes, wondering if she didn't look at her would it be like listening to Mama, but it wasn't. She turned over on her side and tucked Hoppy beneath her chin as the story went on. She knew it by heart. But she still liked to hear it. When she knew how something ended, there were no surprises, which made her feel safe. She liked the way Miss Ruby hugged her. She liked that Mr. Ruby talked to her like a grown-up and not a kid. She liked the way his eyes crinkled at the corners when he smiled.

The last thing she remembered was Miss Ruby saying, "The End," and knowing she was going to see Mama tomorrow.

---

Ladd's partially collapsed lung had reinflated, and he could breathe a little easier now. His head, however, was still one solid throb.

It was sometime around 1:00 a.m. when he rang for the nurse

and asked for pain meds. She showed up a short while later with a syringe full of something she put in his IV, then added some fresh ice to his pitcher of drinking water and checked his vitals.

"Is there anything else I can get for you?" she asked.

"A blanket. I'm kind of cold," he said.

She nodded. They kept the hospital so cold that almost every patient requested warm blankets at night.

"Sure thing. I'll be right back," she said, and left his room.

He shifted position just a little and then eased back down onto the pillow and pulled the covers up over his shoulders. If there was one thing he was going to learn from this incident, it would be to never take a comfortable bed for granted again. This one felt like he was lying on rocks. Or...maybe his back was so beat up from getting stomped that there *was* no comfortable way to lie.

The nurse came back carrying a couple of warm blankets, unfolded them, and then layered them over him, tucking one beneath his feet and pulling it as far up as it would go, and then unfolding the second one at knee level and pulling it up over his shoulders.

"If you were any taller, I'd be layering three on you just to get you all covered up," she said, then laughed softly and turned out the lights as she left.

"Thank you," Ladd mumbled.

The pain meds were kicking in. The warm blankets on his achy body felt so good, and he finally drifted back off to sleep again, then dreamed he was making love with Deborah, naked as the day she was born, lying beneath him on a blanket he'd thrown over a pile of hay up in the barn loft.

Her eyes were closed, her hands locked around his neck. Her legs were wrapped around his waist and she was meeting him thrust for thrust. He was so caught up in the sweet heat of her that he didn't know she was about to climax. And then she did, screaming just enough that he quickly covered her lips with his mouth and came with her. It was the best feeling in the world to come apart in her arms. But when the dream morphed and she disappeared, he began searching for her until he got lost, too, then woke up with a jerk when someone dropped a tray in the hall.

He grabbed onto his chest with both hands, as if that would settle the shards of pain rolling through his body, and looked toward the foot of the bed. That was where she'd first appeared to him after all these years, and with that dream fresh in his mind, he wanted her back. If not beneath him, then at least where he could see her.

Seeing her as she was now—tall and magnificent in a wild, untamed way—reminded him of what he'd lost by not going back to Blessings after her. He didn't know why he'd let her go so easily after dying over and over in her arms. Maybe it was because she'd been too easy to conquer. Too open. She'd hidden nothing from him, and so he thought he'd seen it all. But now, after seeing the woman she'd become, he realized he'd known nothing about her then and knew even less about her now. As for conquering, it was not a word he would associate with the woman who'd saved his life.

He groaned as he reached for his water and took a quick sip. He wanted to roll over onto his side, but broken ribs protested, so he closed his eyes and willed himself not to feel the pain.

He thought instead of where he might go after the farm sold. He'd graduated from college as an architect and had been in a good place in his career when his mother passed away. He came home every holiday after that because he knew if he didn't, his dad would be alone. Then Walt got sick, and Ladd moved home. It never occurred to him not to. He could be an architect anywhere, like he was doing now, and move anywhere he chose to ply his trade.

But he also knew if he sold the property and moved away, he'd be hustling again to find his way back into a firm or have to go out on his own and pay office rent.

Right now he owned and lived rent free on the farm. He could stay there and work a huge portion of his job online. Since he'd left the corporate world, Zoom meetings had taken the place of weekly office meetings. He could work from home, let the land go fallow for a year, and see what happened. He had options. But he had to get well before he acted on any of them.

Deborah was dreaming her alarm was going off and woke up with a start only to realize it wasn't her alarm. It was Dumpling, her mom's old rooster, crowing in the day. She rolled over, smiling, remembering the day long ago when her dad had threatened to wring one particular young rooster's neck and turn it into chicken and dumplings for crowing so loud and long before daylight.

Her mom had countered by threatening to never make chicken and dumplings again if he hurt it. But she did like the name, and so Dumpling it became.

Deborah stretched and then rolled over onto her back to think about the day. No matter what else they did, she was going back to see Ladd. She told herself it was because he had no one to look in on him. But the truth was seeing him had awakened ghosts she thought she'd long ago laid to rest.

She wasn't afraid of them by any means, but she was also a woman who did not run from her own truth. She wanted to see him again.

Carlie woke up to the smell of bacon frying and remembered she was at Miss Ruby's house. She loved bacon but Mama hadn't cooked it for a long time because she got too sick to cook.

And then Carlie remembered the dollhouse and bounced out of bed, dragging Hoppy with her. She sat Hoppy at the end of the other twin bed and raced to the bathroom. When she came back, she headed straight to the dollhouse and got the doll out of bed.

"It's morning, Shirley. Time to get up," she whispered, and began to play, taking "Shirley" to the dollhouse kitchen to eat, and pretending to feed her waffles, which had been her mother's favorite breakfast. Then she walked Shirley to the dollhouse living room, sat her on the sofa, and then whispered to her again—"It's time to go to work"—and handed her a pretend laptop, then went to get dressed.

It was the same routine she and her mother had kept. In her heart, she knew the doll wasn't real, and it wasn't her mother, but reenacting their life gave Carlie a measure of comfort.

Today Miss Ruby said they would go see Mama again, but now that the time was here, she was a little bit scared. What if Mama didn't look right? How would she know it was *her* mama and not someone else's? If there was more than one dead person at the funeral home, did they get them mixed up?

Carlie sighed and plopped down on the floor to fasten the Velcro tabs on her sandals. *Miss Ruby will know.*

She jumped up and as she walked past the dollhouse glanced in to make sure Shirley was still working, and then followed the sounds of voices down the hall and into the kitchen.

Ruby was just taking the last piece of bacon from the skillet and putting it on the plate when Carlie announced herself.

"I'm awake."

"Yes, you are, and already dressed," Ruby said, eyeing the tangled blond curls Carlie had obviously ignored. She pushed the skillet off the burner to the back of the stove and picked Carlie up and hugged her. "Good morning, sweetheart. Did you sleep good? No bad dreams?"

"I slept good," Carlie said.

"Hey! Where's my good-morning hug?" Peanut asked.

Ruby put her down, leaving Carlie to make her own decisions

about who she hugged, but Carlie didn't disappoint. She headed for the table where Peanut was sitting, and when he leaned over so she could reach him, she wrapped her arms around his neck.

"Thank you for my sweet hug," Peanut said.

Carlie nodded, then crawled up into a chair on the other side of the table and sat down.

"Pancakes this morning," Ruby said.

"Yum," Carlie said.

Ruby had two stacks ready and put them on two plates and carried them to the table. She helped Carlie with butter and syrup, then left her with Peanut and went back to make some more.

When they were all at the table, Carlie paused before taking another bite.

"Miss Ruby, is this the day I go see Mama?"

"Yes, it is," Ruby said. "There was a message on my phone when I woke up. We'll go after breakfast, okay?"

Carlie nodded with relief. She took another bite and then glanced up at them.

"Am I doing a good job being a helper?" she asked.

Peanut and Ruby were both startled by the question and hastened to answer.

"Yes, you're a wonderful helper," Peanut said. "You water flowers as good as I do. And you give the best hugs."

"You are the best helper ever," Ruby said. "But you don't have to earn your way to be here. You're here because we love having you and so you'll have a home. And because your Mama knew we would all learn to love each other. Okay?"

Carlie nodded, but her place here in this house had yet to be determined. She didn't belong to anyone in this town. Except Mama. And she needed to talk to Mama about that. She didn't know how this all was supposed to work. If Mr. Ruby and Miss Ruby were guarding her, how long did they have to do that? If they got tired of it, then what?

She put her fork on the plate, with half the pancakes uneaten.

"I'm full, Miss Ruby."

"Okay, honey. Go wash the sticky syrup off your face and hands, and I'll take you to see your mama."

Carlie slid out of the chair and left the room.

As soon as she was out of earshot, Ruby looked at Peanut.

"That makes me sad. I don't know how to assure her she's not just on loan somewhere. She must be so confused."

He shrugged. "She could be no other way. Our job is to give her all the time and love she needs to feel secure about her place with us."

Ruby nodded. "I know you're right, but her world is so broken."

"And it will heal," Peanut said. "Go get yourself together. I'll clean up the kitchen. I don't have an appointment until ten. It doesn't matter if I go in to the office a few minutes late."

Ruby got up from her chair, walked up behind him, and kissed him on the cheek. Her voice was shaking, and there were tears in her eyes.

"You are my heart. You can't ever leave me. I don't know how to be in the world without you anymore."

Peanut pulled her into his lap, wrapped his arms around her, and held her close.

"Nobody's leaving anybody here. Just go be my happy girl and we'll find our way to Carlie, too. Having my two girls happy is all I need."

"Okay," Ruby said. "And thank you for cleaning up."

He swatted her on the backside as she got up.

"You can pay me back later," he said, and winked.

———

Bart Carlson had been on the road since early morning, and would be in Blessings by midafternoon. As he drove, he thought about what he was doing.

Did he want to be a father? Was his concern for the child's well-being honest, or did he just want access to her money? He wasn't sure how he felt. He'd only seen the kid once or twice, but this was why he was going to see her for himself. He had this romantic vision of rescuing her from a disadvantaged family, but as the old saying went, "Only time would tell."

He had called Mila before he left the motel, but the call went to voicemail. She was not an early riser, so he just assumed she was still sleeping. When she woke up and saw she'd missed his call, she'd check in.

---

The trip to the funeral home was silent. Ruby was torn about inflicting all of this trauma on a child so young, but at the same time, Carlie deserved the right to see her mother. Maybe it would satisfy the uncertainty of it all for her. If not, the graveside service tomorrow should confirm that her mother's absence in her life was a final one.

They parked and got out, and when they started inside, Ruby took Carlie's hand and gave it a quick squeeze.

"Are you okay?" Ruby asked.

Carlie paused. "Will Mama still look the same?"

"She'll look like she's asleep, and you can talk to her all you want, but she won't be able to answer," Ruby said.

"Mama told me she will hear me, but she'll be too far away for me to hear her," Carlie said, and then her eyes welled. "I want to hear her."

"I know, darling. But you won't be able to. Are you going to be okay with that, or is this too hard? We can go home if you want."

It was the word *home* that settled it for Carlie. She needed to talk to Mama about that.

"I am going to be okay," Carlie said.

"I'll be right beside you every step, and if you want to talk to your mama in private, I can step out of the room. All you have to do is just tell me I need to leave."

Carlie nodded. "I'm ready," she said, and they walked in together.

One of the employees met them at the door. "Good morning, Ruby. Good morning, young lady."

"We came to see Carlie's mother, Shirley Duroy."

"Yes, ma'am. Right this way," he said and led them to the first viewing room on the right. "Take your time. We won't allow the public in until you give permission."

"Thank you," Ruby said, and led the way into the room.

The flowers they'd ordered for the casket were all white, with gold ribbon and a banner with the word *Mother* draped across it.

"That word says 'Mother,'" Carlie said.

"Yes. Those flowers are from you for your mother," Ruby said.

Carlie liked the white roses and paused at the foot of the casket to run the tips of her fingers across the fragile petals. Then she looked up at the white clouds on the inside of the open lid and tried to see in, but all she could see was part of her mother's forehead and hair.

"Miss Ruby, I can't see her," Carlie said.

"Oh, I'll get this folding chair and you can stand on it," Ruby said, then grabbed it and set it at the head of the casket.

Carlie climbed up with Ruby's help, and when Ruby put her arm around Carlie to steady her, she took comfort from it.

It was the first time Ruby was seeing Shirley as a grown woman, and she was immediately struck by how pretty she was and how little she had changed in looks. "She looks so pretty. Just like I remember her," Ruby said.

Carlie didn't know what to think, but when she reached for Shirley's arm and felt the stiff, cold flesh, she yanked her hand back. Her voice was trembling as she looked up at Ruby.

"Her arm is...is hard and cold, Miss Ruby. They need to bring her a blanket."

Ruby sighed. She was scrambling to come up with an answer that would satisfy a child and went for the truth.

"She doesn't need a blanket, honey. She doesn't feel hot or cold anymore...or pain, or sick, or weak. She's well and happy now. Her body feels stiff and cold because her soul, which was the warm, soft part of her, is not in her body anymore. It's in heaven."

Carlie started. "But why didn't she take her body with her?"

"Because it was broken and sick, remember?" Ruby said.

"Then why did she need the little house if she's already there? I thought it was for her to live in on her way to heaven."

"The little houses are for what's left of us here."

Carlie thought about that for a few moments. "I need to talk to Mama. By myself."

Ruby gave her a quick hug, then pointed at the door.

"See that chair?"

Carlie nodded.

"I'll go sit there. I'll be too far away to hear you, so you can talk all you want. When you're through, we'll leave."

"Okay," Carlie said, then waited until Ruby was sitting down before she turned to her mother. The moment she looked down at her, she was once again in tears. "Mama, I don't know what I'm supposed to do. Miss Ruby's job is to guard me. But what do I do for her?"

She closed her eyes then to listen, praying she would hear an answer, but all she heard was the distant mumble of voices in another viewing room, so she kept talking.

"I help do stuff. I work hard, Mama. Mr. Ruby and Miss Ruby are nice to me. But they're not you, and everything is different, and I'm scared all the time that I'll do something wrong and they'll give me away. I don't know what to do, Mama. Can you dream it to me? I don't want to mess up and go to the fosters." She paused, then leaned a little closer. "You didn't tell me that when you went to heaven part of you stayed behind."

Again there were no answers, but she was all talked out and she wanted to be someplace where people answered when you asked them questions.

She turned and looked at Ruby.

"Are you ready to leave?" Ruby asked.

Carlie nodded, then climbed down from the chair and went straight into Ruby's arms. The warmth of her skin, the faint scent of her perfume, and the gentleness in her touch were what Carlie had needed from her mother. But the reality of that never happening again had just come full circle. She got it. It was a hard, horrible thing to know, but she got it.

They walked hand in hand out of the building and into the sunshine.

Carlie paused and looked up, staring past the treetops, past the birds soaring on the air currents, beyond the tufts of cottony clouds.

"What do you see?" Ruby asked.

"Nothing. I was just looking for Mama, but I think she's already gone."

━━━━━━━━━

Bart Carlson stopped about an hour outside of Savannah to refuel and eat lunch. He was a little worried that Mila hadn't returned his call. She was hot-tempered and had knee-jerk reactions to being threatened. And Bart had given her an ultimatum she'd not only rejected but countered by throwing down one of her own. She had no intention of playing mother to anyone's kid—not even one of her own—and he either agreed, or she was gone.

A car pulled up on the other side of the pumps while he was refueling. It was a beat-up old SUV with three kids in the back and a couple sitting in front with both windows rolled down. The day was hot, and from the sweat on their faces and the clothes sticking to their bodies, they were feeling it. They all looked like they could do with a bath and clean clothes.

And then the mother got out and opened the door for the kids, who piled out like puppies, rolling over each other and talking and laughing.

He watched, wondering why people had children they couldn't afford and was judging everything about them, when the youngest one, a little girl, suddenly tripped and fell on the concrete, immediately skinning her knee and making it bleed.

Before she could cry, her mother scooped her up in her arms and started hugging and petting her and telling her how sorry she was that her sweet baby was hurt.

The little girl was concerned about the blood, but her mother just gave her a kiss on the cheek.

"We'll wash that blood off in the bathroom, and then you'll be good to go. And if you'll be a big girl for Mommy, we'll ask Daddy to get a Coke from that machine. It'll have lots of ice and three straws, and all of you can have a cold treat on this hot day, okay?"

The little girl nodded and hid her face against her mother's neck as they all went inside.

It was a minor injury, and something that happens to children all over, countless times. A skinned knee. A hug and a kiss, and all is well. Except Bart kept remembering how hateful Mila was about bringing a little girl into their home. Who would comfort Carlie when Bart was at work? They would have to hire a full-time nanny, and would she be any more trustworthy than Mila? All of a sudden, he was doubting his intentions. Mila hadn't returned his text from this morning, so instead of texting her again, he called.

She was laughing when she answered, and he could hear voices and more laughter in the background.

"Hello," Mila said.

Bart frowned. "Hey. I was just checking in to make sure you were okay. You didn't return my text this morning."

"I didn't have anything to say," Mila said. "You're on your fucking quest, and I'm having lunch with friends."

The hair crawled on the back of Bart's neck. He looked toward the building, thinking of how loving that mother had been, and knew in his gut he had to stop this right now.

Instead of pandering to the fight he knew she wanted, he disconnected. He was so pissed he couldn't think, but it had come home to him the hard way that chasing after someone else's child was a mistake.

The tank clicked off. He turned and looked. His gas tank was full. He hung up the hose, screwed the gas cap back on, and then drove to the nearest fast-food place to get a burger to go and headed home.

He truly hoped Shirley Duroy's kid was in a good place, but if she wasn't, it was God's fault for letting her mother die. As for Mila, he wasn't going to tell her he was coming home. He was just going to show up and see what there was to see.

She called twice as he was driving and eating, but he didn't pick up. Then she called two more times and he let them go to voicemail. She sent a text, which he also ignored and just kept driving. But he wasn't going to stop overnight again. He was driving straight through. Didn't matter what time he got home. He had a feeling that whatever time it was, there was going to be a surprise waiting.

---

Ruby and Carlie needed something to take their minds off of the visit to the funeral home, so Ruby drove to the Crown to get cookies.

Carlie was immediately taken with the bakery and the deli, and was pointing out things she liked when she heard a familiar voice and turned around to see Melvin Lee pointing and talking about her.

"Hey, Mama! There's my new friend, Carlie. Hey, girl, this is my mama and little brother."

Carlie smiled and waved, entranced by her new friend's ability to talk so loud and so fast, and also by the toddler. She hadn't been around any babies before.

Junie turned to look, curious to finally see the orphaned child everyone was talking about, and immediately saw beyond the blond hair and blue eyes to the sadness within her. The mother's heart in her broke, thinking of how scared and unsettled the child must be.

"Hello, Carlie. I'm glad to meet you. My boys mentioned you all played together at the park. You'll have to come to our house some day and play. We have a big backyard with a sandbox and swings."

"Yeah, but we hafta be careful of the cat poop in the sandbox," Melvin Lee said. "If the boys leave the lid off of it, it's poop city in there."

Junie blushed. "Well, Lord have mercy, Melvin Lee. What a thing to say."

Melvin Lee shrugged. "Can't be havin' my friend gettin' into cat poop. It stinks to high heaven."

Carlie was nodding as if she understood everything he was saying, but they'd never had a pet of any kind and she was unfamiliar with cats and their penchant for digging holes to poop in, then covering them up.

It was all Ruby could do not to laugh out loud. Melvin Lee was, in the best of Southern terminology, *a caution*.

"We're getting cookies," Carlie said.

Melvin Lee looked wistful, but he didn't ask. "I think my granny is making us cookies." He looked up at his mother. "Ain't that right, Mama?"

"Isn't that right," Junie corrected.

Melvin Lee frowned. "I don't know. I was asking you."

"We need to get home with this stuff. Lucy's sick, and Arnie is coming down with the same thing. Some kind of stomach bug."

"I ain't gettin' no bugs," Melvin Lee said, and waved. "Bye, girl. I'll let you know when it's safe to come play."

Junie frowned. "I do say, Melvin Lee. Exactly how do you plan to do that?"

"Well, heck, Mama, I reckon I'll be callin' her. Miss Ruby's got a phone. I reckon she'll let Carlie talk on it."

Ruby grinned. "I reckon I will. Your mama's got my number."

Carlie seemed uplifted by the run-in with her new friend and was holding Ruby's hand when they went out the door with their bag of cookies.

They were on their way across the parking lot when Ruby saw Elliot Graham get out of his car then stop and stare at Carlie, but thought nothing of it. She was new in town, and so far nearly everybody was staring at her.

But then Elliot started toward them, intercepting them before they got to the car.

"Good morning, Ruby. I have a message for your girl. May I?"

Ruby sighed. "It needs to be a good one. We're having a hard time here."

Elliot looked down at the little blond beside Ruby.

"Good morning. My name is Elliot. Are you Carlie?"

Carlie looked up at Ruby.

"It's okay. He's a friend," Ruby said.

Carlie looked back at the old man. He had kind eyes and wrinkles at the corners of his eyes, and his hair was thick and white like snow.

"Yes, I'm Carlie."

Elliot nodded. "Good. I have a message for you from someone named Shirley. Do you know someone by that name?"

Carlie's eyes welled. "That's my mama's name. But she died and went to heaven."

Elliot nodded. "I know. Sometimes people in heaven talk to me because I have ears that can hear them."

Carlie gasped. "You can hear my mama?"

"Yes. She said you asked her questions this morning. I have her answers. She said you won't need to worry about asking her questions anymore. She said when you have problems, you are to ask Miss Ruby. She will always help you, just like she's helping your mama by taking care of you. Understand?"

Carlie nodded.

"She also said...that the longer you are together, the more you will learn to love and trust each other. She said you do not have to earn your right to live with Miss Ruby. That is already settled, and you are safe. She also said nobody is going to get tired of you, and that you would understand what that meant."

Ruby wanted to cry. Now she knew what Carlie was talking to her mother about this morning. *God, please help me take away her fears of being unwanted.*

Elliot looked up at Ruby and winked. "He will. You have to be patient and trust, too."

"Is my mama safe now?" Carlie asked.

"Safe and well. She's sorry she couldn't stay, but she just couldn't get well here."

Carlie leaned against Ruby's leg. This she understood.

"Well, it's been a pleasure meeting you," Elliot said, then looked at Ruby. "Stay aware of jealous tongues. They can cause trouble. But you will persevere."

And then he was gone before Ruby could get him to explain.

Carlie turned around and hugged Ruby's legs.

"I got my wish. I got my wish. Mama heard me."

"And are those the answers you needed?" Ruby asked.

Carlie nodded.

Ruby walked Carlie to the car and got her buckled in the back seat, then sat down in the seat beside her.

"I'm sorry you are afraid, and I'm so sorry you don't trust us to keep you safe. But honey, I promise you... You are a treasure to

# CHAPTER 9

RUBY DROVE HOME WITH ANTICIPATION. CARLIE HAD already explored and fallen in love with the garden in the back of their house. But she'd shared it with Peanut. Today, Ruby would be the one sharing the garden with her.

As soon as they got back in the house, Ruby kicked off her shoes and grabbed bottles of lemonade from the refrigerator.

Carlie was delighted that Miss Ruby was barefoot and immediately kicked her shoes off as well.

"You bring the cookies. I have the lemonade," Ruby said, and out the back door they went.

Carlie was immediately animated and began identifying flowers as they passed on the way to the gazebo.

"Those are 'zaleas, and this is a snow bush," she said.

"Snowball bush," Ruby corrected.

Carlie nodded and kept chattering. "You have lots of roses, and those. I can't remember what you call them, but they're blue and I like blue."

"Those are called bachelor buttons. I like blue, too," Ruby said, then stopped and pointed. "Look! There are hummingbirds at that feeder."

"Looks like they're air dancing," Carlie said.

Ruby smiled. "It does look a bit like they're dancing. That's called hovering. Their wings are moving so fast that it keeps them in place without falling. That's kind of magic, don't you think?"

Carlie stared. "Like fairies?"

"Yes, if there are fairies in my garden, that would be magic, too," Ruby said. "Now let's get in the gazebo where it's shady."

"Yes, where it's shady!" Carlie said, and took off running toward it.

Mr. Ruby and me. And maybe one day, when our house fe
your house, too, you won't be scared anymore."

Carlie heard the words. They sounded good, and maybe
she wasn't so sad in her heart, she would feel all of what Miss  
promised.

"Okay?" Ruby asked.

Carlie nodded. "Okay."

"Now let's go home. We have cookies, and we also have col
lemonade in the refrigerator. How about we go sit in the gazebo
in the backyard and watch the hummingbirds, and you can look
for fairies. Maybe leave a cookie crumb for them somewhere. I've
heard they like sweets."

"Yes. I want to do that, Miss Ruby."

"Then we'd better get going," Ruby said, and drove home
thinking of the wonder of Elliot Graham and the gift he was to
the world.

Ruby's heart skipped, watching her go, running to something and not away from it.

───────────

Deborah went to Ladd's place right after breakfast. She got yesterday's mail out of his mailbox and took it in the house, checked to make sure everything was okay, then saw a phone charger lying on the cabinet, and it occurred to her to look for his phone. Maybe it was in his truck. If it was, he'd probably like to have it. So she went into the garage and began looking in his truck. She didn't remember seeing it when she was cleaning up the blood but then thought of the console and opened it.

And there it was. She grabbed it, took it and the charger to her SUV, and headed to the barn to feed Sam. Afterward, she drove to the pasture below the house to check on the cattle, counting thirty head and fourteen calves. She'd ask him next time she saw him if that was the right head count.

Maggie was waiting for her when she returned home. Deborah took Ladd's phone to her room, plugged it in to charge, and then went with her mom.

They walked the barns and the machine sheds, making lists of the machinery to sell and notes about what Maggie wanted to keep, then came back through the garden and picked the tomatoes that were ripe.

"Those green beans are ready to be picked again," Maggie said. "I'm going to get the bucket."

"I can do it, Mom," Deborah said.

Maggie smiled and shook her head. "I know, honey, but I like working in the garden. Getting my hands in the dirt is calming to me."

"Understood," Deborah said, and went into the house with the tomatoes while her mother went to the shed to get a bucket for the beans.

After leaving the tomatoes in the sink, Deborah got the riding lawn mower out of the toolshed and mowed the front and back yards. By the time she was finished, her mom had the green beans picked and was in the house making chicken salad for lunch.

"Something smells good," Deborah said as she walked in the back door.

"Chicken salad on fresh lettuce leaves and peach hand pies," Maggie said.

"Oh wow, Mom, that all sounds so good, and I haven't had a hand pie in ages. You make the best. I want dessert first."

Maggie laughed. "You always wanted dessert first."

Deborah grinned. "And you always told me no because it would ruin my meal. Only it never did."

"I know. You just kept growing and growing and I couldn't fill up those long legs, no matter how hard I tried. You got your Grandpa Ryman's height," Maggie said.

"And your dark hair," Deborah said.

Maggie ran her fingers through her hair. "Used to be dark," she said. "Too much gray in there now."

"Your hair is pretty, Mom. It suits you."

Maggie rolled her eyes. "It's growing old with me, but I'm not complaining. It's where I am in life, that's all. Go wash. Everything is ready."

Deborah took off at a lope. She didn't have to be told twice. She was hot, tired, and hungry. Cooling off at the table and having good food with her mom. What more could she want?

Ladd Daltry popped into her thoughts as she was washing up, but she let them go. Now was not the time to pursue thoughts of old flames when she was trying to cool off.

———

Maggie and Deborah had just finished lunch, and as they were putting dishes in the dishwasher, Deborah brought up the move.

"Hey, Mom. You know this move would be easier if you were already in town. We could move whatever furniture you want to keep into the house you choose and just leave the rest to sell with the house and property."

Maggie nodded. "I know, but I still don't know if I want to buy or rent when I move."

Deborah paused. "You hate giving up the farm, don't you?"

Maggie's shoulders slumped. "I do. Everything I love is here... except Josh. Everything I love *to do* is here. My garden. My chickens. The flowers. It's home."

Then, before Deborah could respond, Maggie's phone rang. She glanced down and frowned.

"It's from the nursing home," she said, and clutched it against her chest.

"Well, answer it, Mom," Deborah urged, and finished loading the last of the dishes as Maggie answered, then sat down.

"Hello. This is Maggie."

"Maggie, this is Loyal Prevet."

The nursing home director was a long-time friend, but he rarely called.

"Hi, Loyal. Is everything okay?" she asked.

"No, ma'am, it is not. I'm so sorry to tell you that Josh had a massive heart attack about fifteen minutes ago. We worked hard to bring him back, but were unable to revive him."

"Nooo, nooo, I should have been there," Maggie said, and started to cry.

"We are all so sorry here, Maggie. Please accept our sympathies."

Deborah panicked. "Mom? What happened?"

"Your daddy...he's gone. He had a heart attack. They couldn't revive him. You talk to Loyal. I can't think," she said, and gave the phone to Deborah.

Deborah felt like she'd been kicked in the stomach. It hurt to breathe and tears were already welling. She thought she'd been prepared for this, but she wasn't. She wiped her eyes and took a deep breath.

"Mr. Prevet, this is Deborah."

"We are so sorry for your loss."

"Thank you, but what happened?" she asked.

"He didn't want to eat. We were taking him back to his room when he slumped in the wheelchair, unconscious. He never woke up, despite CPR."

Deborah was sick to her stomach.

"Where's Dad now?"

"The ambulance took him to the hospital, but it was just a formality. He was pronounced here by our nurse and then by the EMTs."

"We're coming to Blessings. Please tell the hospital not to take him anywhere."

"Yes, ma'am, I sure will," he said, and hung up.

Deborah was swallowing back tears when she handed the phone to her mom.

"I need to see him," Maggie said.

"I know, Mom. I told them we were coming. Go do what you need to do. We'll leave when you're ready."

Maggie got up, then reached for Deborah and hugged her. Deborah was all she had left now of Josh, and she didn't want to let her go.

Deborah felt the panic in her mother's grasp. There was nothing she could say that would make this easier for either of them, except speaking her truth.

"We both knew this day was coming and that he was getting weaker. It's part of why you wanted to move to town. My heart is so sad for us, but I will not wish Dad back the way he was. He was trapped, Mom. And now he's free."

"I know, honey, I know. It's just…it's a shock. Every day I miss the man he was, but that man has been gone for years. I held onto what was, and pretended we were fine. But we weren't, and I saw it in his eyes. I'm just sad. So sad."

"So am I…but we'll figure this out together. I love you."

"I love you, too, and I'm so glad you are here. Give me a couple of minutes to change shoes."

Deborah watched her walking away and knew she was crying, but she also knew tears were healing. Then she looked down at what she had on and ran to change into something clean.

Within a few minutes, they were on their way to town, and all the way there Deborah was thinking that she didn't want to leave Blessings when this was over and then spend the rest of her life waiting for a phone call like this about her mother. She thought of Ladd, alone in the hospital without one living family member to comfort him. Unless she changed what she'd been doing, that could easily be her one day.

She needed to rethink her future.

———————

While Deborah and her mother were on their way to Blessings, Darren and Cheryl Payne were already in town. Darren dropped Cheryl and the boys off at the Crown to get groceries and went straight to the hospital to check on Ladd. Among other things, apologies were in order.

———————

Ladd was up, walking like an old man because it hurt like hell when he tried to straighten up, but the partially collapsed lung had reinflated, and the pain in his head was somewhat better. The nurse had walked him down the hall, and they were on their way to his room when he looked up and saw Darren Payne coming toward him with a look of horror on his face.

He sighed. Obviously, Darren had found out.

Darren stopped a few feet away for them to catch up and started apologizing the moment Ladd was close enough to hear him.

"Oh my God, Ladd. I'm so sorry. I'm so, so sorry."

Ladd nodded. He had one hand on his chest and the other on the nurse's shoulder.

"Can't talk and walk at the same time. Follow me," Ladd said, and so Darren did.

The nurse got him into his room and settled back in his bed.

"It's time for your meds. I'll be right back," she said, and nodded to Darren as she passed him on the way out of the room.

As soon as she was gone, Darren moved to the side of the bed.

"I can't tell you how sorry Cheryl and I are that this happened. When Deborah came and—"

"Deborah told you?" Ladd asked.

Darren shrugged. "You could call it that. Basically, she read me the riot act for ever buying the bull. It was a mistake. I'll be the first to admit it. And it nearly got you killed. Just so you know, the fence is fixed, the bull is gone...sold...and that won't ever happen again."

"Good to know. Why did you buy something like that?" Ladd asked.

"I had this idea to raise bulls for rodeo stock. They pay good money for them. But I didn't take into consideration that buying an aggressive breed would be dangerous. That's the stupid Southern farm boy in me. In my head, livestock was livestock, except when they're bred to fight and buck and stomp the shit out of people. So it's gone, and you'll be safe now anywhere on your own land," Darren said.

"I'm happy to hear this," Ladd said.

"I have to ask you something else," Darren said. "Do you have health insurance?"

"Yes. It'll cover most of the costs," Ladd said.

"Well, just know that whatever it doesn't cover is on me. I'll be letting the business office here know to send me the bill for the balance due."

"You don't have to do that," Ladd said.

"I do if I want to look at myself in the mirror again," Darren said.

"Then the offer is accepted," Ladd said.

When the nurse came back with Ladd's pain meds, Darren stepped aside.

"Looks like you're going to get some relief in a few, buddy. I'm going to leave now, but is there anything I can do for you at your place?"

"No, Deborah is taking care of things."

"Are you selling out?" Darren asked.

"I haven't decided. Thanks for coming by," Ladd said.

"Sure thing, and again, I'm so sorry," Darren said, and left with his head down and his shoulders slumped.

The nurse eyed Ladd's color as she was taking his pulse.

"Is he the guy who owned the bull that hurt you?" she asked.

"Yes," Ladd said.

"He's lucky it didn't kill you," she said.

"Luck had nothing to do with it. I'm alive because my neighbor, Deborah Ryman, happened to witness the attack. She ran the bull off, dragged my sorry ass into the truck, and got me to the ER."

"Sounds like quite a woman," the nurse said. "Now try and get some rest."

Ladd sighed, then closed his eyes as she left the room, unaware that Deborah and Maggie were in the parking lot below, on their way inside.

---

Maggie was pale and shaking, and Deborah was hanging onto her every step of the way inside. She didn't feel strong and competent. She felt about ten years old and scared to see her father's face, and was thinking how glad she was that she'd stopped on her way through town to see him when she first arrived, even before she went home.

She'd known almost instantly that he didn't know her. The first time she called him Dad and she saw the look of panic flicker in his eyes, she saw no need to push the issue—and now he was gone. She shook off the memory and kept holding onto her mother's hand as they walked inside.

Maggie went straight to the desk clerk.

"My husband, Josh Ryman, is here. Where is he?"

Deborah saw the panic on the clerk's face and added, "We already know he has passed."

"I'll get a nurse," the clerk said, and bolted from the desk, coming back moments later with a nurse at her heels.

"If you ladies will follow me," the nurse said, and led the way to a bay in the ER. She opened the door and walked them in, pulled the sheet back to the top of his shoulders, then looked up. "Please accept our deepest sympathies. We are so sorry for your loss," she said, and shut the door behind her when she left.

Maggie didn't hear her. She was locked into the face of the man before her, remembering when they met. Their first date. Their first kiss. The wedding. Becoming parents and doting on everything Deborah said and did. She remembered every laugh, every tear, every hardship they had endured together. She patted his arm and smoothed a lock of his hair away from his forehead.

"Oh, Josh…this is not how I thought we would end," she said, and then she started to cry.

Deborah kept remembering all the things her dad had taught her. To love with every aspect of your being, but be strong enough to be happy alone. To believe in herself no matter what others thought she should be doing with her life, because she was going to waste it if she didn't. At every milestone of her life, he'd been there, except for one. If she married, she would walk down the aisle alone.

She hung onto her mother and let the wash of memories roll through her, both of them broken by this new hole in their world, weeping until their eyes were swollen and there were no more tears to cry.

---

Evan Morris, Ladd's doctor, was making evening rounds and came in while Ladd was poking at the food on his tray. "Evening, Ladd. Are you finding fault with your dinner?" he asked, smiling.

Ladd frowned. "Trying not to," he said, and laid his fork aside as the nurse moved his tray table so the doctor could check him.

"I like to look at my handiwork," Morris said, and pulled out his stethoscope. "How's your breathing? Still hurt to inhale, or are you getting good breaths now?"

"Yes, it hurts to inhale, but I can."

Morris nodded. "I'd blame that on the broken ribs, then," he said, and raised the head of Ladd's bed up a little more so he could get a better look at the staples in the back of Ladd's head. "These still giving you a lot of trouble?"

"The only way I can lie without messing up the broken ribs is on my back. But I have staples in the back of my head and hoof-prints of the bull that tried to kill me all over my back, so I'm not comfortable, if that's what you're asking."

"I'm sorry," Morris said. "There's not a lot I can do about that except continue pain meds for a while longer and order some ice packs. You can put them on the most painful areas. That and the meds will help reduce inflammation."

"Then ice me down, please," Ladd said.

Dr. Morris ordered the packs to be given as requested, and then moved the table with Ladd's food tray back across his bed.

"Eat. You need to keep up your strength," he said.

"I'd trade you an ice pack for some salt," Ladd said.

Morris grinned. "I eat in the cafeteria every day. Salt doesn't help."

Ladd started to laugh, then grabbed his belly and groaned.

"Feel free to skip the jokes."

"Sorry," Morris said. "I'll see you in the morning."

"When can I go home?" Ladd asked.

"Do you have anyone at home who can help take care of you?"

Ladd sighed. "No, but—"

Dr Morris shook his head. "Then I'm sorry. You have to be in better shape than this to go home on your own. Eat your food. Get strong. Then we'll talk."

Ladd stared at his tray as the doctor left, and then picked up the plastic fork and knife and cut a slice off the baked chicken breast, put it in his mouth, and chewed. It still needed salt, and it had gotten cold, but a trip to Granny's Country Kitchen when he was well would wipe away the memory of the taste.

---

Bart stopped a couple more times on the trip home. Once to get something with caffeine to drink to keep himself awake, and the last time to refuel again. He was wishing he'd never left home and was looking forward to getting back and sleeping in his own bed, so he kept driving on the interstate, sometimes trailing semi trucks, but always pushing the speed limit.

It was after midnight by the time he hit the city limits of Little Rock, and then it took almost forty minutes more to drive through the city to the upper-class neighborhood in which they lived. But the closer he got to their street, the bigger the knot got in his stomach. He had a horrible feeling that surprising Mila wasn't going to be exactly what he hoped it would be.

Their house was the first one on the corner of the block. As always, the security lights were on outside, and he knew the security system would be on. What he didn't know was who owned the sleek, black sports car in the driveway. So unless Mila was having a pajama party with girlfriends, his wife was cheating on him.

He pulled up to the front of the garage and parked beside the sports car, then turned off the security alarm with the remote and went inside.

He paused in the foyer, listening, but he didn't hear voices or the television and took off his shoes before heading upstairs. His heart was pounding, and he felt like throwing up as he stopped in the hall outside their bedroom and listened again. Someone was snoring, and it wasn't Mila. The urge to turn around and walk out was strong, but he also knew he'd never be able to forget or forgive this. And with that, he opened the door, slamming it back against the wall, and turned on the lights, then strode to the foot of the bed, shouting.

"What the hell, Mila? You are one worthless bitch!"

Mila screamed when the lights came on, staring in horror at the rage on Bart's face as the man beside her flew out of bed naked.

"I'm sorry. I'm sorry, man," he kept saying as he grabbed his clothes and darted out of the room and down the hall.

Mila sat up in bed, going on the defense.

"What do you think you're doing, sneaking in like this?" she screamed.

"I didn't sneak anywhere. This is my house. I live here."

Mila threw back the covers and got up, flaunting her nudity. She worked hard to stay fit and knew she looked good. She flashed a look at Bart he recognized all too well, but instead of turning him on, it disgusted him.

"Come here, baby. He means nothing to me. Just someone to play with. I'm sorry. It won't happen again," she drawled.

"I know that for sure because you turn my stomach. Get dressed, pack a bag, and get out. I hope he was worth it, because I'm filing for divorce and I don't want to see your face in this house again."

Mila snarled, and then she laughed. "What happened to your little dream? Did you get run out of town?"

"It was your phone call. You are a coldhearted, hateful bitch, and I realized then that bringing a broken and innocent child into this home would be doing her a disservice. Nobody should be subjected to you and your ugly, selfish ways. Now get dressed and get out, or I'll drag your ass out of the house and throw your shit out the window and give the neighbors something to talk about."

Mila began screaming as she dressed, then threw some of her things into a bag. "I'll destroy you. I'll take you for all that you're worth!"

"Nope. You won't. Remember that prenup your daddy wanted me to sign? The one that states if we dissolve our marriage, I get nothing of your money? So, if you will remember...I said I'd sign it, but the same went for you. If we divorced, the house was mine, and you got no alimony...no nothing. And we both signed it."

In that moment, Mila knew she'd been bested. She threw back her head and screamed. "Daddy will destroy you!"

"Not when I tell him you fucked his best friend in our bed. Take the security remote and the house key off your key ring now."

The thought of facing her father with that news made her pale. She did as Bart asked and then grabbed her jewelry box and stuffed it into her bag, threw the strap of her purse over her shoulder, and left the room cursing him at the top of her voice. He was on her heels all the way, and when she got into her car, he leaned in and grabbed the garage remote from the visor of her car and then opened the garage door for her.

She was still cursing him when she started the car, then accelerated backward out of the garage like she'd been shot out of a cannon and disappeared.

Bart pulled his car into the garage and shut the door. He was shaking as he changed codes on the garage-door opener, then changed the codes on the remote on his key ring. Then he went into the house, changed the security codes on the alarm system and reset it, then sat in his house, weeping and waiting for sunrise.

A few hours later, when shops opened for business, Bart called a locksmith.

Within a couple of hours, all the locks had been changed on the house.

Afterward, he showered, shaved, dressed in one of his good suits, and headed to the bank. There he removed everything from the safe-deposit box, rented a new one, and put everything in it, with him as the only person with the right to access it.

Then he transferred their money into an account she could not access and left the bank. He got in the car and picked up his phone and called his father-in-law, Milos Greco.

The man answered quickly, with a delighted tone in his voice.

"Good morning, Bart!"

"Good morning, sir. Something has happened between Mila and me, and I want you to hear it from me first. I had been out of town on business and came home unexpectedly last night and caught her and Ricky Adler, your golfing buddy, in bed together. She laughed it off. Said it was just for fun and meant nothing and wanted me to forget it."

The gasp of dismay in Bart's ear was unmistakable, but he just kept talking.

"I told her to get out and don't come back, that I was filing for divorce. She threatened to, as she put it, 'take me for everything I had,' at which time I reminded her that according to our prenup, if we divorced, she got nothing from me, and I asked nothing monetary from her. So, she's out of my house. I'm on my way to the lawyer's office with my copy of the prenup, and I just wanted you to know I have no intention of trying to lay claim to anything that belongs to your family…including her."

Milos groaned. "She did this? Truly?"

"Yes, truly, and I'd bet if you made a call to Rick Adler about now, he'd start apologizing when he answered the phone. He kept saying he was sorry to me, but at that point, I no longer cared. I'm sorry this is going to end our friendship. I have appreciated your wisdom and being part of your family," Bart said.

"I am sorry, too," Milos said. "If there's anything I can—"

"No, sir. I don't need help. I don't need money. I just want her out of my life."

Milos sighed. "Understood."

Bart disconnected. That was the last tie to cut.

He started up the car and went straight to his lawyer's office, told him what had happened, and asked him to draw up the divorce papers.

"This is my copy of the prenup we signed, verifying Mila has no claim on the house or anything we jointly owned," he said.

His lawyer arched an eyebrow.

"How did you get her to agree to that?" the lawyer asked.

"Oh, that was her and her daddy's idea. They're rich as sin and so worried about someone getting their hands on even a penny of their money that they demanded the prenup before we were married. I added my little part to it, and everyone agreed, laughing as they did at what a good joke it was that I would think they'd want anything I had."

"Well, I'm sorry for what's happened, but good job on protecting your back," the lawyer said. "Can I get you some coffee while you wait?"

"Yes, sure," Bart said.

He sat sipping coffee and waiting for the lawyer to finish up the papers he had to sign, and thought of Shirley Duroy—who tried so hard to stay alive—and made a vow.

*I will never, as long as I live, live for money again. So help me God.*

After he left the lawyer's office, Bart had one last thing he wanted to do before he put this nightmare to rest. He wanted to send a message to the guardians Shirley had chosen, just to put his mind at rest. But without names, or any way to identify them, he decided to contact the Blessings Police Department and ask them to deliver the message for him.

He googled the PD, got a phone number, and with the sun glaring off the hood of his car into his eyes, he turned up the air-conditioning and made the call.

"Blessings Police Department. This is Avery."

"Uh…Avery, my name is Bart Carlson. I worked with Shirley Duroy at the CPA firm in Little Rock. We all knew about her health issues but are still saddened by what happened. The reason I'm calling… We've been told Shirley designated a guardian for Carlie, and that's a relief to know…that the child would not automatically wind up in foster care. I don't wish to interfere, but I'm asking you to pass this message to her guardians. Tell them Bart Carlson sends his condolences, and if Carlie has needs that they cannot or chose not to meet, I will help. This is my phone number. Please give it to them with the message. Can you do that for me?"

"Yes, sir. I'll see that they get the message and the number," Avery said.

"Thank you," Bart said, and the moment he hung up, the weight of guilt lifted from him.

He'd finally done the right and honorable thing.

# CHAPTER 10

MILA HAD BEEN IN SHOCK WHEN SHE LEFT THEIR HOUSE. She'd played this game once too often, and it had blown up in her face in a way she never expected. There was no way she was going to show up at her father's estate in the middle of the night. He was old school about everything and she wasn't in the mood for another fight, so she took herself to a hotel. When she got to her room, she threw herself on the bed and cried herself to sleep.

The next morning, she woke before eight, ordered room service, then showered, and was still in her bathrobe when the food came. As she ate, she thought about how to tell her father, Milos, that her marriage was on the rocks, and why.

A short while later, she checked out and headed to the family estate. Her stomach was in knots all the way there, but when she saw Rick Adler's car parked in the drive, she tried not to panic. Rick and Milos were friends. He was often at the house.

*Don't make a big deal out of nothing.*

She got out and carried her bag in as far as the foyer, where she met up with the housekeeper. "Good morning, Thea. Where is Milos, and please take my bag to my room."

"Yes, ma'am. Your father is in the library with Mr. Rick."

Mila strode down the hall with her chin up, in her usual take-charge way. But the moment she entered the library and saw her father and the expression on Rick's face, she knew lies would not be necessary.

"What?" she drawled.

"You do not speak to me!" Milos shouted.

"And you don't tell me what to do!" Mila fired back.

"Then know that while I cannot change anything about your mother's trust fund that you inherited, I can change the heir in my will with nothing more than a phone call! I did not work this hard all my life to have a whore of a daughter destroy the Greco name. Sit down and shut up. I have things to say to both of you."

Mila's face flushed an angry red, but she sat because she knew her father never threatened. When he made a decision, he stood by it, and she didn't want to hear him tell her she was disinherited.

Rick glanced at her, but she lifted her chin and looked away. His pretty-boy face and great body no longer held interest for her.

Milos stood, looking at the faces of the two people he cared for the most.

"You have both disappointed me in ways I cannot express. After my son-in-law's phone call this morning, I must confess I was sick to my stomach. Rick, I called you here because what I have to say to you, I will say face-to-face. You were a trusted friend, and you betrayed that in an unforgivable way. You are no longer a part of my circle, and I will make it my business to see that your membership at the club is revoked."

Rick groaned. "Milos! Please. I do most of my business meetings at the club."

"You should have kept your business out of my business, and none of this would have happened. Get out of my house. You are no longer welcome here."

Rick walked out of the room with his head down, his feet dragging.

Mila leaned back, thinking now that her father would relent. But she realized she was wrong when he turned and looked at her as if he'd never seen her before.

"You will be leaving the country. During the time that you are gone, if your name becomes attached to even one more shocking escapade, I will remove you as my heir. You shamed me and you shamed yourself when you broke your vows to your husband. And if you think I won't know what you're doing and who you're doing it with, you are more foolish than I believed."

"Since I will be divorced, what I do as a single woman is my business," Mila said. "You have no voice in that, just as I said nothing about the women who have come and gone in your life since Mother died."

Milos face turned red, but he said nothing.

"And my passport is in the safe at our home," she added.

Milos nodded. "I will text Bart to have your things sent to this address. You do not contact him ever again. You do not cause him one more moment of distress, or I will make you sorry." He sighed and ran a hand through his hair. "When you two became engaged, I did not think him worthy of you. But he has proven to me that was not the case. It is you who was not worthy of him. Now go to your room. You have clothes and luggage here. Start packing. I'll see to the tickets."

Mila stood up in defiance, visibly shaking with rage.

"I am thirty-seven years old, and you are treating me like some wanton teenager. I am an adult, with all the rights to make my own choices."

"Then you are a wanton adult who has made choices that could ruin our family name," he said.

Mila's hands curled into fists. "This is not like when you were young. This is not the old country. People have sex. It is not a mortal sin, for God's sake."

"You were married in the church. You made vows to God and your husband, so yes…what you've done is a sin. I never cheated on your mother, God rest her soul. I honored her and our vows. I don't want to look at your face right now. Go do what I say, or suffer the consequences."

She blanched. "So where exactly am I being exiled to?"

"I will put you on a plane to Paris. After that, I don't care where you go."

Mila got up and walked out of the library with her head up and her shoulders back, shouting as she went. "I hate you for doing this. I will never forgive or forget!"

Her father followed her into the hall. "Stop acting like a child. You aren't losing anything you wanted, and you know it. You are my blood. Act like the Greco you are."

Mila stormed all the way up the stairs, but by the time she got to her room and started packing, the truth of what he'd said set in. He was right. She hadn't lost anything she treasured. She didn't love Bart. She didn't love Rick. But she did love the Greco money.

———————————

Ladd learned of Josh Ryman's passing by accident. The door to his room was open, and when he heard two nurses talking about a man dying at the nursing home, and then he heard one mention Maggie Ryman's name, his heart sank. It must have been Josh.

The next time a nurse came in to check on him, he asked outright, "Did Josh Ryman pass away?"

When she hesitated, Ladd persisted. "He's my neighbor. I grew up with his daughter. She's the one who saved me from the bull and got me to the hospital. I have to know."

She nodded. "Yes. They brought him to the ER but it was too late. He'd already passed."

"Damn," Ladd muttered. "Thanks."

Even after the nurse was long gone, Ladd was still thinking of Maggie and Deborah. He knew Maggie had been planning to move to Blessings to be closer to Josh, but now he wondered if her plans would change—and if Deborah's plans would change, too. Would she leave again, or would this be a reason she'd choose to stay?

He wanted to call her, but he didn't know where his cell phone was, and he didn't remember Maggie's number, which was in his cell. At that moment, he wished for the old days when calling information or using a phone book was an option and was frustrated that he wasn't physically able to just get up and drive to their house. That damn bull had sure put a kink in his world. Now, all he could do was wait and hope Deborah came back to see him. But after what he'd just learned, the chances of that seemed slim to none.

———————

Deborah was up. She could hear her mother moving around in her bedroom, but she had yet to come out. Neither of them had slept well. They'd stayed up into the wee hours talking about the good times, planning the service, and crying on each other's shoulders.

And now it was another day and life had to go on. She still had Ladd's stock to check on, the cat to feed, the mail to bring in, and her father to bury. It felt like too much to deal with at once, but she knew that was just grief. She'd do whatever she had to do, and do it the best way she knew how, because that's how she'd been raised. To always do the best she could, and that would be enough.

They both needed food, so Deborah stirred up some pancake batter and fried a few sausage patties. She had pancakes warming and the sausage coming out of the skillet when Maggie finally appeared.

"I skipped the one-cup Keurig this morning and made a pot," Deborah said, pointing to their old coffeemaker.

Maggie's eyes were red and swollen, but she managed a smile and took a cup of coffee to the table. "You made breakfast," she said.

"We didn't eat supper last night, and we won't get through all we have to do today on empty stomachs. I know you don't feel like it, but you have to eat some of all of this, Mom."

Maggie nodded. "It looks good, and I will. You're a darling to do this."

"We'll get through this together," Deborah said. "As soon as we finish breakfast, I need to run over to Ladd's place and do his chores and bring in the mail. It won't take long, and then I'll be home with you the rest of the day."

"Have you talked to him?" Maggie asked.

"Not since day before yesterday."

"Then, when we go into town to the funeral home, we will also go by the hospital before we leave. I'll wait in the car, but I want you to check on him for me. We kind of looked after each other after Walt died, so I feel responsible to make sure he's doing okay."

"I will," Deborah said. "But right now, we're going to focus on food."

"I'll take two of those fine-looking pancakes," Maggie said.

Deborah took two off the platter and added a sausage patty, then pushed the butter and syrup within Maggie's reach.

Maggie was still making notes on her list as they ate, and after they finished and cleaned up the kitchen, Deborah left her mom adding to the growing list of "things to do to bury Josh" and headed to the Daltry farm.

As she turned off the main road onto the blacktop, she stopped and got Ladd's mail. Coming here used to be almost the same as going home. For the longest time she'd thought of this place as her second home and, in the throes of teenage passion, assumed she would grow old here with Ladd.

That didn't happen.

She shrugged off the fantasy, got back in her car, and kept driving, checking the cattle in the pasture near the road as she went. As she pulled up to the house, she half expected to see Ladd come out the front door grinning, and again shook off the fantasy. She went in long enough to leave the mail with the growing stack and locked the house before heading to the barn on foot.

Today, Sam came to meet her, his long yellow tail stuck straight up in the air like a flagpole.

"Well, hello, pretty boy," Deborah said. "So, you want a ride to the barn, do you?"

Sam meowed, and butted his head against her chin, so she secured him carefully against her and scratched his head as they walked.

Once they were inside in the shade, she put the cat down and headed for the granary.

"It's already getting hot today, Sammy boy. How about some fresh water to go with breakfast?" Deborah asked. She got the big metal water bowl, refilled it at the outside faucet, and then got his food dish and filled it, too.

"Breakfast is served," she said, and when Sam hopped up in the granary, she closed the door.

She was on her way out of the barn when she heard footsteps and then voices, and turned around to see two men walking into the breezeway from the other end. One was tall. One was not. One had a length of rope over his shoulder; the other had a big hunting knife riding in a holster on his hip.

Her heart stopped. This wasn't happening. This wasn't happening.

"Well, lookee here, buddy. Looks like we found the icing on the cake, and I'm in the mood for something sweet."

Deborah's heart skipped a beat. It was happening, and that must have been what Ladd thought when he saw the bull. He'd made a run for the trees and lost. But Deborah was less than five feet from the ladder on the barn wall that led up to the loft, and they were at the far end of the barn, at least fifty feet away.

She leaped toward the ladder, caught the steps in midflight, and started climbing up as they bolted toward her. But she was all the way up in the loft and looking for weapons before they reached the ladder. There was a scoop shovel and a bucket of roofing nails. Not much to fight a war, but she grabbed them and ran toward the opening in the floor.

She'd just set the bucket aside when the first man's head popped up through the opening. She swung the scoop shovel like a ball bat and hit him square in the face. She heard his nose crack and his lips pop, and then he was falling, knocking down the guy behind him as he went.

She looked down through the hole, saw both of them on their backs in the dirt, groaning and cursing, and picked up the bucket of roofing nails and then leaned over the hole and yelled, "Hey!"

They looked up just as she upended the contents of the bucket into their faces.

At that point, mass screaming ensued. Knowing this was her only chance, she came down the steps running, grabbed the rope one man had dropped, and before they even knew she was down, she had both of them hogtied—hands tied behind their backs, and their knees bent back, with rope looped around their ankles, and then around their necks. If they kicked, they choked themselves.

They were bawling and cursing and going nowhere. She pulled out her cell phone and called 911.

"911. What is your emergency?"

"This is Deborah Ryman. I need two ambulances at the Daltry farm. That's 19922 County Road West, and I need the county sheriff, as well. I'm not injured, but two trespassers are. Haste would be appreciated."

"Yes, ma'am. Are you in a safe place?"

"I am now," she said. "I'm fine. We're all in the barn having a grand old time," she said, and then disconnected.

The men were still moaning and cursing. But they were fighting with each other now.

Broken Nose whined. "You said Daltry was in the hospital."

Nail Face groaned. "He is."

"Then who's she?" Broken Nose shrieked.

Deborah kicked Broken Nose's knee. "I am your worst enemy," she said. "Shut up. Don't look at me. Don't talk to me. Don't talk to each other."

Except for moaning and groaning, silence ensued.

She opened the door to one of the granaries and sat down on the threshold. When she did, Sam came meandering over to her, crawled up in her lap, and started purring.

"Where were you when I needed you, boy?" Deborah said, and gently scratched him behind his ears.

Sam meowed, then jumped down from her lap, walked over to where the men were lying, sniffed both of them, then leaped over Nail Face to the soft dirt near the pilings, dug himself a hole and proceeded to poop, then neatly covered it up and slipped into the open space beneath the granaries and disappeared.

"Oh my God! What is that? What do I smell?" Nail Face moaned.

"That would be cat shit. Don't move or you'll roll in it, and stop talking," Deborah said.

Silence settled around them, and about fifteen minutes later, two patrol cars from the sheriff's office arrived, followed by two ambulances.

Deborah walked to the entrance to the barn and waved.

Two deputies emerged from the patrol car with their weapons drawn and came hurrying toward her, followed by the sheriff, Joe Ryman.

The sight of her uncle's face made Deborah feel like crying. She didn't have to be tough anymore now that the cavalry had arrived.

"Hi, Uncle Joe," she said.

Joe Ryman wrapped her in a hug.

"When I found out about this, I couldn't get here fast enough. Are you okay?"

"Yes, I'm okay…and your deputies won't need those," Deborah said, pointing to the guns in their hands. "The perps have been contained."

The deputies ran past her into the barn, then stopped short, staring in disbelief.

"Who are they?" they asked as Deborah and her Uncle Joe followed.

Deborah shrugged. "We never got a chance to introduce ourselves. When they came at me, I climbed up into the loft and took out the first one who climbed up with a scoop shovel. He fell on his buddy, and they both hit the ground. Then I dumped a bucket of roofing nails in their faces before climbing down and tying them up with their own rope."

The EMTs had been given the all-clear sign to proceed and were backing the first ambulance into the barn when Deborah remembered the nails and yelled, "Stop! Don't come any farther! There's a bucket of roofing nails in the dirt."

"Oh. Good call," one deputy said, and then looked up at her and grinned. "Nice hog-tie," he said. "Do you rodeo?"

"No. I'm a veterinarian. I've tied up my share of critters."

The other deputy was asking the trespassers their names. When they wouldn't answer, he dug the wallets from their pockets and took down the information.

She heard him mention the names, but they weren't locals. Then she realized the other deputy was talking to her.

"Did they say why they were here?" he asked.

"I assume to steal. Ladd Daltry owns this place, and he's in the hospital. I'm his neighbor. I get his mail. Check on the cattle. Feed the cat. That kind of thing. I heard them talking, one saying to the other that he thought the place was deserted. The other one said he thought it was, too, because he'd called the hospital this morning to verify that Ladd Daltry was still there. They didn't expect me…but thought we were going to have a little party. I did not expect them, either, and declined their invitation."

"They're going to have to go to the hospital before we take them in," the deputy said.

Deborah nodded. "Just make sure you don't turn around and let them out, because I won't come over here unarmed again."

The two thieves heard her and groaned.

"Bitch," Nail Face muttered.

"Dead shot," Deborah countered, and toed his knee with her boot.

Sheriff Ryman loomed over both of them. "Just like I taught

her. You mess with my niece again, and you'll never find a place safe enough to hide."

The men looked at each other, then groaned. "Niece?"

"Karma's a real bitch," Deborah said.

While the EMTs were loading the handcuffed men into the ambulances, one of the deputies found a truck hidden in a thicket of trees at the gate leading into the pasture.

After that, the truck got towed.

The would-be thieves were hauled off in ambulances, with a county sheriff's car bringing up the rear.

Deborah got in her car to go home.

She was halfway down the driveway when she started shaking. And by the time she got to the blacktop and drove the half mile to the road leading up to their place, she was choking back tears.

What if that had happened to her mother?

What if Ladd had been home, healing, and they'd attacked him?

She couldn't be in two places at once during this transition.

How the hell could she fix this mess?

———————————

Peanut and Ruby were dressed. Carlie was in her Easter dress and white sandals, and Ruby was brushing her hair up into a ponytail.

"Want a ribbon?" Ruby asked.

Carlie eyed the array of colors and pointed to a pink one.

"Good choice," Ruby said, and as soon as she had the ponytail in place, she wrapped the shiny pink ribbon around it, and tied it into a bow. "You look so pretty."

Carlie touched the floral fabric of Ruby's dress. "It's like your garden," she said.

Ruby smiled. "It sure is. Now, do you need to use the bathroom before we leave? There's no place at the cemetery to go."

"I'll go here," Carlie said, and slipped into her bathroom.

Ruby was sitting on the bed, looking at the dollhouse, when she came out.

Carlie walked over to the dollhouse, picked up the doll, and moved her from the sofa to the bedroom, and laid her down.

"She's gonna sleep now," Carlie said.

Ruby held out her hand, and they left the room to find Peanut.

He was sitting in the living room, reading the paper, and when they walked in, he laid the paper aside.

"Two beautiful girls. Are you ready to go?" he asked.

"We're ready," Ruby said, and they traipsed out to her car.

Carlie buckled herself into the booster seat, while Peanut and Ruby got in the front.

Peanut glanced over his shoulder to make sure she was safely buckled up and then started the car and backed out of the drive and headed for the funeral home.

As soon as they arrived, they got in line behind the hearse and headed toward White Dove Cemetery.

To Ruby's surprise, cars began coming out of side streets and driveways and got into line with them, all following the hearse.

"Why are the cars following us?" Carlie asked.

"They're coming to your mama's service. She lived here a long time. People remember her."

Carlie sighed. She liked knowing that.

And so they drove through the gates of White Dove and up the hill to a spot out in the sunshine. The grave had already been dug, but Carlie didn't see it. Only the little tent and a handful of chairs in the shade beneath it.

Peanut parked, and then sat with the car running as a handful of police officers pulled the casket from the hearse and carried it to the grave.

"Oh, Peanut. Look! The policemen are serving as pallbearers. There's Deputy Ralph and Chief Pittman and four more."

"Well, she took her last breath in the lobby of the police station.

I guess they offered as a way of honoring that," he said. "And it's time to get out."

Carlie unbuckled her seatbelt, then waited for Miss Ruby to open the back door. She didn't know what was going to happen. Everyone kept talking about burial, but it had gone straight over her head as to what was going to be buried.

She'd watched the policemen carry Mama's little house beneath a tent. But when Mr. Ruby and Miss Ruby started toward the tent, she stopped. The uncertainty of what was coming was scary. Without putting a name to it, Carlie feared what would happen when they buried her mama. When Carlie was no longer able to see her mama, would she forget her? Would she forget herself? Would their past disappear?

Peanut and Ruby immediately stopped. They saw the fear and uncertainty in Carlie's eyes, and without saying a word, Peanut picked her up.

"Do you want to go home?"

Carlie shook her head.

"Are you afraid?" he asked.

She nodded.

"Don't be, honey. Remember, you're not alone. You have Miss Ruby, and you have me. Now, we're going to do this together, and then we're going to go home together, and tomorrow morning we'll wake up in the same house like we always do, and it will be okay."

Carlie sighed, then nodded. That she understood. That felt safe. That she could hold onto, just like the death grip she had on the back of Mr. Ruby's collar.

"Then let's do this," Peanut said.

The sun was in Carlie's eyes as they approached the tent. She squinted, then turned away from the glare and closed her eyes. When she looked back again, they were in the shade. There were folding chairs. And flowers. And Mama's little house. When they sat, she was between Mr. and Miss Ruby, and there were flowers at their feet. Like Miss Ruby's garden, but not because they were not growing. They were wilting, and like Mama, they would die.

Carlie watched other people getting out of their cars and walking toward the tent. She didn't know them, but they were all looking at her. She looked down at the flowers so she wouldn't have to look at the strangers' stares.

Finally, the pastor from Ruby's church stepped up to the microphone and started speaking.

Carlie looked up. She didn't know him, either, and she didn't understand much of what he was saying. When Miss Ruby's arm slid around her shoulders and pulled her close, she leaned against her breast and closed her eyes. No more little house. No more dying flowers in front of her. No more strangers' eyes on her. She was just Carlie, wanting to hear Mama's voice and knowing that time in her life was gone. And so she sat, listening to the drone of the preacher's voice and hearing someone behind her crying, and wondered why.

Then all of a sudden the man stopped talking. She opened her eyes just in time to see people moving toward the preacher, then getting in line. They were shaking hands with Mr. Ruby as they passed by, and more than once, someone patted the top of her head. She didn't like it, but before she could object, Miss Ruby did it for her.

"Thank you for your concern, but this is too much. Peanut, I'm going to the car with Carlie."

He nodded and handed her the keys.

"Chief Pittman said he had a message for us. I'll be right behind you."

Ruby took the keys in one hand and Carlie in the other and began moving through the crowd of people trying to get her attention. Some she knew were sincere. Other she knew were just nosy.

And then she heard voices behind her that did not bode well.

She remembered Elliot's warning about sharp tongues, as she recognized the voices. Mary Faye Giles and Petula Young—best friends who lived up by the golf course. She'd seen them at the service, and she knew their tendency for gossip and snark was at the top of their list of fun things to do.

"I heard Ruby will be looking for someone to adopt the girl," Mary Faye said.

"Oh really? I just assumed she and Peanut would keep her," Petula drawled.

Mary Faye snorted. "They're a little long in the tooth for parenthood, if you ask me. But I'm just telling you what I heard."

"There are people who would pay big money for a kid that pretty," Petula said.

Ruby turned abruptly. "Carlie, wait here," she said, and walked five steps back and pointed a finger in both women's faces. "Both of you. Shut your mouths and I better not ever hear that again," she said softly.

Mary Faye suddenly realized she'd just insulted her hair stylist and began trying to backtrack. "I'm sorry, Ruby. I just—"

Petula was also anxious. She didn't want to be driving all the way to Savannah to get her hair done. "I misspoke, too," she mumbled.

Ruby turned and walked back to Carlie, took her hand, and kept walking. It was only after they got to the car that Carlie asked, "What happened, Miss Ruby?"

"Nothing, baby. It had nothing to do with us. We're fine," she said. She got in the front seat with Carlie in her lap, and then she put the key in the ignition and started the car so the air conditioner would come on.

Ruby was angry and trying to hide it. "Do you want a drink of water?" she asked.

Carlie nodded and took the bottle of water and drank thirstily and then handed it back.

"Is Mama's buryin' over?" she asked.

Ruby nodded.

Carlie leaned against Ruby's shoulder.

"What happens to Mama and her little house?"

Ruby hesitated. *This is what I've been dreading.* "They will put it in the ground for safekeeping."

Carlie's eyes widened. "How will she breathe?" she whispered.

Ruby patted Carlie's leg and snuggled her closer. "She doesn't need breath now. Remember?"

Carlie shuddered. "Because she died?"

Ruby sighed. "Yes, darling. Because she died. This is what that means."

Carlie felt the knot in her chest getting tighter and harder, and there were tears burning the back of her throat. When they finally bubbled over into her eyes, she let go again, weeping for what was gone and knowing it was never coming back.

# CHAPTER 11

PEANUT EXCUSED HIMSELF FROM ALL THE WELL-WISHERS AND headed for the chief's patrol car as the mourners began getting back into their vehicles and driving away. The chief was directing traffic as Peanut walked up behind him.

"Hey, Lon. They said you have a message for me."

"Oh, yes…we got a call at the office this morning." Lon handed him the paper with the message and the info on it. "It was from a man named Bart Carlson. Said he and Shirley Duroy worked for the same CPA company. Anyway, this is the message, and his contact info if you happen to need it."

Peanut remembered that name. It was the man Shirley warned them might make a claim on Carlie for the money.

"Thanks," he said, and put the paper in his pocket. "I'll read it with Ruby later. I think we need to get our girl home, but I wanted to thank you for you and your men serving as pallbearers. That was unexpected, and most touching," he said.

Lon nodded. "She came to us for help, but we couldn't save her. It was the least that we could do. You're all in our prayers," he added. "Take care."

"Thanks," Peanut said, and then headed back to the car.

When he saw Ruby and Carlie both in the front seat, he knew there were tears, but it was to be expected. Hell. He cried when his mama died, and he was a full-grown man when that happened.

He got in the driver's seat, shut the door, and then leaned over and gave both of them a quick hug.

"Miss Carlie, you were very brave today. Your mama would be proud of you," he said, and handed the both of them a handful of tissues.

"She's going to sit in my lap with me," Ruby said, and began wiping Carlie's face as Peanut started the car and drove out of the cemetery.

Ruby gave her a quick kiss on the cheek.

"Mr. Ruby is right. You are a very brave girl, and the rest of today is for celebrating your mama's life and what a special woman she was. All day today, every time you think of something special about her, I want you to tell us the story. Tell us the funny stuff, even the sad stuff, if you want. Tell us what your favorite things to do were. We're just going to talk about Mama whenever you want, because it is better to celebrate a life than to mourn a death."

"Okay," Carlie said.

She missed having Hoppy to hug, so she pulled Miss Ruby's arms around her instead and held on as they drove. She closed her eyes, just to rest them, and the last thing she remembered was how good Miss Ruby smelled, and how smooth and soft the skin was on her arms.

She was asleep when they got back to the house. Peanut carried her into her room, took off her shoes, and tucked Hoppy in her arms, while Ruby covered her up.

"She needs to sleep worse than she needs lunch," Ruby whispered as they went across the hall to change clothes, and she backed up to Peanut for help unzipping her dress. She didn't have to ask, and he didn't need prompting. He just stopped what he was doing, unzipped the dress, then leaned down and kissed the back of her neck.

"My beautiful Ruby. Do you want me to go pick up some food somewhere?"

Ruby shook her head. "The other day Carlie and I had such a good time having cookies and lemonade in the gazebo that I think having lunch out there today is the perfect shift from where we've been."

"Oh, good idea, sweetheart. What can I do to help?"

"You can taste test," Ruby said, and winked.

"My favorite job," he said, and hurried to finish changing.

A short while later, they were in the kitchen.

Ruby grinned and then turned around and began digging out lunch meat and cheeses from the refrigerator, while Peanut got the bread and mayo.

"Do we do lettuce and tomatoes?" he asked.

"A little lettuce on Carlie's but no tomatoes."

He nodded, and then they began making sandwiches and piled them on a platter, then wrapped it in plastic wrap and set it aside. Then they bagged up chips, cookies, and a handful of napkins and packed all of it into a big picnic basket.

"What are we drinking?" he asked.

"I'll take a Coke, and lemonade for Carlie."

Peanut finished packing up the basket and then turned around.

"What else do we need?" he asked.

"Our girl," Ruby said, and they went to get her.

As they approached her door, they heard Carlie talking and paused in the hall to listen.

"Okay, dolly… Your name isn't Shirley anymore. Shirley is gone. Your name is Girl, and we're going to the park. Playing at the park is fun. We swing and go down the slide, and sometimes our friends come and play with us. And we have picnics in the gazebo with Miss Ruby."

"Oh no," Ruby whispered. "I asked her the other day what she named her doll and she said it was a secret. Now I know why. The doll was a stand-in for her mama, and the hard truth of the funeral has ended the fantasy that Shirley could ever come back."

Peanut slipped his arm around her and gave her a quick hug.

"I love you, Ruby. We can do whatever it takes to help her, but ultimately, it will be Carlie who shows us she's ready to move on."

"I love you too," Ruby said. "And you're right. You're always right when it comes to calm and reason."

She turned in Peanut's arms and leaned into his kiss, then smiled when he turned her loose with a little swat to her backside.

"Cutest little butt in Blessings," he said.

Ruby smirked. "If you say so," she drawled. "Now let's get Carlie and get that picnic started."

Carlie was sitting on the spare bed talking to Hoppy and Girl when they walked in. She'd taken off her Easter dress and was in shorts and a T-shirt.

"Picnic is ready. We're heading to the gazebo," Ruby said.

Carlie's eyes widened as she jumped off the bed.

"Are you hungry, honey?" Ruby asked.

Carlie nodded.

"Then off we go," Ruby said, and smiled to herself when Carlie bolted out ahead of her, her bare feet making little slapping sounds on the hardwood as she ran.

Peanut laughed at her.

"Hey, sugar… You don't always have to be barefoot when you go outside. It's just a good idea when we're watering stuff."

Carlie shook her head. "I have to be barefoot so I can feel where the fairies have been walking."

"Is that so?" Peanut said.

She nodded.

"Then barefoot it is," he said, and kicked off his shoes.

Ruby laughed. "I'm not going to be the only one with shoes," she said, and left hers by the door.

"I've got the basket," Peanut said.

"I'll get the door," Ruby said, and opened it wide.

Carlie went through first, tiptoeing off the patio because the concrete was hot beneath her feet and then bouncing when she hit the grass.

Before long, the trio was in the shade of the gazebo with their picnic spread out before them, watching birds in the birdbaths, the squirrels in the bird feeders, and hummingbirds in the flowers.

The beauty of their surroundings and the food they were eating was a welcome diversion from the morning they'd had. Once they were finished, Ruby gathered up the bits of bread crusts that Carlie had picked off her sandwich, wrapped them in a napkin, and handed them to her.

"Why don't you go scatter these crusts out beneath the big oak. The birds will love them."

"'Kay," Carlie said, and left the gazebo for the path that led her straight beneath the trees at the corner of the yard.

Peanut was sitting, watching her, when he remembered the message Lon Pittman had given him.

"Hey, honey, I almost forgot. The chief had a message for us. Remember that man Shirley warned you about in her letter...Bart Carlson?"

"Yes. Oh lord, please tell me he's not going to be a problem."

"It doesn't appear so. He called the police station because he didn't have contact info for us, and basically just sent his condolences and how to locate him in case we ever needed financial help taking care of Carlie. Here, read for yourself."

Ruby scanned the message quickly, then breathed a sigh of relief.

"Thank goodness. I guess Shirley read him wrong."

"I guess," Peanut said. "At any rate, I do not detect any kind of threat or trouble in this."

"Neither do I," Ruby said, and handed him back the message.

"I'll put it in Carlie's file," Peanut said, and then turned to see what Carlie was doing.

She was on the other side of the yard. It appeared she had already tossed the bread and meandered off to the azalea bushes and was on her hands and knees, poking around beneath them.

"I wonder what's she doing?" Ruby asked.

Peanut grinned. "Oh, she's convinced fairies live there. She's always looking for tiny footprints in the dirt beneath."

"Oh my," Ruby said. "The belief in magic is one of the joys of childhood."

"Making love with you is magic and the joy of my life," Peanut said.

Ruby sighed. "Keep talking pretty to me, darlin', and you might get lucky tonight."

He grinned. "It had already crossed my mind."

Ruby laughed, then got up, circled the table, and sat down in his lap and put her arms around his neck.

"Now, you know Widow Parsons can see into this backyard from her upstairs window, so don't do anything that will scandalize her."

Peanut threw back his head and laughed, then wrapped his arms around her and kissed the back of Ruby's neck until she was laughing and squealing and telling him to stop.

Carlie paused from her investigations and crawled around the azalea bush on her knees until she could see the gazebo, and rocked back on her heels. Mr. Ruby was kissing Miss Ruby and she was laughing.

Carlie sat, listening to the joy, and wanted to be a part of that, but she didn't know how. Being here was too new, and they were still strangers. But it made her feel good.

She got up, brushed off her hands and knees, and then took off for the rose garden to see the bees. If she stood real still and watched very close, she could see the bees crawling deep into the petals and coming out with little yellow dust on their legs. Then they'd fly over to other flowers and crawl into them, too, and come out with even more yellow dust on their tiny legs. She thought it made them look like they were wearing yellow socks.

She wondered where they went when they flew away. Maybe they were going home. If they were, did the yellow dust fall off on the way?

She was still in the garden when Peanut got up and carried their picnic stuff back into the house, leaving Ruby in the gazebo, watching Carlie flitting about her garden like the bees and hummingbirds.

---

The ambulances were gone from the Daltry property. The county sheriff's car was gone, following along behind them, and Deborah was about a quarter mile from home when her cell phone rang. When she saw it was her mom, she sighed. She'd been gone a long time and guessed Maggie was worried. She answered quickly.

"Hey... I'm almost home," Deborah said.

"Thank goodness," Maggie said. "You were gone so long I thought something had happened."

"Something did happen, but I'm fine. I'll tell you all about it when I get there."

"Okay," Maggie said, and disconnected.

Deborah accelerated up the long drive leading to their house, and when she finally pulled up and parked, she relaxed.

Home had never looked so good. She ran up the steps onto the front porch, entering the house in long, hurried steps.

Maggie came out of the kitchen.

"You have been gone more than three hours. What happened?"

"Give me a minute," Deborah said, and went to the sink to wash up, then drank a full glass of water before she stopped and dried off. "Oh my God," she muttered, and sat down at the table.

Maggie sat. "I'm waiting."

Deborah didn't pull any punches. "Two men were on Ladd's property. They walked in on me while I was in the barn, obviously intent on taking whatever they could from the place because they knew Ladd was in the hospital."

Maggie gasped. "You saw them?"

Deborah grinned. "More or less," and then proceeded to tell her what happened—from the frantic climb up into the barn loft to watching the county sheriff and two ambulances driving away.

Maggie's eyes welled. "You could have been killed."

"Pretty sure that's not what they had in mind," Deborah said. "But this is what's dangerous about living alone anymore...especially in the country. And it's solidified something I've been considering. Dad's death and then this confirmed it. If I came home to live and work, would you still stay on the farm?"

Maggie gasped. "Oh, honey! I don't want you to give up your career to satisfy a whim."

Deborah frowned. "Mom! You and home are not whims. You're all I have in this world. And my career is the kind that travels well. There are vet clinics within ten miles north and south of Blessings, and there are never enough vets."

Maggie started crying. "I don't know what I did to deserve such a good daughter, but this would be wonderful!"

Deborah smiled. "Then it's settled. And I want you to know, saying this aloud and you being in agreement takes such a burden from me. I want to be here when you need me every day. Not just when the disasters happen. And I miss being here. Louisville was the place I needed to be at the time, but not anymore. I'll call the clinic there in the next few days, and I'll have to deal with my furniture and my apartment, but I'm staying here." Then she reached across the table and grabbed her mother's hands. "We can do this."

Maggie's eyes welled. "Thank you, baby."

"You're welcome, Mom. Now, do we go into Blessings, deal with the funeral home stuff, and then grab something to eat at Granny's, or eat here and then go?"

"There's not much funeral home stuff to deal with," Maggie said. "I knew this day was coming. I did all of the hard stuff over a year ago. All there is left now is to just take them the clothes they'll need to bury him in and set the day and time."

Deborah nodded. "I should have known. You are always prepared."

"Well, I'm not prepared to talk to a bunch of people today,"

Maggie said. "Let's eat here and then go. I made potato salad and fried bacon. We can make bacon and tomato sandwiches."

"Sounds delicious," Deborah said. "And I will need to stop by the hospital and check on Ladd. I'll have to let him know what happened on his place this morning. It's going to bug him, not being able to be there to tend to things, but even after he goes home he won't be able to tend to livestock for a while. So I won't be doing any job hunting until he's well. Someone has to help take care of him, and we're the closest and oldest friends."

Maggie nodded.

"I'll stay in the car when you do all that."

"It won't take long," Deborah said. "But it's his place, and he has a right to know."

"Agreed. Now let's get lunch and then head into town. There's no need for you to go with me into the funeral home, so I'll drop you off at the hospital, then do what needs to be done. You call me when you're ready to leave, and I'll come pick you up."

"If you're sure," Deborah said.

"I'm sure. Now, if you'll slice one of our fresh tomatoes, I'll get the bread and mayo."

Deborah hugged her mom. "Will do," she said, chose a big red one from the bowl sitting on the counter, and a couple of minutes later, lunch was served.

———————

Ladd was up and walking the halls. He wasn't ready to run any races, and he still couldn't fully straighten up, but he was healing. He wasn't much worse off than the professional bull riders who got stomped during a ride. Most of them managed to get their own asses out of the arena and went to the hospital later. He, however, had come close to getting his skull split. He gingerly traced his fingertips over the staples in the back of his head and sighed. Damn bull.

He paused at the end of the hall to catch his breath and glanced out the window to the parking lot below. When he saw Deborah get out of a car and head for the hospital, his heart skipped a beat. She was coming to see him. Probably an update on the farm… nothing personal. But he still didn't want to miss her.

He turned around and headed back to his room. It was slow going, and he was gritting his teeth from the pain by the time he reached his bed and eased down on the side of the mattress.

And then the door opened, and Deborah paused on the threshold. "Okay to come in?" she asked.

"Absolutely. I heard about your dad. I'm so sorry. Come here," he said, and held out his hand.

Her breath caught. She wasn't prepared for instant sympathy. *Okay, girl, you do not cry.*

She closed the door behind her and walked toward him. She was not expecting him to stand up, but he did. She was not expecting the gentle, one-armed embrace, but he did it.

"He fought the good fight, honey. You and Maggie have my sympathies."

She loved the feel of his arm around her.

"I would hug you for the sweet words, but I'm afraid to touch you," she said, and then looked up, straight into his gaze. "Thank you. Now, please get back into bed."

"I was walking. I'm okay for a few minutes more. Sit beside me," he said, so she did. "Darren Payne paid me a visit. I understand you told Darren Payne what happened?"

She nodded.

He grinned. "He mentioned something about you reading him the riot act. I appreciate you having my back…again. He apologized profusely, said the bull was sold, the fences fixed, and he's paying for what my insurance doesn't."

Deborah nodded. "Good to know he's being upright about the mess he caused."

"At any rate, thank you," Ladd said.

"You're welcome. I have something to tell you. Actually, several things to tell you," Deborah said. "First, everything is okay at your place. At least it is now, but there was a situation there this morning."

Ladd frowned. "What kind of situation?"

"Um, well, I was at the barn feeding Sam this morning when a couple of men walked into the breezeway from the north end. They did not expect to see me. In fact, they did not expect to see anyone, because they knew you were in the hospital."

Ladd grabbed her arm, then winced because he'd moved too fast.

"Oh no! What happened? Did they hurt you?"

"They did not lay a hand on me, although they tried."

Ladd put a hand in the middle of his chest to steady the wild thump of his heartbeat. "Start over, and tell me what happened to you."

"They started after me. I got to the ladder and up to the loft first. Grabbed the scoop shovel, and when one of them popped his head up through the opening and grinned, I hit him in the face with it and broke his nose. He fell backward onto the guy coming up behind him. They were flat on their backs in the dirt when I yelled at them. They looked up. I dumped a bucket of nails in their faces, then hog-tied them with their own rope. Two deputies from the sheriff's office arrested them, and they were hauled off in two ambulances. And…I'm not going back to Louisville. Mom's staying on the farm, and we're not selling the property. I'm moving home."

"Oh my God, Deb. Oh my God. I'm sorry." He clasped her hand to his chest, and then lifted it to his lips and kissed it. "If anything had happened to you, I would never have—"

She put a finger across his lips.

"Shush. Don't give life to the words. Nothing happened. I'm fine. I've counted thirty head of cattle and fourteen calves every time. Are any missing, or is that the right count?"

He nodded. "It's right."

"All right, then. That's good," she said, and cupped the side of his face. "Stop worrying. I'm a big girl. And I'm tough. And when you get to go home, you still won't be able to do much for yourself, so be prepared to see my face every day until the doctor releases you. Understand?"

"You'll be busy taking care of Maggie," he said.

Deborah grinned. "Maggie can still take care of herself just fine. I just don't want her to grow old alone. I'm not even going to go job hunting for a while."

"There are never enough vets around here. I'd bet money the two in this area will be fighting over you, once they know you're job hunting," Ladd said.

"Good to know," Deborah said. "What does the doctor say about your progress?"

"That I'm doing good and luckier than I have a right to be," he said. "I'm hoping to go home in a day or two."

"Oh… I almost forgot," she said, and unsnapped her bag and pulled out his phone and charger. "I thought you might be needing this." She reached across him to lay them on the tray table, and when she did, he slid his arm around her and hugged her close.

"I don't have the right to expect this, but you would be doing me the biggest favor in the world if you would turn and face me. For so many reasons, I have this need to kiss you," he said.

Deborah never hesitated. She was curious to see if there was anything left of the magic that had been between them. In fact, she was the one who initiated the kiss—carefully settling her mouth on his lips—and then waited.

All of a sudden, his hand was on the back of her head, and he was pulling her closer, increasing the pressure of his lips until he heard her groan. At that point, he eased back and traced the shape of her chin with his finger, like he used to do so long ago.

"Lord, Deb. I have to be the biggest fool on the face of the earth for letting go of you."

"At the time, I thought you were," she said. "Now, I'm wondering if it wasn't the best thing that happened to both of us. You know…you never fully appreciate something until it's gone."

"Can I ask you something? And I want an honest answer. Whatever you say, I will accept with all the love and appreciation I have for what we've shared in the past."

"You can ask," she said.

"I was thinking of putting the home place up for sale because there's nothing left for me there. I'm alone day and night, and it's hard. I don't have anyone I belong to, or anyone who belongs to me. But if you're moving home, and if I happened to decide to stick around, would you be open to seeing where this goes…again?"

"Why now? Because it's convenient?" Deborah asked.

He frowned. "No, but that's a fair question, and I don't take offense. The truth is I've thought about you pretty much nonstop since Dad died. Being alone gives a person a lot of time to think about the past…mistakes and all. And I'd already come to the conclusion that letting you go was the stupidest damn thing I've done to date. I would take it as a huge favor if you'd just give me one more chance to do it right."

She was staring at him, and he was holding his breath. When her eyes narrowed, his heart sank.

"Yes," she said.

Ladd blinked.

"Yes? You said yes?"

Deborah sighed. "Yes, please."

And then she heard her phone signal a text and glanced down at it. "Mom's in the parking lot. She's ready to go home."

"Tell her you're on the way down. I'm so sorry I won't be able to be with you at the funeral. Oh…and I guess I need your phone number so I can call you when they're going to let me go home."

"It's in your contact list."

He grinned. "It is?"

"Yes. I was already going to give you another chance. You just didn't know it yet."

He started to laugh, and then grabbed his ribs and groaned.

She stood. "You know what we've never done together?"

"What?" he asked.

"We've made love in the bed of your old truck. We've made love in the barn loft. We've made love on the banks of the creek between our homes. But we've never made love in a bed. When we get to that point again...and we will...I want the mattress please." Then she leaned forward until their foreheads were touching. "You and that bull scared the holy crap out of me. Thank you for not dying," she said, and then she was gone.

Ladd's eyes welled with unshed tears as he eased his way back beneath the covers.

*And thank you for not quitting on me.*

———————————

Deborah and Maggie talked all the way home about the services for Josh. They'd set their headstone the year after Deborah graduated from college and bought prepaid funeral policies, never thinking how soon one would be needed. But their foresight then eased her duties now.

It wasn't until they were home and getting ready to go out to the garden to pick produce that Maggie asked about Ladd.

"Is he healing okay?" she asked.

Deborah nodded. "I think he's hoping to go home within the next couple of days."

"But can he be home alone?" Maggie asked.

"I'm not sure," Deborah said.

Maggie paused, and then looked up. "Next time you talk to him, tell him we have two spare bedrooms and one of them is his if he wants it. He can stay here until he's a little stronger."

Deborah thought about what it would be like to be under the same roof with him and decided she liked the thought.

"I'll mention it, but after he found out that thieves had already been on his property, I'm doubting if he'll be willing to abandon it for a longer period of time."

Maggie sighed. "Dammit. There's no easy way to fix this, is there?"

"No, and don't think I haven't been worried about this, too," Deborah said.

"Well, knowing Ladd, he'll figure it out," Maggie said.

Deborah nodded, but she also knew she would play a part in whatever Ladd decided to do. They had given each other permission to have another go at a relationship, and there were two farms, and two homes, and one person at each farm who was going to be needing her. She could not be in two places at once and had some figuring out of her own to do as well.

# CHAPTER 12

THE DOCTOR RELEASED LADD SATURDAY MORNING, AND JOSH Ryman's funeral was Saturday afternoon. Deborah was a wreck. Maggie was quiet, but accepting of what lay ahead.

It was just after 9:00 a.m. when Deborah took off to Blessings to get Ladd. Maggie was puttering around the house, trying to focus on what she needed to do, but she kept going from one task to another without finishing any of them. Finally, she went out on the back porch, sat down in the porch swing, and just cried because she felt like it.

This was it. The period at the end of the sentence that was their marriage, and the end of the story of their life together. Whatever happened from this day forward was all on Maggie, and she was trying not to be bitter.

She didn't want to be in charge. She didn't want to make all of the hard decisions. And she wasn't sure what she and Deborah could actually accomplish. She just wanted her house and garden and to be able to look out across the pasture in the evenings and watch the sunset. She needed to talk to Deborah about the pasture that was going to seed. And then she remembered Ladd had spoken to her months ago about the wisdom of trying to take care of it all on his own.

A thought occurred to her then, but this was not the day to think about it. Maybe in a week or so, when the funeral was behind them and Ladd was feeling better. For now, she was right where she wanted to be, out on her porch, on her own.

―――――――――

Unaware of what her mother was dreaming up, Deborah drove with single intent all the way to the hospital. She needed to get

Ladd without delay and get him home, settled, with food in the house and everything at his fingertips, because the afternoon belonged to her and her mom.

She was a little bit sick to her stomach, but she knew it was nerves. She dreaded that funeral more than anything she'd ever dreaded in her life. This was her daddy. It wasn't fair that such a good man would have had to suffer so long, only to have his life come to this end.

She'd cried twice on her way to town, and now her eyes were red-rimmed and slightly swollen. Ladd would see them. And he was going to feel bad that her day with her mom had been inter-rupted to bring him home. But the truth was this break from what was looming was saving her sanity.

Deborah got out on the run and went straight up to the nurse's station on his floor to make sure Ladd's discharge papers were ready. And they were.

"Give me about fifteen minutes to get him into these clothes, and then bring the wheelchair. We'll be ready to go," she said.

"Will do," his nurse said.

Deborah turned away from the desk and headed down the hall to his room. The door was open. She walked in, closing the door behind her as she went to the bed where he was sitting.

"Hey, you. I brought clothes for you to go home in."

"Oh, thank God," Ladd said. "All I have is this hospital gown that leaves me bare-assed."

She smiled. She knew what his bare ass used to look like, and it was fine—however, not for public viewing.

"Sorry, but I dug around in your closet until I found a pair of sweats and some house shoes. I also got a shirt that buttons up, so you won't have to put your arms up over your head."

"Do not apologize for anything," he said. "This is all perfect."

"Do you need help getting dressed?" she asked.

"Honestly, I don't know."

She laid the clothes down, then grabbed the sweats and started putting them on him, one leg at a time. Once the waist was up past his knees, she stepped back.

"You're going to have to stand up now so I can get the sweats the rest of the way up."

He eased off the bed, then held onto her shoulders as she pulled them up.

She reached behind him, untied the gown at the back of his neck, and let it fall to the floor, then helped him into the shirt, one arm at a time.

"I can button it," he said, and sat down on the mattress and went to work.

As he did, Deborah bent over and slipped the house shoes on his feet.

"You're not ready to go out dancing, but you are clothed enough to make a public appearance now," she said.

"Thanks to you," Ladd said, then tilted up her chin, forcing her to look at him. "This is a hard day for you and Maggie. You both have my love and sympathy. I wish I could be there for you."

Deborah sighed. "Thanks. I have a question to ask you."

"Ask away," he said.

"Mom says to tell you that we have two spare bedrooms on the first floor that are waiting for company. They share a bathroom, so you would have that to yourself. It would be so much more comfortable for you to be where we could help, and you could have decent food while you're still at this healing stage. But nobody's feelings will be hurt if you'd rather go home. Just know that I'll probably spend most of the next few days with you, if you won't stay with us."

He frowned.

"Maggie needs you."

"And so do you," Deborah said. "So you see my predicament. If you stay with us, then you can ride with me every day to count cattle and feed Sam and get the mail. You'll know when you're strong enough to be on your own. The last thing you want to do is set yourself back. Until you get the staples out of your head and can dress yourself without breaking out in a cold sweat, you don't have any business being alone."

Ladd sighed. He was going to need help, and Deborah and Maggie were the only ones offering. If he insisted on going home, it was going to make it harder on Deborah.

"If you weren't both grieving, this decision would be easier," Ladd said. "If I go stay with you and Maggie, I feel like I'll be adding to the burden."

Deborah frowned. "The burden of what? You'll just be sharing our food, and we'll be the extra pair of hands when you need them."

"Okay then, but if I see I'm in the way, I'll take myself home, even if I have to cross a creek to do it."

Deborah rolled her eyes.

"It would be in your best interests to stay away from pastures and creeks until you're well enough to run again, and then be certain you can outrun the next critter after you. Do you hear me?"

He grinned.

"Loud and clear," he said, and then looked toward the door as a nurse came in with a wheelchair.

Within minutes, Deborah had him in the car, reclined in the passenger seat, and they were headed out of town. She knew the ride was going to be hard on Ladd, but there was no easy way to do it.

He was grim-lipped and silent as she drove on the highway, but once she turned up onto the blacktop leading to their home, the road was rougher and bumpier. She slowed down considerably, and still she heard the occasional gasp and groan.

"I'm so sorry," Deborah said.

His face was ashen, his teeth gritted.

"No, no…you're doing fine, love, and we're almost there."

Deborah gripped the steering wheel a little tighter, as if she could hold the car wheels up out of the potholes, and kept driving. A couple of minutes later, the two-story farmhouse came into view and she breathed a sigh of relief.

"We're home," she said, and drove around the house and pulled up near the back porch.

Maggie had been watching for them and was relieved Deborah had talked him into staying with them. He was almost as dear to her as her own daughter, and so alone. She opened the back door as they were coming up the steps.

"Welcome, Laddy. I have your room all ready. Deborah, the big one…that used to be your grandpa's."

Deborah nodded. "Lean on me, Ladd. You need to lie down and let all those tight muscles relax."

"Was it a hard trip?" Maggie asked.

"It was fine," Ladd said.

"No, it wasn't fine, Mom, but we're here. What time do we need to be ready for the family car from the funeral home to come pick us up?"

"They'll be here at eleven. There's a dinner at the church and then the service is at two. It will probably be close to four o'clock before we get home. I'm worried about leaving Ladd alone that long."

Ladd shook his head. "No, no, I can get around on my own. I have orders not to lift anything but a fork to my mouth. I'll sleep. And gratefully. The nurses never let me alone long enough to do anything but nap."

"There's food in the refrigerator for you. Ham sandwiches, some potato salad, fresh sliced tomatoes, and there are peach hand pies on the counter in that covered dish."

"Oh wow, Maggie. That sounds amazing. Now stop worrying about me."

Deborah gently slipped her arm around his waist. "Lean on me just a little bit longer, and I'll get you down the hall to your room."

Ladd did as she asked and a few moments later gratefully collapsed on top of the bed. Deborah pulled off his shoes, covered him with the quilt at the foot of the bed, and handed him the remote to the TV. Then impulsively, she leaned down and kissed his forehead.

"Rest. Eat. Do not leave the house for any reason. Here's your phone. Call if you need us, and I'm serious. Dad doesn't need us. This process we go through to bury our dead is all for the family and propriety's sake. If you have a problem, call me. I have to get changed now. I'll check on you before we leave."

She ran her finger down the side of his face, then turned and walked out of the room.

"Thank you," Ladd said, but she was already gone, and he felt like he'd just run the longest race of his life.

The central air was humming. The ceiling fan above him was spinning, and the quilt she'd pulled up over him was just enough to keep his feet from getting cold. Within seconds, he was asleep.

As promised, the family car arrived at the farm at 11:00 a.m. Deborah was wearing a little black dress that was far shorter than she would have liked, but long legs were a curse when it came to short dresses.

She ran down the hall to check on Ladd, and when she saw him sleeping soundly, she hurried back to the living room, grabbed her purse, and out the door they went.

She and Maggie sat side by side, holding hands—each lost in memories of the man they were laying to rest—and when they reached the church, they became overwhelmed by the number of friends who'd come to support them.

By the time they served the food at noon, Maggie was emotionally exhausted and Deborah knew it. She hovered at her mother's side throughout the meal, interacted with the countless

THE BEST OF ME

friends who came by to speak to them to give her mother a break, and then both of them listened to the stories their friends told about Josh. Some talked about him as the kid who'd grown up in Blessings. Others told stories of what a good neighbor he'd been, and always the good friend. But it was the man who'd been best man at their wedding that broke her. When he came to give her a hug and retold the story they all knew so well, of how Josh thought he'd lost the wedding rings and then found them pinned to the inside of his tuxedo, right where his mother told him she'd put them, they all had a good laugh.

"It didn't take much to get Josh sidetracked," Maggie said, and then got teary again thinking of him in past tense.

Finally, they were escorted into the sanctuary and the service began. At that point, Deborah began to lose focus. And then right in the middle of a prayer, someone sneezed. Twice. While everyone's heads were bowed and their eyes were closed.

When the pastor finished, he said, "Amen," then looked up at the congregation. Then glanced down at the closed casket before he turned to the pianist.

"Geraldine, was that you who sneezed?"

She nodded, her cheeks flushing in embarrassment.

The preacher looked out across the congregation as he took his handkerchief out of his pocket and wiped his forehead.

"Thank goodness. For a minute there, I thought that sneeze came from the casket. I was just making sure."

There was a shocked moment of silence, and then Maggie laughed, and Deborah grinned, and the congregation erupted in laughter.

Everyone who'd known Josh Ryman knew how much he liked a joke. He'd pulled many on the pastor over the years on Sunday morning. Either he was unplugging the sound system or playing Van Halen over it instead of spiritual songs before services started. It was just the right touch to carry through the rest of the service because no one was sad that Josh had finally broken the chains of helplessness from the aftereffects of the stroke. They were there out of respect for the man he'd been, and for Maggie and Deborah.

Everything Deborah had been dreading was over in less than an hour, and by the time they were seated in the family car and on their way to the cemetery, Maggie was shaky.

Deborah got a bottle of water from the console between them and handed it to her mother.

"Drink some, Mom. It's hot and you're getting dehydrated. You look like you're going to pass out."

"I feel like it," Maggie said, and took several sips before she put the bottle back in a cup holder. "Thank you. For everything."

Deborah's eyes welled. "Oh, Mom, I feel lost, too. We'll get through this and figure out where we go from here, and we'll do it together. Okay?"

"Okay," Maggie said, and then leaned back and closed her eyes.

---

Ladd woke up a little after one, and thought about the food in the refrigerator, and got up. The nap had been rejuvenating. He was slow but steady on his feet as he made his way to the kitchen.

After poking around a bit, he got a ham sandwich, potato salad, and sliced tomatoes on a plate and carried it to the table, then got himself something to drink and sat down.

The house was quiet but familiar, and he could see Maggie's garden through the kitchen windows. It was lush, neatly weeded, and obviously watered when necessary. At fifty-four, she was a fairly young widow. She might marry again one day.

Then he thought of Deborah, wondering how this relationship experiment was going to play out. All he knew was that he was going to give it his all and hope for the best.

He ate all he could, carried his dirty dishes to the sink, and thought about the peach hand pies then decided to save that for later. The thought of going back to bed beckoned. He got situated in bed, propped up with pillows behind him so he could watch some TV, and fell asleep watching a game show and dreamed of men chasing Deborah in his barn. He could hear her screaming for help, but he couldn't walk.

He woke up again, bathed in sweat and shaking, grateful that it was just a dream. Just to break up the memory of that nightmare, he went to get a hand pie. He put one on a little plate and carried it back to his bed, then sat up in bed and channel surfed until he found a movie. The peach filling in the pie was sweet, the crust flaky, and he was confident that the spy thriller he'd chosen to watch would be short on jokes and pratfalls—nothing that would aggravate the broken ribs.

———

The funeral was over, and Deborah and Maggie were on their way home with boxes of fried chicken, a multitude of sides boxed up in to-go containers, and an indecent number of desserts.

They had a few pots of flowers Maggie wanted to replant and had requested all of the other flowers be taken to the nursing home where Josh had spent the past four years, to be distributed in the rooms of the other residents.

Now that the service was over, Maggie seemed at peace. She'd honored her husband and their life together. It was the last thing she would do for him, and it was enough.

As for Deborah, she had already shifted focus to the man waiting for them at home, and it appeared so had her mother.

"I hope Ladd has managed okay on his own," Maggie said. "I mean…he was just released from the hospital, and we basically dumped him off and left him on his own."

"I'm betting he's been resting and eating," Deborah said.

Maggie sighed. "We're going to be a while eating up this food they sent with us."

"The Ladd I remember was never full," Deborah said.

Maggie glanced at her. "Is there anything left of what was between you?"

Deborah shrugged. "Maybe. We've kind of agreed to see what happens."

Maggie reached for her hand and gave it a squeeze.

"I'll wish you both the best, whatever you decide, but you know nothing would make me happier," she said.

"I know, Mom. Ah…and we're home," she said.

As soon as the driver parked, he helped them carry in the food and flowers, expressed his condolences one last time, and drove away.

Deborah watched from the front porch until he was out of sight, then went inside.

Maggie had gone to her room to change, but Deborah wanted to check on Ladd before she did anything. His door was ajar, and she could hear the television. But when she peeked in, she found him asleep with the remote loose in his hands and thought if he was well and if they were alone, she would crawl right into bed beside him and wake him up.

Satisfied that he was okay, she hurried to her room to change, and then went to the kitchen. When she saw the dirty plate, fork, and glass in the sink, she knew that he'd eaten, too.

Good. Eating and sleeping would help him heal. Then she began getting food into the refrigerator and freezer. When Maggie came back, she dealt with the desserts, keeping out what wouldn't freeze to be eaten first, and packaging and storing the rest.

Maggie was looking longingly at a coconut cream pie and then impulsively got two forks out of a drawer and carried them and the pie to the table.

"Hey, Deborah, I need your help," she said.

Deborah was in the pantry and called out, "I'll be right there." But when she came out and saw her mother at the table with a whole pie, eating from the dish, she grinned.

"Looks like you're doing okay on your own," she said.

"Don't be a party pooper," Maggie said and handed her a fork.

Deborah laughed and sat down beside her, ready to dig in.

"Hey! Where's my invitation?" Ladd asked.

They both jumped up and then led him to the table.

"You're family. Family doesn't need invitations," Maggie said, and went to get another fork.

Ladd eased into a chair with a wince. "It's a damn shame I had to get stomped by a bull to get some attention around here."

Deborah handed him the fork. "It's also a shame you couldn't run faster," she said.

Maggie frowned. "Deborah. What a thing to say."

Ladd laughed, and then groaned and grabbed at his ribs. "This is the Deborah I remember, but can we save the jokes until laughing doesn't hurt, and push the pie a little closer? My reach has been seriously restricted."

Deborah moved the pie and then they both moved their chairs closer.

Ladd took his first bite, then rolled his eyes. "Mmm, this is so good."

"I'm pretty sure it came from Granny's, which means Mercy Pittman made it. She is one fine baker," Maggie said.

"You're no slouch, Miss Maggie. I ate one of your peach hand pies. It was delicious," Ladd said, then glanced at Deborah. "Do you like to cook?"

"I feed myself, but I'm better at healing animals than making pie crust, so if one of your prerequisites is fine dining, then you need to mark me off your list."

Ladd's eyes narrowed. "I never cared if you could cook before, and nothing has changed. I'm not picky about what I eat, so get that chip off your shoulder, dip it in chocolate, and pass it on over."

Maggie sighed. It appeared there was far more than sparks between them. But they were going to have to work out their past on their own. She took one more bite of pie and then stood.

"I'm going to the garden. Tomatoes need to be picked. I'll be up canning again before long."

"I can pick them for you, Mom," Deborah said.

"You have to go check on Ladd's cows and feed Sam. I like my alone time in the garden. It gives me time to think."

Deborah knew her mom. She never said anything she didn't mean.

"Yes, ma'am," Deborah said, then watched as her mom picked up a bucket in the utility room and went out the back door.

"I'll go with you," Ladd said.

Deborah frowned. "You just got out of the hospital today. You can go with me in the morning, okay?"

"It appears I don't have a choice," he muttered.

"You have a choice. I'm expecting you to make the wise one," she snapped. "I'll gather up all the mail and bring it back with me. Is there anything else you want?"

He sighed. "I'll have bills to pay, but my laptop is probably dead."

"I'll go rummage around in your business until I find it, or we can get it in the morning. Your call," Deborah said.

He grinned. "I look forward to you rummaging around in my business, but it can wait."

"I'll get us some supper together after I get back," Deborah said. "The church sent a lot of food home from the dinner. Fried chicken and scalloped potatoes are on the menu later."

Ladd held out his hand. "Are we good? No hard feelings?"

"No hard feelings, and we were always good together," Deborah said, but instead of taking his hand, she cupped his face and kissed him, then stopped abruptly. "You have your cell phone. My number is in it. I won't be long. I'm going to get your mail, count the herd, and feed Sam."

"Thank you," Ladd said.

"You're welcome. Please go lie back down for a while. I don't want to get in trouble with your doctor."

"Going now," Ladd said, and left the room.

Deborah grabbed her keys and her phone, then went out the back door, waving at her mom.

"Back soon," she said.

"Be careful. No more bad men," Maggie said.

Deborah gave her a thumbs-up and then got in the car and drove away, unaware her mother was watching her from the garden, and inside the house Ladd watched from the window. They both loved her, and she'd just given up everything she'd built and worked for to stay home with them.

———————

Deborah had her routine down pat.

She stopped to get the mail and was looking for the herd out in the pasture along the road, but they were nowhere in sight.

"Oh great. Just when I don't have time to be delayed," she muttered, but her mood immediately shifted when she realized the whole herd was up at the barn by the main gate.

She did a quick head count, then went in the house to get the mail she'd been gathering and took it to the car, then drove to the barn. If she needed to make a run for it again, wheels would be close at hand.

Sam was waiting for her when she walked into the barn and came toward her, meowing a welcome.

"Hello, pretty boy," she said, and scooped him up in her arms. He was purring softly as he head-butted her chin.

She grinned, scratching his ear as she headed toward the granary, thinking Sam was as smooth as his master. When she passed the steps leading up to the loft, she thought about the nails beneath her feet and made a mental note to check about getting a roofing magnet to sweep the ground for all the nails she dumped on the two thieves then opened the granary and set Sam down inside. He meowed and chirped as she filled his bowl with cat food, then refilled his water bowl before shutting him inside.

Anxious to get home, she was on her way out of the barn when there was a loud and sudden bang behind her. She spun, her heart pounding, only to realize the wind was coming up and one of the granary doors wasn't fastened.

"Oh my lord," she muttered, and ran back to latch it. As she did, she glanced out. The sky was getting dark, and the wind was rising.

A thunderstorm was coming!

She turned and ran to the other end of the barn, jumped in her car, and was almost to the highway when the first raindrops hit her windshield.

Lightning flashed somewhere up ahead, followed by a loud crack of thunder. They needed the rain, and she loved a good thunderstorm. When she reached the turnoff to their house, she accelerated into the turn, hoping she could get home and inside before it unloaded.

The house was just ahead, and Maggie was standing on the front porch. Deborah honked as she drove past and pulled up beneath the carport. Her mom loved storms as much as she did.

Within seconds, the rain turned into a deluge, blurring the trees surrounding the farm, but she was home. She got out, grabbed the bag with Ladd's mail, and walked up onto the porch and hugged her mom.

"I should have known you'd be out here," Deborah said, and then turned around and faced the storm.

Wind was blowing the rain up beneath the overhang on the porch and onto her boots, washing off the dust from the barn.

The front door opened behind her. She turned just as Ladd walked out.

"I had a suspicion you two would be out here," he said, and walked in between them.

"Here's your mail," Deborah said.

"Thank you. I, too, love the smell of rain," he said.

It was the perfect end to a long, sad day.

"Am I mistaken, or did you mention fried chicken for supper?" Ladd asked.

All of a sudden, Maggie had something to do. Purpose was what was going to get her through this. "I'll get the chicken out of the fridge. Do you want it heated up, or—"

"I like it cold just fine," Ladd said.

"So do we," Maggie said.

"There are scalloped potatoes to reheat," Deborah said. "Let's go inside. For the first time today, I'm hungry."

A short while later, Ladd was seated at the kitchen table watching Deborah peeling tomatoes and listening to their voices and thinking how wonderful it was not to be in a house all alone.

The rain was blowing against the windows and hammering upon the roof, but the homey atmosphere and the scent of warming food was comforting. Now that Ladd was here, he was glad he came. Getting to see Deborah again in this setting was like old times, and it made him want her even more.

He was locked in on the shape of her backside and her long legs when he realized she'd turned around and caught him staring. Their gazes locked. Memories flooded, followed by the curiosity of what it would be like to make love again.

Then she turned away, brought a little plate of deviled eggs to the table and a glass of iced tea and set it in front of him.

"You have some serious healing to do first," she whispered.

"So, you can read minds now?" he asked.

"Only yours," Deborah said.

Maggie was lost in thought and missed the whole byplay, and then the timer went off. She took the potatoes out of the oven and carried them to the table, gently patted Ladd on the back, then went back to help Deborah get the rest of the food on the table.

The wind whipped around the corner of the house, slamming branches of the lilac bush against the outer wall.

"Goodness. My poor tomatoes," Maggie said.

"They'll survive," Deborah said. "They always do."

———————

The thunderstorm hit Blessings just as people were sitting down to supper, while others were getting off work. Lights flickered a couple of times when lightning was close, but the power stayed on.

Carlie was in her room playing when the first clap of thunder sounded. She got up and went to the window to look out. Mama used to say it was God giving everything a bath. She thought about where Mama was now and wondered if she was getting rained on, and then decided the little house she'd picked out for her would shelter her, just like this one was keeping them safe and dry.

She crawled up on the window seat with Hoppy and sat watching the downpour. Someone's dog was running down the street, soaked to the skin, with its tail tucked between its legs.

"Poor puppy," Carlie muttered.

A car drove past, splashing the dog even more, but before she could work herself up into dismay, a boy came out of a house and called out to the dog, who ran toward the boy and up onto the porch out of the rain.

Carlie sighed. Problem solved.

Then she heard Miss Ruby call out, "Carlie! Supper is ready!"

She gave Hoppy a hug, then left him on the window seat and skipped out of the room. Something smelled good. Maybe spaghetti. She loved spaghetti.

"I'm here," she said as she skipped into the kitchen.

Ruby turned and smiled. "Yes, you are, and we are happy you are!"

"Is that spaghetti?" Carlie asked.

Ruby nodded.

"Yum," Carlie said.

"Yum, indeed," Peanut said. "Grab a chair and get comfy. Supper's coming."

They sat, made their plates, and began eating, talking about everything from the thunderstorm to enrolling Carlie in school on Monday.

"I'm in second grade," Carlie said.

"We know, honey," Ruby said. "Your mama sent all of your school info. You'll be enrolled here to start third grade when school starts."

"Oh yes. I forgot," she said, then forked up a bite of spaghetti noodles and sucked them into her mouth, like sucking soup up a straw.

Peanut grinned and started to do the same thing, then caught the look on Ruby's face and stopped.

"It was just a thought," he said.

She rolled her eyes.

He winked.

And supper continued.

# CHAPTER 13

LADD WOKE UP IN THE NIGHT AND THEN COULDN'T GET BACK to sleep. The staples in his head felt like nails. His back hurt. And he couldn't roll over on his side without hurting. He got up and turned the light on, trying to remember where he'd put the pain pills, and was banging doors and opening drawers when Deborah walked in.

"I'm sorry. Did I wake you?" Ladd asked.

"It doesn't matter. What's wrong?" she asked.

"I was looking for my pain pills."

She frowned. "I think you had them in the kitchen. Maybe on the sideboard? I'll check," she said, and hurried out of the room.

Ladd sat down on the side of the bed and closed his eyes. His head was pounding and he was hoping Deborah found them. Otherwise, sleep tonight was over.

As luck would have it, she came back with the pill bottle in one hand and a glass of water in the other.

"Found them," she said, and handed him the water, then shook out two pills into his hand.

He downed them and half a glass of water, and then set it aside.

"Thank you, Deb."

"Lie down. I'll sit with you a bit until the pills take effect," she said.

"You don't have to," he said, but he was already back beneath the covers and holding her hand.

Deborah smiled. "I know that, but maybe I want to. I kind of like you, you know."

Ladd eyed all of the long, dark hair hanging loose around her face and down the back of her neck, then the gym shorts and over-size T-shirt she was wearing.

"Nice pj's," he said.

"You aren't looking at my pj's. You're looking at my bare legs."

He grinned. "And that's your fault for having legs too long and shapely to ignore." But he was still looking, this time at her face. "You've changed looks so much. Besides the fact that you grew six inches after I left, you went from cute and adorable to a stunning, confident woman. You are a real Wonder Woman. You even look a little like her, except you wear more clothes than she does."

Deborah smiled. "I think your pain pills are kicking in. Wonder Woman, indeed. Hush now and try to relax," she said, and got up and began turning off lights before coming back to sit on the side of the bed. He was still watching her. "Ladd, you have to close your eyes to sleep."

"You're so beautiful," he said.

Deborah sighed. "Why did the people we love have to die for us to come to this place again?"

Ladd felt like crying. Instead, he threaded his fingers through hers.

"I don't believe that. I believe they had done everything they'd come to do and their jobs here were finished. Regardless of how their lives ended, that's why they're gone now. The fact that our paths have crossed in life not once but twice tells me we're not through. I just don't want to mess this up again."

Deborah was stunned by the depth of his beliefs—beliefs she didn't even know he held. Their years apart had turned the hotheaded boy she remembered into an intelligent and thought-ful man. And like him, she didn't want this second chance to go wrong.

"We're going to be fine. You just need to get well. I give you my word I will not leave you."

"Like I left you?" he asked.

"We were kids. Now we're not." She got up and kissed his forehead, and then his lips. "Close your eyes, love."

His eyelids drooped. The pain pills were kicking in.

"Love," he mumbled.

"You love. I love. We love," she said softly, then sat without moving until she knew he'd fallen asleep.

Only then did she go back to bed, but now she couldn't sleep. She knew her mother was most likely awake and grieving. She also knew that sometimes grief was best dealt with alone.

Over the past four years, once it became obvious her father was not going to recover from his stroke, Deborah gave herself permission to face the truth of his declining health, while her mother who was with him every chance she had was less aware. For Deborah, knowing now that her father was no longer of this earth left her with a sad, empty feeling.

Finally, she fell asleep, and dreamed she was standing at a crossroad. There were no signs to indicate where either road would lead, and her dilemma was knowing she still had to choose.

When she woke, it was morning.

The rain had stopped sometime during the early morning hours, and she could hear Dumpling crowing somewhere in the distance. Then she remembered Ladd was in a bedroom down the hall, and jumped up and hurried to dress.

She could smell coffee, which meant Maggie was up.

Today was the first day of the rest of their lives.

Once she was dressed and her hair pulled back in a ponytail, she went to check on Ladd.

She could hear him moving around and knocked on the door, then called out. "Good morning. Do you need any help?"

"No. I've got it," Ladd said.

"Okay. Going to check on Mom," she said, and headed for the kitchen.

Maggie was taking bacon out of the skillet when Deborah walked in, gave her a hug, and kissed the side of her cheek.

"Morning, Mom," Deborah said.

"Good morning, sweetheart. Did I hear you up with Ladd in the night?"

"Early this morning, and yes. He'd left his pain pills in the kitchen last night and was looking for them. I sat with him until he went back to sleep. With where his injuries are, I don't know how he ever gets any rest. Did you get any sleep?" she asked.

Maggie shrugged. "Some. I just wanted the sun to come up. Things never seem as bad after sunrise. Biscuits are in the oven and I'm making gravy. Do you want any eggs?"

"I don't. I'll settle for biscuits and gravy."

Maggie nodded. "Same for me, but I'm going to fry a couple for Ladd. I seem to remember he likes his eggs well done. No runny yolks for him."

Deborah smiled. "How do you remember stuff like that?"

Maggie shrugged. "If you ever cook for someone, you remember their likes and dislikes, so you better start taking notes."

Deborah laughed. "Lesson noted."

Maggie winked and then turned back to the stove and began making roux for the gravy. By the time Ladd walked into the kitchen, she was taking his eggs out of the skillet and the biscuits out of the oven.

"Good morning, honey. Your timing is perfect," she said.

A wave of emotion washed through him. Walking into a kitchen and seeing Maggie at the stove and Deborah carrying food to the table was just like old times. Until all of this happened, he didn't know how much he'd missed being with people.

"It all smells so good," he said.

Deborah could see the tension in his face and the way he was favoring his left side as he stood. Getting dressed alone was probably more than he should have tackled.

"Sit. I'll bring your coffee. Did you take pain pills this morning?" Deborah asked.

"I just took a couple. By the time we eat, they will have had time to kick in so I can ride with you to my place."

She nodded, and then Maggie talked about what a beating her vegetable garden had taken during the storm.

After they'd eaten, Maggie sent them on their way, with Ladd sitting on one pillow, another behind his back, and carefully buckled in.

Deborah drove much slower to the Daltry farm than she had the day she drove him to Blessings bloody and unconscious.

"Are you doing okay?" she asked as they reached the highway and then crossed the bridge over the creek and headed south.

"Yes. It feels good to be outside, but it looks like the creek was out of its banks last night. There's a lot of debris caught up in the tree roots."

"There's something to be said for living on a hill," Deborah said.

Ladd grinned. "We might not have to deal with flooding, but we're a sitting target for tornadoes."

"Is the basement under your house still good?" Deborah asked.

"It's dry and sound, but not used much now. Some of Dad's stuff is stored down there."

"I remember those shelves lined with your mother's canning. All those pretty quarts of peaches, green beans, and tomatoes. And the pickles. She made the best pickles."

"I hadn't thought of that in years, but she did have the touch when it came to pickling stuff." Then he leaned back against the pillow and glanced out the passenger window. "I sure do miss them," he said, and closed his eyes.

Deborah reached for his hand and gave it a quick pat, then took the turn from the highway to the blacktop leading to his place. Ladd felt the turn and sat up. This was all Daltry land now, and he was glad to be on it again.

They were still on the blacktop when Deborah suddenly pointed. "There's the herd...on the other side of the pond."

"If you honk, they'll come up to the barn," he said.

She arched an eyebrow. "Now you tell me."

He looked a little startled. "I'm sorry. I didn't think."

She laughed. "I was just teasing you," and then she braked, honked the horn a couple of times, and then drove a little farther before honking again. By the time they reached the house, the herd was at the corral behind the barn.

"There are some cattle cubes in the granary closest to the corral," he said.

Deborah nodded, drove past the house and all the way to the barn, then parked at the fence so he could watch.

"You are not allowed to get out," she said.

"But—"

"Not today, mister. You can watch from here, but I'm feeding Sam first."

He sighed but didn't argue. She was right. Not today. So he watched as she disappeared into the barn and waited until he saw her coming out of the other end of the barn pushing a wheelbarrow with three bags of cattle cubes.

She opened the first sack and slipped through the gate, then began pouring the cubes out in a row, moving quickly to keep from getting jostled. Then she ran back to get the second bag, poured it out the same way, and then did the same with the last one. Now that the whole herd was strung out in a line across the pasture with their heads down, counting them was a breeze.

She refastened the gate, pushed the wheelbarrow back into the barn, and then headed back through the breezeway. Sam came out from beneath the granary, meowing, and she swooped him up.

"Wanna go see your Laddy? You are such a sweet boy. I know he misses you," she crooned and carried him to the car, opened the door, and got in with him in her arms.

The big yellow tom leaped out of her arms and into Ladd's lap, then began head-butting Ladd's chin and begging for pets.

"Aw, hey, Sam. Have you been a good boy? Did you miss me? I sure missed you," Ladd said.

The cat purred and purred, and then settled into Ladd's lap and began licking its paws. Ladd was stroking him gently and scratching the cat's head.

"Thank you for this, Deborah. Sam has been my confidant for quite a while now."

She nodded. "Hang onto him. I'm going to drive back to the barn and let him out, then we'll go to the house."

Ladd nodded, cuddling the cat as she started the car and put it in gear.

"You can drive all the way in if you want," Ladd said, as she parked just outside the breezeway.

"Not until I get a magnet to remove all those roofing nails from the dirt. There's a guy coming out to sweep it tomorrow," she said. "We don't have to be here. He'll just call me when he's finished."

He paled. "Sorry. I completely forgot what you went through here. Blame it on drugs and pain."

She leaned over and kissed him square on the lips.

"Stop apologizing and give me your cat."

She opened the door, took Sam out of his arms, and got out, talking baby talk to the cat all the way back inside, then set him down beneath the granary door. He meowed and then wandered off.

She ran back and jumped into the car.

"I love your cat," she said, then headed for the house.

"How about me?" he asked as she pulled up and parked.

"You already know the answer to that, or we wouldn't be here," she said. "Here are the keys to your house. Let's go get your stuff."

Ladd was slow, but walking into the house felt good. He was home. No surprises to be had here. The place needed a good cleaning, but other than that, all was well.

"You said you wanted your laptop. Where might I find that?" Deborah asked.

"I turned Mom's sewing room into an office the year I moved home. If it's not in there, it might be in my bedroom. I'm going to get my shaving kit and some more clothes. I'll look there."

Deborah frowned. "Okay, but leave it all on your bed. I'll pack it up for you. No lifting anything beyond the clothes you put on, remember?" She was starting to walk away when she heard him sigh and then a frustrated response.

"Yes, ma'am."

She stopped, turned, and then very gently wrapped her arms around his waist and laid her cheek on his chest.

"I'm sorry. This is me being forthright so I don't cry at every little thing. It's the price of being a female in a field that is mostly men. You're hurt. I do love you, and we have both been reminded of how fragile and fleeting life can be. Ignore the tone of my voice and remember if I didn't want you back in my life, we wouldn't be here right now."

Ladd tilted her chin just enough and kissed her. Tentatively at first, testing. But when he heard her moan beneath her breath, he deepened the kiss, and as he did the years fell away, and she was shaking from want of him and he was aching in places that had nothing to do with being hurt.

Finally, it was Deborah who stopped.

"We can't do this yet. We just can't. I'm not having sex with a man with broken ribs and staples in his head. We both have better sense than that, and we both want you well."

He sighed and rested his forehead against hers.

"Well, you have better sense. I was willing to give it a try."

She laughed out loud. "Spoken like a true man. Sex wins out over good sense."

"Every time," Ladd said, and then grinned and gave her backside a quick pat. "Now, where were we?"

"Laptop. Shaving kit. Clothes," she said.

"Right. Going to my bedroom," he said, and went down the hall as Deborah turned around and headed for a small room just off the foyer and across from the living room.

It didn't take but a few moments to spot his laptop, and it was plugged in which meant it was already charged. She spotted a small briefcase, dropped the laptop and the charging cord into it, then zipped it up and headed for his bedroom.

Ladd was in the bathroom gathering up his shaving kit when she entered.

"I found it. Do you want more sweatpants for ease in dressing?"

"Yes, and short-sleeved T-shirts. The sweats are folded up on a shelf in the closet, and the T-shirts are folded up in the top drawer of my dresser."

"I see them," she said, then spotted a large duffel bag in the bottom of his closet and carried it to the bed.

Before long she had it packed, and his shaving kit was tucked in with the clothes.

"Okay, I think this is it," Deborah said. "And if there's something we missed, we'll get it later. I'll still come over to check on everything before sundown."

She shouldered the long strap on the briefcase and picked up the duffel bag, then led the way out of the house, put everything in the back of her SUV, and went back to make sure the house was locked up before leaving the farm. She stopped at the foot of the hill to get the mail, handed it to him, and then they headed home.

Maggie was outside weeding flowerbeds when they drove up. She rocked back on her heels and waved as they got out.

"Everything okay there?" she asked.

Ladd nodded. "Sam was glad to see me."

"I'll bet he was," she said. "How do you feel after the ride?"

"I'm good," Ladd said.

"Good. Then sit out here and talk to me while I weed. You need some fresh air and sunshine, and I hate this job, so you can help me pass the time."

"I'll take that job," he said. He handed Deborah his mail and eased down on the steps.

"I'll help, Mom. Just let me put this stuff inside first."

A short while later, they were laughing and talking about old times and remember-when. And every once in a while Deborah would glance up and catch Ladd watching her, and her pulse would quicken.

He wanted her. Maybe as much as she wanted him.

———

That evening after supper, they drove back to check on the cat and the cattle. The herd was near the fence, grazing, and as Deborah and Ladd were coming up the driveway, Deborah spotted a cow with a long gash on the side of her hip.

"Ladd! Look! That cow has a huge cut on the side of her hip."

Ladd frowned. "We need to get her into the corral."

"Does she have a calf?" Deborah asked.

"Yes. A little red and white one with a red heart over one eye."

"Oh, I know that one," she said. She drove on to the barn, got a bucket with a few cubes in it, and a length of rope, and started out into the pasture.

The cattle saw her and started toward the barn, thinking they were going to get cubes.

"I'll get the gate," Ladd said.

Deborah frowned. "Please be careful. You're just now beginning to heal."

"I will," he said, and opened the corral gate, knowing the cattle would funnel into the corral and then they could separate the injured cow from the others and get her doctored.

The sound of cubes rattling in the bucket was all it took to get the herd moving toward Deborah, and as soon as she knew they were on the move, she turned around and led them in.

As soon as the injured cow and her calf came in, Ladd slammed the gate shut, leaving the rest of the herd out in the pasture.

"I'm going to get a rope on the cow and tie her up, then we'll let the others back out," Deborah said, and slowly moved around the interior of the corral until she got close enough to the injured cow to slip a rope over her head, then quickly tied her up short to one of the panels. "Okay, open the gate and I'll run the rest of them back out."

Within minutes, she was checking out the wound.

"The debris in here looks like tree bark. There's got to be a broken limb about *this* high somewhere in the woods. She could have been jostled against it, or if the herd got spooked she ran into it. I can clean her up, but I'll come back tomorrow and see if I can find it and saw it off clean."

Ladd frowned. "I need to be doing stuff like this," he muttered.

"Well, right now you can't, and I can. Do you have any kind of wound salve on the place?"

"Yes, in that first granary. There's an old wooden box with a hinged lid. I keep all of the vet meds in there."

She ran into the barn, located the box, and found what she needed, along with a handful of paper towels that she tore off a roll. She thought of all the meds she would have had at her disposal back at the clinic in Louisville and then shrugged it off and hurried back.

Ladd had hooked up a hose to the faucet by a stock tank and had a thin stream of water running, washing off the wound.

"Good job, honey," Deborah said, and checked the wound again. "I think you've got it cleaned out."

Ladd turned off the water then draped the hose over a post, while Deborah wiped down the area on the cow's hip with the paper towels.

The cow bawled and kicked, showing her disapproval with what was happening. Ladd slipped a hand beneath her jaw and started talking to her, calming her.

Deborah was applying a good amount of an antibiotic salve to the jagged cut when the little calf butted her knee.

"What's the matter, bud? Am I in your way?" she said, and tried to scratch him on the head, but he wasn't having any of it and butted her again. "I don't think he likes me messing with his mama," Deborah said.

Ladd was on the other side of the cow, making sure the rope was taut enough to keep her from tossing her head.

"We all have our limits of what we'll put up with," Ladd said.

Deborah looked up at him and grinned. "You weren't referring to me, were you?"

He laughed. "Hell no. I do not bite the hand that feeds me. You're my Wonder Woman, remember?"

Deborah's eyes narrowed. "I thought that was the drugs talking."

"Oh, the drugs were talking, all right, but all they did was remove my inhibitions. I'm still in shock at what an awesome freaking woman you grew up to be."

"Well, thank you, kind sir. And you'll have to show me your etchings one day soon. I saw a couple of drawings on your table. Are they of something you're working on, or something that has already been built?"

"Etchings?" He grinned. "They're a little of both, but surely you aren't insinuating that I have ulterior motives on you."

"Nothing ulterior about them," Deborah said. "You've been honest with me from day one. And all teasing aside, I'm in this with you all the way. Not everybody gets a second chance with their first love, but we did…we are. Now, let's get this girl and little butthead here in one of the stalls inside the barn for the night. If you'll open up the stall door, I'll lead her in."

"We'll need to leave her some hay and water," Ladd said.

"I know. Let's just get her inside. It's going to be dark soon."

And she was right.

But by the time night fell, they were already on their way back home.

Maggie was waiting for them on the porch as they drove up, then got out.

Deborah sighed. "Sorry, Mom. I should have called, but we found an injured cow and had to get her up and doctor her. Then we put her in the barn for the night."

Maggie frowned, then shook her head.

"Daughter, we're farmers. Something is always happening or delaying us, and nobody owes anyone else an explanation. If I was worried, I would have called. I love this time of day, when it's coming to a close. I always have. You two go on inside and get washed up. I took a pie out of the freezer. It's on the counter if you want some. Help yourselves. I'm just going to sit out here a little while longer."

Pie was eaten, and Maggie finally came inside. She went to watch television in her room, leaving them on their own.

They wound up playing poker in the kitchen. When they finally quit and went to bed, Deborah owed Ladd twenty thousand dollars and gave him an IOU.

She kissed him goodnight at his bedroom door, then dreamed about him all night long.

The next morning they were back at the farm, checking on the cow. Then she left Ladd in the house, borrowed his four-wheeler, and took off to the woods with a handsaw and her rifle.

As it turned out, she didn't need the rifle, but she did finally find a rather deadly looking stub on a chestnut tree that was about the right height to have caught that cow on the hip. The limb that had broken off was on the ground beneath and in varying states of decomposition, while the stub had aged and hardened, turning it into a deadly weapon. She got off the four-wheeler and sawed the stub off all the way down to the trunk, then tossed it in the back of the four-wheeler and headed back to the house.

Ladd heard her coming and walked out to meet her.

She pulled up and stopped, then pointed at the chunk of wood behind her.

"What do you think?" she asked.

Ladd frowned. "I think you found it, and damn! That would rip the hide off of any of us. Good job, honey."

"I'll park the four-wheeler. Do you want to leave the cow put up another day or so?"

"Yes, but let's turn her out in the corral for the day so that little bull of hers has some wiggle room."

"I'll toss down a bale of hay from the loft," Deborah said.

"And I'll fill up the water trough. We'll put her back up tonight."

"Deal," Deborah said.

He rode down to the barn on the four-wheeler with her, and then helped her get the cow and calf settled.

Sam came out to see them and wound himself around Ladd's ankles until Ladd relented and picked him up.

"I created a monster here, didn't I?" he said.

Deborah shook her head. "Sam is lucky to have you."

"You could have me, too, and you don't even have to kiss my ankles to do it," Ladd said.

Deborah threw her head back and laughed and laughed, and then threw her arms around his neck and kissed him until his ears were ringing from the blood-rush.

"You are such a man," she said.

He grinned. "Would you have me any other way?"

She pointed a finger at him in warning, and then climbed the loft to get the hay.

She could still hear him laughing all the way up there, and it made her heart sing. It had been a long time since she'd felt this alive. Strange how death in a family could do that, but it had. Maybe it was nature's way of reminding people not to miss out on what was left of their own lives.

# CHAPTER 14

DOWN IN BLESSINGS, A WHOLE NEW ASPECT OF LIFE WITH Carlie was about to begin. Peanut was back in the office, and Ruby was going back to work at the Curl Up and Dye, with Carlie in tow.

Carlie was just beginning to settle in at the Butterman home, but going to work with Miss Ruby was a whole new thing. She had her coloring book and crayons packed. A pillow and a blue blanket that she was going to leave at the shop, and an iPad for playing games.

And yesterday when Miss Ruby took her to pre-enroll in school, Carlie met her new teacher, Lena Schultz. She liked Mrs. Schultz. She had a nice, quiet voice and a kind smile. To her delight, Melvin Lee appeared with his grandma, Minna, as they were leaving.

"Hey, girl! Are you gonna be in Miz Schultz's class, too?" he asked.

Carlie nodded.

Melvin Lee grinned. "Hot dang! I'll be seeing you every day!"

Minna hid a grin and then winked at Carlie.

"Are you excited? I always loved school," she said.

Carlie nodded. "I like school, too."

"We'd better get out of the way. Looks like a line is forming," Ruby said.

"Bye, girl!" Melvin Lee yelled.

Ruby and Minna shared a laugh, and then Ruby and Carlie walked out into the hall and began walking toward the front exit. Their footsteps echoed in the building as they passed the other rooms, hearing parents and kids talking to their new teachers.

Carlie was a little anxious, but she was also excited. School was something she was good at. She looked up at Ruby as they walked, and thought how pretty Miss Ruby was, and how good it felt to hold her hand. It made her feel safe, and right now, safe was at the top of Carlie's list.

"Guess what?" Ruby said.

"What?" Carlie asked as they left the school and headed to the parking lot.

"We're going to meet Mr. Ruby at Granny's Country Kitchen and eat lunch together, and then Mr. Ruby is going to go up to the shop with us. Tomorrow, I go back to work, and he's going to hook up a television in the break room for you so you can watch your shows if you get tired playing. Does that sound okay with you?"

Carlie nodded.

"Good," Ruby said. "We're going to have a great time, you and me. I've never had a buddy to go to work with before. I know you'll start school soon, but until you do, we're a team, okay?"

Carlie beamed. "Yes…a team."

"And when you start school, it will always be either me or Mr. Ruby who takes you to school and picks you up. Okay?"

"Okay," Carlie said, and sighed with relief. One more question answered that she hadn't even asked but had wondered about. "Mama used to eat at Granny's. She told me."

"And now you'll find out for yourself that it's a pretty fun place to be and the food is very good."

"Will that Granny lady be there?" Carlie asked.

"You mean Lovey? She usually is. We'll find out when we get there," Ruby said. She buckled Carlie into her booster seat, then got in and drove away.

Carlie glanced at her reflection in the window as they drove. She looked the same, which was weird because everything about her world had changed.

Ruby saw Peanut's car as soon as she pulled into the parking lot, and smiled. This was their first meal out as a family, and he'd made sure not to be late.

"Looks like Mr. Ruby got here before us," Ruby said. "There's his car."

Carlie sat up and smiled. She'd never had a daddy before, and she liked to pretend he was hers. Then they got out and went inside.

Lovey was at the front register. She came out from behind the counter and gave Ruby a hug and then leaned over and hugged Carlie, too.

"I'm so happy you came to see me," Lovey said.

"My mama used to come here," Carlie said.

Lovey nodded. "I know, sugar. Her and your grandparents. Every Sunday after church. Mr. Ruby is already here. I'll show you where he's sitting."

They followed Lovey into the dining room, and as soon as Carlie realized people were looking at her, she reached for Ruby's hand.

Ruby gave it a quick squeeze and led her toward the booth where Peanut was waiting.

"There are my girls!" he said. He got up and gave Ruby a quick kiss on the cheek, and then helped Carlie up into the booth and gave her a quick kiss on the top of her head. "Did you get enrolled in school, honey?"

She nodded. "My teacher's name is Mrs. Schultz. She has happy eyes."

Peanut watched the expressions changing on Carlie's face and thought what an amazing child she was. Her life had been one hardship after another, and she still saw the world through the eyes of fairies and hummingbirds and gardens full of flowers.

"I know Lena Schultz. She's a nice lady," Peanut said.

Carlie glanced at Ruby. "Does she come to the Curl Up and Dye, too?"

Ruby nodded. "About once a month. Let's look at the menu and see what the special is today."

At that point, their waitress arrived with biscuits and took their drink orders, giving them time to decide what they wanted to eat. When Peanut squirted some honey on a biscuit for Carlie, she forgot about the strangers looking at her. She forgot about everything except the excitement of eating out and seeing her friend, Melvin Lee.

But Ruby hadn't forgotten a thing. She was thinking how swiftly a life could change. This time last week Carlie had watched her mother die, and now she was in Granny's eating honey on her biscuit and eyeing her Mr. Ruby with unabashed adoration. Ruby saw the times when sadness was with Carlie, but the times were becoming shorter and less intense. She felt like they were doing good, considering all that had happened.

———————

There were plenty of diners who were curious about the pretty little blond, although now they all knew her story and that Ruby was her legal guardian. They'd heard rumors that the child might be up for adoption, and other rumors that Peanut and Ruby were going to raise her. They might still be talking about that in the privacy of their own homes, but not in public. Not anymore. Not after word got around at how Ruby had cut Mary Faye and Petula off at the knees for speaking out of turn at Shirley Duroy's funeral. Nobody with a brain wanted to make an enemy of Ruby. Her hair salon was the only place to get hair done this side of Savannah, and that included barbering for men.

And it was plain to see the happiness between them. The little girl was obviously being well cared for, and they felt sorry for what had happened to her mother, and today was the day Mercy Pittman made pecan pies for Granny's. It was more important to get a piece before they ran out than it was to meddle in someone else's business.

Carlie was still licking honey from her fingers as Peanut and Ruby began making plans.

"I'll go to the shop and hook up the TV. It's in the back of my car, and I have the snacks you wanted for the shop as well. I'll put them in the mini-fridge," Peanut said.

"Thank you, darling," Ruby said. "We're going to the library. We need some new books for Carlie to have at the shop while I'm working."

Carlie leaned against Ruby's shoulder without thinking, but Ruby didn't miss the implication. Carlie was getting used to them. Comfortable with them. She felt safe with them. *Please, God, don't let anything happen to take that away from her.*

Later, as they stopped by the shop to drop off some books and check out the new TV, Ruby went to her workstation to check her appointment book. The girls had been making and moving appointments for her all week, but it was time to play catch-up. No surprises needed. She had to know what was on the week's agenda so she could prepare.

She was looking forward to getting back to work, but a little anxious as to how this would all play out. Only time would tell.

Tuesday dawned to a wall of heat and an inconvenient lack of moving air, which led most everyone with good sense to find something to do indoors.

It was a busy day at the Curl Up and Dye.

Ruby and Carlie arrived early to open up, to get Carlie settled and Ruby's workstation ready for her first appointment. She worked for almost an hour before she was ready to sit down, and was in the break room with Carlie when Vera and Vesta arrived.

Their delight at seeing Ruby and Carlie was real.

"Sister! It is so good to see you here again! We missed you. And we have been looking forward to having Carlie here with us."

Carlie looked up from her coloring book. "Just until I start school," she said.

Vera smiled. "Did you already get enrolled in school?"

Carlie nodded, and kept one eye on her cartoons as she continued to color.

Ruby leaned over and kissed the curls on Carlie's head.

"I'm going to work now, but if you need me, you know where to find me, right?"

Carlie nodded. "At your station."

"Good girl," Ruby said, then got up.

Vera and Vesta put their lunches in the refrigerator and then left the break room, talking in their twin-speak shorthand—finishing each other's sentences and laughing at inside jokes only they understood.

A couple of minutes later, Mabel Jean arrived, peeked in and waved at Carlie, gave her a thumbs-up, and hurried to her station because she had an appointment due to arrive in minutes.

The anxiety Carlie had felt quickly disappeared and she soon lost interest in the people coming and going. She was in her own little world in the back room, coloring pictures and watching old Looney Tunes cartoons.

---

Bart Carlson was back at work, and his boss none the wiser that Bart's marriage had blown up in his face. As for Bart, he couldn't quit thinking what might have happened if he'd pursued trying to take custody of Carlie Duroy.

Last night he'd awakened from a nightmare of epic proportions. In the dream, he'd walked in the house to discover Carlie sobbing and on her own, and Mila nowhere in sight.

The dream was so real that he'd thrown back the covers and walked through the house and out onto the patio, then took a deep breath and looked up. There wasn't much to see of the night sky for the glow of security lights and night-lights around his neighborhood, but he felt the vastness above him just the same.

Bart knew he had a really nice house, but he didn't live in it. He just slept here. His first try at making a family had been an abysmal failure, and he'd come far too close to ruining what was left of Carlie Duroy's life in the process.

"I hope you're happy, little girl. You damn sure deserve to be," Bart said softly, then went back into the house, reset the security alarm, and glanced at the time.

It was a quarter to four in the morning. Too late to go back to bed, but too early to get ready for work. He poked around the kitchen, then made coffee while eating peanut butter toast. When it was done, he sat down in his recliner, turned on the TV, and kicked back to watch one of the national news shows. And not once did he wonder where Mila was or what she was doing, because he didn't care.

———————

Mila had been in Paris two days.

She'd pouted throughout the entire flight over, wreaked havoc among the flight attendants, and woke herself up during the flight by crying in her sleep.

She was at a hotel for now, but she was already in contact with a Realtor. She was going to spend her way through Europe and make Milos sorry he'd done this. She was thinking of leasing for at least a year and using Paris as a base so she could travel to the countries of her choice to suit herself.

The problem was that traveling alone was boring. But she'd soon take care of that. There were pretty boys all over the world who were willing to hook up with anyone if the money was right. None of this was her idea. She'd gone along with it to soothe her father's rage, but she wasn't about to isolate herself for anyone.

And all of this happened because some stupid nobody of a

woman had a bad heart and died, leaving her daughter an orphan. If only Bart hadn't gotten it into his head to fight for custody, none of this would have happened. She just wasn't cut out to be the motherly type.

The sun was shining. The sidewalks were filled with throngs of people, and the streets were full of cars all going hither and yon, and the noise and the colors of the city were everywhere. She gave herself a quick glance in the mirror.

"You've got this," she said. "Paris awaits."

Then she slung the strap of her handbag over her shoulder and left the hotel.

———————

It was nearing lunchtime when Carlie came out into the salon and went over to where Ruby was sweeping up hair from a haircut she'd just finished.

"Are you getting hungry?" Ruby asked, as she hung up her broom. "I know I am."

"Yes. Can we eat our lunch now?" Carlie asked.

Ruby nodded. "I have a whole hour before my next appointment. I'm so ready to sit down and eat. Ladies, we'll be in the break room."

Carlie skipped on her way back. "I cleaned up the table," she said.

Ruby stopped and hugged her. "You are such a good helper. Thank you. Why don't you get our lunches out of the fridge while I wash up."

Happy to be in charge, Carlie hurried to the fridge and got the two plastic containers with red lids and carried them to the table, then got her lemonade and Miss Ruby's Pepsi and sat down to wait.

Ruby came out, plopped down on the sofa beside Carlie, and opened the lids on their containers.

"Mmm, ham and cheese for you. Ham and cheese for me. And these are our chips. Help yourself, sugar. I'm starved."

Carlie smiled. "I'm starved, too," she said, and to prove it, popped a potato chip in her mouth while Ruby unscrewed the lid on her lemonade.

As they ate, Ruby admired the pages she'd colored in her coloring book.

"Have you read any of your library books yet?" Ruby asked.

"Not yet. I'm saving those for after lunch," Carlie said, and then leaned over, her nose wrinkling as she whispered, "What's that funny smell?"

Ruby grinned. "Vera is giving her client a perm. Do you know what that is?"

Carlie took a bite of sandwich and shook her head.

Ruby ran her fingers through Carlie's soft white-blond curls.

"Well, not everyone is as lucky as you to have natural curls in their hair. So, for the people with straight hair who want curls, we roll their hair on different-colored rods, then put this stinky solution on the rolled-up hair. When we take out the rods, their hair is curly. Perms are smelly at first, but that goes away, and then the lady has pretty curly hair, just like you."

Carlie listened, then took another bite of sandwich as she digested that info. She was learning lots of new things with Miss Ruby.

They were still in the break room eating when the back door opened and Peanut appeared in the doorway, carrying a bag from the Crown bakery. "There's my two best girls!" he said. "I brought you a surprise. Snickerdoodles! Enough for everyone…including me!"

Carlie took another bite of her sandwich. "I like snickerdoodles," she said, talking around the food she was chewing.

Peanut laughed. "So do I, sugar. So do I." He snagged a cookie from the sack, kissed Ruby, and thumped the top of Carlie's head and winked, then took a bite of cookie as he walked out the door.

"I sure do like Mr. Ruby," Carlie said.

Ruby grinned. "So do I. Finish up your lunch, and if you're too full to eat a cookie now, we can take one out for you right now, wrap it up, and save it for later."

"Okay," Carlie said, but as soon as Ruby bagged up her cookie, she took it and put it on top of her box of crayons. "For later," she said, and took a big swig of lemonade.

At that point, the twins came into the break room, got their lunches to eat at their stations, and saw the sack.

"Help yourselves," Ruby said. "Peanut brought one for each of us."

Carlie sat quietly, absorbing the laughter and the happy sounds in the salon.

"Oops, my next client came early," Ruby said. She wrapped up what was left of her food and put it back in the fridge. "Take your time, honey. Want the TV back on?"

Carlie nodded, then packed up what was left of her food, too, put it in the refrigerator, and crawled up on the sofa. She sat for a moment, looking at the shelves with salon supplies, the pale-pink walls, and the old gray sofa on which she was sitting. She still thought about their apartment in Little Rock and the friends she'd had since pre-K. Sometimes it made her sad to think she would never see them again, and today she was sad she'd never see Mama again, either.

Then she sighed. But Mama was in her little house and Carlie was in the Curl Up and Dye watching Road Runner cartoons. Mama used to laugh and laugh at the Road Runner and the Coyote. Carlie liked Tom and Jerry better, but today, watching Road Runner almost made it feel like they were still connected.

Someone out in the salon said something funny, and all of the women laughed. Carlie liked being where people were happy. Even if she didn't know them, the laughter felt good, like a hug.

She turned the sound down a little bit on the cartoon and

then tucked Hoppy under her chin, pulled up the blanket they'd brought from home, and stretched out to watch her show.

The vent from the air-conditioning was just above her head. Her tummy was full, and the blanket was soft. She sighed and closed her eyes.

Just for a moment.

And fell sound asleep.

———————

Ruby's day at the Curl Up and Dye came to an end at just after 3:00 p.m. Normally, she would have stayed and chatted with the other customers as she did laundry, but not today. This had been a long day for Carlie, and she needed to be outside in the fresh air and run and play before bedtime.

Ruby had washed a load of towels earlier, and now they were nearly through drying. She was sweeping up around her station and waiting for the dryer to go off, so she could fold them and have them ready for tomorrow.

Vera and Vesta were working late, and Mabel Jean's last customer wasn't due for another hour. And then the dryer went off.

Ruby got a laundry basket, emptied the towels from the dryer to the basket, and carried them to the table in the break room to fold.

The TV was still on, the cookie Carlie put back to eat later was still on her coloring book, and she was curled up on the sofa with Hoppy under her chin, fast asleep.

"My poor baby," Ruby whispered. "Such a long, long day for you, and not a whisper of a complaint."

She grabbed a towel, still warm from the dryer, and quickly folded it, and then went through the basket, folding the rest without thought, and carried them into the salon and stacked them in the cupboard.

"Okay, girls, that's it for me. I need to get my little Sleeping

Beauty home for the day. Thanks for everything. Whoever is out last, lock up and turn out the lights as you go."

"No worries," Vera said. "We've got this. Tell Peanut thanks for the cookies."

"I sure will," Ruby said, then went into the break room, got her purse out of her locker, and sat down on the sofa beside Carlie. "Wake up, sweetheart. Work is over. It's time to go home."

Carlie stretched as she opened her eyes, and then sat up on the side of the sofa. "Home?"

"Yes. Somebody needs to go check on the fairies and see if the birds have water. And somebody needs to make supper."

"I'll do the fairies and the birds," Carlie said, and slid off the sofa with Hoppy under one arm.

Ruby smiled. "Then I'll make supper."

"Maybe Mr. Ruby is home already," Carlie said.

"I hope so. I like it when all my family is together, don't you?" Ruby said.

Carlie glanced up at Ruby. "Am I your family?"

"You bet your bottom dollar," Ruby said and wrapped her arms around her and hugged her tight.

Carlie giggled, but she was hugging her back. "What's a bottom dollar?" she asked.

"It's the last one. The one on the bottom of your purse, and I'm betting my last dollar on you, sugar. You're our girl forever...if you want to be."

Carlie sighed. She must have done all the right things after all because Miss Ruby didn't want to give her away.

"I want to be your girl and Mr. Ruby's girl. Mama said you would be a good guard, but I think you're the best guard ever."

Ruby was blinking furiously, doing everything she could not to cry.

"Thank you, honey. Thank you. We love you a bunch. Now, let's go home, okay? You can leave your coloring book and crayons here if you want, or pack them up in your tote and take them with you."

"Are we coming back here tomorrow?" Carlie asked.

"Yes. Tomorrow is a workday, too."

"Then I'll leave them here," Carlie said. She grabbed Hoppy and slid off the sofa.

Ruby took her by the hand as they slipped out the back door.

———

Peanut was home when Ruby and Carlie pulled up beneath the carport. He was looking forward to seeing them and anxious to give Carlie her surprise.

Earlier in the day he'd had to go to the courthouse in Savannah. When he was finished, he'd stopped by Walmart again, but this time he'd skipped the toy section and gone to the garden department, specifically to the area where little fairy houses made of pottery were displayed.

He picked out one that looked like a mushroom, one that looked like a tiny English cottage, one that was covered in colorful flowers, and one that looked like a stalk of broccoli with a little door and window. Then he picked out accessories to go with them, and a little garden gnome, a fairy, a little elf pushing a wheelbarrow, and a little mouse wearing a dress, a bonnet, and an apron. Carlie had been looking in vain for fairies. Maybe they just needed to know they were welcome.

And then he heard them coming in the back door and got up from his recliner and went to meet them.

"I'm so glad you're home early," Ruby said.

"Me too," Peanut said. He swooped her up in his arms and danced her around the kitchen, with her feet dangling above the floor.

Carlie laughed, and Peanut saw the delight in her eyes and put Ruby down.

"Next!" he said, and scooped Carlie up and danced her around the kitchen table.

Her giggles and laughter were music to their ears. He gave her a quick kiss on the cheek and then put her down and pointed at the sack on the table.

"I had to go to the courthouse in Savannah today," he said. "I brought you something for the garden."

"For Miss Ruby?" Carlie asked.

"No. For you. Look and see."

She was still giggling when she climbed up on a chair and began pulling out the items inside the sack.

She gasped when she saw the fairy. She hugged the little mouse, then danced the elf across the table to meet the fairy before pulling out the little garden gnome.

"There's another sack," Peanut said, and picked it up from beneath the table. "They need their own little houses, right? So, now you have four houses for your little people. I thought you could find places to put them, like under the bushes or in a flower bed…whatever you think they'd like."

"Thank you, Mr. Ruby! I love them. So much!"

Ruby was beaming. "Peanut Butterman, you are the best."

"That's what I hear," he drawled. "Do you want me to help you carry them outside?" he asked.

Carlie glanced up at Ruby.

"Run on," she said. "I'll let you both know when supper is ready."

"What are we having?" Peanut asked.

"Pork chops, mashed potatoes and gravy, and green beans."

"Yum," Peanut said.

"Yum," Carlie echoed, and kicked off her shoes before putting her little people back in the sack.

"You carry that one. I'll carry the heavy one," he said, and out the door they went, both of them barefoot. Both of them laughing and talking like best friends the same age.

Ruby sighed. It was part of Peanut's gift. It was why he got people to confess their guilt on the stand. Why everyone loved him. Why he had the dumbest name in the world and was still sexy as hell.

She watched them for a few moments and then turned away from the window and went to change clothes. Those pork chops weren't going to cook themselves.

———

Peanut watered while Carlie went about matching up houses and little people, then set them up in the gazebo before going on a search to find where their homes should be.

She was down on her belly, clearing off a space beneath the lilac bush for the mushroom house and the garden gnome. Then she slipped between a cluster of azaleas and put the little mouse and the English cottage beneath the lowest branches for safety and shelter.

The little house that looked like a stalk of broccoli with a door and a window was the little elf's house, because the elf was wearing green and the little house was green. She found a place in Miss Ruby's tulip bed for that one, and when she stepped back to look, it blended in so well with the tall green leaves that she couldn't see it.

The last one was the little house that looked like a tree. It also had a tiny door and window, and she was certain the fairy would like living there. She put them in the flower bed with the blue bachelor buttons and the pink phlox and sunny-yellow marigolds, because she was certain fairies liked the tiny flowers best.

Then she sat cross-legged in front of the fairy's house and "flew" the fairy over the blossoms and slipped her in among the greenery beside it. Resting her elbows on her knees, she leaned forward, whispering, "I think you might have a sister here, but I can't find her. If you see her, tell her I said hello."

A butterfly flitted across her line of sight, and for just a second she imagined it was the fairy, finally coming to say hello. And then she sighed and looked up. Mr. Ruby was finished watering and sitting on the gazebo steps, watching. He waved.

She gave her fairy one last look. "I'll see you tomorrow evening. Have a good night." Then she got up and went running to where Peanut was sitting.

"Did you get them all fixed up?" he asked as she slid to a stop in front of him.

Carlie nodded.

"I'm hungry. How about you?"

"Yes. For pork chops."

He grinned, then stood up and took her by the hand.

"How about we go see if Miss Ruby has supper about ready? We're both pretty dusty, so we'll need to wash up really good before we sit down at the table, right?"

"Right," Carlie said, and off they went, walking in companionable silence.

Ruby was at the stove, taking the last pork chops out of the pan, when they came in the back door.

"Did you get everybody moved into their new houses?" she asked.

"Yes!" Carlie said and held up her grimy little hands. "I'm going to wash myself," she added, and ran out of the room.

Peanut held up his huge hands. "I'm going to wash myself, too," he said, and winked at her as he walked past.

Ruby sighed. *So this is what it feels like to have children. I like it.*

———————

Supper was long over.

Ruby washed Carlie's hair to get the leaves and grass out of it, then let her play in a bubble bath while her hair air-dried. By the time she got her out of the tub and into pajamas, Carlie almost fell into bed.

"Here's Hoppy," Ruby said. "Are you too tired to hear a story?"

"No. I want a story," Carlie mumbled, and pulled Hoppy up beneath her chin.

Ruby dug out *Frog and Toad Are Friends*, one of the books Carlie had brought from home, tucked her in, then began to read.

Carlie's eyes were closed, but she was listening. They were the same words in the same book when Mama had read them, but Miss Ruby's voice was not Mama's voice. And every day that passed, it was becoming a little bit easier to accept the difference as okay.

By the time Ruby finished, Carlie was sound asleep. Ruby leaned over and kissed her forehead, then whispered near her ear, "You are loved, little one. Sleep well."

# CHAPTER 15

THE REST OF THE WEEK AT THE CURL UP AND DYE PASSED LIKE clockwork. By Saturday, Carlie had her hair trimmed, her fingernails painted, and was far beyond the shy little girl who'd hidden out in the break room the first day.

She was mindful, and helpful, and folded towels like a pro. She kept the magazines stacked neatly up front in the waiting area and took the feather duster to all the bare surfaces.

She was among women, and in her element.

And it was good.

Carlie Duroy was getting her sass back.

---

The Buttermans went to church on Sunday.

Within seconds of them walking over the threshold, Melvin Lee saw them and came running.

"Hey, girl! Hey, y'all," he added, making sure to include Peanut and Ruby in his greeting.

Peanut grinned. "Good morning, Melvin Lee. Are you looking forward to going back to school?"

"Yep," Melvin Lee said, and then gave them all a big smile. "Look. No teeth."

There was a gap where two teeth should have been.

Carlie gasped. "What happened?"

"They just fell out. I'm a late bloomer. Getting ready to get my man teeth. No more baby teeth for me, I tell ya."

Ruby grinned. He was such a delight that she wanted to hug him, but Melvin Lee wasn't a hugger. "Congratulations," she said. "Did you leave them for the tooth fairy?"

"Yes, ma'am. A dollar a tooth. I'm saving my money. Once they all fall out, I might have enough to get me a new bike."

About that time, Minna came up the aisle with an irked look on her face.

"There you are. Come on, Melvin Lee. It's time to sit down. Church is about to begin."

"Okay, Grandma," he said, and then pointed at Carlie. "When it's time to go to our Sunday school class, I'll come get you. You don't know which room it's in, but I do." Then he gave Peanut a toothless grin. "Don't worry about your girl. I got this."

Peanut was still shaking his head when they slid into their seats, with Carlie between them.

"Hey, Carlie. What do you think about Melvin Lee?"

"He's my first friend in Blessings. He's smart and he don't take no guff."

Ruby blinked. "Uh, when did he tell you that?"

"When we were going up and down the slide at the park. He's smart, Mr. Ruby. Mama always said leave the dumb boys alone, but Melvin Lee is smart, and he's my friend."

"Good enough," Peanut said, and put his arm over the back of the pew. That way he had Carlie in the shelter of his arm and his hand on Ruby's shoulder.

And then the service began. About thirty minutes later, everyone began moving to their respective classrooms for Sunday school.

As promised, Melvin Lee came after Carlie with all the fervor of a knight in shining armor on a charging horse and grabbed her by the hand.

"Let's go, girl. We don't want to be the last ones in the room, or we'll wind up havin' to sit beside Keith Dillon."

"What's wrong with sitting beside Keith?" Peanut asked.

"He farts!" Melvin Lee said.

"Eww," Carlie said.

"'Zackly," Melvin Lee added. "I'll bring her back when it's over, Miss Ruby. Don't worry."

"I know," Ruby said. "You got this."

Melvin Lee nodded, and off they went, with Carlie hanging onto his hand as if her life depended on it.

"You think she'll be okay?" Ruby asked.

Peanut arched an eyebrow. "My money's on Melvin Lee."

Ruby sighed and looked back down the hall, trying to find them in the melee of heads and kids all moving into three separate classrooms.

Peanut gave her a quick hug. "Ruby, honey, she's about to go into third grade. She's been taking care of her mother for two solid years, and Melvin Lee Wilson is holding her hand, and she's under the Lord's roof. I think she's gonna be fine."

---

And Peanut was right.

When Sunday school classes ended and they all began making their way back up toward the sanctuary, they started looking for Carlie.

Instead, they saw Melvin Lee standing outside the ladies' restroom with his arms folded, looking like every married man waiting on his wife to come out. All he needed was to be holding a purse.

"Where's Carlie?" Ruby asked.

"In there with Grandma. She had to take Lucy, so Carlie went, too."

"I'll just go in and check on her," Ruby said.

Melvin Lee sighed. "There's a line. There's always a line in the ladies' room. Mama says it's a woman's curse to have a little bladder."

Peanut burst out laughing.

Ruby frowned and pushed her way inside, coming out moments later with Carlie in hand.

"Thank you, Melvin Lee. You are a good friend," Ruby said.

"Yes, ma'am," he said, and then waved at Carlie. "Bye, girl."

"Bye, Melvin Lee. Do unto others."

"Just like they do to you," he said, and then followed Minna and his little sister, Lucy, up the hall.

"Is that the verse they taught you in class today?" Ruby asked as they headed back into the sanctuary.

"Mostly," Carlie said, and skipped once, just before they reached their pew.

"Mostly," Peanut echoed, and then grinned.

———————————

One week later, Deborah and Ladd were at his place before 8:00 a.m., watching the roofer she'd hired using his big magnet to pick up the roofing nails she'd dumped in the breezeway of Ladd's barn. He'd been delayed from his previous appointment, and she was glad it was finally happening. Then she would be taking Ladd to get the staples out of his head and hoping he'd be released to drive again. His ribs didn't hurt nearly as much as they had in the beginning and only when he tried to lift. The roofer finally left with twenty bucks in his pocket for about fifteen minutes' work, and Ladd had his bucket of roofing nails back.

"I hope he got them all," Deborah said.

"We'll know soon enough next time someone drives into the breezeway," Ladd said. "So let's get back to your mom's. I need to change clothes before we go into town."

Deborah nodded, and then got in her car and drove home. She was driving him into town, but she was torn about what the doctor would say about his healing. If Ladd was well enough to move home, that meant she wouldn't be seeing him as often, and she'd gotten used to his face, and his hugs, and his kisses.

When they got back home, they found Maggie getting ready to go to the truck garden, which was a larger patch of garden fenced off between the chicken house and the barn. The fruit trees were in that plot of ground, as were the rows of potatoes and field peas. The rows of purple hulls were loaded and ready for a first picking.

Deborah liked crowder and black-eyed peas just fine, but purple hulls were her favorite. She eyed her mother as she put on her old gardening shoes and got her wide-brimmed straw hat to keep the sun off her face.

"How about I drive the Gator up from the shed, and you can haul the peas back to the house in it. I'll help you shell later."

"That would be helpful, darlin'," Maggie said.

Deborah grabbed the Gator key from the key rack by the door. "Tell Ladd I'll be right back," she said, and took off out the door at a lope.

Maggie shook her head as she watched her go, envying her daughter's long legs, then dug around on a shelf by the back door for mosquito spray. She was spraying the arms of her shirt and the legs of her jeans when Ladd walked up behind her.

"Want me to spray your back, too?" he asked.

"Yes, please," Maggie said, and handed him the can. "Mosquitoes and gnats love to chew on me," she said.

Ladd sprayed her from her shoulders all the way down to her ankles, then handed her the can. "You're good to go, Maggie. Hey, where's Deborah?"

Maggie pointed at the green John Deere four-wheeler that came shooting out of the shed and the dark-haired girl driving it.

"She's bringing up the Gator for me. I'm going to the truck garden to pick peas."

"I love those peas. I'll help you shell," Ladd said.

Maggie grinned. "I won't say no. They're tedious to get out of their shells, but they're also tasty. I hope you get an A-okay from the doctor today. It will be a relief to sleep without staples, right?"

"Yes, ma'am," Ladd said, and then watched Deborah come to a sliding halt outside the back porch and put the Gator in park.

When she swung her leg over the steering wheel and jumped off, his gut knotted. He dreamed of making love to her. Nightly. Surely to God, that was going to happen soon.

"Hey, Mom, your ride awaits," Deborah said as she came into the kitchen. "I put a couple of bushel baskets in the back for you. Don't get too hot, and if you think of something we need from town, call me. If we're still there, I'll pick it up before we leave."

"Will do," Maggie said. "Drive safe. I'll see you both later." She blew them a kiss before heading out the door.

Deborah stood for a few moments, watching to make sure Maggie was safely aboard and on her way to the truck garden, then turned around.

"Let me wash my hands and change shoes, then I'm ready. Are you?"

"More than ready," he said, still thinking of making love to her.

A few minutes later, they were out the door and heading into town.

"You know, I was just thinking, we could have had your roofer use that magnet on my head and pull out the staples, and we wouldn't be going into town," Ladd said.

Deborah frowned. "What a horrible image that just put in my head. Uh…no…and hell no."

Ladd laughed and then rubbed his hand over the staples.

"I'll be so glad to get them out. It feels like I have a zipper on the back of my head."

"I can only imagine," Deborah said. "I'll be glad for you, too."

"Do I get sympathy sex when they're out?" Ladd asked.

Deborah laughed.

Ladd sighed and spoke to his reflection in the passenger side window. "She laughed. I fear that may mean no."

Deborah was still grinning when the highway below finally came into view. She was braking to a stop to check for traffic when a truck pulling a horse trailer passed in front of them, heading toward Blessings.

"That driver has a heavy foot," Deborah said. "He's pulling that trailer too fast."

She looked both ways before pulling out behind it, but the truck and trailer were swiftly disappearing into the distance.

All of a sudden, the truck swerved toward the ditch, then over-corrected, which made the trailer swing from side to side. To their horror, the horse trailer suddenly flipped over on its side, while the truck was still moving. Sparks from the metal scraping on concrete began flying out from under it, like sparks from fireworks on the Fourth of July.

"Oh my God!" Deborah cried and accelerated. "Call it in, Ladd. The truck is going to flip, too. There's no way it can't."

And she was right.

Ladd was on the phone with 911, giving directions and a play-by-play of what they were witnessing. Even with the windows up and the air-conditioning running, they could hear the squeal of metal on the highway and see the sparks flying up from the pavement as both truck and trailer were now sliding down the highway.

Finally, everything came to a stop with the trailer on the shoulder of the highway and the truck upside down in front of it, still connected to each other. Smoke was boiling up from the truck when Deborah slammed on the brakes and put her car in park.

"Stay here," she said.

Ladd frowned. "Hell no, I'm not—"

Deborah grabbed his arm. "Ladd! Please! I can't help them if I'm worrying about you. Just stay on the phone with the police. We have one lane of traffic blocked, a driver trapped in a truck that might burst into flames, and there's a horse in that trailer. We need the highway patrol, an ambulance, the fire truck, a tow truck, and a vet ASAP."

"Shit…but understood," Ladd muttered, and started making calls back to 911 to add to their initial report.

Deborah opened the back of her SUV, grabbed a tire iron and a length of rope, and started running.

—————

Roy Andrews had been working his roping horse, Fancy Dancer, ever since just after daybreak, and was just getting ready to head for the stables with him when he noticed blood on the ground.

He dismounted and got down to look, and when he did, blood dripped on his arm.

"What the hell?" he muttered, and then turned around.

That's when he saw blood pouring from Dancer's nostrils. Scared, he headed to the stables with him at a walk and quickly put him in a stall, then called his vet, only to find out the vet was twenty miles away on an emergency. He glanced back in the stall and was horrified to see Dancer standing with his head down and a growing puddle of blood near his front hooves.

Roy didn't hesitate. He made a run for his truck, hooked up the horse trailer, and then walked Dancer into the trailer, shut and locked the trailer gate, and jumped in the truck.

It was over a half-hour drive to Dr. David Angelos, the vet on the other side of the county, but Roy was too worried to wait. He took off out of the driveway, calling the clinic as he went to let him know he was coming.

"Bring him straight in to the big barn," Dr. Angelos said.

"Will you be there?" Roy asked.

"Yes. We'll be waiting," Angelos said.

Roy disconnected, and took off down the driveway from his ranch to the highway. Dancer was his best roping horse, and this had come out of nowhere. Roy was sick about how long it was going to take him to get to the clinic north of Blessings and scared to death they couldn't fix Dancer, even after he got there.

The first fifteen minutes on the road felt like an hour, and he imagined Dancer bleeding out in the trailer. Then he got behind three cars in a no-passing zone and nearly lost his mind.

Finally, he pulled out around them on a flat stretch of road and accelerated, and even after he'd passed them, he just kept going. Both hands on the wheel and his gaze fixed on the highway in front of him, counting down the mile markers as he passed them, and praying.

He was about three miles outside of Blessings when his back tire blew. The disintegrating tire pulled him toward the ditch, and as he was trying to slow down, he overcorrected. In the rearview mirror, he saw the trailer jerk and then start shaking and knew instantly that some part of the tongue hooking the trailer to his hitch had either broken or come undone.

He was trying desperately to stop when he saw the trailer tip, and then it was on its side, sparking metal to concrete as he was trying to bring the truck to a halt. But when he stomped the brakes, the truck flipped, and everything went black.

---

Deborah glanced into the two-stall horse trailer as she ran past. The back gate had popped open, and she could see a big black horse on its side, kicking and screaming.

"Oh my God…poor baby," she muttered, but the truck was smoking, and she needed to get the driver out first.

Because it was upside down, she had to get down on her knees to get a good look at the driver, and what she saw stopped her heart. The windshield was shattered, but still in place. The driver was still buckled in, but hanging upside down. He wasn't moving, and she didn't know whether he was dead or just unconscious.

She crawled back out, then began trying to open the doors, but they were both jammed, so she crawled back to the windshield with her tire iron and began stabbing and swinging at the windshield until it finally began coming out of the frame.

Smoke was boiling up around her, blinding her when she

needed to see, but she didn't hesitate and crawled into the cab of the truck to feel for a pulse. To her relief, the driver was alive, so she began feeling along the seatbelt for the release. Once it was beneath her fingers, she gave it a pop.

Within seconds, the man began sliding down and out of the seat belt, until he was lying unconscious on what was actually the roof of the cab. She grabbed both of his arms and began pulling, and kept pulling until she had him out of the cab, then began trying to drag him away from the wreck.

All of a sudden, Ladd was beside her. "I've got one hand, you get the other. We need to get him farther away in case this thing blows!" he said.

Deborah panicked. "Dammit! I told you to—"

"Pull, baby, pull," Ladd said. "We can fight about this later."

And so they pulled until the man was a safe distance away.

"Stay with him," Deborah said, and ran back to get her tire iron and rope, and then headed for the horse trailer.

There was blood everywhere, and the horse was still screaming and kicking. It was in the stall that was flat against the highway, which meant the only thing between the horse and the pavement was the metal of the trailer. She had no way to tell if it had peeled back the metal as it was being dragged, because if it had the horse would be seriously wounded.

Even if she could get to the rope at the front of the trailer to untie him, he was flat on his side. She couldn't get him out, and watching the horse suffer was maddening.

And then all of a sudden, a multitude of things began happening at once.

Two pickup trucks going in different directions pulled up at the crash site and stopped. The drivers got out on the run. One was Duke Talbot. The other was Jake Lorde.

They both recognized Ladd kneeling beside a man in the ditch, and then they saw Deborah.

"What can we do?" Duke yelled.

Deborah ran toward them. "I need to pull this trailer upright or we'll never get this horse out alive. There's blood everywhere inside."

"I've got a log chain in the back of the truck," Duke said, and ran to get it.

Duke and Jake threaded the chain through the broken windows on the side of the trailer, then hooked it to Duke's truck. At Deborah's direction, Duke began to back up.

At first it appeared as if the metal on the horse trailer would just pull off the frame, and then the chain reached its length and held firm. After that, the horse trailer began to tilt. As that was happening, the tow truck arrived from Blessings and a highway patrol car from the direction of Savannah.

The patrolman took over directing traffic.

The tow-truck driver hooked onto the other end of the trailer, and as they began to pull in unison, the trailer came upright, rocked on its wheels, and then settled. The moment the horse was upright, Deborah bolted into the empty stall beside it to assess its injuries.

While she was inside with the horse, the ambulance arrived from town, followed a couple of minutes later by Dr. Angelos, the vet, pulling a horse trailer.

The EMTs headed for the victim as Angelos got out on the run and headed for the trailer. He didn't know there was a woman inside until he stepped in and saw her.

"Hello there," he said, eyeing the blood all over her. "Were you in the truck with Roy Andrews?"

Deborah realized this man knew the driver.

"No. We just happened to witness the wreck. I'm a vet. My name is Deborah Ryman. I haven't found a wound, but there's blood coming out of both nostrils, and blood everywhere inside here."

"My name is David Angelos, and this man was on his way to my clinic when this happened. All he said was his horse was bleeding profusely from both nostrils and it wouldn't stop."

Deborah nodded. "Well, we witnessed the wreck. Not sure what happened, but one tire is shredded so I'm guessing a blow-out. Anyway, the truck swerved, causing the trailer to roll over on its side. It got pulled at least fifty yards on its side before the truck rolled and stopped, and this horse has been kicking and screaming from ever since I got here until we pulled the trailer upright."

"Oh hell," the vet muttered, then ran back to his truck to get his bag.

Deborah moved closer to the horse, who was standing with his head down, shaking in every muscle.

"Easy, boy, easy," Deborah said, and scooted through the tiny aisle at the front of trailer then eased into the stall beside the horse, still talking as she ran her hand along the side he'd been lying on. She couldn't see any obvious wounds or breaks, but blood was still dripping from the horse's nose. She tugged on his halter just enough to get him to lift his head, and as she did, a foul odor drifted up her nose.

Frowning, she ran her hand along the underside of his jaw and then back down his neck.

"You are such a beauty," she said, still stroking and talking in a calm, even tone.

Dave Angelos stepped into the trailer again, and when he did, Deborah moved back to the empty stall and then out of the way.

"There's a pretty foul odor coming out of his nose or mouth, can't tell which. Might be polyps. They'll cause bleeding like this, but I'm not telling you anything you don't already know. Do you need help loading him into your trailer?"

Angelos shook his head. "There are plenty of people here to help if I need it," he said.

Deborah nodded. "Then, since this is your client, I'll get my friend and we'll go on our way. He's supposed to be getting a bunch of staples out of his head today."

"Good lord," David said. "What happened to him?"

"He got tossed by a neighbor's bull. He's still healing, but not patiently. I hope you can help this big fella. He sure is a beauty."

"Do you live around here?" the vet asked.

"I grew up on a farm south of here. I've been working with a big-animal clinic in Louisville for several years, but I just moved home to be with my mom. My dad just died."

"I'm sorry for your loss," he said. "If you're looking for a job, come see me. Angelos Veterinary Services. We're online. Give me a call."

"I'll keep that in mind," Deborah said. "And good luck with the horse and its owner."

She walked out of the trailer and looked around for Ladd, but he was nowhere in sight. She started walking through the crowd of people and emergency vehicles, and then saw him sitting in her car, right where she told him to wait.

She breathed a big sigh of relief and hastened her stride. When she got in, he handed her a whole handful of wet wipes from the canister on the floor of her SUV.

"You're a mess," he said.

She grinned. "Last time I took you to the doctor, the blood all over me was yours, and I showed up in a bra but no shirt. And now I'm bloody all over again. You're gonna have to go in by yourself to get the staples out. I can't be seen in public like this." She began cleaning the blood and dirt from her hands as best she could. "How's the driver? Do you know?"

"He hadn't regained consciousness when the EMTs left with him."

"The vet knows him. The driver's name is Roy Andrews, and he was on his way to Dr. Angelos's clinic when he wrecked. Now, let's go get those staples out," she said.

Ladd buckled up as Deborah wove her way through the chaos. Once the highway was clear ahead of them, she sped up.

Ladd was quiet for a couple of minutes, and then he reached over the console and lightly touched her arm.

"I'm pretty sure I've said this before, but it bears repeating. You are an amazing woman."

She sighed. "I didn't do anything amazing."

"Yes. Yes, you did. I'm alive because of you, and now so are that driver and his horse."

She shrugged. "You do what's needed when the time arises, right? And there's the city limit sign. I'll have you at the hospital in no time. They told me to just bring you into the ER to get the staples out rather than sit and wait in one of the doctors' offices. I'm going to drop you off at the entrance, then wait in the parking lot."

"I was expecting you to be at my side, holding my hand," he said.

"So was I. But plans change. Find out when they want to see you again about your ribs, and make an appointment."

Ladd just sat and nodded, letting her direct and order because he knew that's what she needed to do to calm down.

And then they were driving up Main. Someone honked at them, and Ladd glanced up just as Peanut Butterman drove past them.

They waved back, and passed Granny's and Crown Grocers before turning off Main toward the hospital. Deborah pulled under the covered entrance long enough to let him out.

"I'll be right out here," she said.

Ladd paused, his hand on the door handle. "It's all good, baby. Just take a deep breath and give yourself time to regroup while I'm inside. Hopefully, it won't take long."

Then he closed the door and went inside.

Deborah hated that she was leaving him to do this on his own, but she was nothing short of a bloody mess. So she drove away from the entrance and found a place near the front so she could watch for him to come out.

# CHAPTER 16

IT DIDN'T TAKE LONG FOR LADD TO BE TAKEN BACK TO THE exam area. His procedure was a simple one, and at the moment they only had one other patient in the ER—the driver Deborah had pulled out of the wreck.

Ladd saw him in an exam room as they were walking past, and the man was hysterical.

"Please! Somebody tell me if Dancer is okay," he kept saying.

Ladd paused and glanced at his nurse.

"I was at the scene of that wreck. I know the vet has his horse. Hearing that might calm him down a little."

"Wait here," she said, and darted into the exam room and whispered in Dr. Quick's ear. A few moments later, she came out to get Ladd. "Dr. Quick said for you to come in."

Ladd stepped into the room and then to the foot of the bed.

"Hey, dude… My name is Ladd. My girl is a vet. We witnessed the wreck. She pulled you out of your truck and then helped get the horse trailer on its wheels. Your vet arrived while she was inside with your horse. It was on its feet and the vet was loading it up in his trailer when we left, so if it helps, I know it's in good hands."

"Oh my God! Thank you," the injured man said. "My name is Roy Andrews. I rodeo, and Fancy Dancer is my best roper. Tell your girl I said thank you…for everything."

"I will," Ladd said. "Good luck," he said, and then followed the nurse down to another exam room.

The nurse eyed him as she seated him on the bed. "Dr. Frank is subbing here today for one of the other doctors. He'll be here shortly to remove your staples. We may have you lie down on your stomach to—"

"Nope. That's not happening," Ladd said, and patted his chest. "Broken ribs are still healing. I can't even sleep on my side yet."

"Oh. Wow. Sorry. I didn't know. No problem. I'll just have you sit down in that chair so Dr. Frank has a better view."

"That I can do," Ladd said, and took a seat in the straight-backed chair beside the bed.

"He'll be right here," the nurse said, and left to go get a tray set up.

Within a few minutes, a middle-aged man with a face as red as his hair walked in wearing a white lab coat. The nurse was right behind him, pushing a cart with an assortment of instruments and disinfectants.

"Good morning. Ladd Daltry, is it?"

"Yes, sir," Ladd said.

"I'm Dr. Frank. I understand we're removing staples from your head. Let's have a look."

He walked behind Ladd, checked out the staples and the stage of healing his head was in, and then nodded.

"Yes, they're ready to come out, so let's get started."

Ladd didn't look. He didn't need to see what they were doing. He just wanted them out.

He barely felt the first two they took out, but there were a couple that stung pretty good, and then again the last one nearest the bottom of his hairline. The whole time the doctor was taking them out, Ladd was getting an earful about the softball league Dr. Frank's teenage daughter had played in last night in Savannah and that she was the star pitcher for her team. They'd won their game by three runs and had another game tonight.

Ladd closed his eyes, letting the conversation roll over him while thinking how freaking good it was going to feel not to be sleeping with metal in his head tonight.

"Okay, that's the last one," Doctor Frank said as he dropped the staple into the pan with a clink. "Now, what's this about broken ribs, too? How about you get back up on the bed for me and pull off your shirt."

Ladd traded the chair for the bed, then pulled the T-shirt over his head, leaving his upper torso bare.

Doctor Frank eyed the fading bruises as he felt along Ladd's upper body.

"How's the pain level?" he asked.

"It's pretty good. I quit the pain pills and take over-the-counter stuff now when I need it."

Frank nodded. "So, continue as you were directed. Ribs take a while to heal, so no heavy lifting, for sure. And I'd check back with your regular doctor in a couple of weeks. He might want to x-ray you again to check progress. For now, take it easy when you wash your hair. You still have a few places that need to heal a bit more, okay?"

"Yes, sir," Ladd said, then ran his hands lightly over the back of his head. The absence of metal felt amazing. "Am I good to go now?"

Doctor Frank nodded. "I'd say so. But you know what to do if you start experiencing any trouble. If you start feeling congestion in your lungs, or like you're getting a fever, don't fool around. Get to your doctor."

Ladd nodded, then put his shirt back on.

The doctor signed off on his visit, and the nurse walked him out. When they passed Roy Andrews's room again, he was on the phone. Ladd heard Roy's side of the conversation as he was passing.

"Yes, baby, they're going to release me soon. You'll have to come get me. I totaled the truck. Don't cry, sugar. I'll be okay. I just want to go check on Dancer."

At that point, Ladd thought of the woman waiting for him out in the parking lot and walked faster.

Deborah was on the phone with her mom, telling her all about the wreck, when she saw Ladd coming out of the ER. "Hey, Mom, gotta go. I see Ladd coming. We'll be heading home now."

"Take your time, honey. Stay and have lunch at Granny's if you want."

Deborah laughed. "No way. When I said I had blood on my clothes again, I meant it."

"Oh dear," Maggie said. "Well, maybe another time. See you soon."

"Yes, ma'am," Deborah said. She started the car, then backed out of the parking place and started driving toward Ladd. He met her halfway and got in.

"Everything go okay? Are you all right?" she asked.

"A-okay. Right as rain," he said.

She smiled. "That sounded like your dad."

Ladd reached for the seatbelt and buckled up. "It did, didn't it?" he said, and then leaned across the console and kissed her. "Roy Andrews says thank you for saving him and his horse."

"Oh, you talked to him?" Deborah said.

"Long enough to let him know the vet has his horse. He was raising all kinds of hell about it, wanting to know what had happened to him. It appears Fancy Dancer is his best roper."

She grinned. "Nice name. So he rodeos?"

"Apparently. And I have a favor to ask," Ladd said.

"Name it," Deborah said.

"Go through the drive-through at Broyles Dairy Freeze. I'm buying drinks."

"Ooh, I would love a Coke, and hopefully they can't see much of the blood on my clothes."

He winked. "Well, you could take the shirt off like you said you did last time, but they might arrest you for indecent exposure."

"I was decent enough," she muttered.

"I'm just sorry I missed it," he said.

"Patience, Ladd. I'll take it all off for you one of these days."

He groaned. "Let's go get those Cokes. I need something cold in my belly to offset the fires you keep starting."

She laughed as they drove away.

They got their cold drinks and then headed home, retelling the story of the wreck as they went, and still marveling that both man and horse had lived through it. But while Deborah was driving, Ladd was thinking.

The removal of the staples and the thumbs-up from the doctor about his ribs pretty much removed the reasons he'd been staying with Deborah and Maggie.

When it finally went quiet between them, he brought it up. "Deb, honey...I think it's time I go home. I don't want to outstay my welcome."

Deborah's heart skipped a beat. She didn't want him to leave. "That would never happen," she said.

"Your mom is the best, but I remember how Dad was after Mom died. I was there, but he had a terrible time trying to make conversation. Finally, I realized he just wanted to be alone. He needed to work things out his own way without worrying about how I was feeling about her death, too."

Deborah frowned. "Do you think Mom wants to be alone?"

"I don't know. But you could ask. You'll know by the way she hesitates...or not...before she answers."

"Then what do I do? I have already given my notice at the clinic back in Louisville, and any day now a small moving van will be arriving with my things."

"You could tell her you're moving in with me because we want to try this relationship thing again as adults and not two dumb teens."

"You were dumb. I was just young," Deborah said.

Ladd grinned. "Duly noted. And while we're together, we'll

figure out how to make both of our careers work without losing our homeplaces."

"You've been thinking about this for a while, haven't you?" she said.

"Just about every night I've been under your roof, wondering what it would take to get you under mine."

"All you had to do was invite me," Deborah said.

"And I did. Now, you and Miss Maggie talk, and if you think you need to stay a while longer with her, then I'll accept whatever you think is best and wait for the day when you realize you can't live another moment without me."

"Don't leave just yet. Give me a day or so to talk to Mom. I really don't want you living on your own. There are chores that will need to be done that require lifting, and you'll do it anyway if I'm not there to help."

"Deal," Ladd said. "In the meantime, I promised to help shell purple hulls."

"And so did I," Deborah said. "I also think your mama cow is healed up enough to turn back in with the herd."

"We'll do that this evening when we go get mail and feed Sam," Ladd said.

Deborah nodded, then finished off the last of her Coke. By the time they reached the drive leading up to the Ryman farm, the sun was blistering hot and glaring off the hood of her car.

"I hope Mom's not still out in this heat," Deborah said.

"We'll soon find out," Ladd said.

When they got back to the farm, Deborah parked beneath the carport. "Oh, good. The Gator is parked in the backyard. At least I know she's in the house," Deborah said.

They walked in to find Maggie sitting in the living room with her feet up on the footstool and a huge bowl of peas in her lap, watching TV and shelling away.

"Oh! You're home!" Maggie said, and set the peas aside and

got up. "Turn your pretty self around, Ladd Daltry, and let me see your head."

Ladd grinned. "Dang, Deb. Your mother appreciates me more than you do," he said, but he gladly turned around to give her a clear view of his head, minus the eleven staples.

Deborah ignored him, watching as her mother gently ran her fingers through the hair at the back of his head.

"Your hair grows so thick and fast, I can't even tell where they shaved it. I'm so happy that healed," Maggie said. "I'd hug you, but you're not all put back together yet," she added, and patted Ladd's cheek. Then she eyed Deborah's appearance. "Lord, child. You look like you've been butcherin' hogs."

"So does that mean you don't want to hug me?" Deborah asked.

"Pretty much. Have you two had lunch?"

"No, ma'am," Ladd said.

Maggie nodded. "I have stuff in the refrigerator. Why don't you come help me while Deborah cleans up and changes?"

"I was thinking Deborah might need help, too," Ladd said.

Deborah turned a vivid shade of pink, and Maggie burst out laughing.

"I cannot believe you just said that!" Deborah mumbled, and walked out of the living room.

"Was it something I said?" he asked.

Maggie was still laughing and shaking her head. "Yes, you're getting well. To the kitchen, mister."

"Yes, ma'am," Ladd said, and followed.

Deborah was in her room, peeling off the bloody clothes and thinking this was like coming back from a vet call. Even when she wore coveralls over her clothes and rubber boots instead of her regular shoes, she still came back in a mess. Right now, she had blood and horse manure on her jeans, and blood all over everything else. The fact that Ladd didn't blink an eye riding home with her in that condition spoke well for their future relationship.

She turned on the shower, then stepped inside, even before the water ran hot, and started with her hair, squirting a dollop of shampoo in her hand and washing it, then rinsing.

Once she was through with her hair, she scrubbed her skin until it was pink and tingling. Only then did she turn off the water and get out. She towel-dried her hair, then herself, and went to get some clean clothes.

After she dressed, she went barefoot through the house, following the voices and the laughter. Ladd's deep, husky laugh rolled through her like waves of energy. She wanted him. She wanted him and the fire he lit inside her. She sighed. All these years, and he still turned her on.

"There you are!" Maggie said. "Clean, shiny, and smelling oh so good!"

"Happy to oblige," Deborah said, eyeing the table laden with food. "I'm starved."

"There's plenty to choose from," Maggie said. "Let's sit. I have things to tell you."

Deborah frowned and glanced at Ladd. He shrugged and shook his head.

Maggie poured cold sweet tea over the ice in their glasses, then sat down and took half of a chicken salad sandwich from a platter of sandwiches. They added sides and chips as they wished, then settled down to eat.

Deborah took two bites, chewed and swallowed, and then put her hands in her lap and eyed her mother. "I'm waiting for your news," she said.

Maggie also paused, took a sip of her iced tea, and then leaned back in her chair.

"Nina called me after you two left this morning. She was checking up on us to see how we were faring since Josh's passing. Worried that I might be afraid to be on my own."

Deborah interjected briefly for Ladd's sake: "Nina is Mom's sister. I didn't know if you would remember her."

Ladd nodded. "Vaguely."

Maggie sighed. "I explained that you were moving back to the area but would most likely be living nearby, so technically I wasn't going to be alone like I have been for the past four years. It's weird how people thought just because Josh was alive that he was still company for me in any way. We haven't been under the same roof since his stroke."

Deborah and Ladd glanced at each other. So Maggie was well aware of where their plans were leading them.

"Are you, Mom? Afraid to be on your own?" Deborah asked.

Maggie rolled her eyes. "Well, good lord, no! My brother-in-law is the county sheriff and everyone in the area knows it. I've been winning our Thanksgiving turkeys for years at the American Legion turkey shoot, so nearly every man in the county knows I'm as good if not a better shot than they are."

Ladd's eyes widened. "Really?"

Deborah laughed. "I didn't get the way I am by accident."

Maggie smirked. "Anyway...back to Nina. With her recent divorce and her kids and grandkids all out of state, she's lonely. After hemming and hawing around the subject for a while, she finally came out and asked if I would be amenable to an extended visit."

Deborah leaned forward. "What did you tell her?"

Maggie shrugged. "She's my baby sister. I told her yes, she was welcome to stay as long as she wanted."

"And what if she decides she doesn't want to go back to New Mexico?" Deborah asked.

"I won't care. Her living here won't be a burden. I own the farm. I own the house. Do you mind?" Maggie asked. "I mean, you just gave up a career to stay with me, and now—"

"Mom! Of course I don't mind!" Deborah said. "Besides, you were right. Ladd and I talked. When he moves home, I'm going with him. Either we make it work this time or let go of the past."

Maggie glanced at Ladd. "If you break her heart again, I will break both your arms and toss your body in the patch of poison ivy down by the spring."

Ladd threw back his head and laughed and laughed, and then every time he glanced at Maggie he started laughing again.

"Oh lord! Oh, Miz Maggie! I swear to God and to you and to Deborah, that's never gonna happen. Besides, she saved my life, remember? So according to legend...I now owe her mine."

Maggie pointed her fork at him. "I don't think that's a real thing."

Ladd's smile faded. "It's real to me, Maggie. Loving Deborah is easy. Getting her to trust me again is not. But I have the rest of my life to work on that. All you have to know is that I'd die to keep her safe."

Deborah frowned. "No. I worked too damn hard keeping you alive the first time. Enough of promises and threats and fake Chinese proverbs and dying from the both of you." She reached across the table and took her mother's hand. "I want to grow old with him. That is all that needs to be said."

Ladd's eyes filled with tears.

Maggie swallowed past the lump in her throat.

Deborah sighed. "So, when is Aunt Nina coming?"

"In a couple of days," Maggie said.

"Good. Just enough time for me to clean up the spare bedroom and do up the laundry. Ladd needs to be home. I need to be with Ladd, but close to you. Aunt Nina's insecurity is a lifesaver for all of us, including you, whether you'll admit it or not," Deborah said.

"She's never lived in the country in her life," Maggie said.

"Then Dumpling will give her the old Ryman welcome, and you can take her to the truck garden to help you pick peas," Ladd said.

"She'll catch on to what matters, and you can leave her to cleaning house when you want your alone time outside," Deborah said.

"Then that's settled," Maggie said, then picked up what was left of her sandwich, and they finished their meal before settling in to shell peas.

————————

That evening after supper, when Deborah and Ladd went over to get his mail and check on the cattle, the mood between them was light and upbeat. All of the maybes were out in the open, and Deborah had said aloud the thing Ladd wanted to hear most.

She wanted him.

Deborah felt like her life had just opened up to new vistas. She had admitted her deepest desire, and the freedom of being open left her feeling giddy. Like she was a teenager again, but smarter and confident of who she was now.

After stopping for mail, Deborah drove straight to the barn to check on the mama cow and calf. Ladd got out with her and smiled when Sam came running.

"Hey, Sammy, how are you doing?" Ladd said, then picked him up and carried him back into the barn to the granary. They fed the cat first, then headed for the corral.

Deborah opened the gate, and when she walked in, the cow saw her and mooed, hoping for cubes. The little calf saw her and started running and kicking up its heels.

"Well, the calf is ready for greener pastures, but it's Mama that matters. Let me see how that wound looks," Deborah said, and moved around to the other side of the cow to check.

The cut had granulated to a thick scab and the torn hide was already healing.

"What do you think?" Ladd said.

"I'm going to put one last dose of salve on it and then let them go," Deborah said.

Ladd nodded. "Agreed. I'll get the big gate, and once we let Mama and her calf out, the herd will come up. I'll count them then."

He walked to the big gate, then opened it all the way.

The old cow saw daylight and started toward it at a steady clip with her calf beside her, bawling and calling the others as she went.

"They hear her," Deborah said, and pointed toward the trees. "Look. Here they come."

Ladd hurried back inside the corral and closed the gate, then stood and watched as the herd welcomed back their own. Then he climbed up on the rails of the corral to get a better view and counted out the herd.

"All here," he said. "Sam's fed. Cow's back with the herd. Now come to the house. Everything in there is at least thirty years old, except the cookstove. It's older. Let's talk about what stays and what goes."

Deborah slid her arm around his waist and then laid her cheek against his chest. "I'm staying, no matter what it looks like. And there's a van with my stuff en route to Georgia. It's supposed to arrive in a couple of days. Not much. Just some living room furniture, my bed, and my clothes. I can contact the company to change the delivery location."

"Is your bed bigger than Dad's?"

"It's king-size," Deborah said.

"Hot damn," Ladd said, then tilted her chin up just enough. The kiss was a vow and a promise, and he was so full of love for her that he couldn't catch his breath.

Deborah's eyes were closed, but she'd loved this man for so long that it felt right to be here again. "We can look at furniture tomorrow," she said. "I'm tired. I feel like I've been wrestling tigers."

Ladd hugged her. "Then let's go home. Your mom is waiting and will continue to wait as long as you reside under her roof. She won't rest until we're back."

"How did you get so smart about women?" Deborah asked.

Ladd ran a finger down her cheek, wondering how anyone as tough as she was could still feel so soft. "By remembering what I'd had before I lost them."

That night, when Ladd went to bed, it didn't hurt when his head hit the pillow, and when he slept he dreamed of being in a room of shadows and Deborah coming toward him. In the dream he knew she was nude, but he'd only seen her naked when they were teens so his dream wouldn't let him go farther than the shape of her coming out of the dark.

And then she was with him, wrapped around him, sinking into him, and fading as shadows do when there is no more light. He could feel himself inside her, her arms around him, and then her legs wrapped around his waist as he started to move.

Then Dumpling crowed, and Ladd woke up in a state of frustration and expectation. "Damn rooster," he muttered. "No wonder Josh threatened to wring its neck."

He got up and showered, and by the time he was dressed he could smell coffee. The Ryman women were up, and he wanted to go home. But he wasn't going without his girl. He was never leaving her behind again.

Today was for getting ready for Aunt Nina.

Day after tomorrow, Deborah's things would arrive.

He thought about what to do with the old stuff they were getting rid of, and then thought of Dan Amos. He had rental properties, some of which were furnished. He'd give Dan a call, and if he wanted the bed and living room furniture, he could have it.

There were things to be finished before something new could begin.

Deborah and Ladd were at his farm, helping Dan Amos and his crew load up the furniture Ladd was giving them. She was cleaning where the furniture had been when her phone signaled a text. She put down the mop to read the text, then looked up.

"Aunt Nina has arrived."

Ladd nodded, then hurried to hold the door open as Dan and his crew carried out the last piece of furniture. As soon as they had it loaded, Dan came back to the porch.

"I sure appreciate this," Dan said. "And I don't care what you said, I'm not taking it for free." He handed Ladd a check. "Having furnished rentals is a rarity these days, and anytime I can offer one is a good thing for me and the renter."

"Thanks," Ladd said, and put the check in his pocket.

"Tell Deborah I said goodbye. I want to get this stuff unloaded before noon," Dan said.

Ladd waved them off and went back inside to where Deborah was cleaning.

"You don't have to do this now. Your aunt just arrived. We can come back later," he said.

She shook her head. "I want to get this done before my furniture arrives tomorrow. I'm almost through. We'll deal with cleaning the rest of the house after I move in."

"Can I help?"

"Um...you can put the broom back in the utility room. I'm almost through mopping."

He got the broom, and when she turned around he swatted her backside with it. Deborah spun around, the mop still in her hands.

"Do you really want to do this...considering you're the one who'll be going home wet?"

"Sorry. Too tempting to ignore," he drawled.

Before Deborah could respond, her cell phone rang. She set the mop aside to answer as Ladd was walking away. When he came back, she was smiling.

"Guess what? That was the moving company. The moving van is a day ahead of schedule and already in Savannah. They'll be here in about an hour."

Ladd grinned. "Does that mean there will be a bed in this house tonight?"

"I guess it does," Deborah said. "Glad I decided to start cleaning. Timing is everything."

"Today is going to be the beginning of our life together. We're sleeping here tonight. In a king-size bed. And we're going to make love and heal every crack I ever put in your heart."

Deborah's eyes welled.

"You were worth waiting for," she said, and then threw her arms around his neck and kissed him until her ears were ringing from the blood-rush. "Oh lord… No time for this right now. I need to finish mopping that corner before they get here," she mumbled, and reached for the mop. "You. Go sit outside on the porch swing and watch for them. I can't think when you're this close."

Ladd cupped her face. "Then you're going to lose your mind when I get you in bed. Grab a Coke when you come join me. We'll toast to new beginnings."

Deborah slung water and mopped until she was done, then dumped the mop water down the drain and left the wet mop on the back porch to dry. After that, she grabbed a Coke and headed for the front porch.

Ladd was sitting in the porch swing, talking on the phone. He disconnected when she came out.

"That was my boss in Savannah. He was checking on how I was doing and asking me if I was ready to take on a new project. I said yes. They're emailing the details. I'll work up some ideas, and then we'll have a Zoom meeting next week."

Deborah sat down beside him, curious now to be seeing this side of him. She unscrewed the cap off her bottle of pop, then lifted it in a toast.

"To old loves and new beginnings," she said.

"I'll drink to that," Ladd said. "And you'd better call Maggie to let her know what's happening."

"I was just about to do that," Deborah said, and then called Maggie to fill her in on the change of plans.

Maggie was helping Nina unpack when Deborah called. "Hey, honey. Did Dan come get the furniture yet?"

"Yes. He's already gone. I was cleaning up when I got a phone call from my movers. They're a day ahead of schedule and already on their way here from Savannah. Are you and Aunt Nina okay?"

"Of course we're okay. We haven't stopped talking more than long enough to take a breath. As for your movers, did they get the change of address?"

"Yes. They know to come here. I spoke to the driver. So, Ladd and I are on the porch waiting. I didn't want you to worry that something happened, but it's going to be a while before we come home."

Maggie laughed. "It's going to be longer than that, sugar. Your new home is where you're sitting right now."

Deborah blinked. The reality of that had not sunk in until her mother said it. "I guess you're right. Anyway… We'll be back later to get our clothes and say hello to Aunt Nina."

"We'll be here," Maggie said. "Happy new first day, darling. I love you both."

"We love you, too, Mom. See you later."

Ladd put his arm around her shoulders. "Everything okay?"

"Yes. She and Aunt Nina are about to start living their best lives, I think."

"Good for them," Ladd said.

Deborah nodded. "And good for us," she said, and laid her head on his shoulder.

They were swinging and talking, and touching, and teasing— basically foreplay for the night ahead—when Ladd suddenly stood.

"I hear a truck."

Deborah paused, then smiled. "I hear it, too!"

A few seconds later, it appeared.

"There comes our bed!" Ladd said.

Deborah rolled her eyes. "There is more in that truck than sex."

Ladd laughed out loud and hugged her. "You're so right. They're bringing the rest of our lives."

Deborah sighed. "You always did know how to sweet-talk the pants off me."

"It's a skill I promise to use wisely," Ladd said.

And then the truck was at the house, and they went out to meet the movers.

———————

It took about an hour for them to unload the boxes, unload and set up the bed, and carry the living room furniture into the house. Deborah signed off on the delivery, and the movers were gone.

Then, with Ladd at her heels, she went straight to the boxes labeled SHEETS AND TOWELS and pulled out a set of sheets and pillowcases, then dug until she found the comforter she used as a bedspread, and they made up the bed.

Ladd eyed the comforter. "It looks like a garden."

"It is a garden. See the hummingbirds?"

"I like flowers. I like birds. It's a hit with me," Ladd said. "Now. We do either one of two things. We tear up what we just made in a frenzy of hot sex, or we go to your mom's, say hello to Aunt Nina, and get our things."

Deborah smirked. "You are going to be so much fun to grow old with. I guess we'd better do the adult thing and go say hello and get our things."

"I guessed you would say that," Ladd said. "But I'm driving my truck."

Deborah started to argue, and then stopped. If he was well enough to make good on tonight's promise, he was well enough to drive.

"Okay. Your keys are on the peg. Let's go."

# CHAPTER 17

IT WAS THE FIRST DAY OF SCHOOL, AND CARLIE WAS DAWDLING through getting dressed, then dawdling through breakfast. Peanut had already left for the office, and Ruby needed to get Carlie to school so she could get to the shop.

This was all a learning experience. Carlie was going to a new school, and Ruby, who was now an acting parent, was getting her little girl, who wasn't really hers, off to start a new school year.

Ruby sensed Carlie's delays all had to do with a reticence to face yet another unknown and kept watching her face as she was brushing her hair.

"Are you nervous?" Ruby asked.

Carlie shrugged.

"It's okay if you are. Being the new kid is never easy, but after you make some more friends, you won't be new anymore," Ruby said, and put two pink butterfly clips in the girl's hair to keep the curls out of her eyes.

"Were you ever the new kid?" Carlie asked.

Ruby sighed. "Yes. We moved a lot when I was growing up. I didn't like it much then, but now I like meeting new people. You still want to eat in the lunchroom, right?"

Carlie nodded. "Melvin Lee eats in the lunchroom, so I will, too."

Ruby nodded. "Just know that you have lunches paid up until the end of the month."

"Okay," Carlie said.

"Get your backpack. We've already packed all of the school supplies you were supposed to have with you, so I think we're good to go." Then she gave Carlie a big hug and a kiss on the cheek.

"Mr. Ruby and I are so proud of you. You are the best, Carlie Jo. Remember that."

Carlie beamed. Remembering her mother's last words—*"the best of me"*—made her feel better. "I'm not scared, Miss Ruby."

"Good. Let's get loaded up and be on our way so we aren't late for school or for work."

Carlie grabbed her backpack, and Ruby slung her purse over her shoulder, and out the door they went. They buckled in and backed out of the drive, but Ruby kept glancing in the rearview mirror as she drove.

Carlie might not be scared, but Ruby was a nervous wreck. This was her first time to be leaving Shirley's daughter in someone else's care.

*Being a mother is hard. I'm going to have to toughen up, for sure.*

Ruby already had instructions on where parents got in line to drop off their kids and where they parked to pick them up in the evening, so when they reached Blessings Elementary, Ruby put the car in park. But before she could get out, Carlie had the door open and was climbing out, dragging her backpack with her.

*Oh lord. Okay. Don't make a scene,* Ruby told herself.

"Bye, sugar! I'll pick you up when school is out. You watch for my car, and mind the teacher."

"Yes, ma'am. Bye, Miss Ruby. Have a nice day!" Carlie said. She was smiling as she shouldered her backpack and started up the long walk toward the school.

And then Ruby saw Melvin Lee on the front steps. When he saw Carlie, he came flying off of them like he'd been launched and met her halfway and took her backpack. Ruby knew he was talking because she could see his lips moving, and then they turned their backs on her and joined the rest of the children walking into the school.

"And that's how that goes," Ruby muttered. She put the car in gear, and as soon as she was cleared to move, she drove away.

She got to work and her first customer arrived. But with every passing hour, her anxiety grew, and she knew she would not relax until she knew if Carlie's first day was a good one or a disaster.

———————

Thanks to Melvin Lee, Carlie found her room and then her teacher, Mrs. Schultz, whom she'd met during enrollment. She put the contents of her backpack in her desk and hung her backpack on an empty hook beside the others.

"Girl, I gotta sit over there. But you got this," Melvin Lee said.

Carlie nodded. She'd already decided if somebody tried to get bossy with her, she was gonna be like Melvin Lee. She wasn't gonna take any guff.

"Thank you, Melvin Lee."

He flashed his missing-teeth smile. "Welcome, girl."

And so the day began.

The Pledge of Allegiance.

Roll call.

Sorting kids into groups and centers.

Carlie soon figured out that school in Blessings wasn't all that different from school in Little Rock. Just different names and faces, but she already knew the routine.

Be quiet.

Listen.

And be polite.

Mama always said good little girls were just ladies in waiting. Carlie didn't know exactly what that meant, but she was good at following 'structions.

———————

The girl sitting next to Carlie in reading center was staring at her, eyeballing her hair, her clothes, and the fingernail polish on her nails. Carlie knew it, but she was doing what Teacher said, which was to read to herself until told to stop.

When the teacher moved to the far side of the room to help another student, the girl pointed at Carlie's nails. "My name is Johnetta. I'm named after my daddy. My mommy doesn't allow me to paint my nails."

"Too bad. I get sparkly ones next time," Carlie said, and turned the page.

That wasn't the reaction Johnetta expected—and she was jealous of the new girl's blond curls, blue eyes, and pretty nails.

"My mommy says you ain't got no parents. My mommy says you're an orphnant."

Carlie rolled her eyes. "Or-phan. Not orphnant."

Johnetta blinked. "Whatever."

The teacher turned around. "Johnetta, please stop talking and read the pages I assigned."

"I wasn't talking, Mrs. Schultz. It was this new girl."

Carlie's eyes widened. She had been talking, but in response to Johnetta's questions. Suddenly, she was frozen in fear. First day of school and someone had already told a lie about her.

But Lena Schultz wasn't fooled. She'd been watching from across the room from the beginning and knew Johnetta's tendency to embroider the truth.

"I'm sorry, Johnetta, but you must be mistaken because I saw you speak first. And I know Carlie responded, but she has not denied it, and you lied to me. I think we all need to stop right now and think about how we use our words. Because this is the first day of school, I want all of you to know that lies are not accepted in my classroom, and the next person who lies to me will stay in at recess. I don't care if it is the first day. I believe how you begin leads the way for how you proceed. Now, Johnetta, since you are ready to talk, please stand and tell the class about the first three pages of the chapter you were reading."

Johnetta ducked her head. "I didn't read it yet," she mumbled.

Lena Schultz looked at Carlie. "Carlie, can you please stand and tell the class about the first three pages?"

"Yes, ma'am," Carlie said, and recited the plot and characters' names, and what had happened so far, and what was going to happen after that.

Lena smiled. "My goodness, you must already know that story. Have you read it before?"

"No, ma'am. I like to read. I read ahead a little. I'm on chapter four. Was that okay?"

Lena sighed. "Yes. That was just fine."

Carlie sat down, relieved she wasn't in trouble.

At that point, the bell rang.

"Put up your books, get in line, and we'll go out for recess. Remember, no talking in line," Mrs. Schultz said.

Carlie put up her book and got in line.

Johnetta pushed the boy behind Carlie out of the way so she would be behind her. They filed out of the room and then down the hall, with Johnetta purposefully stepping on Carlie's heels until she tripped her.

Carlie fell flat.

Johnetta laughed.

Melvin Lee came flying out of the line, his eyes wide from the panic of seeing blood coming out of Carlie's mouth.

Mrs. Schultz came running. "Carlie, are you okay?" she asked. "Oh no, your lip is bleeding. Come with me, and I'll wash it off for you."

"I'm fine, Mrs. Schultz. I'll just go on out with my friend, Johnetta, if that's okay with you?"

Lena Schultz nodded. "If you say so."

"Yes, ma'am. Thank you," Carlie said, and when she smiled at Johnetta, blood was pooling between her lip and her teeth.

Johnetta was beginning to realize the new girl wasn't as easy to bully as the other girls she didn't like. But she'd made her bed, and she had a horrible feeling Carlie Jo Duroy was about to lay her in it.

The class all filed outside, and as soon as they left the building, Carlie spat out the blood in her mouth right on top of Johnetta's shoes, then swiped her arm across her mouth, leaving a bloody streak on it, too.

"I just told a lie about you, so we're even," Carlie said. "You're not my friend. You are never going to be my friend. And if you ever do that to me again, I will bust your nose so hard it splits all the way in two."

Johnetta was horrified. She was half a head taller than this new girl. She'd made her fall and bust her lip. She was still bleeding and not a tear in her eyes. And she'd just threatened her. Nobody had ever challenged her before.

And then, as if that wasn't bad enough, Melvin Lee came at her with his fists doubled, zeroing in on her like a flogging rooster.

"Hey, you stupid old girl. You leave my friend Carlie alone, or you'll be sorry."

Johnetta turned and ran.

Melvin Lee put his arm around Carlie's shoulder, then handed her an almost clean handkerchief. "You're a'bleedin' on your shirt, girl."

Melvin Lee's sympathy made Carlie want to cry, but she didn't.

"I know. But I didn't take no guff," she said.

"She won't bother you no more," Melvin Lee said. "Johnetta's a bully. And now she's scared of you. My daddy always says, 'Stand up to a bully, and they'll leave you alone forever.' You'll see. My daddy knows guy stuff real good."

"But I'm not a guy," Carlie said.

"No, but you're good as one, and I'm not lyin.'"

Carlie started to smile, and then winced when it pulled.

"I need to rinse out my mouth."

"Go tell Mrs. Schultz. She'll send someone in with you so's you don't get lost."

Carlie nodded. "Thank you for being my friend, Melvin Lee."

"Welcome, girl. There's some nice girls in class. You'll figure it out."

"Yes. I'll figure it out," Carlie said, and began looking around the playground until she spotted their teacher and took off walking toward her.

Lena saw her coming and went to meet her. "Are you okay, honey?"

"I want to go rinse out my mouth now," Carlie said.

"Absolutely," Lena said, and signaled to one of the other teachers on playground duty that she was taking Carlie inside.

After they were inside one of the girls' bathrooms, washing the blood off her shirt and her mouth and arm, Lena glanced around to make sure they were alone and then asked, "What was Johnetta talking to you about?"

Carlie shrugged. "It doesn't matter. I think something's wrong with her."

Lena asked another question. "Did she trip you?"

"She won't be doing it again," Carlie said. "I don't take no guff."

Lena blinked, and then bit her lip to keep from laughing. That sounded just like Melvin Lee. If he had decided to be Carlie's champion, then she was going to be fine, because they all knew Melvin Lee didn't take no guff, either.

———

Ruby had her eye on the clock all afternoon, and she'd just finished up with the client who was walking out the front door. It was time to go pick up Carlie, and she had an hour before the next client was due.

"Ladies, I'm going to get my girl. We'll be back soon."

"Can't wait to hear all about her first day," Vera said.

"Me either," Ruby said, and grabbed her purse on the way out the door.

She knew the rules for where to drive and where to park. The school had had a little boy hit by a car a while back, and ever since then their routine had been tightened up, and there were no exceptions.

She drove straight to the school, then parked in the pickup line and settled back to wait. It was hot, and the air conditioner was blowing the hair off Ruby's neck, which made her think about cutting it shorter or starting to wear it up again.

She heard the bell begin ringing to dismiss school and saw kids coming out and starting to walk home. Then teachers were taking their bus riders to the proper buses and making sure the littles who were at school for the first time got on the right buses. Then the car riders came out, and Ruby started searching the faces.

It took her a couple of minutes to spot Carlie, but she wasn't alone. Not only was Melvin Lee walking with her, but so were Willie, Arnie, and Lucy, all with solemn expressions on their faces. Like they were bringing her home from war.

And then Ruby saw Carlie's face and groaned.

"Oh no," she moaned, and got out of the car and opened the back door. "Carlie! Honey! What happened?"

Melvin Lee waved his hand. "I'm talkin' for her, Miss Ruby, 'cause her mouth hurts." He saw his grandma get out of the car and he waved. "Come get these kids, Grandma! I'll be right there."

"I'm okay," Carlie mumbled. "Didn't take no guff." She climbed in the back seat, tossed her backpack on the floor, and buckled herself up as Melvin Lee began to explain how Carlie got hurt.

"Teacher got onto Johnetta Kilby for lying on Carlie. So Johnetta tripped Carlie when we were going out for recess. That old Netta is a bully. Only Carlie didn't cry. She just told Netta if she touched her again, she'd punch her in the nose so hard it would split it in two. And Netta ran off 'cause that's what bullies do. Carlie did good. Netta won't bother her no more. Bullies are scared of people who stand up for themselves. Gotta go. Grandma's got that look. See you at school tomorrow, girl."

Ruby didn't know whether to laugh or cry, but she had to move out of the line so she shut the door, jumped back in the car, and drove away so the cars behind could pull up.

As she was driving, she kept glancing up in the rearview mirror again, expecting to see devastation on Carlie's face. Instead, it looked more like satisfaction.

"I'm so sorry, darling. I'm so sorry. We'll get some ice on that and it'll help take the swelling down."

"Okay," Carlie said. "School was good. Mrs. Schultz is nice. Lunch was hard to eat. I mostly drank milk and could only eat the mac and cheese."

"What did that Johnetta girl say to you?" Ruby asked.

"She said her mother didn't let her paint her nails, and that I was an orphan. But she's not very smart. She said 'orphnant.' Sounded like she was trying to say 'elephant' or something. Then Teacher got onto her for talking during reading time, and she stood up and lied and said she wasn't talking, it was me. And Mrs. Schultz knew she'd lied because she'd seen it all, and I'm not in trouble and Johnetta is. I'm fine, Miss Ruby. I stood up for myself. Melvin Lee says she won't bother me no more."

"Anymore," Ruby muttered.

"Yes, anymore," Carlie said.

"Mr. Ruby is not going to be happy that someone hurt you, and neither am I," Ruby said. "What did you think about being called an orphan?"

Carlie leaned back and for a few moments was silent. "Well, I don't like being called names. But that isn't a lie, is it? Orphans don't have any family. So that's me, right?"

Ruby frowned. "We'll talk more about this tonight. Are you okay to be at the shop for a bit? I have one more client and then we can go home."

"Yes. I can watch cartoons, and if you have a straw, I can drink a chocolate milk."

"I have straws," Ruby said. She was blinking back tears when she pulled up to the back of the shop and got out. "Just leave everything in the car. We won't be here for long."

Carlie nodded, then calmly clasped Ruby's hand as they walked in the back door and then into the salon to say hello.

It didn't take but seconds for everyone to see the horribly swollen lip and Carlie's scraped elbows, and then everyone was talking at once.

"Oh no! Oh, sweetheart! What happened? Are you all right?"

"She don't take no guff," Ruby said. "Is my client here yet?"

"No," Vera said.

"Then I'm going to get Carlie settled. I'll be right out."

Carlie bounced up onto the sofa, then pulled the blanket over her legs and leaned back as Ruby dug around for a straw, then opened a little box of chocolate milk, popped in the straw, and handed it to Carlie.

"Yum," Carlie said as the first little sip went down.

"Your regular cartoons?" Ruby asked.

Carlie nodded.

Ruby found the channel with Looney Tunes cartoons, handed her the remote, and then leaned down and gently kissed Carlie on both cheeks.

"I love you, Carlie Jo, and I am so proud of you. I won't be long."

Carlie took another sip of her chocolate milk, but there was a funny feeling in her chest, and it was suddenly hard to swallow.

Tom and Jerry cartoons began, and she was still sipping chocolate milk and watching through a veil of tears.

Miss Ruby loved her.

She didn't know if it was the same way Mama loved her, but hearing the words made her feel all sad and good at the same time.

Peanut, like Ruby, was anxious to know how Carlie's first day at school had gone. When his day came to an end, he grabbed his briefcase, then paused at his secretary's desk.

"Let's go home, Betty. Whatever's left over will still be here tomorrow."

Betty Purejoy nodded.

"You don't have to say that twice," she said. "You go on. I want to save this file, and then I'll lock up."

"Have a good night," Peanut said, and left the office.

There was a bounce in his step as he left the building and waved at the groundskeeper at the courthouse as he got in his car.

He drove straight home with a smile on his face, thinking about the evening awaiting him. He wanted to hug Ruby until her cheeks turned pink and then spend some time out in the garden with Carlie. She loved to check her fairy houses while he watered, and he was anxious to hear all about school.

When he reached the house and pulled up in the drive, no one came to meet him. He didn't think much of it, but when he got in the house and it was quiet, he frowned. He could smell food cooking, so he left his briefcase and jacket in the living room and headed for the kitchen.

Ruby was at the stove making noodle soup for Carlie, and when she saw Peanut walk in, she turned the fire out from under the pan and burst into tears.

Peanut's heart skipped a beat as he quickly wrapped her in his arms and pulled her close. "Hey, hey, baby…what's wrong? Are you okay? Where's Carlie?"

"No, I'm not okay. I'm so mad I could spit nails. Carlie's in her room playing with her dollhouse. Her mouth is swollen, and she has a big cut on the inside of her lip, but she swears she's fine. Her byword for the week is she don't take no guff and we have Melvin Lee to thank for that."

"Why does she have a fat lip?" he asked.

"John Kilby's girl, Johnetta, took a dislike to her because she's the new girl. She lied about Carlie to the teacher and got caught doing it, so she got in trouble and Carlie didn't. When they were going outside for recess, she purposefully tripped Carlie and made her fall. When she did, Carlie hit her chin and her elbows and bled all over the place. Teacher got out most of the blood on her shirt, and she's going to be okay. Me, not so much. I want to go to Johnetta Kilby's house and yank her bald-headed for hurting my baby. She made fun of her finger-nail polish, called her an orphan, and made her bleed. Carlie shrugged it off because, as she says, that was the truth. Kids who don't have family are orphans."

"Lord. Girls are vicious, aren't they?" Peanut muttered.

Ruby sighed. "Yes, they can be."

"So what do you want me to do about it?" Peanut said. "I don't much like Kilby. He's the biggest know-it-all on the City Council, but I don't think we should get involved here. Sounds like Carlie took care of business on her own."

"I agree, but I think Johnetta's bullying days with Carlie are over. Carlie put the fear of Jesus in her."

Peanut grinned. "She did?"

Ruby rolled her eyes. "You don't have to be so proud of that."

"I like all my girls with a little sass," he said.

Ruby shook her head and then wrapped her arms around him. "Where are we with all the paperwork on Carlie?" she asked.

"Well, once we got a death certificate, I sent it off for Shirley's life insurance. We'll put all of that in a trust fund for Carlie, and you are her official legal guardian. That about covers all of it. Why?"

"What would it take to adopt her?"

He grinned. "Well, asking her what she thinks would be the first step. What prompted this?"

"Hearing the sadness in her voice when she said she didn't

have any family. We're already her family. Just not in the eyes of the law."

Peanut hugged her again. "I'm going to talk to Carlie about her fat lip. We'll feel our way around the rest of that."

Ruby wiped her eyes and nodded.

"I've got to finish this noodle soup. Carlie's lip is too swollen to chew."

Peanut frowned. "Well, damn. I didn't think it was that bad."

"Go look for yourself," Ruby said. "And supper will be ready in about ten more minutes."

"Got it," Peanut said, and headed for Carlie's room.

Ruby was right. He wasn't prepared for the extent of the swelling. It made him hurt just looking at her.

"Hey, sugar," he said, and sat down on the side of the bed next to where she was playing.

"Mr. Ruby!" Carlie cried. "You're home! I got a fat lip!"

Peanut frowned. "I see that. I'm so sorry. It makes me sad to know you got hurt. Can I have a hug?"

Carlie threw her arms around his neck, and when she did, Peanut pulled her up into his lap and just held her.

"I'm sorry someone was mean to you," he said.

Carlie nodded and tucked her head beneath his chin. "Me too. But Melvin Lee says it won't happen again. He knows that Johnetta girl. He says she's a bully."

"Did what she said hurt your feelings?" Peanut asked.

Carlie shrugged. "Maybe a little. But she's dumb, so I forgive her."

Peanut chuckled. "That's really big of you."

Ruby came into the room to tell them supper was ready, then realized they were in the middle of a discussion and sat down beside them and listened.

"Do I need to go talk to the principal tomorrow about this?" Peanut asked.

Carlie shook her head. "Nope. I spit blood all over Johnetta's shoes and told her if she messed with me again, I would hit her so hard it would split her nose in two."

"Wow! That's pretty scary talk," Peanut said. "I can see where you've got her on the run."

Carlie nodded.

Peanut glanced at Ruby and then patted Carlie's back. "Miss Ruby said that girl called you an orphan."

"Yep," Carlie said, and then shrugged. "But I can't get mad about that because I am."

"You wouldn't be an orphan if you were adopted by a family," Peanut said.

Carlie frowned. "Are you gonna give me away?"

Peanut hugged her again. "No! Never! We were kinda hoping one day you'd want to adopt us, because we sure do love you."

Carlie's eyes widened. "I can do that?"

He nodded.

Carlie looked at Ruby. "Do you want to be adopted, too?"

"More than anything," Ruby said.

"Then why didn't you say so?" Carlie asked.

Peanut sighed. "Because we didn't want to be rude to your mama's memory. We didn't want you to feel rushed into doing something you didn't want to do."

"Then I say yes!" Carlie cried. "If I adopt you, and you adopt me, then what would I call you?"

"What would you like to call us?" Ruby asked.

"I never had a daddy. I want to have a daddy," she said.

"I'd be honored," Peanut said.

"What would you like to call me?" Ruby asked.

Carlie's chin quivered as her eyes suddenly welled.

"I want a mommy. I miss mine. Could I call you Mommy?"

"I would love it if you called me Mommy," Ruby said. "But don't worry about it all just yet. Mr. Ruby will have to file adoption papers at the courthouse, and that takes time."

"How much time?" Carlie asked.

"It's hard to say," Peanut said. "But if you want that, then I'll start the paperwork tomorrow. Okay?"

Tears rolled as Carlie nodded. "Yes. I don't want to be an orphan anymore."

"Then it's settled," Ruby said. "And supper is ready. I made noodle soup. You can drink the soup through a straw and then eat the soft noodles afterward."

Carlie's tears kept rolling. "You do good things for me, Miss Ruby."

Ruby hugged her. "You do good things for me, too, baby girl. You make my heart happy, and you make every day one to look forward to."

"Do I make you happy, too, Mr. Ruby?" Carlie asked.

Peanut nodded. "So happy. Instead of one girl, I have two to come home to. And I can't wait for someone to call me Daddy."

Carlie shuddered as if the weight of the world had just left her shoulders.

"I'm gonna have a family again."

Ruby grabbed a handful of tissues and wiped Carlie's face.

"There. All better now," she said. "Let's go eat soup."

# CHAPTER 18

LADD AND DEBORAH WALKED INTO THE HOUSE TO THE AROMA of fried chicken and biscuits baking in the oven.

"Oh my gosh, this house smells good," Deborah said. "Mom went all out for Aunt Nina."

"She went all out for us, too, honey. I suspect this is our send-off," he said, and he was right.

"There you are!" Maggie said as she came to meet them. "I guessed you two would be hungry after all the moving and cleaning. Go say hello to your aunt Nina. I'm running out to the garden to get a few tomatoes to slice."

"Yes, ma'am," Deborah said, and took Ladd's hand as they entered the kitchen. Nina was at the counter mashing potatoes, and when she saw them, she turned off the immersion blender and came running.

"Deborah! Sweetheart! It's been ages!" Nina said, and gave her a quick hug. "And who's this gorgeous man?"

"I like her already," Ladd said.

"Aunt Nina, this is Ladd Daltry. Ladd, this is my aunt, Nina Stone."

"Nice to meet you, Miss Nina," Ladd said.

Nina sighed. "I love Southern men…and their sweet Southern ways." Then she frowned. "Why is his name familiar to me?"

Deborah grinned. "Possibly because we grew up together. His family farm abuts ours. And maybe because he's all I talked about when I was growing up."

"She was my best girl," Ladd said. "Life kind of separated us… and then death brought us back together again. We definitely got the message that time waits for no man."

"Ladd's father died last year, and he stayed on at the farm. If he hadn't, we might never have seen each other again," Deborah said.

"Oh, I think fate would have shown us the way, regardless," Ladd said. And then Maggie came back, and the two sisters and Deborah finished preparing the meal while Ladd sat at the table with a glass of iced tea, watching the three women with a mixture of respect and delight.

Nina was a faded version of her older sister, Maggie. Similar size and looks, but less assertive. Maybe it had to do with being disrespected by her husband of thirty years—and then the ultimate betrayal of being dumped for a younger woman. And Ladd learned from listening to them talking that it was entirely due to Maggie's advice that Nina didn't let herself be cheated out of a proper divorce settlement.

As it stood, Nina was financially secure. It was just her heart that had been shredded, but it was his personal opinion that Nina would come into her own here. Maggie and Deborah were perfect examples of strong women, taking care of business.

The conversation continued over the meal, and then a clock chiming down the hall reminded them of the time.

"Mom, this was the best, but we need to get our stuff together and get back in time to do chores," Deborah said.

"Do what you need to do," Maggie said, and so Ladd and Deborah retreated to their respective bedrooms in the old house and began to gather up their things.

Most of Deborah's things had arrived in the van. She only had what she'd brought for her visit. And Ladd only had what Deborah had brought over for his stay while he was healing.

Once they had all of that packed and loaded in his truck, there was nothing left to do but say goodbye.

Maggie smiled as she watched them standing at the doorway, just as they'd done countless times before when he'd come to take Deborah out on a date.

"Well, I guess I don't have to be reminding you of your curfew this time," Maggie said. "I always thought this is where life would take you two, but I never imagined it would take this long." Then she took a deep breath, blinking back tears. "All I have to say is, don't waste a minute being angry with each other. Life is too damn short for that. And…I fully expect to see you two for Sunday dinners…when time permits. You are still my children, whether you like it or not."

"We like it," Ladd said, and gave her a quick hug.

Deborah wrapped her arms around Maggie and hugged her fiercely. "And…you're still my mom, which means when you need help with anything, we are who you call first. Understood? We're just across the dang creek…not in another state. Not anymore."

"Understood," Maggie said. "Now get. And just know if you need extra grazing land for your cattle, the grass isn't doing anything but growing on my side. No need letting it go to seed and weeds."

Ladd sighed. This might be the difference between keeping his cattle and selling them like Maggie had. If he had room for the herd to grow and didn't have to buy hay, it would make a huge difference.

"Thank you, Maggie. You know I'm likely going to take you up on that," Ladd said.

"With a vet in the family and extra land and grass, I'd say your days of raising cattle are about to get a whole lot easier. You might even get a chance to design the next Taj Mahal," Maggie said.

Ladd grinned. "That's doubtful, unless it's meant to be a casino somewhere."

Nina clapped her hands. "I *love* going to casinos."

Maggie rolled her eyes. "Lord, lord, what have I gotten myself into?"

"We're going now, Mom. Love you bunches. Love you, Aunt Nina. You two take good care of each other." And then they left.

Deborah glanced back as they were driving away. Her mother and aunt were standing on the porch waving. She waved back, then sighed.

"They'll be fine," Ladd said. "I predict they'll become notorious in their old age."

"You're right. It's just my instinct to be caring for something... or someone."

"I've already volunteered for the job, and I can promise I'm going to be needy as hell," he said.

Deborah glanced at him then. At the black hair with a tendency to curl, at the strong jaw and a nose she vaguely remembered him breaking more than once. And then he caught her staring and winked. And when he did, she was sixteen years old all over again, riding in the truck with her first love, knowing it was exactly where she belonged.

---

That night, she came to him from the shadows, wearing nothing but a smile. Regal in her demeanor, with a lean body toned to perfection. She crawled into bed and then gave herself up to the fire within them.

Making love had always come as natural to them as breathing. There had never been a moment of awkwardness, and tonight was no exception. All those years apart had only sharpened their desire for each other.

The blood was racing through Ladd's body at breakneck speed, and Deborah felt like she was coming undone. And then he was inside of her, hard and aching, and she was whole again.

They lost control of the pace within moments, and it was nothing but a body-slamming free fall to the climax.

"Too fast. Couldn't stop," Ladd mumbled as she lay on her side, her hand resting over the thunderous pace of his heartbeat.

"I didn't want to stop," Deborah said. "I still don't."

"Then come here to me," Ladd said. "We have a lot of catching up to do."

They made love until they were dripping wet with sweat, then got up and showered together at three in the morning, went back to bed, and passed out in each other's arms.

The next morning, Deborah woke up with Ladd already inside her, and so their day began.

By the time they made it to breakfast, Sam the cat was on the back porch, meowing. Ladd laughed.

"He knows I'm home," Ladd said. "I'll walk down to the barn to feed him."

"And I'll see what we have in the way of breakfast food here, but I know there's a shopping trip to the Crown on the agenda. You were gone so long a lot of stuff spoiled."

"Then let me feed Sam, and I'll take you to Granny's for breakfast. We can get groceries and anything else before we come home."

"Check to see if you need feed. We can get that at Truesdale's," Deborah said.

Ladd paused. "This is really nice. Having someone to plan with."

Deborah hugged him. "We're going to be spectacular together," she said. "I'll make lists. You go do your thing. But don't dawdle. Last night was an epic marathon of sex, and I'm starving."

Ladd went out the door smiling. A job well done was most satisfying, and he aimed to please.

---

A short while later, they were on their way to Blessings, and once again Ladd was behind the wheel. They'd taken his truck to haul back feed, and Deborah had the grocery list that included both food and cleaning supplies.

There was a lot to be done, and the rest of their lives to do it, but right now all they wanted were some of Mercy Pittman's heavenly biscuits and some bacon and eggs.

They drove straight into town and up Main to Granny's, found a place to park, and went inside.

Sully was working the front and greeted them with a smile. "Good morning. Deborah, you just missed your mom and her sister, and I hear congratulations are in order for you two."

Deborah rolled her eyes. "She couldn't let it be even one day."

Ladd thought that was funny, but he wasn't about to deny it. "It took us long enough to make it happen. We'll take all the best wishes we can get. Right, honey?"

"Definitely," Deborah said. "And we're starving. You'd better not be running out of biscuits yet."

"We never run out of biscuits here," Sully said. "Follow me."

They were seated and had coffee and hot biscuits on the table in no time.

"Your order will be coming right up," their waitress said, and then hurried off to another table as Deborah and Ladd quickly became the topic of conversation.

Jake Lorde was getting up to leave and stopped at their table. "Congratulations, you two."

"Thanks," Ladd said.

"Hey, Deb, did you hear anything about that guy you pulled out of the wreck?"

"Ladd saw him at the hospital later," Deborah said.

"Yes, I did," Ladd said. "He was talking when I saw him, mostly worried about his horse. But I passed on the info I had, and he was relieved to know a vet came to get it. I think his injuries were minimal."

"That was a mess," Jake said. "It's sure a good thing you two were there. Well, I'd better get going. I have a big ad campaign due in a couple of days. I have to get back to work."

"Where do you work?" Ladd asked.

"Oh, I work from home. I do ads for a lingerie company in another state. The joys of technology and Zoom meetings," Jake said. "See you around."

"I guess if he can do it, so can I," Ladd said.

Deborah frowned. "Do what?"

"Work from home. I can design and draw blueprints from anywhere. I don't have to always be on-site."

"We can do whatever we want and need to do," Deborah said. "That vet who came and picked up the horse told me to come talk to him if I wanted a job."

"So? Are you going to?" Ladd asked.

"Eventually, maybe...but on my timeline. I'm not interested in seven days a week and on call every night. I did that and nearly burned myself out. Right now, I just want to get us settled and the cattle taken care of, and decide what we're going to do with two farms. Do we make it into one big one and increase the workload, or do we get your smaller one up and running, and both of us working at our chosen careers? It's all stuff we have to decide together, but not today."

"*We.* That's one fine word, and I do love it when you talk sexy," Ladd said, then looked up. "Ooh, here comes breakfast."

Deborah chuckled. "You are so easily distracted."

"No. I have laser focus, and it's always on you. You said you were starved. So, here comes our food."

---

When the alarm went off at the Butterman house, Ruby jumped out of bed and went to wake Carlie. "Good morning, angel. Time to get up," she said softly and kissed her cheek.

Carlie opened her eyes, rolled over, and started to talk, and then winced.

"Ow," she said and felt her mouth. "It's still swollen," she said.

"It'll take a while for it to get well," Ruby said. "In the meantime, I'm going to make us some oatmeal and we can put brown sugar and cream on it. That will be something good that's easy to eat. Go wash your face and then come to breakfast. We'll do clothes and hair later."

"Okay," Carlie said, and crawled out of bed as Ruby headed for the kitchen.

Later, after they'd eaten, Ruby made a point of fixing Carlie's hair into a cascade of curls, added a pink bow, and then helped her dress in one of the new outfits from the school clothes they'd bought—pink shorts and a pink and white polka-dot top.

"Want to wear your new light-up mermaid sneakers?" Ruby asked.

Carlie nodded, then shivered with anticipation as Ruby got them out of the box.

"I love new shoes," Carlie said.

Ruby grinned. "So do I, sugar. Here you go. Put these on, then grab your backpack. It's about that time."

Carlie adjusted the Velcro strips to tighten the shoes on her feet, then stood up and stomped around the room, laughing.

"Look at me. Just like a fairy. Just like Tinkerbell in *Peter Pan*."

Ruby frowned. "Just remember…you can't fly like a fairy. But you can run fast."

"Right," Carlie said, and grabbed her backpack, then looked at herself in the mirror. "My mouth still hurts."

Ruby rubbed a little bit of lip balm on it to soften it up, then dropped the lip balm in Carlie's pocket. "For later if you need it," she said. "I also made your lunch today, honey. It's in your backpack. All kinds of soft stuff that you can eat."

"Thank you, Miss Ruby. You're my best guard ever," Carlie said, and hugged her.

"And you're my best girl," Ruby said. "Now let's get a move on."

"Move on," Carlie echoed, and out the door they went.

————————

Melvin Lee was standing on the front steps of the school, watching the kids getting out of cars.

Every morning during the school year, Arlene Winston, the

principal, stood on the steps welcoming students into the building, and now, for the second day in a row, Melvin Lee Wilson had lingered beside her instead of going to his classroom.

"Melvin Lee, you need to go on inside," Mrs. Winston said.

"I can't, Miz Winston! I'm a'waitin' for Carlie. She's new. She ain't got no friends yet but me, and Johnetta bullied her yesterday, so I don't want her to be afraid to come back."

Arlene sighed. She was a sucker for knights in shining armor, even if they were in the third grade and missing teeth. But she hadn't heard about any bullying incident, and after an incident with the Pine brothers being bullied a few years back, she didn't want to relive that again. She needed to speak with Mrs. Schultz, for sure.

All of a sudden, Melvin Lee let out a whoop. "There she is! Hey, girl!" he cried and took off down the steps at breakneck speed.

"Be careful!" Arlene cried, but he'd already cleared the steps and was racing down the walk, dodging between other students coming in. She watched as he slid to a stop, took the backpack from a little blond dressed all in pink, and up the walk they came. "New girl, and cute as a bug," Arlene muttered. "No wonder she was picked on."

As they started up the steps, Arlene saw the girl's swollen mouth and stifled a gasp. *What the hell happened to this child?*

"Hey, Miz Winston. This here is Carlie."

Arlene looked down, straight into the bluest eyes she'd ever seen, and smiled, because the delight in this child's eyes gave her no choice.

"Hello, Carlie. I believe we met when you enrolled. You sure look pretty today."

"I got a fat lip," she said.

"I see that. I'm so sorry," Arlene said. "You two better hurry and get in your room before the bell rings."

"Yes, ma'am," they echoed, and hustled inside.

As soon as the last student was in the building, Arlene went inside and then hurried down the hall to Lena Schultz's classroom.

Lena was standing in the open doorway, greeting her students. "Good morning, Mrs. Winston," she said.

"Good morning, Lena. Do you have a moment before class begins?"

"Of course," Lena said.

"What happened to Carlie Duroy?" Mrs. Winston asked.

Lena frowned. "Johnetta Kilby is what happened. She took an instant dislike to Carlie yesterday and kept grilling her during quiet time, then lied and said it was Carlie talking and not her." Then Lena proceeded to tell the rest of the story, all the way to Carlie's comment, "I don't take no guff."

Arlene Winston frowned. "Keep an eye on Johnetta. I do not want this to become a daily ritual of bullying. I won't tolerate that."

"Yes, ma'am, and neither do I," Lena said.

Arlene stepped into the room, looked around for Johnetta, and caught her glaring at Carlie as if she was an abomination.

Fortunately, Carlie didn't seem bothered by Johnetta's attitude and was making her shoes light up for the little girl beside her.

Johnetta glanced up, saw the principal watching her, and quickly looked away, but her heart sank. Now she was on the principal's radar, too.

Maybe she didn't care about that stupid new girl anyway. Her old mouth was swollen up like a pissed-off toad frog, and she acted like it was nothing. That new girl came from a big city. And her mama was dead. Maybe she was tougher than she looked. Maybe she just better leave that ol' girl alone.

Then, to add insult to injury, Melvin Lee stared hard at her as he passed her on his way to his desk. Of all the kids in class, Melvin Lee was the one she didn't want to cross. And he was the new girl's friend. Yes. She was just gonna pretend that girl didn't even exist. Mama called that "the cold shoulder." So she wasn't ever going to look at her or say her name again. And if that girl wanted to sit with her at lunch, she wouldn't talk.

Johnetta's plan worked fine in her head, but when lunchtime came, Carlie was sitting at a table with three other girls and two boys, one of whom was Melvin Lee, and Johnetta wound up sitting at a table with a conglomeration of kids from three different classes, including Keith Dillon, who farted all the way through lunch.

Some of the kids made fun of him as they ate.

A couple of girls picked up their trays and moved to another table, leaving Johnetta the only girl left at the table. She couldn't even taste her food for the smell and was already in a mood. Then Keith let another slow, quiet fart slip, and Johnetta had had it.

"Keith Wayne, I'm trying to eat my food, and all I taste is your stink. If you fart again in front of me, I will tell everyone you pooped your pants."

Keith blinked, startled by her rage. The other boys were eyeing Johnetta as if she'd just grown horns. They didn't know what the fuss was about. Farting and farting contests were part of their lives. But they also knew enough to give Johnetta Kilby a wide berth, so they shoved the rest of their food into their mouths and got up and went outside to play, preferably somewhere Johnetta Kilby was not.

Johnetta finished her lunch without looking up, then carried her tray to the counter and walked out of the lunchroom with her head up. This was not an auspicious beginning to her third grade experience, and she was wishing that new girl had never come to Blessings.

She stomped out of the lunchroom and out onto the playground with her lower lip hanging and a frown on her face. She kept thinking how unfair this was, and how nothing bad had happened to her before that ol' girl came.

Normally, she would have been playing volleyball with the big kids, because she was tall, but it appeared they'd already formed a team and were playing without her, and that Carlie girl was on the merry-go-round, so that was out too.

She walked over to the benches beneath a large shade tree and plopped down, her shoulders slumped, her whole demeanor one of dejection.

———————————

Carlie wasn't stupid. She'd been keeping an eye on Johnetta's whereabouts all through lunch, and also after she came out on the playground. She didn't want any trouble, but she also didn't want that girl to come up behind her when she wasn't looking and hurt her again. Her mouth couldn't take any more abuse.

Mr. and Miss Ruby were so good to her, and she couldn't quit thinking about adopting them so she'd have a family again. This was a good day. Even if she still had a fat lip and the mean girl was still glaring at her when she thought Carlie wasn't looking.

Carlie watched Johnetta go from group to group out on the playground and then finally go sit down on the bench by herself. She felt kind of sorry for her that she wasn't playing. She looked sad and lonesome. Carlie knew what it felt like to be sad and lonesome.

Then all of a sudden, she saw Johnetta scream, then jump up and slap her arm. Carlie got off the merry-go-round, her heart pounding, knowing something was wrong. When she saw Johnetta start fumbling in her pocket, and then stagger and fall to the ground, Carlie gasped. All she thought was *just like Mama.*

She ran toward Johnetta as fast as her light-up mermaid sneakers would take her, and when she got there, Johnetta's face was already beginning to swell. Her lips were puffy, and she was gasping for air.

Carlie dropped down on her knees and grabbed Johnetta's arm. "Did you get stung? Are you 'llergic?"

Johnetta nodded and tried to reach for her pocket again, and that's when Carlie got it. "EpiPen? You have one?"

Breath was barely more than a wheeze coming out of Johnetta's mouth when she nodded.

Carlie rammed her hand into both of the pockets, and then realized there was a zipper inside one of them. She unzipped it, pulled out an EpiPen, and shoved the orange tip against the outside of Johnetta's upper thigh, then pushed hard. The needle popped out into the muscle, injecting lifesaving epinephrine into Johnetta's body.

All of a sudden there was a crowd of kids around them, and teachers went running toward it, thinking there was a fight. But what they found was Carlie on the ground, holding Johnetta's hand, and Melvin Lee standing behind her with a "get back" look on his face.

Lena was the first teacher to arrive.

"What happened here?" she cried.

"Wasp," Johnetta gasped.

"She got stung," Carlie said. "I saw her scream and slap her arm. Then she staggered and fell down. I ran fast."

Lena looked up at one of the teachers. "Call the office. Tell them we need an ambulance. Allergic reaction to a wasp sting," she said, then looked back at Carlie. "Honey. How did you know to do this?"

"My mama was 'llergic like this. She taught me how to use her EpiPen so she wouldn't die." Her eyes welled. "Then her heart got sick and she died anyway, and I couldn't save her."

Tears rolled, and Carlie wasn't the only one crying.

The ambulance came and took Johnetta away, and all the kids went back to playing, except Carlie. It was a hard reminder of her mother's absence in her life. Even after the bell rang and they went back to their classrooms, Carlie's focus was elsewhere, and Lena let her be. Her whole class was distracted. Johnetta's near-death experience had rattled all of them.

Finally, Lena stopped their last class of the day.

"Okay, boys and girls. I know we're all feeling bad for Johnetta, so let's make her some get-well cards."

She began dragging out art supplies and scissors and glue, and when the chatter began, she let them talk. They needed to rationalize what they'd seen in their own way.

Carlie chose white construction paper, folded it in half to make her card, then began cutting out all colors of flower shapes and gluing them to the front of the card. She glued one big flower cutout inside and drew a fairy sitting on a toadstool beneath it.

Then she wrote: "Get well soon. Love, Carlie."

"As soon as you've finished, bring them to my desk. I'll take them to Johnetta after school."

Carlie carried her card up and laid it down, then lingered. "Mrs. Schultz? Is Johnetta going to be okay?"

"Yes. We got a text that she is at home and will be fine, thanks to your quick actions. You saved her life, Carlie. You are a very brave girl."

Carlie nodded, then went back to her desk.

What Lena didn't tell Carlie was that she'd called Ruby and told her what happened, and what a wonderful and smart little girl Carlie was. They had debated whether she should stay at school or go home. But it was Ruby who made the decision.

"If she's not hurt, then let her stay. The sadness she feels of Shirley's absence is going to be part of her life for a long time. She'll do better being distracted by the other kids."

"Yes, ma'am," Lena said, and the notification of the incident was complete.

When the final bell rang to dismiss for the day, Carlie gathered up her backpack, and Melvin Lee gathered her up with the rest of his siblings, and they headed out the door together.

"You're gonna be okay, girl," Melvin Lee said. "Sometimes we get sad, and then we get over it. And sometimes we get sad again, but it keeps going away."

Carlie nodded, but when Melvin Lee reached for her hand, she didn't pull away. She held on as tight as she'd held onto Mama. As tight as she'd held onto Johnetta. And then when Miss Ruby got out of the car and got down on her knees and hugged her in front of everyone, Carlie held onto her just as tight.

"Thank you, Melvin Lee. You are truly one of the best friends I think I've ever known," Ruby said.

Melvin Lee nodded, then waved at Carlie. "See you tomorrow, girl."

"Okay," Carlie said, and got up into the seat and buckled herself in.

Ruby put her backpack in beside her, then cupped the side of her cheek.

"Let's go by Broyles Dairy Freeze and get a malt on the way home," she said.

Carlie nodded. "Can mine be vanilla?"

"Yes, ma'am, it sure can," Ruby said and got in the car.

As soon as the crossing guard waved them on, they drove away.

Once they got their malts, Ruby drove to the park. They got out and went straight to the gazebo, carrying their cups. After they sat down and had a couple of good sips, Ruby reached for Carlie's hand.

"I am so proud of you for what you did today," Ruby said.

Carlie nodded and took another sip.

"We made get-well cards. I put flowers all over mine and drew a fairy," she said.

Ruby smiled. "That sounds like the perfect card. I know she will like it."

Carlie drank a little more and then looked up.

"Why didn't she like me?"

Ruby sighed. "Oh, honey, sometimes people don't like them-selves. I think maybe she just wished she was more like you, instead of herself. Being jealous is something we all have to deal with. Some people just take it to extremes."

"Why would she be jealous of someone like me? I have problems."

"All she sees is a pretty little girl who's trying really hard to be happy, and I think she doesn't feel pretty or know how to be happy."

"Oh," Carlie said and took another drink, then laid her head against Ruby's shoulder. "I cried for Mama today."

Ruby swallowed back tears. "I know, sugar, and that's okay. It's always okay to feel what you feel. But I want you to think about something for me. Your mama was allergic to insect stings, too, right?"

Carlie nodded.

"So, if she had not shown you how to give her a shot when she needed it, Johnetta might have died today. What your mama taught you saved someone else's life. Knowledge is special. That's something your mama gave you that will always be with you. Even after you adopt us for your family, it will change nothing that had to do with you and your mama. She's always going to be yours. Like we will be yours. People shouldn't have to be alone if they don't want to."

"I don't want to be alone. I want to be your girl, too."

Ruby swallowed back tears. "That's what we want, too. So we're good about that, right?"

"Yes. Good," Carlie said, and took one more sip. "I'm full now."

"So am I. Let's go home. You have lots of time to play before supper and bedtime. You can tell Mr. Ruby all about your day later."

Carlie sighed. "Maybe…could you tell him for me? I don't want to talk about it anymore."

"Yes. I'll tell him for you. Now let's gather up our trash. We can dump it on our way back to the car."

"I'll do it," Carlie said, and took both their cups and carried them to the trash, then raced off toward the car, her shoes flashing with every step.

As soon as they got home and Carlie changed clothes to go out and play, Ruby sat down and called Peanut. As soon as she heard his voice, she began to tell him what had transpired. By the time she was through, she was crying again.

"Oh, Peanut. This child is so special. She's an old soul in this tiny little body, and I don't know why her life had to start off so awful and so hard, but I will spend the rest of my life trying to make up for that."

"As will I," Peanut said. "Her misfortune has been a blessing we never saw coming. Just remember, this too shall pass. I'll be home soon, and we can water stuff together and she can tell me what she wants and we'll ignore the rest."

"I love you," Ruby said.

"I love you, too, pretty lady. And we keep doing this, one day at a time."

———————————

That evening, Lena Schultz stopped by the Kilby house to check on Johnetta. She was sitting on the sofa by her daddy, watching cartoons, when Lena was escorted into the living room.

"Mrs. Schultz! I didn't know you would come see me," Johnetta said. "You can sit by me…if you want."

"I would like that," Lena said, and smiled at John Kilby as she sat down. "How is she doing? Were there any lingering aftereffects?"

"No, thanks to the child who gave Johnetta her shot. She's going to be fine. We're keeping her home tomorrow, but just as a precaution. Mrs. Winston assured us she was getting pest control out to the playground tomorrow to find the wasp nests and get rid of them."

"Good to know," Lena said, and then handed Johnetta a little gift bag. "The kids made get-well cards for Johnetta. They were really scared to see what happened to her. We had a big lesson about allergies after that."

Johnetta took the cards out of the sack and began shuffling

through them, looking at the designs and the signatures, and then she found the white one with all the flowers. She opened it, read the name, and then started to cry.

"I didn't think she would send me one," Johnetta said as her parents gathered around her, unaware of what was behind the tears.

"Who? Who is she talking about?" John asked.

Lena glanced at Johnetta. "I think Johnetta should tell you."

John looked at his daughter. "What's going on, sweetheart? Was someone mean to you?"

Johnetta's tears rolled faster. "No. I was mean to her."

"To who?" her mother asked.

"The new girl. The one whose mother died. She's in my class. I wasn't nice to her. I tripped her and she fell and hurt her face. And then she saved my life, Mama. She's the girl who knew how to give me my shot. She said her mama taught her how to do it because she was allergic, too. She cried after she helped me. She cried so hard because she could save me but she couldn't save her mama. I was so mean. I was a bully. And she made me this pretty card anyway."

"Oh lord," John said, and looked at his wife, and then at Lena. "Thank you for coming. This is something we needed to know. I can assure you there will be no more bullying, and Johnetta will be at school as soon as we get the all-clear from Mrs. Winston."

Lena patted Johnetta's arm.

"You are going to be fine. You told the truth. That's a very powerful thing. Just remember, how someone looks has very little to do with what their lives are all about. Carlie's had a very hard life. She needs friends. Maybe you two could be friends, if you tried."

"I will do better," Johnetta said.

"No. You will do your best," John Kilby said.

His daughter nodded. "Yes. My best."

# CHAPTER 19

Carlie was quiet on the way to school the next morning, and Ruby was worried.

"Are you feeling okay?" she asked.

Carlie nodded. "I'm just remembering my spelling words."

Ruby sighed. Her little perfectionist.

"Oh, good job," Ruby said. "Do you have a test today?"

"No. We have to make sentences with the words. I know all the words and how to spell them, but I'm not sure what a meadow is. I think it's like grass, but I don't know how to use it."

"I can help," Ruby said. "A meadow is like a pasture… Cattle or sheep or horses eat grass there and wildflowers grow."

Carlie's eyes lit up. "Oh! I know the word 'pasture.' I get it! Thank you, Miss Ruby. Now I won't make a mistake. I don't like to be wrong."

Ruby laughed. "You and Mr. Ruby are certainly a pair. He doesn't like to be wrong, either, so his solution is to always be ready with the right answers. Like you. You like to be ready ahead of time."

Carlie's whole demeanor shifted. She liked being like Mr. Ruby.

Ruby smiled to herself as they pulled up at the school. Carlie was already in launch mode. She unbuckled herself and had her backpack in her hand when Ruby put the car in park.

"Got everything?" Ruby asked.

"Got it!" Carlie said, then opened the door, jumped out, and slammed the door shut.

Ruby waited, watching to make sure Melvin Lee had her in his sights, and only after he shouldered her backpack and grabbed her hand did she feel confident enough to drive away.

As for Carlie, she was getting far more attention just getting into her classroom than she had the day before. Big kids were patting her on the head or on the back, telling her "good job" for what she'd done yesterday, and giving her a high five as they passed her in the hall.

Carlie was relieved when she and Melvin Lee finally reached their classroom. She emptied the books out of her backpack and took her seat. Mrs. Schultz took roll call and then made the announcement that Johnetta was fine, she loved her get-well cards, and she would be back in school as soon as the pest control company located and got rid of the wasp nests on the playground.

Then, before their first class began, Mrs. Winston buzzed the intercoms in all of the classrooms for an all-school announcement, and everyone in each of the rooms got still.

"Good morning, students. As you all know, Johnetta Kilby, one of our third-graders, who is allergic to insect venom, was stung by a wasp on the playground yesterday. And I want to recognize Carlie Duroy, also a third-grade student, for her quick action in recognizing that Johnetta Kilby was in distress and for knowing how to inject the EpiPen that saved Johnetta's life.

"We are proud of Carlie for her heroism, and I am designating this as Carlie Duroy Day. She gets to be first in line today and will get a certificate at the monthly assembly, along with our undying gratitude for her quick wit and swift action. That is all. Have a great day."

Carlie was embarrassed to be the center of attention, but she took it in stride. And as the day went on, it became obvious that it was also a turning point for Carlie. She was no longer the new girl. She was the girl who'd saved someone's life.

At noon, she ate a vanilla-and-chocolate-swirl pudding cup and mac and cheese, and she had chocolate milk to drink through a straw. She ran fast in her light-up shoes out on the playground, and the light tinkle of her laughter as she came flying down the slide was nothing short of miraculous. No one fully understood how far Carlie Duroy had come from the devastated child she was a month ago.

All outside activities for the playground ended after the noon recess, because pest control had arrived to locate the nests and rid the school ground of wasps.

They found a medium-size nest of red wasps up under the eaves of the roof and a larger nest of yellow jackets in the trees near where Johnetta had been stung, then removed them and sprayed both areas thoroughly before calling it a day. Mrs. Winston was satisfied and announced regular recesses resuming tomorrow.

Carlie went home with a note to give to Peanut and Ruby regarding her being honored and the certificate she would receive at the monthly assembly. Parents were encouraged to attend.

She handed it to them as they sat down to supper and then grinned shyly when they began to praise her. She took all the praise like the flowers soaking up water tonight from the downpour happening outside.

"Well, sugar, we sure don't have to water anything this evening," Peanut said. "Our flowers are getting a big drink from God."

Carlie liked that.

"I will play dollhouse instead," she said and took another small bite of cloud-soft stewed chicken and dumplings.

"Oh… How did that test on using spelling words go?" Ruby asked.

Carlie's eyes twinkled. "I got an A."

"Awesome," Ruby said, and winked.

"Hey, what am I missing?" Peanut asked.

"A lesson about meadows," Ruby said.

"Ah, sounds intriguing," Peanut said. "I'll have to look that up for myself."

"See, Carlie? I told you Mr. Ruby is always looking things up, so that when he needs the information, it's already in his head."

"I have all kinds of information just waiting to be used," Peanut said, and then waggled his eyebrows at Ruby.

Carlie giggled. She didn't know why they were laughing at each other, but she liked it when Mr. Ruby made jokes.

The wind began to blow, and the rain came down harder, and Peanut got up to turn on the TV and check the weather.

"Just a thunderstorm," he said when he returned, and then finished off his last bite of chicken and dumplings. "Is there dessert?"

Ruby shook her head. "You had to ask? There is always dessert in this house. Tonight it's ice cream sundaes."

"Yum," Peanut said.

"Yum," Carlie echoed.

Peanut got up and began carrying dishes to the sink, while Ruby got out the ice cream and sauces.

"Who wants just ice cream, and who wants the works?"

"I'll have the works," Peanut said. "That means everything on mine," he said for Carlie's benefit.

"I'll have the works," Carlie said.

"Coming up," Ruby said, and she soon had a three-scoop sundae with strawberry preserves and chocolate sauce on Peanut's serving, and a one-scoop sundae with the same on Carlie's. "Do we need a little whipped cream on top?" she asked, holding the aerosol can of whipped cream.

Peanut held up his hand.

Carlie held hers up and then giggled. "Just like at school," she said.

Ruby loved hearing the laughter, and gave Carlie two little squirts, and one big one on Peanut's.

"Aren't you having any?" Peanut asked.

"I'm just having whipped cream," Ruby said, and tilted her head back and squirted the whipped cream straight into her mouth.

The shocked look on Carlie's face immediately dissolved into pure delight and then a giggle.

"When your mouth gets all well and you can open it wide, you get a squirt," Ruby said.

That was a promise Carlie could get her head around, and she happily dug into her ice cream.

---

The next morning, Johnetta was back at school, but her mother was with her. They'd already had a conversation with Mrs. Winston and asked permission to apologize to the class and to Carlie in person, and she'd readily agreed, with the understanding that she would be present, too.

Everyone was in their seats and Mrs. Schultz was at her desk waiting for their arrival, when they finally walked in.

Arlene Winston took immediate control. "Students, we are so happy to have Johnetta back at school all healthy and ready to learn, but before you begin, she has something she wants to say to all of you, and in particular Carlie Duroy. Johnetta, you may proceed."

Johnetta was red-faced and sweaty and looking at her mother for moral support. All she got was a frown and a nod, so she turned to the class and then looked straight at Carlie.

"I want to apologize to all of you for being bossy all the time. And I want to apologize to Carlie for everything I did to her. I was mean to her for no reason. She didn't do anything to me, and I was still hateful. I lied to Mrs. Schultz and said Carlie was talking when it was me. I called Carlie an orphan. I tripped her in the hall and made her fall, and it hurt her. So bad. And then day before yesterday, after all the mean stuff I did, she saved my life."

Johnetta was frozen with fear. The whole class was silent. Staring. She had a horrible feeling they were going to hate her forever. "Carlie, I am so sorry. I already promised Mama and Daddy, and I promised God, and now I'm promising you…I will never be mean to you or anyone else again as long as I live."

Then she waited.

The silence was swallowing her by the second, and then Carlie stood up. "I'm glad you didn't die," she said.

Johnetta nodded. "Me too. I'm sorry. I would like to be your friend, if you can forgive me."

"I forgive you. I will be your friend," Carlie said.

Johnetta's sigh was one of relief.

"Thank you, Johnetta. Now take your seat," Mrs. Schultz said. "Thank you, Mrs. Kilby. Thank you, Mrs. Winston. You've both helped restore peace to my classroom."

Johnetta's mother gave her a look and then left the room, and Mrs. Winston went with her.

The school day began on a positive note, and by the time lunchtime came around, Johnetta was once again included at the tables with her friends and in the games being played outside. She was a little leery of anything flying, but she soon got caught up in a volleyball game and forgot.

When the bell rang to go back inside, she ran to catch up with Carlie and chattered all the way inside, then let Carlie get a drink first. She was rocking all the good deeds today, and Carlie was grateful.

But she was also suspicious. Even though she was willing to be friendly, it was going to take more than an apology before Carlie felt like she could trust Johnetta. And that was okay. She was gaining friends every day, but no one was ever going to be better than Melvin Lee. He was her best friend ever.

---

Ladd and Deborah spent two whole days inside the house cleaning and rearranging. The half-ass studio Ladd had set up in a back bedroom was abandoned and moved to what had once been a family room. Deborah made room for his drafting table, then went up into the attic to get it. It had been dismantled, so she carried the pieces downstairs and put it all back together, then added a leather chair, and a Wi-Fi booster to his laptop for Zoom meetings.

Ladd was so excited about his new office that he'd already begun initial designs for his new project, which left Deborah free to explore her options down at the barn.

She finally settled on a room at one end of the barn that had once been a tack room and hired a carpenter to do some repair on the windows and flooring and put up Sheetrock on the walls. After that, she painted the room, put in a window-unit air conditioner, put up shelves, and added a mini-fridge and a good supply of basic meds for injured animals, with Sam the cat overseeing everything she did. Now the next time they had an injured animal, she'd be better prepared to take care of it.

She and Ladd made love when the mood hit them and fell deeper in love with every passing day.

One morning as they lingered at the breakfast table, planning out their day, Ladd brought up her mother's offer to use her land for grazing.

"I have a question," he said.

"I'm listening," Deborah said.

"It's about the land and the cattle. I've been crunching numbers, and my best suggestion is we either take advantage of your mother's offer and use her grazing land so we can increase the herd, or we just agree that we're keeping cattle here to play with because they're not making any money, or we sell them."

"But then what do we do with the land?" Deborah asked. "Look at Mom's land. It's overgrown and weedy, and little trees are sprouting up all over land we used to mow for hay. Even if we have no animals on the place, we'll still be brush-hogging pastures and keeping fences up because our neighbors have cattle in the adjoining pastures."

Ladd nodded. "Exactly. And that will wind up being busywork that generates no income. I can lease the land to someone else to run their cattle on it, but then we run the risk of having them out on our place, or people driving through our place all the time to get to their cattle, and I don't want that happening."

"Neither do I," Deborah said.

"So, what's your first choice?" Ladd asked.

She didn't hesitate. "Using Mom's land and increasing the herd."

Ladd nodded. "Mine too. So the first thing I guess we need to do is let Maggie know we're going to take her up on her offer, and then we need to check the fencing, repair what needs to be fixed, and build some gates between our two properties so we can move cattle back and forth to different pastures to graze."

Deborah sighed. "We just made our first joint decision, didn't we?"

Ladd grinned. "Yes, I guess we did. Does it make you feel like a grown-up?"

Deborah abandoned her chair and crawled into his lap, straddled his legs, and then wrapped her arms around his neck.

"I am already a grown-ass woman, Ladd Daltry, and you know it."

He groaned as she scooted closer to his crotch.

"I need to talk to you about something else," he muttered.

"What's that?" Deborah said, and leaned forward and gently bit the lobe of his ear.

Breath caught in the back of Ladd's throat.

"I need to know how you feel about a quickie before we go talk to your mom."

She rocked against the growing bulge beneath her.

"Well, I know how you feel, and you know how I feel about spontaneous sex, so I'm all about making your day."

Ladd groaned. "Then head for the bed, lady, before we do this on the floor."

Deborah stood, then leaned over and ran her tongue between his lips before turning her back and sauntering out of the kitchen.

"Lord help me," Ladd said, and got up and followed her.

She was naked and flat on her back on the bed when he walked into the bedroom.

Ladd came out of his clothes, crawled onto the bed and slid between her legs. When she wrapped her legs around his waist and her arms around his neck, he took her hard and fast and lost track of time.

Deborah's eyes were closed, her entire focus on the feel of him inside her and what she felt coming. She was addicted to him, to what he could do to her, and how it made her feel. The added pleasure of it all was knowing what she did to him.

And then the climax hit—a blood-rush of sensations that exploded, leaving her with the aftershocks of the best feeling ever.

She was still riding the shock waves when Ladd came inside her. Even after the last waves of their climax had passed, they lay silent within each other's arms, still joined, reluctant to give up the connection.

Deborah groaned, then tunneled her fingers through his thick, dark hair.

"You are my everything," she said softly.

Ladd buried his face between the pillows of her breasts.

"Ditto," he mumbled, and then raised up and kissed her senseless.

They finally dragged themselves out of bed, got dressed again, and then sat within the silence of the bedroom, looking at each other.

Suddenly, Ladd got up and went to his dresser, dug through his socks until he found a little box, and brought it back to the bed.

"We kind of skipped this part, and you don't deserve that," he said and opened the box. "I love you, Deborah. So much. I don't want a life without you in it. This is your official proposal. Will you marry me?"

"Yes, a thousand times yes," she said, and held out her hand as he slipped the ring on her finger.

"This was Mom's ring. She gave it to me a long time ago and said if I had a lick of sense I would give it to you, but you were gone. Thank you for coming back. Thank you for saving my life. Thank you for loving me again."

Deborah was in tears. She remembered his mother wearing this ring and was so moved that even that long ago she'd wanted her to have it.

"It's a treasure, and I can't believe it fits," Deborah said.

He shrugged. "Some things are meant to be."

Deborah reached for his hand. "Let's get married at the courthouse by a judge. We can have a reception at Granny's sometime afterward and serve cake to our friends, then come home, feed Sam, and go to bed."

Ladd smiled. "Sounds perfect, but are you sure you want to give up your wedding?"

"It's our wedding, and I'm not into frills and fuss," she said.

"Then it's a deal," he said. "Your mother may raise a little hell."

"Well, she'll get over it," Deborah said. "I'll leave the cake and the reception business to her and Aunt Nina and Lovey Cooper."

"So let's go talk to your mom and let her know what's going on. Then we can drive over the pasture to check the fences and figure out where the gates need to go."

"Let me make sure she's there," Deborah said, and called.

Maggie answered. "Hello."

"Mom, are you home?" Deborah asked.

"Yes, we're here."

"Okay, we're coming over. Talk to you soon," Deborah said, and hung up.

Moments later, they were in the truck and headed down the drive.

They arrived within minutes and went in the back door. Maggie and Nina were canning tomatoes and up to their elbows in juice and peelings.

"Oh wow!" Deborah said. "You really are having a bumper crop this year, aren't you, Mom?"

"Yes, and last night's rain is only adding to the bounty. You know how tomatoes are. Lots of hot sun and plenty of water and they go wild. Can you talk while we work?" Maggie asked.

"We sure can," Ladd said. "We discussed it. We want to take you up on the offer of using your pasture for grazing."

Maggie paused, flashing them a big smile. "I'm so happy to hear this!" she cried. "It will be wonderful to look up on the hill and see cattle again."

"Of course we'll take care of all the fencing…any repairs along the way, and we're going to build a couple of gates between the property so it will be easy to move the herd back and forth. We plan to expand the herd, too," Ladd added.

"And there's more," Deborah said, and showed them her ring. "Ladd proposed. Of course I said yes."

Maggie squealed, and she and Nina high-fived each other, splattering tomato juice over both of them.

"Oops," they said, and then laughed.

"Now, before you start dreaming about big weddings, we don't want one. We're going to get married by a judge at the courthouse. We will need two witnesses. I am assuming you and Aunt Nina will do this for us?"

"Yes, of course," Maggie said. "But no celebration at all?"

"We want to have an impromptu reception at Granny's in one of the banquet rooms. Wedding cake and punch. And I'm putting you and Aunt Nina in charge of the cake. Pick out the flavor, the way you think it should look, the groom's cake, too. The whole thing. Ladd and I will pay for it, but we just want to show up and have fun with our friends."

"Awesome," Maggie said. "You give us a date, and we'll take care of the rest."

"Check to see what dates Lovey has open for a Saturday evening in September, and we'll take the first one. Likely, we'll already be married before the reception happens, but doing it all in one day seems too stressful," Deborah said.

"We can do that," Maggie said. "I'm so happy for the both of you, and I'm happy for me, and your daddy would be so happy to know the land was in use again."

"Dad would feel the same way, knowing his legacy will go on," Ladd said.

"So, we're going to head up into the pasture," Deborah said. "Happy canning."

"Just remember it came a good rain last night. There are a couple of low spots that you could get stuck in."

"I remember them, Mom. We'll be fine."

Maggie stood at the back door, watching through the window at the pickup going up through the pasture. She had a moment of heartache, knowing it wasn't Josh in the truck, and then she let it go. It wasn't lost to her. It was just the next generation picking up the torch to carry on.

———

A week later, there were two new gates in the fence line separating the two farms. One led to the northwest pasture. The second led down the hill to the pasture to the east that was just above the house.

They'd built both of the gates above the creek that came out of the hill and ran east through Maggie's place. And when they moved the cattle into the east pasture first, the cattle were hesitant until they began moving through the opening and discovered the lush green grass. At that point, they began crowding to get into the new pasture.

When the last one went through, Ladd shut the gate and stood beside Deborah, watching as the herd began making itself at home.

"Look, the bull found the pond," Deborah said. "He's already waded off in it to get a drink."

"This is wonderful," Ladd said. "Now let's go get ourselves a marriage license. After that, we can schedule a time with a judge and get Maggie and Nina in on it."

They turned and looked down the hill to the farmhouse in the distance.

"Look, Ladd! There's Mom on the back porch. She's waving. She's going to love seeing the cows up here again."

They waved back, walked back to the truck, and drove back to their house. It didn't take long to change clothes before they headed for the courthouse in Blessings.

---

Getting the marriage license was simple. Finding a judge who wasn't in court, not so easy. Finally, they made their way to Judge Garfield's office in the courthouse, knocked, then entered.

His secretary looked up. "Good morning. Can I help you?" she asked.

"We'd like to schedule a time in the next couple of days for Judge Garfield to marry us," Ladd said. "We already have the license."

His secretary smiled. "How fun. Let me check his schedule," she said, and pulled it up on her computer. After scanning through it, she looked up. "He can do it either tomorrow morning at ten, or the day after at four in the afternoon."

"Let's do tomorrow morning," Deborah said.

Ladd nodded. "Agreed. Tomorrow morning at ten."

His secretary made the notation in his schedule, then added, "You will come back here. He'll perform the ceremony in his chambers."

"Yes, ma'am. Thank you," Ladd said, and then left the courthouse and got back in his truck. "Hey, honey. Would you like to eat lunch at Granny's before we go home?"

"Yes," Deborah said. "You drive and I'm going to text Mom so she and Aunt Nina can put that time in their social calendar."

Deborah sent the text while Ladd drove them to Granny's.

"Okay, they're notified," Deborah said, and dropped her phone back in her purse. "Since this is my last day as a single woman, I will eat pie."

Ladd frowned. "You are not being shot at sunrise. This is not your last supper."

Deborah shrugged. "I'm still having pie."

He just shook his head and got out of the truck, then came around the cab and opened the door for her.

"Come on, darlin'. Let's go eat pie."

---

That night after her shower, Deborah came out of the bathroom wearing a nightgown.

Ladd frowned. "That's the most clothes I've seen on you at night since you moved in. What's up?"

"I thought we would call a moratorium on sex until we are married."

"But that's tomorrow," Ladd said.

"I know, and I'm a long way from being a virgin because you took care of that when I was fifteen, but I thought it would be a nice symbolic way to honor the tradition."

Ladd looked at her for about five seconds, then pulled her nightgown over her head, tossed it on the bed, and laid her down on it.

"I retract my statement," she said.

Ladd leaned down, rolled his tongue around her nipple and licked, then did the same to the other one before sliding his hand down her belly.

"This is called foreplay," he whispered, and proceeded to set her on fire, and then he paused. "Still want to call this off?" he asked.

She moaned. "Don't you dare. Finish this."

"It will be my pleasure," he said, and did as he was told.

The next morning they were up before daylight, rushing around to do chores and then racing back to the house to get ready.

Deborah got a text from Maggie. "Mom and Aunt Nina are already on their way to town. They don't want to be late," she told Ladd, and then she laughed. "This is definitely not a traditional wedding, but I'm glad we're doing it this way."

"Me too," Ladd said as he came out of the office, brushing a piece of lint off of his black suit and then dusting off the toes of his Justin boots.

Deborah sighed. "Lord, but you are a beautiful man."

Ladd eyed the dress she was wearing with appreciation. He knew the sheer perfection of what was beneath the cream-colored sheath.

"And you, my love, are stunning. Let's go. We don't want to be late for our own wedding."

They got in Deborah's SUV, with Ladd behind the wheel, and drove away.

Deborah clutched her hands against her breasts, feeling the steady thump of her heartbeat, then turned to look at him.

"I dreamed about this happening a thousand times in my life, and now that the day has come, it doesn't seem real."

"Are you happy?" Ladd asked.

She smiled. "So happy."

He reached for her hand. "So am I."

As it turned out, the ceremony was pretty cut and dried.

Maggie had a bouquet of flowers waiting for Deborah. She shoved it in her hands just before they moved before the judge.

He said a few words, then went straight to his business.

"Do you, Deborah, take Ladd to be your lawfully wedded husband, to love and to cherish in sickness and in health, to be faithful to one another until death do you part?"

Deborah lifted her chin and looked straight into Ladd's eyes. "I do."

The judge nodded and turned to Ladd.

"Do you, Ladd, take Deborah to be your lawfully wedded wife, to love and to cherish in sickness and in health, to be faithful to one another until death do you part?"

"I do," Ladd said.

"Who has the ring?" the judge asked.

Ladd pulled the wedding ring out of his pocket and slipped it on Deborah's finger.

The judge smiled. "By the power vested in me by the State of Georgia, I now pronounce you husband and wife. You may kiss your bride."

Ladd leaned forward, and Deborah met him halfway. The kiss was brief, and then Ladd pulled her back, cupped her cheeks, and kissed her again, longer and tenderly.

"Congratulations, Mr. and Mrs. Daltry. I wish you a long and happy life," the judge said.

Everyone signed the marriage license, and the deed was done.

"Congratulations!" Maggie cried and hugged the both of them. "I have a son-in-law! I couldn't be happier for you both. I'll call you tomorrow with details about the reception. Go celebrate," she said. Then she and Nina left the courthouse and went straight to Granny's for lunch and to spread the word.

Deborah and Ladd were married.

They went home, and as they approached the door, Ladd paused.

"This is the first time we'll walk into this house as husband and wife, so we cross this threshold together," he said, and took her hand. "On the count of two," he said. "One. Two."

They stepped together, both feet crossing the threshold at the same moment, and then they were inside.

"Welcome home, Mrs. Daltry," Ladd said.

"Welcome home, my darling husband," Deborah said, and then she was in his arms.

---

The following Saturday night, there was a come-and-go reception for Ladd and Deborah in the banquet room of Granny's Country Kitchen.

The dress code was casual. The wedding cake was a white four-tier spectacle of sponge cake and buttercream, for which Maggie was responsible, and a chocolate groom's cake with raspberry filling, covered with a dark-chocolate ganache.

They served cake on little paper plates and drinks in paper cups, and there was continuous music pouring out of the sound system.

When an old Garth Brooks song began, Ladd pointed at Deborah. "Sugar, they are playing our song," he said, and swung her into his arms and out on the floor, singing "I've got friends in low places."

It was pure country all night and set the bar for weddings in Blessings to somewhere between shabby chic and a barn dance.

Her uncle Joe Ryman showed up as a stand-in for the traditional father–daughter dance, which made Deborah cry, and as they were two-stepping around the floor he whispered in her ear.

"Those two guys you took down had priors all over four states and arrest warrants in three of them. They won't be out of prison until your hair turns gray. And that good news is my present to the both of you."

"Thanks for letting me know, Uncle Joe. And thank you for this…for the dance."

"My pleasure, darlin'," he said.

The dance ended but the party continued, and it was a party to remember. It was the only official notification to Blessings that Deborah and Ladd's wedding had taken place, but now everyone knew that the call of Blessings had pulled two strays from their little town back to the fold, and that was enough.

# CHAPTER 20

THE ADOPTION PROCESS WASN'T AS SIMPLE AS RUBY HAD assumed, but Peanut got them through it.

Because there were no living relatives, because there was no one left in the world who would have reason to contest the request, and because Ruby was already named by the deceased parent as the legal guardian, and because Peanut knew all the right people to make it happen, less than two months after filing the papers they got a notice for a date to appear before the court.

It was October—a couple of weeks away from Halloween and the annual school carnival. Carlie had a fairy costume hanging in her closet for the event, unaware that something else, something far more wonderful was about to take place.

It was Friday when the letter arrived at Peanut's office in the mail, and he had it in his pocket when he came home from work. He knew this news was going to set the tone for the night and was preparing himself for some kind of Ruby-worthy celebration. She was the best at impromptu parties.

He parked under the carport and then headed up the front steps and let himself in.

Ruby was in the living room on the sofa with her feet up, and Carlie was curled up beside her, her head in Ruby's lap. She'd fallen asleep in the middle of cartoons with her blankie over her shoulders and Hoppy tucked tight beneath her chin, and Ruby was dozing, tired from a long day at work.

When he saw the two of them asleep on the sofa, he thought to himself how utterly beautiful the sight. He tried to be quiet as he closed the door, but Ruby heard the click and opened her eyes.

Peanut put a finger to his lips and then pulled an envelope out of his pocket and handed it to her.

She frowned, opened it, then began reading the letter inside. All of a sudden she gasped. Her eyes widened, and then she clutched it against her breasts.

"Oh, Peanut. Finally."

He nodded, then sat down in the chair next to them.

"It's this coming Monday. Carlie will have to miss school."

"Oh, she won't care. She's going to be over the moon."

Carlie woke up when she heard her name. She opened her eyes, stretched, and then saw Peanut and popped up from Ruby's lap like a jack-in-the-box.

"Hey, sugar," Peanut said. "We have some good news for you."

"What is it?" Carlie asked.

"Next Monday, which is just three days from now, we're going to court for your adoption day."

Carlie leaped up from the sofa and into Peanut's arms and hugged him. "Thank you, Mr. Ruby, thank you."

Ruby was blinking back tears. "Yes, thank you, Mr. Ruby. Thank you for negotiating the legal system for us."

"It's the best thing I ever got to do as a lawyer," he said. "I'm as excited as you two are."

And then Carlie turned to Ruby, her eyes twinkling.

"What am I going to wear?"

Peanut laughed. "Perfect question for a very important day."

"We'll figure it out," Ruby said.

———————————

The following Monday was overcast and promising rain, but it didn't dampen spirits in the Butterman house. Everyone was up early because they had to be at the courthouse in Savannah by 11:00 a.m.

It was Ruby's day off, but she called the school to let them know Carlie would be absent. She made pancakes for breakfast and made one in the shape of a heart for Carlie.

"My pancake is a heart!" Carlie cried.

"Because we love you," Ruby said.

"Then you all have to take a bite of my pancake, because I love you, too," she said.

So they did, with Carlie giggling when Peanut pretended he was going to take the biggest bite. After they ate, they went to their rooms to dress.

Peanut dressed for work…a suit and tie.

Ruby's hair was currently a gorgeous shade of brown with auburn highlights, so she'd pulled out brown slacks and a white blouse.

Carlie chose her favorite purple knit pants and a lavender long-sleeved T-shirt with a sparkly fairy on the front, and her light-up sneakers in case she had to run fast.

When they got ready to load up, Carlie was carrying Hoppy.

"So, Hoppy is going along for the ride, is he?" Peanut said.

Carlie nodded. "Hoppy was with me when I came to live with you. I think he will want to be with me when my name changes so he'll know that it's still me."

"I think that's a good idea," Ruby said, but she wouldn't look at Peanut for fear she'd burst into tears.

Everyone got in, buckled up, and then they were off.

Carlie was unusually quiet, but when Ruby glanced in the back seat and realized she'd just dozed off, she relaxed.

"Ruby…darlin'. She's fine. We're fine. This is going to be an epic day for all three of us."

"I love you," Ruby said.

"I love you, and it goes without saying how much," Peanut replied.

They were about halfway there when the first sprinkles hit the windshield. "Oh shoot. I was hoping we could get in and out of the courthouse before this happened," Ruby said.

"We're going to drive out of it," Peanut said.

Ruby grinned. "Oh, we are, are we? And how do you know that?"

"Because I looked at the weather map before we left. We're just catching the edge of the thunderstorm. It's moving away from Savannah right now."

"I hope you're right," Ruby said.

About a half hour later, they were driving into Savannah. The sun was already peeking through the scattering clouds. The streets were wet, but the rain was gone.

"Behold the sun," Peanut said.

Ruby shook her head. "I stand corrected for ever doubting."

And in the backseat, Carlie was waking up.

"Are we there yet?" she asked.

"We're in Savannah and headed to the courthouse right now," Peanut said.

A short while later, they exited the car and headed across the parking lot for the courthouse. Carlie was still carrying Hoppy.

Once inside the building, Peanut led them to the courtroom.

A guard was at the door and greeted Peanut with a smile.

"Morning, Mr. Butterman," he said.

"Morning, George. We're here to see Judge Bailey this morning."

"He'll be arriving shortly. Have a seat."

Peanut escorted them in, then walked them down to the front and took seats in the front row.

Carlie was eyeing the high ceiling, all of the benches, and the big desk at the front of the room, sitting on what looked like a stage. There was a long wall of windows, and everything was made of wood.

"Is this a fence in front of us?" she asked.

"Kind of," Peanut said. "People sit behind it, and the only people who are allowed to approach the bench—that's what the big desk is called—have to get the judge's permission first."

"'Cause he's the boss?" she asked.

Peanut smiled. "Yes, he's definitely the boss."

Ruby was curious, too, but not about the furnishings.

"I expected other people to be in the courtroom," she whispered.

"When it's an adoption hearing, sometimes the judge just wants the family present and not an audience."

Ruby nodded and then settled back to wait, but they didn't have long.

Within minutes, a bailiff appeared. "All rise for the Honorable Judge H. Bailey," he said.

They stood, watching a door open, and then a heavy-set man in a long black robe walked out into the courtroom and took a seat behind the bench.

"You may be seated," the bailiff said.

They sat back down.

Then the judge called all three of them to come forward.

They walked in tandem, with Carlie carrying Hoppy.

After reading the petition for adoption and verifying the papers in the file before him, the judge asked to speak to Carlie and invited her to sit in the chair next to the bench.

"Good morning, young lady. Would you please tell me your name?"

"Carlie Jo Duroy, and I'm eight years old."

"Thank you," Judge Bailey said. "I understand your mother was the one who placed you with Mrs. Butterman."

"My mama's dead," Carlie said, and pulled Hoppy up beneath her chin.

The judge saw a shimmer of tears in her eyes and regretted the question.

"Yes, I know. Let me ask the question another way. Your mother, before she passed, named Mrs. Butterman as your legal guardian, and you've been living with her and Mr. Butterman since her passing. Is that right?"

"Yes, sir. I live with Mr. Ruby and Miss Ruby now. I want to live with them forever. I want to 'dopt them."

Judge Bailey eyed the stuffed rabbit, then pointed at it. "Who's your friend?"

"This is Hoppy. My mama gave him to me."

"Brought him along for moral support, I see."

Carlie frowned. "I brought him so he knows my last name is going to change. I would not want him to think I was lost."

Judge Bailey leaned back, then looked up at Peanut and Ruby. "A most remarkable child you have here," he said.

"You have no idea," Ruby said. "But we love her to distraction."

Bailey nodded, then looked at Carlie again.

"So tell me, Carlie. Why do you want Mr. and Mrs. Butterman to adopt you?"

"'Cause I'm an orphan. I don't belong to anyone anymore. I don't have family." Her chin quivered just a little. "They want me to be their family, and I want to be. Please don't say no. Please let me be their little girl."

"Oh...this isn't a test," Judge Bailey said. "I've already signed the papers. You, my dear girl, are officially adopted. Your name is Carlie Jo Butterman, and they are legally your parents. Forever and ever."

Carlie exhaled and then started to shake.

Peanut swept her up in his arms, and Ruby was hugging and kissing her.

Carlie was so overwhelmed that she just hid her face against Peanut's shoulder and cried into Hoppy's floppy ears.

"Oh my," Judge Bailey said. "I didn't mean to upset her."

"It's not you, sir. You read her file. It's just dawning on her that she is no longer alone in the world," Peanut said.

Ruby gathered up the papers, and Peanut carried Carlie all the way out of the courthouse and didn't put her down until they got to the car.

"Are you okay, sweetheart?" Ruby asked.

"I'm really adopted?" Carlie asked.

"Yes, ma'am. You are really adopted," Ruby said. "You're our little girl now. For always. You can call me whatever you want, and if Miss Ruby still feels better, that's fine with me."

Carlie shook her head. "Miss Ruby was my guard. You're my mommy now, and Mr. Ruby is my daddy, right?"

"That's right," Peanut said.

She smiled, and then she giggled, and then she threw her arms around their legs and hugged them where they stood.

"I think we're all pretty happy here," Ruby said, blinking back tears. "And I think a celebration is in order. Peanut…what is the name of that pop shop where we got those good hot dogs and ice cream that time?"

"Oh, the Soda Pop Shoppe on Bull Street?"

"Yes! Let's take Carlie to lunch there. It's a fun place to eat, and today is all about fun. Carlie, how does that sound to you?"

"I like hot dogs and ice cream…a lot," she said.

"I know, and so do I," Ruby said.

And so off they went, with Carlie taking in the sights of the city, pointing and asking questions, and then upon their arrival becoming fascinated with all of the offerings to be had inside the shop.

And all the while they were there, Carlie never stopped talking. Even when she was chewing, she was quizzing them.

Mommy this…and Daddy that…and they knew it was because she wanted so badly to say the names. To feel them on her tongue and hear how they sounded coming out of her mouth.

Carlie Duroy didn't just get adopted today. She was reborn.

They were finishing up their ice cream when Carlie suddenly gasped and then stopped eating. "Mommy, do I need to tell my mama I have a new name?"

"No, baby. Your mama is an angel now, and angels know

everything, sometimes even before they happen. Your mama knows and is so happy for you that you can't even imagine."

Carlie nodded. "I just needed to make sure. I would not want her to lose me like I lost her."

"That'll never happen," Peanut said.

———————

That night, after the bedtime story had been read and Hoppy was getting as sleepy as Carlie, Peanut and Ruby tucked her into bed.

Ruby leaned over and kissed her on the forehead, then whispered in her ear, "Goodnight, daughter of mine."

Peanut pulled the covers up over her shoulders, then brushed the curls off her forehead. "Goodnight, my little fairy," he said.

Carlie's eyes were closed, and Hoppy was under her chin, just where she liked him to be. Her bed was soft and warm, and she had never felt so safe.

"Night, Daddy. Night, Mommy," she mumbled, and then buried her nose in Hoppy's fur and fell asleep.

Ruby and Peanut were both teary-eyed as they left her room.

"We're parents," Peanut said as he pulled Ruby into his embrace.

"Better late than never," she said.

———————

The next morning, Peanut rode along when Ruby took Carlie to school, just so he'd know the routine, he said. But in truth, he wanted to see for himself the dedication to the routine Melvin Lee had begun on Carlie's first day.

As soon as they pulled up into the line to let kids out, Carlie unbuckled herself, grabbed her backpack, and opened the door.

"Bye, Mommy. Bye, Daddy. See you this evening!" And she was out.

The door slammed shut, but she was already running toward the school.

"There he comes," Ruby said, pointing to the boy running against the tide of kids walking into the building to get to Carlie.

As soon as he reached her, he gave her a pat on the arm, shouldered her backpack, and then grabbed her by the hand and they headed up the walk and into the building.

"Oh wow!" Peanut said. "So this is every day?"

"Every morning and every day after school."

Peanut sighed. "If this is happening now, it's not going away. We're looking at our future son-in-law. I'd bet money on it."

Ruby shrugged. "As long as he finally has all his teeth when it happens."

Peanut laughed, and then they drove away.

---

Mrs. Schultz had been notified yesterday as to why Carlie wasn't in school, and she also knew that Carlie wanted to announce her new name change herself, so as soon as the last bell rang and everyone was in their seats, Mrs. Schultz addressed the class.

"Children, you all know Carlie was absent yesterday, and she has something she wants to tell you herself. Carlie, why don't you come to the front of the room and share your news."

Carlie walked to the front of the room and then turned to face the class.

"Yesterday, I went to Savannah to the courthouse and got a new name. My name is not Carlie Jo Duroy anymore. My name is Carlie Jo Butterman. Miss Ruby and Mr. Ruby aren't my guards anymore. They're my parents. They adopted me. I have a mommy and a daddy. I have a family again."

Melvin Lee let out a whoop. "Way to go, girl!" he said.

The rest of the class was clapping and cheering, and then Johnetta started chanting: "Go Carlie! Go Carlie!" and the class picked up on it.

The roar coming out of Mrs. Schultz's room was only slightly less noisy than a riot. She let it go on for a few moments and then held up her hands and called for quiet.

"That's enough, children. We can't get too noisy and bother the other classes. But we are all so very happy for our friend, and Carlie, I have something for you that we need to change."

Carlie turned around and watched as Mrs. Schultz pulled something out of her desk.

"We need a new name to put on your cubby," Lena said, and handed her the small placard. "Let's take the old one down and put up one that has your new name on it."

Carlie saw the name CARLIE BUTTERMAN written in big black letters on the strip of white poster board and beamed. She watched Mrs. Schultz take down the old name and slide the new one into place.

"Okay, Carlie Butterman. Welcome to third grade all over again. Now take your seat so I can call the roll and get our day started."

"Yes, ma'am," Carlie said, and hurried back to her desk and slid into the seat. Mrs. Schultz was calling out names, and when she called out "Carlie Butterman," Carlie's heart skipped a beat.

"Here!" she said, and then sat silently within the room, watching how the sunlight swept across the whiteboard, and how the dust motes were suddenly visible in that light, hovering and moving with the air flow like hummingbirds moving from flower to flower.

And as she sat, goosebumps suddenly rose on her arms and on the back of her neck. Her heart began to pound and her vision began to blur from unshed tears, because she was hearing her mama's voice and it made everything she'd gone through suddenly be all right.

*Good girl, Carlie. Good girl! You found your place. You can never lose that which is already inside of you. I am you, and you are the best part of me.*

# LETTER FROM
# THE AUTHOR

Dear Readers,

This is the last book in my Blessings series, but just because the stories have ended doesn't mean Blessings has.

The people you came to love in all these stories will live on in your hearts. The memories you have of them and their lives will be what keep Blessings alive.

And somewhere in another dimension, that which was created here lives on.

People coming and going, living and dying.

Being heroic and cowardly, and in the end persevering and overcoming, because the love and care of others is what humanity is all about.

Thank you from the bottom of my heart for all the years you have given to me. I hope, in some small measure, you will remember the stories I gave to you, because they were the best of me.

With love and blessings,
Sharon Sala

*the*
*Next Best*
*Day*

# CHAPTER 1

IT WAS SATURDAY IN ALBUQUERQUE. THE FIRST SATURDAY IN February and it was cold. But weather was not an issue for twenty-nine-year-old Katie McGrath. She awakened in a state of absolute bliss, calm and confident in everything this day would bring, because she was getting married.

And she wasn't just gaining a husband. She was getting a family, something she'd never had. She didn't know where she came from, or who her parents were, or if she had any extended family. All she'd ever known was foster care.

She'd come close to getting adopted more than once, but every time, something would happen. Either the couple changed their minds about adopting, or decided she wasn't the right fit for their family.

By the time she was twelve, she had a chip on her shoulder and was tired of pretending anyone cared about her. At that point, she was just another half-grown kid in the foster care system, made her peace with it, and finally aged out.

Once she graduated high school in Chicago and left the foster care system, she knew exactly what she was going to do. She wanted to be a teacher, and with the help of a couple of grants, and working two jobs for four years, she put herself through college.

Coming to Albuquerque to teach, which is where she was now, was also where she met Mark Roman. He was a farm boy from Kansas who had a junior position in a CPA firm, while Katie taught at Saguaro Elementary. Now, three years later, here they were, ready to take that next step in their relationship, and she couldn't be happier.

She was just getting out of the shower when she got a text from Lila Perry, a fellow teacher who'd become her best friend, and today, her maid of honor.

It was a 'good morning, good luck, see you at the chapel,' kind of message, but it brought reality to the day. It was time to get moving.

After breakfast, she loaded up her things, made a quick trip to her hairdresser, then hurried off to the chapel to meet Lila.

Lila was short, blonde, and curvy—the opposite of Katie, who was tall, with dark, shoulder-length hair and the metabolism Lila longed for.

When Katie pulled up in the parking lot, Lila helped carry in the dress and everything that went with it.

"I love your hair!" Lila said, eyeing the smooth silky strands as they headed inside.

Katie smiled. "Thanks. This style works really well with the veil," she said.

They spent the next couple of hours getting ready in one of the dressing rooms, laughing and talking.

Gordy Thurman, Mark's best man, arrived early too, and popped in to give her a thumbs up.

"Hey, Katie, you look beautiful. So do you, Lila," he said.

"Thanks," Katie said. "Is Mark here yet?"

"Not yet, but we both know Mark Roman is never going to be the early-bird. He'll be here soon," Gordy said, then waved and went to find the men's dressing room.

The wedding chapel was a popular venue, even though the wedding wasn't going to be a large.

Just Katie and Mark.

A maid of honor and a best man...and fifty guests.

The florist stopped by the bride's dressing room to drop off flowers, then scurried away.

Katie was listening without comment to Lila's continuous spiel about what a fun, week-long honeymoon she and Mark were going to have at the Bellagio Hotel in Vegas.

"You're going to be in the honeymoon suite, living it up. That should warrant enough good luck to do a little gambling while you're there," Lila said.

Katie laughed. "We have a little money put aside for that, too."

They were down to finishing touches when Katie finally sat down on a bench so that Lila could fasten the veil to Katie's hair.

Once Lila finished, she eyed the pretty woman before her and sighed.

"You look breathtaking, my friend. Your wedding dress is as elegant as you are. Mark is one very lucky man."

Katie shivered. "I'm the lucky one," she said, then got up and moved to the full-length mirror in the corner of the room, and did a full turn, eyeing herself from front to back. She felt beautiful and loved.

She was still thinking of Mark when her cell phone rang. When she saw it was him, joy bubbled up into her voice.

"Hello darling. Are you as ready as I am?"

"Um...Katie...I have something to tell you," Mark said.

Katie laughed. "Sorry, but last-minute jitters are not allowed."

"It's not jitters, Katie. I'm so sorry, but I can't marry you."

Katie's knees went out from under her. For a few horror-filled moments, this was her childhood all over again. She reached backward for a chair that wasn't there and sat down on the floor.

"What do you mean, you can't marry me?"

Lila saw her fall, and then heard those words coming out of Katie's mouth and gasped, but when she started toward her, Katie held up her hand.

Lila froze in midstep, horrified.

"I can't marry you, because I'm already married…to Megan. We eloped to Vegas last night. I'm sorry but—"

Katie went numb. "Megan who?" Then she gasped. "Megan, your boss's daughter, Megan? You married Walt Lanier's daughter? Just like that?"

Mark Roman sighed. "No, not just like that. We've been seeing each other for a while and-"

Katie's voice rose two octaves. "You've been cheating on me and still playing out this wedding lie? When you knew it wasn't going to happen? What kind of a low-life does that?"

"I know you're—"

Katie interrupted him again. "Oh! Now your unexpected promotion makes sense. Your boss can't have his daughter married to a lowly CPA in the financial department."

"Look, Katie. I'm sorry. I didn't mean to hurt you. It just—"

Tears were rolling down Katie's face, and her heart was pounding so hard she didn't know she was screaming.

"You lie! You don't give a damn about what you just did to me. Just stop talking. I can't believe I was this blind, but I'm beginning to realize how freaking lucky I am to find this out about you now. You are a cheat and a liar, and you just sold your honor and your word for money. You deserve each other."

"I'm sorry…I'm really—"

Katie interrupted him again.

"Not as sorry as you're going to be when you remember everything about today was paid for with your credit card," Katie said, and hung up.

Lila's eyes were wide with unshed tears, and she kept staring at Katie, waiting for the explanation.

Katie looked up. "Mark married his boss's daughter last night. They eloped to Vegas. Our Vegas. Will you help me up? I have to tell the guests."

Lila reached for Katie with both arms and pulled her up and then hugged her so hard.

"I'm so sorry, Katie. I'm stunned. I can't believe he just—"

Katie pushed Lila away and took a deep breath.

"I should have known. I should have known. I have never been enough," she mumbled. "God give me strength."

Then she tore off the veil, tossed it aside, yanked up the front of her skirt with both hands so she wouldn't trip, and strode out of the dressing room.

Gordy had just received the same phone call from Mark and was coming to look for Katie when he saw her storming up the hall toward the sanctuary with Lila running behind her, trying to catch up.

"Katie, I don't know what to-"

She just shook her head and kept walking, unaware Gordy and Lila were behind her. They stopped at the door to the sanctuary, but Katie kept walking down the aisle before stopping at the pulpit and turning around to face the guests.

Her eyes were red and tear-filled, and the splotches on her cheeks were obvious signs she'd been crying. Total humiliation was imminent, but she lifted her chin and met their gaze.

"I have just been informed there will be no wedding today. I'm not getting married. Mark eloped with his boss's daughter last night. They got married in Vegas. Thank you for coming, please take your gifts home with you when you leave. The wedding food will be going to a homeless shelter."

The communal gasp was so loud Katie felt like it sucked the air from the room, and then the buzzing undertone of shocked whispers began.

She went back up the aisle with her chin up and her head back.

"Worst day of my life," she muttered, and walked back to the dressing room, changed into the clothes she'd arrived in, left the wedding dress and shoes in a pile on the floor, leaving Lila to contact the caterers to have them pack up the food and take it to a shelter.

Lila kept telling her not to worry, she'd take care of everything and call her tonight, but all Katie could do was thank her and hug her.

She couldn't face the pity.

She couldn't face herself.

She wasn't enough.

She drove home in a daze.

---

Meanwhile, Mark Roman was alternating between being a happy bridegroom, and feeling like an asshole, which was fair, because he qualified in both categories. When he'd told Megan he had to make the call to Katie and needed some privacy, she'd been more than understanding.

"I totally understand, darling. I have some things to take care of anyway. I'll be back later," she said.

So now he'd made the dreaded call, and Megan was still gone, and he was too rattled to go looking for her, which, as it turned out, was for the best, because Megan was only two floors down, in one of the suites reserved for the big spenders the casinos called whales.

And this particular whale, who went by the name of Craig Buttoni, didn't just gamble with money. He was in the drug game up to his eyeballs and Megan and her father, Walt, were, in a sense, his employees.

Walt Lanier used his CPA business as a front, while he controlled the flow of cocaine coming in and going out of New Mexico. From time to time, Megan had her own little part in the business, and had just fucked it up by getting married to an outsider.

Craig Buttoni was pissed, and when he found out she was honeymooning in Vegas, he sent her a text she couldn't refuse, demanding her presence in his suite.

The moment she knocked on his door, he opened it, grabbed her hand long enough to look at the size of the ring on her hand, rolled his eyes, and then pulled her into his suite and locked the door.

"Is he making payments on that thing?"

Megan glared. Buttoni was in his late forties, with a bulldog under bite and diamonds in his ears. His eyes were always at half-squint, and she was just a little bit scared of him. She didn't like the comment or the tone of his voice, and snatched her hand back.

"I didn't see you offering anything better," she snapped. "I'm happy. Be happy for me."

Craig liked it when she got feisty, but business was business.

"He's not in the loop. He could cause us trouble," Craig said.

Megan glared. "You keep your hands off him. If I think he's dangerous to us, I'll just dump him. I got married in Vegas. I can get unmarried here if the need arises."

Craig held up his hands and took a step backward.

"There's a lot riding on your itch for sex. Just making sure we understand each other," he said.

"I can scratch my own itch," Megan said. "I married him because I love him."

Craig threw back his head and laughed. "Okay. But you're the one with the most to lose. He can't suspect anything. If you fuck up, you know my rule for fuckups."

"Yes. You eliminate them," Megan muttered. "I'm leaving now. Happy roll of the dice," she said, and let herself out.

When Megan got back to the honeymoon suite and saw the look on Mark's face, she knew what she had to do, and it all revolved around getting naked.

Katie holed up in her apartment for the entire week that would have been her honeymoon, and slept away the shock, then ate away the rage, and ignored the phone calls from everyone but Lila. Those, she took, only to reassure her best friend that she was still kicking. By the time she was ready to go back to Saguaro Elementary, she had her game-face on.

It took that week of solitude to remind herself that, in the grand scheme of things, her heart had been broken, but nobody died. She was tougher than some man's lies. She didn't need a man to take care of her. She didn't need anyone. Ever again.

It was time to go back to work. Some would talk behind her back. And some would not. But her first grade students would not know the depth of her heartbreak. She'd been Miss Katie before and she was still Miss Katie, and she would keep their little world safe and secure, and they would know they were loved.

For Katie, it was enough.

*Six weeks later*

Katie was getting ready to walk her class down to the cafeteria for lunch.

"Boys and girls, if you brought your lunch, get it out of your backpack and get in line," she said, and then took a deep breath when two of her six-year-olds suddenly lost their minds, launched at each other, and began wrestling in the floor. "Oh no! Alejandro! Kieran! I'm so sorry, but you forgot the rules. Get up and go to the back of the line."

Alejandro scrambled to his feet, his dark eyes wide with instant distress.

"But Miss Katie, it's my turn to be leader!" he said.

"I know!" Katie said, keeping the tone of her voice between regret and it's out of my hands. "You and Kieran made bad choices. Now, get to the back of the line and do not look at each other. Do not touch each other. And just to make sure, I'll be watching you to help you not forget again. Allison, you will be leader today."

"Yes, ma'am," the little girl said, and strode to the front of the line like she was walking a runway.

Katie sighed again. Three more hours and Saguaro Elementary would be out for Spring Break. It was none too soon.

The past weeks had been stressful beyond words. By the time she'd returned to work, everyone knew what had happened. Half of the staff wanted to talk about it. The other half just gave her sad, hangdog looks. It was the students who'd saved her sanity. They didn't know what happened, and the few who'd asked her if her name had changed, were fine when she answered, "No."

But today, the kids were antsy to be gone, too, and Alejandro and Kieran were examples of the lack of focus within the building.

Katie glanced up at the clock again, then nodded at Allison.

"It's time. Lead the way," Katie said, and watched Allison disappear out the door, with the other students in line behind her. Katie stayed toward the back of the line to make sure her little rebels were still there, and up the hall they went.

They were halfway to the cafeteria when they began hearing popping sounds, and what sounded like a scream in another part of the building.

Before she could get on her walkie to check in with the office, the principal was on the school intercom, and the tremble in her voice was enough to freeze Katie's blood.

"We have an active shooter in the building. Proceed with lockdown procedures immediately."

Katie groaned. She was halfway between her room and the lunchroom, and immediately ran to the nearest classroom, which happened to be Lila's room, and yanked it open.

Lila was already in lockdown mode and running to lock the door when Katie appeared.

"Lila! We need to shelter with you. We were on our way to the cafeteria. It's too far from our classroom to go back!"

"Get them in here," Lila said, even as she was getting her students on the floor against the far wall, away from the door.

"In here! In here!" Katie cried and began hurrying her students into the room.

A series of single shots rang out, as if the shooter was picking targets, but the screams she'd been hearing suddenly stopped, and the silence was more terrifying than the screams.

Katie was counting kids as they entered the room, and then realized she was missing two. In a panic, she spun and saw Alejandro back down the hall, lying on the floor with blood pouring from his nose, and Kieran kneeling beside him.

"Oh no," she groaned. "Lila. Proceed with lock down. I've got two missing," she cried, and turned and ran.

Lila saw the little boys way down the hall, and Katie running in an all-out sprint to get to them, even as the screams and gunshots were getting louder.

"Hurry, Katie! Hurry!" she shouted, and then slammed the door shut and locked it, before running back to the students who were now in a state of panic. Some were crying, and some were too scared to move. She had to get them into the safest part of the room and flat on their stomachs. The smaller the target, the harder they were to hit.

For Katie, the slamming door was a relief to hear. Her students were safe. Now all she had to do was get the last two and get them back inside with the rest of her class before it was too late.

---

Alejandro was crying so loud he didn't hear his teacher calling to them, but Kieran did. When he heard Katie shouting at them, he looked up, realized the other kids were gone, and the hall was empty.

"Get up, Alejandro! Miss Katie said we have to run!" Kieran cried.

At that point Alejandro looked up and realized they'd been left behind.

"Miss Katie...I fell!" he cried, as Katie came to a sliding halt in front of them.

"I see, baby, I see," Katie said. "But we have to run now," she said, and grabbed them both by their hands and started back up the hall with them, moving as fast as their legs would take them.

All of a sudden, she heard the sound of running footsteps behind her and panicked.

*Oh God, oh God...he's behind us. No time to get into another room. No time. No time.*

And then some older students flew past her unattended.

"He got in our room. He shot our teacher," one girl cried, as she flew past.

Katie got a firmer grip on the boys and began pulling them as she ran, but the shots were louder now. The shooter was getting closer.

Then out of nowhere, one of the coaches appeared at Katie's side. Their gazes met as he reached down to help her. His hand was on Kieran when a bullet hit him in the back of the head, splattering blood everywhere as he dropped.

Both boys screamed.

"Miss Katie!" Alejandro cried.

The shock of what Kieran had seen was too much as his little legs went out from under him.

Katie yanked Kieran up into her arms and pushed Alejandro in front of her.

"Run, baby, run!" she shouted. "Go to Miss Lila's room. See the door up ahead! Just run!"

No sooner had she said that when a bullet hit the floor between her feet, and then a second one ripped through her shoulder. It was like being stabbed with fire. She screamed, nearly dropping Kieran, and in a last-ditch effort to save the boys, she grabbed Alejandro and threw herself on top of them.

Kieran was screaming and Alejandro was in shock.

Katie's shoulder was on fire and everything was fading around her.

*God, oh God, please don't let them die.* She wrapped her arms around the both of them and held them close, whispering.

"Alejandro...Kieran. Don't talk. Don't move. I love you."

More gunshots rang out. She heard a body drop beside her, but she wouldn't look. Couldn't look. And then there were more screams, more shots as Katie took a second shot in her back, and everything went black.

Seconds later, police appeared in the hall in front of them and took the shooter down, but the damage was done. Katie was unconscious and bleeding out all over the boys beneath her.

––––––––

The shooting was all over the news, both locally and nationally.

Thirty-six hours later, of the five adults who had been shot, Katie McGrath was the only one still alive.

One student, a fifth-grade girl, died at the scene, and twelve other students had been shot and transported to hospitals. All but two of the surviving wounded were released within a couple of days, and the last two were due to go home tomorrow.

Only Katie's condition was unknown. Her tenuous hold on life was still wavering, and she had yet to wake up.

––––––––

*Four days later*

The news was traveling fast throughout the hospital.

Katie McGrath was exhibiting signs of regaining consciousness.

Lila Reece was all the 'next of kin' Katie had, and she was on her way to the hospital for her daily visit when she got the call.

She cried the rest of the way there out of relief.

Visiting time was in progress when Lila entered ICU. She went straight to the nurse's desk to get the update.

"Her heart rate is stronger. Her pulse is steady, and all of her vital signs show signs of waking," the nurse said.

Lila nodded, too emotional to comment, then hurried to Katie's bedside. She clasped Katie's hand and began patting it and rubbing it until she got herself together enough to speak.

"Hey, Katie honey…it's me Lila. Can you hear me? You have no idea how many people have been praying for you. Your students have been calling me every day, asking for updates. You saved them. They love you so much. We all do. I'm here. Right here. Nothing to be afraid of anymore."

———

Katie was trying to wake up, but she couldn't think what to do, or how to move. She heard a familiar voice, and was struggling to focus on the words, but they were garbled.

Then she heard her name. Katie! Someone was calling her. She wanted to respond, but it was too hard, and so she slid back into the quiet. But the voice wouldn't let her go.

Memories were coming back with the sounds. She'd been running. There was blood. *My students! Where are they?*

She moaned, then someone was holding her hand. She tried to grip the fingers, but moving made everything hurt.

The voice…familiar, but she kept trying to remember what happened. *We were running. Hide. Hide. Hide.*

"Her eyelids are fluttering," Lila said.

The nurse nodded.

Lila leaned down near Katie's ear, speaking quietly.

"It's me, Katie. It's Lila. You were so strong for the little ones. They're safe, Katie. They're all safe… and so are you."

A tear ran down the side of Katie's temple.

Lila's eyes welled. "You hear me. I know you hear me."

It took a few seconds for Lila to realize Katie was squeezing her fingers. Ecstatic, she squeezed back.

"Yes, Katie, yes, I'm here. I have to leave now, but I'll be back. You aren't alone, baby. You are not alone."

Visiting time was over and the floor was still bustling with nurses tending patients, and doctors coming and going.

Katie's imminent awakening brought her surgeon to ICU to check her stats, and someone had tipped off the media. They were back out in the hospital parking lot, waiting for her doctor to come out and make a statement regarding her status, because Katie McGrath's welfare had become the city's concern.

Video from the halls of Saguaro Elementary had shown the panic and horror of that day. There were images of teachers and children being shot on the run, and of the shooter coming out of classrooms he'd just shot up.

Parents were traumatized as they watched their children all running for their lives. And then the blessed relief of the arrival of the police, and the shooter being taken down.

The first funeral had come and gone, and three other funerals were imminent for victims. The grief and horror in the city was real.

There was a clip of Katie throwing herself on top of two little boys, and then getting shot in the back, that someone had leaked to the media. It was viewed tens of thousands of times before the administration realized it, and had it pulled.

The shooter was unknown to the community—a loner who'd been in Albuquerque only three months, and while the authorities were still investigating, his reason for what he'd done died with him.

There were so many people grieving the people who'd died, and others coping with wounded children who were going to suffer lasting trauma to their bodies, and both teachers and children so traumatized by the incident they didn't want to go back to school. They all needed good news, and finding out that Katie McGrath might be waking up, was it.

―――――――

Katie opened her eyes to a nurse and a doctor standing at her bedside.

She recognized being in a hospital, but she was confused about why. She hurt. Had she been in a wreck? What had—?

And then it hit her! The shooting!

"The boys… the boys…" Her voice drifted off, but the doctor knew what she meant.

"Your students are safe. The two little boys you protected…they were not wounded. You saved their lives. All of your students are safe."

Tears rolled down the side of her face. "Died…saw…" she mumbled, and closed her eyes.

"Yes, but you're not one of them. Your wounds were serious, but you're going to heal, and that's what matters. A whole lot of people have been praying for you. They are going to be ecstatic that you finally woke up," he said, and patted her arm.

It was the words, 'finally woke up,' that made her realize she'd been unconscious for a time.

She reached for her mouth. Her lips were dry. The words felt caught in her throat.

"How long…here?" she asked.

"Four days out of surgery," the doctor said. "Welcome back, Katie. Just rest. All you have to do right now is rest and get well, and I have the pleasure of going out to tell the media that you're awake."

---

They moved Katie from ICU to a private room the next day, and Lila was right beside her all the way, quietly celebrating the knowledge that her best friend was still on this earth. As for Katie, she waited until the nurses finally left before she began questioning Lila.

"Are my kids all okay? What about Alejandro? Kieran?"

"They're all good. You saved their lives, Katie," Lila said.

Katie sighed. "Who was the shooter. Why did he do it?"

"A stranger. He'd only been in Albuquerque three months. No one knew him, and as far as I know, his reasons died with him."

Katie's voice was trembling. "I know Coach Lincoln died. He was right beside me when it happened. Who else?"

Lila's eyes welled. "Darrin Welsh, the security officer. Our principal, Mrs. Garza. Ellie Warren, who was one of the science teachers, and a little girl named Barbie Thomas—a fifth grader."

"Oh my God," Katie said, and burst into tears.

Lila held her hand and cried with her. Being a survivor brought its own level of hell. The guilt of being alive.

# CHAPTER 2

After ten days in the hospital, Katie was released.

Lila picked her up from the hospital and took her home, made sure Katie was comfortable, and left to get her some fresh groceries.

Katie was propped up in her bed with a cold drink on the side table, and an enormous pile of mail beside her. According to Lila, they were well-wishes from students and their families, as well as get-well wishes from strangers who'd heard about the shooting and her bravery and sent the cards to Katie in care of her school.

She laid there for a bit, staring at the pile of mail, and then closed her eyes, trying to make sense of what she was feeling. After being jilted, she'd slipped back into the old foster kid mindset, wondering why she was never enough, why there was no one who wanted her, and as she grieved the loss, buried what was left of her dreams in her broken heart. But after she'd gone back to work, the passing days moved into a maze of repetition that began to feel safe again.

Then the shooting happened, and when she took the first bullet, she was so afraid that she would die before she got the boys to safety, they were all that mattered. Now, knowing all twenty of her students had come through that horror without being shot was all she could have asked for. She would have gladly died to keep them safe, only the sacrifice had not been necessary, after all.

There had to be a message in this for her.

Maybe she mattered more than she thought.

She mattered enough to still be breathing.

Her cell phone rang. She glanced at it, let it go to voicemail, and then got up and slowly walked through the rooms of her apartment. They were familiar. Nothing had crossed a boundary here that felt threatening. She'd been alone all her life. She could do this. She could get well here, but going back to bed was the first step. Her legs were shaky as she crawled into bed and began sorting through the pile of mail, until she found names she recognized, and began with those.

Some were from students she'd had in previous years, some from parents, from staff and teachers from Saguaro Elementary, and many from people across the country. Some of them even had money in them, and all of them were filled with love and prayers.

There was a big manila envelope filled with messages and hand-drawn pictures her students had sent to her. She knew them well enough to read between the lines. They were traumatized by what had happened to them and afraid she was going to die.

Katie was in tears as she put them all back in the manila envelope. They wanted to know when she was coming back, and she didn't know if she could. Just the thought of being back in those halls made her nauseous. She was scared to go back, and scared what would happen to her if she didn't. What if she was too messed up to ever work in public again?

She rubbed the heels of her palms against her eyes and leaned back against the pillows, trying to regain her equilibrium as she gave herself a pep talk.

This was her first day home from the hospital.

She was a long way from being healed.

Nobody was pressuring her to do anything, and she had a lot of sick leave built up, so she was still getting paid.

She would figure it out as she went, just like she'd done everything else, only not today. She fell asleep with a pile of letters in her lap, and woke up when Lila came back with groceries.

"Hey honey!" Lila said. "I got that prescription for pain pills filled. Do you need one?"

"Yes," Katie said, and started to get up.

"No, I'll bring it to you," Lila said.

Katie eased back against her pillows as Lila ran to the kitchen, grabbed the sack from the pharmacy, then raced up the hall again.

"Here you go. It says one every four hours, and no more than six in twenty-four hours. I'm going to put up your groceries."

"Thanks, Lila," Katie said, and was opening the container when Lila left.

Katie could hear Lila banging around in the kitchen, and relaxed. Whatever needed doing in there, Lila had it covered.

Katie took a couple of pain pills, and then slid back down in the bed and closed her eyes. The sound of Lila working in her kitchen was comforting as she drifted off to sleep.

---

Lila began by cleaning out the refrigerator, dumping what was bad or out of date, and carried out the garbage, then began putting up the new groceries. When she had finished, she went back to tell Katie she was leaving, only to find her asleep.

She wrote a quick note, turned out the lights, and let herself out of the apartment.

Katie woke some time later, found the note and food ready to eat in the refrigerator, and once again, was so grateful for such a good friend.

She spent the rest of that evening going through the pile of mail. They were unexpected and heart-warming, except for one. Even before she opened it, she recognized the writing.

Mark.

She stared at it for a few moments, debating with herself whether she would even open it, then frowned and tore into it, pulled out a standard get-well card with religious notes, and a brief comment about how proud he was of her. She stared at the signature for a moment, wondering what the hell made him think she ever wanted to hear from him again, and then threw it in the trash.

That night, she dreamed of the shooting and woke up shaking, stumbled to the bathroom and threw up. Afterward, she made her way to the kitchen and got something to drink to settle her stomach. She was standing in the shadows with the glass of Sprite in her hand when she heard sirens in the distance and started shaking. It made her angry that the woman who'd given birth to her had chosen to abandon her in an alley, and that two men, one she'd loved, and one she never saw coming, had come close to destroying her.

*What the hell am I supposed to be learning from all this crap?*

She took a sip of the drink in her hand and then walked to the window and looked out at the city below. The lights of the police car she'd heard were out of sight, but even at this time of night, the streets were still teeming with cars and people. Too many people. Too many loose cannons. She did not feel safe here. Not anymore.

She carried her drink back to the bedroom, took a couple more sips, and then got back in bed and turned on the TV. She finally fell back asleep with a Disney movie playing in the background and woke up after nine a.m. to find a text from Lila, reminding Katie to message her if she needed anything, and that she was bringing fried chicken and sides in time for her evening meal.

———————————

And so Katie's self-imposed isolation and healing began.

They told her to take it easy and rest, and she was trying her best, even though it seemed as if the phone never stopped ringing. She kept wondering how people even got her number, and decided someone in the school system had to have given it out. But if she didn't know the name that popped up, she let it go to voicemail. It was her only defense.

She was mobile, to a degree, but still not released to drive, so she had groceries delivered, and sometimes food delivered, and the only person who came to see her was Lila.

As time passed, her isolation brought home to her, how small her circle of real friends was, and admitted most of that was her fault. She didn't want to be out and about.

However, the faux safety and comfort she felt during the day, ended when the sun went down and the lights went out.

Then, the dreams came as she relived the panic, the pain, the horror.

Some nights she woke up screaming.

Some nights she woke up sobbing.

And every night when she went to bed, there was a subconscious fear that she would not wake up at all.

The toll it took on her physically and mentally was becoming obvious. Her clothes were hanging loose on her body now. Her face was thinner. She jumped at the slightest sounds. She was Zooming with a mental health professional.

She'd survived, but at what cost?

———————

Mark and Megan were living the high life. His new job was fulfilling, and while Megan wasn't exactly the homebody he'd expected of a wife, their time together was everything he'd dreamed it would be.

When Mark went to work, he left his wife in bed. And when he came home from work, she always had a beautiful table set, and good food ordered in. It didn't even matter that she never cooked and didn't clean. She was pretty, and rich, and good in bed, and he knew she loved him.

And then the shooting happened at Katie's school, and the fantasy he'd been living in began to deflate. As soon as he heard about it, he was in hysterics. He and Megan had their first fight about her. He wanted to go to the hospital to see her, and she told him if he did, not to come home.

Mark was pleading. He didn't believe her. "But Megan, it doesn't mean anything other than not wanting her to suffer alone."

And then Megan screamed and threw a plate all the way across the room, shattering it against the wall.

"No, Mark! You left her alone when you married me. She is no longer your business, and neither is her life. You're a fucking fool if you think she wants anything to do with you. Don't you understand that she probably hates you? She'll live or she'll die, whether you're there or not."

Mark was in shock. The woman screaming at him was a stranger. He'd never seen this cold, unfeeling side of her and in that moment, something between them shattered.

He turned around and walked out of the room and didn't come back.

Almost immediately, Megan realized what she'd done and went after him. But it was too late. She saw the shock on his face. The damage was done.

"Look. I'm sorry that felt brutal," she said. "But you aren't seeing this from a woman's viewpoint. You betrayed her. She will hate you forever. And you're betraying me by wanting to rush to her side. How do you think that makes me feel?" she cried.

"Like an insecure bitch?" he asked, and closed the door to their bedroom in her face.

She gasped.

"I won't be talked to like this," Megan screamed. "I'm going to Daddy's to spend the night."

He didn't respond, and he didn't come out. Megan was furious, but at a loss. Instead of following through on her threat, she slept in one of the spare bedrooms and the next morning got into the shower with him and gave him the blow job of his life.

The fight was over.

But neither had forgotten what had been said.

The honeymoon was over, but the marriage was still intact.

It was a Tuesday in late May when Katie got an invitation she couldn't ignore. It was from Boyd French, the new principal at Saguaro Elementary, requesting her presence at a special assembly on Friday to honor those who died, and the victims who survived.

The thought of it made her ill. But she needed to know if she could go back to that school and teach again, so she told him yes, and didn't tell Lila. She could drive herself there. She could walk into that building on her own. After that, she made no promises, not even to herself.

―――――――

Friday came in a burst of sunshine in a cloudless sky the color of faded denim, with the Sandia mountain range delineating the space between heaven and earth.

Katie dressed with care, trying to minimize her waif-like appearance by wearing a long, pink and green floral dress with a black background. The hem stopped mid-way between her knees and ankles, hanging loose upon her slender body. The petal-style sleeves were comfortable, and the sweetheart neckline finished off the look. She chose plain black flats and wore her hair pulled back for comfort against the heat of the day, but her hands were shaking as she grabbed a small pink shoulder bag, then dug her car keys out of the bag, slipped on a pair of sunglasses, and headed out the door.

It was just before one p.m. when she pulled up into the school parking lot, and when she got out, fell into step with a small crowd of people entering the building. She kept her head down and got all the way into the office without being stopped.

Michelle Aubry, the school secretary, looked up just as Katie was taking off her sunglasses, and burst into tears.

"Katie! Oh. I'm so glad to see you."

Katie sighed. *This is why I don't go anywhere. Everyone I see reacts like they're seeing a ghost.*

"It's good to see you, too, Michelle. I was summoned to attend an assembly. I assume it's in the gym?"

"Yes. They have a stage set up and the media is here, too, so prepare yourself."

"Oh lord," Katie said, and then a man came out of the office, saw Katie, and came toward her with his hand outstretched.

"Miss McGrath, I'm Boyd French. Thank you for coming."

Katie shook his hand and smiled. "Katie, please, and it's nice to meet you, sir."

Boyd French shook his head. "Believe me, the honor is mine. It didn't take me long to learn how much you have been missed. I'm not going to pretend this day will be easy for you, but you have no idea how beloved you are here. Your students ask me every day if you're coming back. I think they just need to see your face to know for themselves that you are well."

Katie's gut knotted. Guilt was a hard co-pilot, and knowing her children wanted her back made her feel sorry for them, and for herself.

"I'm looking forward to seeing them, too," she said.

"Well then, if you're ready, I'll be escorting you to the assembly," Boyd said, and then glanced at Michelle. "Call if you need me."

"Yes, sir," the secretary said, and then waved at Katie as the duo left the office, and started down the maze of hallways to get to the gymnasium at the far end of the building complex.

There were dozens of people in the halls, all of them walking toward the gymnasium, chattering with each other, and calling out to friends as they passed.

A sudden screech of laughter made Katie jump.

Classroom doors were banging as lagging students hurried to the gym to get into place. To Katie, it sounded like gunfire.

The first time it happened, she gasped, and for a moment, she was back in that day, looking for a place to hide.

Boyd saw her turn pale and slipped his hand beneath her elbow. "I'm sorry. I didn't think," he whispered.

Katie shook her head. "It's okay. Just nerves," she said, then lifted her chin and focused on the cool air from the air conditioning wafting down the back of her neck.

Boyd wasn't fooled. He'd done two tours in Afghanistan and Iraq and he knew PTSD when he saw it. Katie McGrath was struggling. Maybe it would be better when they got out of the hall.

"We're almost there," he said quietly.

Katie nodded, blinking back tears. This feeling was awful. She was failing horribly. If she couldn't get down a school hallway, how would she ever be able to teach here again?

And then they reached the gymnasium. The bleachers were packed with students and families. And the chairs set up in concert-style out on the gym floor were for victims and their families.

Katie assumed she would be sitting there, until the principal led her up on the stage. And the moment she started up the steps, she noticed cameramen from local news stations aiming their cameras at her. She was trying to come to terms with being the focus of attention when she heard little voices begin calling out, "Miss Katie! Miss Katie!" and lost it.

She made herself smile as she turned and waved, but she couldn't see the faces for the tears.

Boyd seated Katie next to him, handed her a program, gave her a quick nod, and then moved to the podium.

"Ladies and gentlemen, students, teachers, and members of the media, thank you all for coming. Six weeks ago today, a tragedy occurred here at Saguaro Elementary. A stranger came onto our property and shot his way into the building, causing great tragedy. This gathering is to honor and commemorate those wounded and those we lost, and thank you for coming."

The big screen above the stage was suddenly awash in color, with the logo of Saguaro Elementary, and as Boyd continued to speak, the images of those he began naming flashed on the screen behind him.

"As you all know by now, we lost our security officer, Darrin Welsh, a valued member of our staff. He'd been with us for almost eight years, and he lost his life in a valiant effort to stop the shooter. Elena Garza, who had been your principal for thirteen years called the police, then ran out of her office into a blaze of gunfire and died. Coach Aaron Lincoln, who had been your soccer coach and history teacher, died trying to save children caught out in the hall. Ellie Warren, one of our science teachers, had already turned in her paperwork to retire at the end of this school year, and was shot and died in her classroom. And we lost Barbie Thomas, one of our precious fifth grade students, who was looking forward to moving into middle school."

The silence within the walls was broken only by the sounds of weeping.

Boyd French cleared his throat, and continued, and so did the slide show, as he move on to the recognition off each of the twelve students who'd been wounded, and then the last picture was one of Katie.

"All of you...those who were not wounded, and those who were...those who we lost, and those who were saved, are all heroes, because you did everything right. It was the stranger who did everything wrong. But, in the midst of all the tragedy, first-grade teacher Katie McGrath shielded two of her students with her body, took the bullets meant for them, and saved their lives, and for that, we come today to also honor Miss McGrath. Katie, would you please come forward."

Katie stood, her knees shaking. And as she began walking toward the podium, everyone in the gym began chanting her name.

"Katie! Katie! Katie! Katie!"

Boyd held up his hand, then pulled a plaque from a shelf beneath the sound system.

"Katie, on behalf of the Albuquerque public school system, and Saguaro Elementary, it is my honor to present this award. It reads: To Katie McGrath, for courage, bravery, and sacrifice, in the line of fire."

He handed it to Katie, who was visibly overwhelmed as she clutched it to her.

"Are you okay to say a few words?" he whispered.

She nodded, then moved to the microphone and took a deep shaky breath.

"Thank you. This is unexpected, and such an honor. But it feels strange to accept an award for doing the same thing every other teacher here was doing that day. We were all putting ourselves between your children and the danger they were in. Every year, your children, who you entrust to our care, become ours for a little while each day. We work hard to make sure they are learning what matters. Some days we want to wring their necks. Some days we are so proud of them for how hard they try. And every day we love them. Enough to die for them, which is what happened here. I don't know why I'm still here, but all I can assume is that I am supposed to be. Again, thank you for this recognition, and thank you for the hundreds of letters and well wishes that were sent to me."

The audience gave her a standing ovation as she walked back to her chair, wiping tears as she went.

The principal ended the program with a final announcement.

"Earlier this morning, we unveiled five wooden benches on the playground, each bench has a name etched on it to commemorate a precious life that was lost here. Yes, the names will be reminders of our tragedy, but as time passes, the benches will also come to represent a place to rest from the innocence of play, and for teachers to sit while they watch over your children on the playgrounds. We will not forget.

"Now, this concludes our program. Students, unless your parents are here, you will return to your classes. Parents, if wish to take their children home with you at this time, they will be excused. Just notify their teachers before you leave with them. And...Katie, I think your class is going back to their room with their parents and teacher in hope that you will stop by to visit with them before you leave."

Katie nodded, but she was sick to her stomach. How in the hell was she going to get through this without falling apart?

# COMING HOME TO MAGNOLIA BAY

People and pets find their forever homes in this charming
small-town romance from Babette de Jongh

Sara Prather's young son, Max, has fallen in love with Jett—a friendly
bully breed at the Furever Love Animal Shelter. But when animal trainer
Justin Reed chooses Jett for a film, panic sets in. Thankfully Reva, an
animal communicator, agrees to let Jett work on the movie on one condition: Justin must stay in Magnolia Bay and train Jett as a service dog for
Max. And the more time Justin spends with Sara, Max, and Jett, the more
he realizes that he's also looking for a place to belong…

> **"Charming… Just the right blend of
> romance and animal cameos."**
> —Debbie Burns, bestselling author of the Rescue Me series

For more info about Sourcebooks's books and authors, visit:
**sourcebooks.com**

# THE WEDDING GIFT

Heartwarming Southern fiction from bestselling author
Carolyn Brown—available for the first time in print!

Darla McAdams is on the verge of breaking up with her fiancé, Will
Jackson—only a week before the wedding. Darla's sure that her Granny
Roxie will understand when Darla tells her that her first love, Andy, has
come back to town, making her doubt everything.

Granny has been married fifty-five years—she can certainly sympa-
thize with Darla, and she's perfectly willing to share her wisdom. A long
conversation in the bridal room about marriage, anniversaries, and what
saved her own half-century marriage might just help Darla settle those
pre-wedding jitters…

**"[You] will flip for this charming small-town tale."**
—*Woman's World* for *The Sisters Café*

# FIND YOUR WAY HOME

Small-town romance heads to the mountains of New Zealand
in a brand-new contemporary series by Jackie Ashenden

Brightwater Valley, New Zealand, is beautiful, rugged, and home to those
who love adventure. But it's also isolated and on the verge of becoming
a ghost town. When the town puts out a call to its sister city of Deep
River, Alaska, hoping to entice people to build homes and businesses in
Brightwater, ex paratrooper Chase Kelly is all for it. But former oil execu-
tive Isabella Montgomery and her plan to open an art gallery don't seem
up to the test. Now Chase is determined to help her learn the ways of his
formidable hometown.

**"The heroes are as rugged and wild as the landscape."**
—Maisey Yates, *New York Times* bestselling author,
for *Come Home to Deep River*

# HOPE ON THE RANGE

Welcome to the Turn Around Ranch:
charming contemporary cowboy romance from
*USA Today* bestselling author Cindi Madsen

Brady Dawson has been in love with Tanya Greer for as long as he can remember. But running the Turn Around Ranch with his family doesn't leave much downtime for relationships. Now that Tanya is contemplating a move to the city, it looks like he might never get his chance... Faced with the realization that he might lose Tanya forever, he'll have to cowboy up and prove to Tanya that the Turn Around Ranch is the perfect place to call home.

**"Feel-good romance...full of witty charm."**
—A. J. Pine, *USA Today* bestselling author